BETTER OFF DEAD

"Why don't you shift yourself back to a human? You know I can't abide cats," Guthrum declared.

Jafnar would have shrugged at the dwarf if he could, so he did the next best thing by sitting down and licking one paw. It was an odd experience for the human part of him. Then he sauntered over and sniffed at the inert form of Illmuri.

"He's dead as a turnip," Guthrum said, shaking his head. "And the master is gone, I fear forever, and I was able to do nothing about it, nothing at all."

Guthrum mournfully launched himself into a Dvergar lament. There were no words, but the dolorous song conveyed all the grief of a vanquished and disappearing people.

Jafnar's fur bristled.

"Don't grieve yet," Illmuri's voice came faintly. "I'm not entirely dead. Finish me off and then sing your song."

"Alive then, are you?" Guthrum rumbled with a gathering scowl. "Didn't know when you were well off, you poor fool. This world is nothing but a lot of bother."

By Elizabeth H. Boyer
Published by Ballantine Books:

THE SWORD AND THE SATCHEL
THE ELVES AND THE OTTERSKIN
THE THRALL AND THE DRAGON'S HEART
THE WIZARD AND THE WARLORD

The Wizard's War
THE TROLL'S GRINDSTONE
THE CURSE OF SLAGFID
THE DRAGON'S CARBUNCLE

THE CLAN OF THE WARLORD

THE CLAN OF THE WARLORD

Elizabeth H. Boyer

A Del Rey Book
BALLANTINE BOOKS • NEW YORK

A Del Rey Book
Published by Ballantine Books

Library of Congress Catalog Card Number: 92-90624

ISBN 0-345-35966-6

Manufactured in the United States of America

First Edition: October 1992

Chapter One

The Kryppling wind howled down from the fells, honed and stropped the worn corners of the desolate settlements, then blasted out to sea, lashing the firth into a caldron of hissing waves. Its voice was the voice of hopeless grief, keening through the skerries and skarps, or mocking, evil glee trumpeting from the crags of Rangfara. When the wind began, as it did every night, the hard-bitten landholders locked their doors and the thralls curled up close to their meager fires, all wondering if chaos would be held at bay for yet another night, and if the Krypplingur would allow them to see another gray, mizzling dawn.

Mistislaus barred and bolted the door, while the wind blasted at his lamp through the cracks. He left it to shudder and whistle icy drafts into the ruined great hall and took his little lamp to pad slowly up the narrow, broken stairs to the loft room above. Several cats followed him up, knowing about the cozy room underneath the roof-tree, where a small fire burned in Mistislaus' improvised hearth and a pot of something sat simmering on a flat rock. The hearth was a massive kettle, large enough for a man to bathe in, turned on its side against one wall. A gaping crack allowed about half the smoke to escape upward and out through a hole in the turf roof.

Mistislaus sat down in his chair—a chair carved for some long-lost lord of the hall below, who now lay moldering in his barrow, perhaps indifferent to the fate that had beset his land and descendants. Mistislaus eyed his meager supper, and eyed the three cats crouching beside his chair. Their spines were knobbly ridges, their bellies lean, and their heads scarred from their battles with the rats downstairs. For that reason alone, Mistislaus shared his supper with the cats. They were better equipped than he for dealing with the horde of hungry rats. Since the advent of the Krypplingur, rats of all kinds had multiplied and scavenged and despoiled until there was scarcely enough food for anyone.

As Mistislaus was dividing a piece of coarse bread among the cats, the dwarf Guthrum came stalking into the room and flung down a basketful of fresh-cut peat.

"We'll starve to death if you keep feeding those wretched cats," he growled with a black glower at the cats.

"They're the only warlords the settlements can boast of now," Mistislaus replied, shaking the last crumbs out of his white beard and brushing his gown.

Guthrum snorted. His imposing beak of a nose enabled him to utter the most magnificent of snorts, which shot down any absurdities with a report like a cannon.

"Warlords! They're scarcely less pestiferous than the rats! They prey upon men's industry based on a very thinly held notion of domesticity. If we should die—which is rather more likely than not—they'd forget you in an instant and go back to the wild, where the little conniving beasties belong."

The orange tabby cat seated on Mistislaus' knee opened his one green eye to glare back at Guthrum.

"If you're so certain you're going to die," Mistislaus snapped, "why don't you go back to your snug Dvergar halls underground, Guthrum? You'd certainly be more comfortable there with your own people, instead of watching the Ljosalfar here perishing by degrees at the hands of the Krypplingur."

It was a question Mistislaus had skirted tactfully since his arrival at the abandoned house a year ago. He had found Guthrum and three old thralls barely scrabbling out a desperate existence in the wreckage of Ulfgarth, once a prosperous highland farm. The rightful owners of Ulfgarth were dead or vanished into the walls of Rangfara. No one had ever returned from the Dokkalfar fortress to tell tales of the Krypplingur's merciless cruelty, but it was a reality every homestead in the settlements could bear grim witness to. Not a family had gone unscathed since the Dokkalfar had swept into Nordanfirth two winters ago on the teeth of a blistering cold storm to lay seige to Rangfara, battering it with spell and destruction until no one was left to defend it except the frightened farmers and fishermen who had come within its walls for protection. Rather than continuing a futile resistance and perishing, one and all, they had surrendered and sworn serfdom to the Krypplingur.

Guthrum squared his thick shoulders and hoisted one bristling black brow incredulously. "You think that I should go abegging at the doors of strangers, like a homeless cur craving a crust of moldy bread, when this has been my home since I was first formed? You think that all Dvergar are cut from the same mold, like peas in a pod? You think that Dvergar are Dvergar are Dvergar, and there's no differences betwixt them all? What would happen if your precious and parasitical cats were dumped on another farmstead with the cats living there? Would those other cats welcome your cats with open paws? No indeed! Your cats would be attacked and driven out to starve to death on the cold and barren moors, homeless and heartbroken."

Mistislaus waved his hands helplessly, trying to halt the flow of self-righteous wrath being heaped upon his head.

"I'm sorry, I shouldn't have mentioned it," he interjected at last, when Guthrum paused to draw another breath. "Particularly since I'm the newcomer here, and you welcomed me when I was a homeless wanderer."

"It was nothing," Guthrum declared, elevating his noble nose. "It was what Finnkell and his lady Ulf-hild would have done, were they alive today. It was no great generosity on my part, you know, since I'm not the master here, merely the least of the servants. What does it matter now that I was chieftain of the once-mighty Thrumr clan that occupied this portion of Skarpsey for ages and eons, who were driven out by the arrival of the ungrateful Ljosalfar? Ljosalfar whom we protected and taught our finest skills to out of the generosity of our hearts. All that is forgotten now, and I ask nothing except to remain here on the land that was once ours, remain as nothing but the least of the least servants."

Mistislaus sighed gently. He'd heard Guthrum's least-of-the-least and humblest-of-the-humble speech at least a dozen times since his arrival. It was one of the things that seriously caused him to question his wisdom in remaining in the Nordanfirth settlements. The Krypplingur, at least, left him alone most of the time, and he didn't have to listen to their endless justifications.

"Of course, Guthrum," he said kindly. "I can understand how you must feel."

"Oh, can you now?" Guthrum demanded. "Not only must I lose my chieftaincy, my people, my wealth, but now I have to endure your pity? Well, I won't have it, not for a moment. You'll not go stuffing compassion down my throat. Good night, master, I'm going down below."

"Guthrum! Come now!" Mistislaus protested. "It's a miserable night. Why do you always insist upon sleeping downstairs where it's so cold? There's plenty of room up here, and a good deal warmer besides."

"Is it charity you're offering me now?" Guthrum demanded in a voice of horror. "Is that the final insult? Is there no limit to your unkindness?"

"I haven't been unkind! I'd like to be a great deal kinder to you, but you won't have it!" Mistislaus exclaimed, startling even himself with his outburst. Nervously he added, "It gets lonely here, you must know, and I'd like to be able to call you a friend, Guthrum."

Guthrum turned slowly, as if the idea were such a novelty to him that his powers of thought were temporarily stunned. His deep-set Dvergar eyes narrowed, almost completely obscured in folds and creases and a few warty knobs sprouting stiff black hairs.

"A friend, eh?" he growled suspiciously, nodding slightly to himself. "Well, I'd have never thought it of you, Master. You seemed a harmless sort when I let you in here, but I see I was deceived. It's just that kind of generosity that drives the Dvergar farther and farther away from Ljosalfar reach, but I guess that's the way you want it. I hate to leave on such a wild night as this, with who knows what lurking out there, but I see I have no choice, if you're going to insist upon treating me like a friend."

"No! Wait! I take it all back!" Mistislaus shouted, as Guthrum started down the stairs. "I'll do my best not to be kind to you, but I keep forgetting! Give me one more chance, Guthrum! It's this cursed wind that wears away a man's temper and good sense!"

Guthrum answered with a great, wounded snort and kept going. Mistislaus got out of his chair, but he knew Guthrum would find fault with anything he could possibly say to him, so he stalked around the cluttered room in distraction, trying to settle his nerves.

"Blasted dwarf!" he muttered, feeding a bit more peat into the tiny fire under the crucible on his workbench, which was a huge slab of stone braced against the thick turf partition. Guthrum had hauled it up the stairs on his back, uncomplaining, brushing off Mistislaus' thanks with his usual churlish indignation, as if gratitude were the most offensive of Ljosalfar traits.

The distillation in the crucible plopped and burbled sullenly, and Mistislaus heaved another sigh. For a year he had tenderly nurtured this concoction, never allowing the fire to die or get too hot, never stirring the molten mass within, but after a year there was still no sign that he had discovered the secrets of alchemizing gold from dross metals. Nor was it the first of his failures. In a few days, he suspected, the compound would turn to a heavy black sticky lump, which he would have to discard.

Mistislaus put his whale-oil lamp on the workbench and sat down on a stool before a stack of thick old books. They were the only friends and family he possessed, these dry old scholars whose wisdom was preserved on the crumbling pages of vellum, although their mortal carcasses were long since turned to dust—or ash, in some cases.

Just as he was beginning to read, a hullaballo of shouting arose downstairs, and he heard the front door crash open, driven by the wind against the wall repeatedly, like the thrashing of a wounded horse pounding its head against the ground in helpless agony. Wincing, Mistislaus arose and reached into the corner by his kettle-hearth and grasped the smooth wood of his staff. No one ever opened the door after dark, when the chaos ruled. Drawing deep breaths to steady himself, Mistislaus hurried down the narrow stairs.

Guthrum was shouldering the door shut, forcing his way step by agonizing step against the furious wind, which came howling into the deserted hall to tear at the ragged banners hanging on the rafters, racing round and round the room in wild exultation. He barred the door and turned to a knot of dark figures that seemed to be struggling behind him.

"What is this intrusion?" Mistislaus demanded in the sudden calm, and summoned a glowing orb of light, like a hovering ball of lightning, to the end of his staff. It illuminated the hall and its occupants with brilliant white light, making them all squint and throw their arms up to shield their eyes. He recognized Hrysi and Hugi and Thorborg, the three remaining thralls, and they were holding onto a stranger, who ceased his thrashing and shouting the moment Mistislaus summoned his alf-light.

"Don't kill me!" he quavered, venturing to peek out between the fingers of one shielding hand. "I've done no harm! I was only trying to do a good deed, and I don't deserve to die for it!"

"Who are you, then, and what are you doing here after dark?" Mistislaus descended the remaining steps, dimming his light slightly.

"I'm nobody but Gulmr, from Morlandi-stad. I used to be the chief shepherd there, when there were sheep. There's a few of us hiding out at the highest shielings. The Krypplingur don't like to come up that high, much."

"Get on with it," Guthrum growled. "You've got some explaining to do, and you'd better begin with this."

He came into the ring of light, carrying a small bundle awkwardly in his arms—the arms that could grip a horse and fling it off its legs onto its side, or hoist aloft a stone that five ordinary men could not lift.

"Why, it's a little ungbarn!" Thorborg gasped, her scowling mask of wrinkles and warts suddenly transformed into an expression less sinister as she took the baby from Guthrum. "Whatever are you thinking, bringing a child out at night! Is it sick, and you've brought it here for the master to heal?"

"No, she's not sick," Gulmr said gloomily, "but I did bring her to the master."

"And you didn't plan to get caught, either," Guthrum rumbled, folding his arms across his chest and glowering. "Why bring your unwanted brat to us? Do we have any better means of caring for it than you do?"

"At least he didn't abandon her on the fell to die, or be eaten by wolves," Mistislaus said in a grim tone. "Let's have a look at the wee creature, Thorborg."

Mistislaus braced himself, fully expecting to see some horrid deformity in the hapless child. Since the Krypplingur had conquered Rangfara, their dark arts had induced strange occurrences only whispered of and shivered at. Calves and colts were born dead or hideously misshapen, and human infants were not spared similar curses.

He expelled his breath with a sigh when he saw the child unwrapped by Thorborg's old clawlike hands gentled by caution. The others sighed, also, and even Guthrum uttered a small snort of satisfaction. It was a perfectly formed child, less than a year of age, dressed in a lovingly embroidered little red gown with matching slippers and cap.

"A bit thin, perhaps," Thorborg said, "but it's only natural in times like these."

"She's not been starved," Gulmr declared. "Her mother gave her the best of care—up until she died a fortnight ago. There's nothing wrong with the child—nothing like you might fear, since the Krypplingur came." Nervously he made signs to ward off evil, though it did seem a futile gesture. "Her mother wasn't one of us. We found her, not long after Rangfara fell to the Krypplingur. Wandering on the fells she was, wounded a bit and heavy with child. We took her in, of course, thinking she might have been—" He paused and glanced quickly back and forth, before whispering the word. "—from the Skylding clan, child or relative of the warlord Hoggvinn himself perhaps. The hapless wee mother wasn't anyone we'd ever seen, but she had that look, if you take my meaning. Her hair was very light and her eyes blue. But she never told us her real name, nor the infant's. She said only to call her child Skyla. Then the poor woman became ill and died, leaving us her child."

"Then why did you bring it here?" Guthrum snorted. "Do we look like a home for orphan bairns?"

"Or is there something about the child you're not telling us?" Mistislaus asked. In the manner of all clumsy people unacqainted with babies, he had offered her his forefinger to grasp, and now she wouldn't let go of it, and he had no idea what to do to get out of his uncomfortable situation. She gazed at him unblinking, her blue gaze sharp with interest. A gurgle came from between rosebud lips.

Gulmr shifted anxiously from one foot to the other. "Well, we just can't keep her," he said. "She doesn't belong with rough shepherds. What would she grow up like? A young pup, rolling around in the dirt? That's not for her, and it wasn't her mother's wish. I saw her, more than once, just sitting and looking back at Rangfara, holding this child and talking to her. It gave me a peculiar turn, let me tell you. It's just not right that we keep her. I thought the master would know better how to raise her up and teach her to be a lady, like her mother. Besides, if she's a Skylding, and you being a wizard . . ." The whispered suggestion trailed in the silence.

"I'm flattered," Mistislaus said, shaking his head, "but you sadly overestimate my ability, I'm afraid. This child would be better off at Morlandi-stad with shepherds and their wives and children, so she could grow up under somewhat normal circumstances, with companions of her own age. At least she might have a future, safe in the highlands, rough and tumble as it may be. Here, there's no one for her except three old thralls, a grumpy dwarf, and a pothering old wizard who isn't much good at anything. There's not even a woman here to care for a child or keep her company."

"And what am I, then, may I ask?" Thorborg demanded in her harsh voice, shoving her face almost into Mistislaus'. "A two-headed calf?"

It was true, he had forgotten, or ceased to think of her as female, or much of anything except a ragged, stooped figure scavenging the barren farmstead for a handful of grain, a single egg, a few vegetables to make into broth. She attempted to make the old kitchen somewhat clean and habitable for the other two, Hrysi and Hugi. They shared their quarters with the three remaining sheep and a cow and several geese and ducks and chickens—

pitiful remainders of the plentiful flocks and herds kept by Finnkell and Ulf-hild, but each fowl and beast was priceless. The thralls took the animals outside to forage each day and stayed with them to ensure that they weren't killed or stolen.

Mistislaus cleared his throat. "I simply meant that we don't want the poor child here, Thorborg."

"Who says we don't?" Thorborg retorted. "You've seen the way those shepherds live, in hovels and in caves, like wild people. I don't misdoubt that without a chieftain in Nordanfirth, these shepherds will become nothing but savages roaming the fells. They'll be scarcely better than trolls. What kind of life is that for that poor lady's child?"

Mistislaus glanced anxiously at Gulmr. The shepherd's appearance certainly did look ragged and savage, with pelts tied around him and boots made of troll skins.

"Let's go into the kitchen where it's warmer," Mistislaus suggested, tugging his finger away from the child at last. "There's no sense in giving the baby a chill."

The kitchen was fragrant with hay and the sweet breath of the animals, who lay with their knees folded beneath them, gazing at the human visitors and chewing placidly.

Hugi and Hrysi sat down on stools near their livestock, two weatherbeaten old fellows with bright eyes and wind-reddened cheekbones, sly as two aged foxes in their own den. Their beards were sparse and matted, and it was doubtful if either of them had ever owned an entire set of breeches, blouse, and jerkin without holes and tatters. A lifetime of peat smoke had colored them russet from head to toe.

Thorborg sat down beside the fire. Gulmr glanced around, assessing the meager stores visible.

"It seems to me you have plenty to keep one more alive," he said, nodding toward the livestock. "The bairn has been getting goat's milk since her mother died, and seems to be doing well enough on it."

"Aye, she'll have goat's milk," Thorborg said.

"If we keep her, that is," Mistislaus interjected.

"She's healthy and strong," Gulmr continued. "Not half-witted; you can tell it even now."

"I can see that," Thorborg said. "She'll be a fine lass one day."

"I don't doubt that she's from the best stock. Kin of our warlord Hoggvinn himself, I'm thinking. Perhaps even his own child."

"I hadn't heard anything about him remarrying, after the lady Gudlaug died," Thorborg said. "But he did travel to the south and stayed there nearly a year after she died. It's a pity we'll never know for certain who this child's parents were. I don't suppose you found any clan genealogy scroll about the baby's mother when you buried her?"

"Not a scrap," Gulmr replied. "Nor would she breathe a word of it to us. This child has no pedigree to speak of."

"All the more reason that you should keep her," Guthrum said. "What use is a pedigree to shepherds? Sheep don't care who herds them. One day you'll be nothing but nomads anyhow, when there's no one to teach you your letters."

"Even shepherds like to know who their ancestors are," Gulmr retorted. "There are old loyalties and traditions that must not be forgotten. No matter what our lives might be in the future, the marriage lines must be kept."

"All your careful record keeping of marriages and clans won't be worth the sheepskin it's written on," Guthrum grunted. "The Krypplingur will see to that. What's the use of your pedigrees and records when you're probably going to be destroyed anyhow?"

"Hem! We don't know that for certain, just yet," Mistislaus said. "You dwarfs take such a dark view of things, Guthrum."

"As well we should, considering what has happened to our clans and families," Guthrum said. "Scattered, dead, broken up, and forgotten, and the future doesn't look any better for you Ljosalfar. The Dokkalfar will get you all, eventually."

"Thank you for your encouragement," Mistislaus said dryly. "We can always count on you to give us hope. What do you think we should do about this child?"

Guthrum shrugged his shoulders. "You can either drown it or send it back where it came from, I don't care. Just don't try to keep it here. I can't put up with its squalling at all hours of the night and day."

Mistislaus turned to Hugi and Hrysi. "What do you say, Hugi, Hrysi? What's your vote?"

They both shrugged their sharp shoulders and stared at the toes of their boots, embarrassed to be asked the question, as if it implied that they were capable of giving any opinion.

"It's not our place to decide," Hugi said.

"Thralls don't vote," Hrysi added. "You're the master, you decide."

Mistislaus swallowed his exasperation. "In times like these we have to forget who's master and who are thralls," he said. "Our mutual situation has made us equals."

"We've been thralls all our lives," Hugi said in an injured tone, as if Mistislaus were trying to foist something undesirable upon him. "Our ancestors were mostly thralls, except the ones that started out as criminals. We don't mind belonging to this bit of earth, while you folks make the decisions and fight the battles. In fact, it's much easier that way."

"So it makes no difference to you whom you serve, Ljosalfar masters or Dokkalfar," Guthrum snorted.

"Not much," Hrysi answered. "Since we'll all likely end up as thralls together, why don't you just give the child to the Krypplingur now and be done with it? They can raise her up in the kitchen or stables or pigstys as they please, or cut her throat."

"No one's going to cut her throat or raise her to keep pigs," Thorborg said with a menacing gleam in her eye. "You dolts may be thralls and content to be so, but I wasn't born to this lot. I started out as a pickpocket when I was scarcely old enough to walk. I earned my lot as a thrall all right, but I didn't give up my courage, at least. We're going to keep this child and raise her up the best we can. She won't be a thrall and she won't be a shepherd or a half-wild scraeling. Whether or not she's got a pedigree, she'll be a Ljosalfar, and the master will teach her how to use the powers she was born with."

Mistislaus shook his head, as did Guthrum and Gulmr, and said, "That sort of teaching is strictly forbidden by the Krypplingur, and you know it well, Thorborg. The only reason they allow me to live is because I seem harmless to them—and I truly am, there's nothing I could do against them—and I treat the illnesses of the people with my cures. I can't teach anyone about powers. You shouldn't even say such a thing, unless you want listening ears to carry back word to the Krypplingur that I'm starting an insurrection, and you know where that would put me. Dead, or imprisoned, and I hope you don't want that."

"No, I don't want anything to happen to you," Thorborg said. "This child will need you, one day."

"I'll fetch her bundle of things," Gulmr said. "It's just outside the door."

"I don't remember voting on this matter," Mistislaus protested, rather feebly, as the bundle of clothing was brought in and opened and examined, clothes, trinkets, and one gold ring.

"Your vote isn't required," Thorborg said. "We're keeping the child. Skyla, he called her. A nickname obviously. Probably short for Skylda. It means 'duty,' or 'a binding promise.' I wonder why her mother chose such a name, and what she was binding this child to."

"The Skylding clan, perhaps," Mistislaus murmured. "She may be the last of it."

"Hush!" Thorborg hissed. "Don't mention that name! It's bad luck, and we don't want this child to be unlucky."

"Raising a child is a lot of work," Guthrum said, rather gloomily.

"Don't worry, I shall do it all myself," Thorborg said sharply. "I raised quite a few of my own quite some time ago. I doubt if the procedure has changed much."

An old basket was brought to serve as a cradle and Thorborg settled down to rock it. Mistislaus stooped to take one last look at the child.

"What's this in her mouth?" he asked, reaching down to pull something from her lips.

"A feather," Thorborg said in surprise when he held it up, wet and bedraggled. "I wonder how she got it?"

Mistislaus made no answer. There was another feather in her mouth, and another after that. In silent horror, Thorborg watched as he pulled a large wad of feathers from the child's mouth, one after the other, until she finally fell asleep, which seemed to put an end to the phenomenon.

"She's bewitched," Thorborg said in a whisper.

Mistislaus pried a pebble out of each of the baby's hands, examined them, and placed them on the worn table, where they sparkled like clear drops of dew in the firelight.

"Raw gemstones," he said softly. "Keep watching, I suspect there will be more. She's not bewitched. Rather, I'd say she's something of a little witch herself."

"Natural skills, untaught?" Thorborg asked in awe.

Mistislaus nodded. After a long moment of silently watching the child sleep, he sighed gently and went upstairs for a last despairing look at his crucible. Deprived of his full concentration, the substance within invariably changed to something else. As he suspected, it had turned pitch black already, sooner than he had feared.

Chapter Two

Despite the best efforts of Thorborg, Skyla grew up as blithe and free as one of the wild ponies who roamed the moors and fells of Nordanfirth. At a tender age she first began her explorations toddling at Thorborg's heels as she harvested herbs and wild onions and tended to the vegetable plot, carrying a little basket that she filled with small smooth stones and bits of sticks, and flowers when she could find them. Then she discovered the larger world beyond the crumbling walls of Ulfgarth by following Hrysi and Hugi out with the cattle. After that, there was no longer any contentment to be found for her in pottering around the house and garden.

Nor was there any keeping her in the little dresses and gowns Thorborg rummaged out of the old trunks and linen presses in the rooms that once belonged to Ulf-hild, the last hereditary mistress of Ulfgarth. With difficulty, Mistislaus persuaded Thorborg that there was no sense in wasting good cloth and workmanship, so Skyla was dressed in the clothing of Ulf-hild's vanished children. Skyla, however, discovered the trunks, also, and found plenty of shirts and trousers that fitted her and suited her far better than the skirts whose hems got encrusted with burrs and caught on things as she climbed over.

"She might as well have stayed with the scraelings!" Thorborg declared, throwing up her hands in despair. "What would her poor lady mother say? I've done the child no good to speak of!"

"She's healthy enough," Mistislaus observed dutifully. "Fresh air and exercise is always good for a child."

"But I can't get her to sew a stitch, and as for teaching her to cook, why, I'd just as well tie up a colt in the kitchen and expect it to make a pastry. I can't even convince her to wear girls' clothing, let alone to take a bath once in a while. And that hair!"

Mistislaus carefully put his sharp hair-trimming knife away in his satchel. Cutting Skyla's hair was like shearing a wild goat, and it pained him to make her so angry with him. As he looked out the kitchen door, Skyla vaulted over the garden wall and loped toward the moors, still indignant from her haircut. Her hair was almost pure white and had seemed to grow at an amazing rate from the time she was a year old. When Mistislaus cut it short, it formed a halo of curls around her pointed little face, lending her a deceptively innocent expression. When it grew out longer, as it inevitably did between shearings, it was more like a pony's mane, falling into her eyes and down her neck in witch locks. Then her true nature was more apparent, with her sparkling eyes showing cunning behind the screen of curls, her chin more pointed-looking than ever. The best time to capture her for a shearing was early in the morning before she escaped to the moors, carrying her breakfast in her hands as if she had just stolen it.

Cutting the hair seemed to put a temporary halt to the endless array of feathers, blades of grass, seeds, pebbles, bits of glass, and simple dirt that collected around Skyla's presence. Over the past twelve years, Mistislaus and the others had gotten accustomed to her strange talent for generating peculiar objects. Guthrum, however, had remained aloof and suspicious since the day several score of fresh, live herring showered down upon him. Nor would he have the slightest thing to do with enchanted food, even though Thorborg assured him it was no different from any other ordinary herring out of the firth.

Thorborg stooped to sweep up the white locks, taking care not to leave a single hair where it might be found by evil-wishers. She put the hair into a bag, which had grown quite fat after twelve years, intending one day to weave a garment from it. A cloak imbued with such power would enhance Skyla's natural abilities and serve to protect her against evil spells others might cast at her.

"At least she'll be more biddable for a while, now her hair's cut off," Mistislaus said encouragingly. Covertly he rubbed the place on his knee where she had bitten him.

"She's liking it less and less, though," Thorborg replied. "And she's getting bigger. In another year, when she turns thirteen, she might be too strong for us."

Mistislaus nodded, his expression rather bleak. Before long she would be taller and faster, and it would be more difficult to cut her hair. When it was long, mischief enveloped her like a cloud, and manifestations of her power accompanied her every action. Of late, she was starting fires accidentally, and no door could remain shut or locked when she was near.

Talking to her was useless; she had no more idea where the manifestations came from than a young goat might. She had not discovered the power of speech until she was nearly four years old, and even now she seldom spoke. Mistislaus had no idea what thoughts revolved behind her wide gray eyes. Among the peasant folk who came to Mistislaus for cures and charms, her silence and abstraction had earned her the undeserved label of being a witling.

Her passion for being outdoors amounted to an obsession. Mistislaus stepped outside, watching her race straight to the top of the fell. She halted and stood with her arms out from her sides, turning slowly around as if surveying her lonely kingdom of black skarps and emerald hollows, embracing her freedom in the pale sunshine. She whistled, and over on the next fell a band of wild ponies flung up their heads, snorting and lashing their long tails before racing away with a thunder of hooves to vanish over the skyline like a particolored stream of smoke.

"When are you going to teach her, wizard?" Thorborg demanded softly, after first glancing around warily to see that no strangers had come into the yard. "She's a Skylding and deserves her heritage."

Mistislaus shook his head at her tireless question.

"I'm not the one to teach her," he said. "She's not even remotely interested in practicing magic; we're lucky she even learned to read. If you can't get her into a house, how can she be taught anything? She languishes, sitting on a chair. You should know, from your hopeless attempts at teaching her anything about fancy stitching or cooking."

"We should've kept her locked up," Thorborg said. "The madness of the moors has gotten into her. It's nothing but pure chaos, started by the Krypplingur, and unless you do something about it, she's going to be lost to us."

"Well, you might have spoken a bit of truth about the moors," Mistislaus admitted uneasily. "I'll speak to her when she comes in tonight. That's one thing that always will bring her in."

Skyla's terror of the dark had enlivened the nighttime house with her screams since the first night Gulmr had brought her to Ulfgarth. All she required to comfort her was a tiny wick burning, but in the drafty old kitchen a stray puff of wind from under the door was likely to blow it out. Soon after the flame vanished, Skyla inevitably awakened, wracked by some hideous nightmare, shrieking and flailing around as if fighting trolls or Dokkalfar. With the wick relit, she gradually stopped her sobbing and gasping, staring into the little flame until her eyes grew heavy. In the morning, she had no recollection of awakening, nor of the dreams that had so terrified her.

The nightmares troubled Mistislaus more than he cared to admit to Thorborg. Secretly he suspected that the cause of the dreams was a potent carbuncle stone growing somewhere in the child's body, or perhaps it had been sewn under her skin by her mother soon after her birth. Most Alfar were born with a tiny grain of the magic substance, which was usually allowed to die with them. But occasionally a stone was formed of unusual size and power, a stone that was passed down from generation to generation, imbuing each successive owner with all the knowledge and skills of its past owners. It was a stone most coveted by the workers of magic, the darkest of whom were willing to commit all manner of crimes to obtain such a stone.

But without a pedigree and a genealogist to record her birth in the long scrolls of clan history, Skyla would never know the name of the stone she possessed. Without a parent or other historian to teach her of the stone's history, she would never understand the images it put before her, or the emotions it caused to burn within her. She would be blindly driven by forces she could never understand. Her mother had been foolish and cruel to have kept her lines a secret. Skyla needed her own kin to teach her what she needed to learn about herself, her history, and her future.

Mistislaus anxiously watched her, biding his time.

Instead of waiting to confront Skyla at night, when her fears were waiting to surface like hungry sea monsters, Mistislaus went in search of her on the moors. He took his staff and satchel and lunch enough for two, even though he knew that she would not be found if she didn't want to be. The moors were wild and dangerous, overgrown with bracken and thistle and thorn that hid deep crevices in the earth. Once the sheep and cattle and goats of the settlements had kept the wild growth down, in addition to occasional burnings to encourage the grass for the livestock. Now that the Krypplingur had taken command, no one burned fields any longer, and noxious vegetation ran rampant in once-fertile pastures. The few cattle and sheep picked out a meager existence close to the houses and walls and barns of the homesteads, under the watchful eyes of their herders. The lush highlands, where the trolls and wolves vied for possession of the dark kells and ravines, were left vacant.

Mistislaus walked along whistling tunelessly and rapping his staff on the path with every other step. When he reached an open place, he sat down upon a large flat stone and opened the bundle of bread and cheese. As an especial lure, he had brought along a fruit bread, made with as many dried plums and berries as could possibly be pressed into the dough. It was sweet and sticky with a fruity syrup poured over it. He broke it in half and sucked the syrup off his fingers, one by one. By the time he reached the fourth finger, Skyla had materialized, crawling out from under a large thorn thicket like a fox scenting a strayed goose.

"Plumabrot, my favorite," she declared, helping herself to the larger share and garnering half the bread and cheese while she was chewing. "How did you know I was hungry, Mistislaus? All my traps were empty this morning, and something got into the berry bushes in the night. Do you think there are any bears in our fells?"

"It would not surprise me, the way the Krypplingur are changing the land," Mistislaus answered. "It used to be quite safe to go roaming about, but now you never know what you'll find. Snakes, wolves, hostile landvaetir—and all may be eyes and ears for the Krypplingur. Which brings me to the point. The moor's such a dangerous place—"

"Yes, it's lovely, isn't it?" Skyla wolfed down the plum bread and started on the bread and cheese. "The Krypplingur vaetir are easy to recognize. There's always something not quite right about them—too many spots, not enough, the wrong color of eyes, the wrong number of toes—that snake by your foot, for example, should have four brown stripes down its back, with a spotty stripe in the middle, but you see they've got the middle stripe wrong."

Mistislaus leaped to his feet at the first mention of snake. He thrust at it with his staff and watched it slither away like a ribbon in the rank grass. Skyla laughed and commandeered the rest of the cheese.

"What I usually do is toss them into running water," she said. "They melt away like mist. Sometimes they explode with a bang and a cloud of smoke. Those are the ones I like the best."

Mistislaus sat down, after a quick look around the rock to make sure there were no more snakes.

"You needn't fear them," Skyla said. "Especially the normal snakes. Most of the time they're more frightened of you than you are of them."

"Snakes are potent magic," Mistislaus replied. "It's never a good idea to mess with them, unless you know exactly how to handle them, especially the venomous ones."

"I handle them all the time," Skyla said. "You've got to know how to speak their language, Mistislaus, so they won't bite you. Would you like for me to teach it to you?"

"I don't think so," Mistislaus said nervously. "I've never really felt the need to be conversant with snakes."

"They know a lot about healing," Skyla said, "and you are the only healing physician for the settlements of Nordanfirth, so I think you ought to know snake language."

Mistislaus looked at her dubiously, an uneasy sensation tiptoeing down his spine. She was searching around among the black rocks, making little chirping noises between her teeth.

"Here you are, my little fellow," she said, kneeling down, and when she stood up, she had a slender, very poisonous viper twining around her wrist. "Now then, all you've got to do is keep him close to you and talk to him like I was doing, and gaze into his eyes, especially at midnight or noon, and he'll begin to talk to you. I always bring my snakes mice and crickets. This gentleman likes small frogs the very best of all, though he says he can't catch them often enough—Mistislaus, whatever is the matter with you?"

Mistislaus backed away as she came toward him. "All right, you've had your fun," he said, trying to keep his tone of voice even and friendly. "Put him down now and let him go. You've frightened me enough to last you for a month. I know how you enjoy terrifying Thorborg with toads and lizards, but you shouldn't endanger yourself just for the sake of a joke, Skyla. We would all feel terrible if you were hurt."

"It's not a joke, Mistislaus," she protested earnestly, her light eyes wide with innocence. "At least, not this time. The toads I put into Thorborg's bed weren't really cold. In fact, they didn't like her bed at all, and were angry that I'd lied to them about the bedbugs. There wasn't a one. They were almost as angry as Thorborg."

Mistislaus hesitated a moment. If it hadn't been a snake, and a venomous one, he would have taken it home just to humor her. She was always trying to convince him he could make some little creature talk, and he was soft-hearted enough to half believe her. Often his workbench up in the loft resembled a menagerie, although he secretly suspected she was laughing at him when he sat down and solemnly attempted to converse with a squirrel.

Skyla also conversed earnestly with their domestic creatures, and had done so from the time she could walk among the beasts, never with the slightest suspicion that the huge, muddy hoof of a cow could crack her skull. The farmstead now boasted eight cows with the creamiest milk in all the settlements, a dozen goats, thirty sheep, and flocks of geese and hens, none of which beasts or birds every strayed far or fell ill or failed to produce.

"Skyla," he began patiently, "I think the snake would be happier if you left him here."

"No indeed, Mistislaus, he's quite anxious to teach you all he knows and he's not the least bit frightened. Just hold out your arm and let him slither onto it."

"I'm far more afraid of him than he'll ever be of me," Mistislaus said. "I fear I'll never know what wisdom lies within that little skull of his."

"But Mistislaus, you're being foolish—" she began, then halted suddenly, lifting her head to listen, wide-eyed with growing alarm. "Ho, Mistislaus! Krypplingur are coming!"

"I've nothing to fear from them, even if they were coming," Mistislaus said severely. "I think you've tried to frighten me enough for one day, don't you, Skyla? It's rather an undesirable characteristic of yours to want to scare the liver and lights out of people—especially people who care about you."

Skyla bent down to let the snake uncoil from her arm.

"You'd better get out of sight," she said. "The Krypplingur are going to come around that hill in just a moment, and you'll be in full view."

"They don't come out very often in full sunlight," Mistislaus scoffed, taking up his staff. "I shall return to Ulfgarth now, and tell Thorborg that you'll be inside well before the supper hour for your lessons."

Skyla made a face. "Lessons? Tell her I learn all I need to know from the living things, not dead things woven into cloth or boiled into soup. You'd better go the long way around, or you'll run into the Krypplingur."

"Well, I won't go the long way around," Mistislaus declared, and started away, his back stiff with indignation. She was the most exasperating child he had ever encountered, and somehow he always ended up feeling like a fool when he tried to reason with her. She was far too clever, and knew herself to be too clever, and never failed to take advantage of it.

He heard the drumming of horses' hooves behind him and assumed it was the herd of wild ponies he had seen earlier, so he did not bother to look back. Striding along smartly, swinging his staff, he suddenly became aware of a chill, misty cloud overtaking him and the slow dimming of the sun. Glancing over his shoulder, he saw a band of horsemen sweeping down the side of the fell, following the faint track Hrysi and Hugi took each day with the cattle. About a dozen Krypplingur were riding toward him, clad in their long cloaks and carrying an array of weapons. Tassels of hair and bones and teeth dangled from their sword hilts, knife handles, and headgear—relics from vanquished enemies. Their faces and hands were wrapped with strips of black cloth to protect them from the sun, weak and muffled as it was by a cloud of dank mist.

The riders plowed to a halt all around Mistislaus, almost running him over and peppering him with bits of turf and dirt from the horses' skidding hooves. The horses snorted and caracoled, threatening to tread on him, while the riders laughed and pretended to menace him with their lances and maces.

"It's just old Mistislaus," one of them jeered. "For a moment there I thought he was an actual wizard."

Mistislaus looked around at them carefully, trying to recognize them by their armor or trophies, or the design of their saddles. He was no stranger to harassment by the Krypplingur, who were reputed to be the most savage of all the Dokkalfar family clans. All were descended from a single ancestor who bore the epithet Kryppling because of a hump on his back. Banished from the warrior clan, he had started his own clan, passing on to his descendants the hereditary hump and an accompanying ruthless ferocity that made the clan Krypplingur dreaded even among the Dokkalfar.

"Ah, Othefur, is that you?" Mistislaus inquired of the foremost Kryppling, maintaining his aplomb even when one of the Dokkalfar tried to hoist up his long gown with his sword to see what he wore underneath.

"Othefur? Othefur? Is that what I am to you? A bad smell?" the Dokkalfar leader demanded, giving his bristling mace a threatening brandish near Mistislaus' left ear. "It's Ofarir, you fool, and don't you forget it next time, or you'll learn why I'm called the Disastrous."

"I fear I'm somewhat forgetful, especially when it comes to names," Mistislaus answered contritely. "I'm sure I'll remember next time, when I have the pleasure of your company, and that of your esteemed companions."

The Dokkalfar all laughed nastily. One of them who stood apart watching the antics of his cohorts nudged his horse a few steps nearer. He was not a Kryppling, nor was he dressed as a warrior, favoring instead a plain black cloak and hood, covering a long gown and leggings beneath. At a glance Mistislaus would have recognized a wizard, even without the sensations of power and evil that radiated from his presence.

"So this is what the Ljosalfar wizards have come to," he said coldly, surveying Mistislaus through a slit in his wrappings. "They used to be a haughty lot, but this one looks more like an old beggar."

"He wandered in here like a stray cat looking for a warm barn," Ofarir answered. "Soon after the siege of Rangfara. We permitted him to stay, since he does seem to have a small talent at healing sickness and injuries and diseases of cattle. We can't allow all the Ljosalfar to die, you know, or our larders would be getting slim."

"You think too much of your bellies and larders," the stranger said contemptuously. "You should remember how the Dokkalfar are meant to live—underground, and without the dainty Ljosalfar fare you've learned to crave."

"Meistari Illmuri," Ofarir said with a deprecating shrug of his shoulders, "it's nothing we couldn't give up at a moment's notice, should my father Herrad command it. But it seems to please him that we enslave these dayfarers on the face of the land, so we do it, and if we learn to eat their food and enjoy a few of their foolish and comfortable ways, there's no harm done."

"You'd be comfortable with a halter around your neck, too," Illmuri said. "I can see why Herrad has need for me. Rangfara and its comforts has spoiled even the Krypplingur, who once fancied themselves the most savage of the clans."

"We didn't fancy ourselves anything," Ofarir snarled, giving his mace a shake so the knuckle bones and teeth clattered. "Krypplingur are the most savage, and everyone knows it and trembles. Shall I gut this wretch to prove it?" Without taking his slitted gaze from Illmuri, he gestured with the mace at Mistislaus, missing the end of his nose by inches.

"Only the unsure need to prove themselves," Illmuri said in a silky tone, gathering up his reins and starting his horse forward. "I wish to examine this fellow's living quarters. I want to see whether or not he's got some dangerous evidence lying about to incriminate him."

"What do you need with evidence? Just kill him, if you're suspicious," Ofarir suggested, glaring at Mistislaus and spurring exasperatedly after the wizard.

They cantered away, pelting Mistislaus again with turf and pebbles from the horses' hooves. Gripping his staff, he strode after them as fast as he could go, dreading what he was going to find when he got back to Ulfgarth.

In a moment he saw Skyla's russet hood bobbing above the

thistles as she came out of hiding and planted herself in the middle of his path.

"Mistislaus!" she spat angrily, giving his chest an accusing poke. "How could you behave like—like a craven coward to those Krypplingur? You almost kissed their feet! You sounded so fearful and polite to them!"

"Skyla, that's the way one does when one is surrounded by twelve or thirteen of one's enemies," he said, a trifle irritated. He had never seen her so angry, trembling and pale, and her eyes were flashing. "What should I have done? Flown in their faces and called them names and invited them to open my skull and look at my brains?"

"That would have been better than being such a buffoon with them," she said earnestly, falling into step beside him. "Why didn't you blast them with alf-light? Why didn't you shift shapes and fly away? One of these days you'll have to challenge that Illmuri to a duel, I think, to teach him a lesson."

"If I had been foolish enough to attempt any of those absurd plans, I would now be nothing but a puddle in the road," Mistislaus said in mild exasperation.

"They are hateful," Skyla said through her teeth, clenching her fists. "I would fly at them myself if I had a proper weapon. But I despise the feel of metals in my hands. Mistislaus, we must destroy them, you and I!"

"Child, if we tried, I at least would be killed, if not all of us," Mistislaus said. "And if you were spared, what would you do without me to pester and frighten, I might ask? So we will not be attacking Rangfara or Illmuri in the foreseeable future. You must put that notion out of your head entirely. Our freedom is gone, and the time for war is past. Now we simply endure."

Skyla cocked her head and looked at him curiously, like a cheeky wild bird singularly lacking in fear.

"Mistislaus," she said, as if she were speaking to a stubborn child, "the time for war is never past, as long as Ljosalfar are not free of the Dokkalfar oppression. The land surrounding Nordanfirth is our land, Ljosalfar land, and these misshapen Krypplingur are enemies, intruders, usurpers, and murderers of all that's good and natural. Besides murdering people, Mistislaus, they're murdering the very earth that gives us what miserable life we have. They are poisoning it in ways you can't dream. We've got to stop them before it's too late."

"Skyla! What can the two of us do?" Mistislaus demanded in righteous indignation, more than a little alarmed at her sudden interest in the Krypplingur. Her exact birth date was unknown to him, but its proximity was certainly bringing her Skylding heritage into her consciousness. "Storm their gates? Lay in ambush for Krypplingur warriors, who would, incidentally, be fifty times a match for us, and our lives would be poured out in the dirt very promptly? Or would you rather rot away in a tiny dungeon cell, locked away from the daylight and the soft earth, with the cold sweating stone pressing around you, and bars of metal on the door?"

He knew she would shudder at that idea, and she did. It was all she could do to sleep and eat indoors most of the time, as a civilized being should do. Often he thought she would have fared better with the shepherds. As he had suspected, Gulmr and his band had indeed reverted to the wild in the twelve years since they had given Skyla away. Perhaps Gulmr had even back then had some inkling what trouble Skyla was going to cause and wisely had wanted nothing to do with it.

"They are evil," Skyla said in quiet, cold vehemence after walking in silence a few moments, giving time for Mistislaus to start thinking he had made an impression on her with his sensible arguments.

Mistislaus sighed. "Yes, they are evil. And so terribly powerful. This Illmuri gives me a very unpleasant feeling. Skyla, I want you to stay out of their sight. I'd hate for them to carry you off to Rangfara."

When they came into sight of Ulfgarth, they saw a cloud of black smoke rising up from the dooryard. Thorborg stood helplessly twisting her hands in her frayed apron, watching from the kitchen doorstep. One of the Dokkalfar appeared at the loft window and threw down an armful of books in a fluttering cascade of ancient papers and crumbling leather spines. Below, a fire smoldered and flames licked greedily at the old brittle vellum pages, eating away centuries of wisdom. The wizard Illmuri poked at the fire to keep it burning properly, stooping to pick up a page to read for a moment, then holding it carefully in the fire to be sure it caught.

With a strangled cry, Skyla started forward, but Mistislaus caught her arm and held her back.

"It doesn't matter," he said gently. "They are, after all, nothing but books. Most of their knowledge is outdated now, nothing that anyone can practice anymore. Just dusty old friends, and I've got them safe up here." He tapped his temple with one thick finger.

"But Mistislaus! Your books! The people who wrote them will be lost forever now! All that wisdom!"

"Yes, it will be gone. Maybe for the better, too," Mistislaus said, unable to keep the sorrow from his tone. "The Ljosalfar are a failing race."

"Only because they've given up!" Skyla snapped angrily. Twisting out of his grasp like an eel, she bolted away down the path that led past the old fallen-down cow byre.

After watching a moment to make sure she was completely gone, Mistislaus heaved a sigh and shrugged his shoulders and turned back to the scene of the burning that awaited him. He trudged forward and halted at a modest distance from the fire and the wizard Illmuri, not near enough to imply any criticism, but close enough to show that he was interested in what was happening.

"So we meet again," Mistislaus greeted him politely. "I see you've found my old books. I'd never thought any of them were particularly worth burning, though."

Illmuri looked up sharply from ripping out priceless pages and dropped the ruined book at his feet, the fire forgotten. His piercing eyes swept over Mistislaus in sudden suspicion and disbelief.

"Who—what are you?" he said, as if speaking to himself, and his gaze went opaque, sliding away over Mistislaus' head unheedingly.

"Nobody and nothing in particular, except a rather useless old wizard with a lot of dusty old books no one cares to read anymore," Mistislaus answered, stifling a sigh as he gazed at his books.

"Silence!" commanded Illmuri. "I know what you are. But for a moment, there was something here."

"Shall I get rid of this old bag of uselessness for you, my lord?" Ofarir inquired in a tone of exaggerated politeness. "I say we burn him along with the books, just in case there's a faint residue of knowledge or power somewhere about him. You never know when it might surface, like a nasty rash."

Illmuri swept a glance of pure contempt over Ofarir and beckoned peremptorily. "Get away, you lump of ignorant spite," he barked. "If I want this old fool killed, I shall do it myself, at my own leisure. Perhaps one day I shall, when I'm in need of amusement."

Mistislaus chuckled and shook his head, as if appreciating a good joke. "My young friend, if you want to frighten me, tell me that I'm going to live forever. Death holds no fear or awe for me any longer. It's this continuous struggle to stay alive that is so wearisome. What to eat. What to wear. How to find it. It's all so ignoble, somehow, don't you agree?"

Illmuri looked at him intently, removing his gaze suddenly from a point somewhere beyond Mistislaus' back. "What's your name, old man?" he demanded.

"Mistislaus," Mistislaus answered innocently. "The Cloudless One. I chose it when I was a youth in a small and obscure wizards' school. It seemed such a good name for a wizard, at the time. I fear you may think it doesn't fit very well now, nor did it ever."

"No, you're not cloudless," Illmuri said, scowling in concentration as he stared at Mistislaus. "In fact, I can discern nothing of you except clouds and fog and fat. If there is a spark of power in you, it's obscured by smoke."

Mistislaus waved his hand to fan away some of the smoke of the burning of his books. "Well, if ineptitude was a crime, there'd be more gibbets than kings and chieftains."

Illmuri threw back his head and uttered a bark of grim mirth. "You may be old and foggy, but you speak the truth."

"I do my best," Mistislaus replied with a touch of worry in his tone. "But sometimes, these days, one scarcely knows whether or not to be truthful and hang himself, or remain silent and live."

"Who lives here with you?" Illmuri inquired, neglecting for a moment to poke more books into the fire, thus allowing certain precious truths to survive a few moments longer in Skarpsey. Mistislaus could scarcely keep his eyes off his beloved books, tumbled around so precariously.

"Besides myself, there's two outside thralls, Hrysi and Hugi, and one old woman who keeps the kitchen, Thorborg, and one ill-tempered old dwarf who skulks about doing what he chooses." Mistislaus paused a moment.

"And? Is that all?" Illmuri's eyes probed Mistislaus suspiciously.

"No, of course not. I was merely composing myself to continue. One must catch one's breath, you know. Did you really believe I was going to skip someone?" A note of reproach crept into his tone. "Didn't I tell you I always tell the truth?"

"I was going to test you. There's a lad in a russet hood peering at you from the top of that ruined barn behind you. I trust he belongs to you?"

"The lad? Oh, of course," Mistislaus said.

"Who are his parents?"

"Parents?" Mistislaus repeated. "Nordanfirth possesses a sad legacy of orphans, young man, and you should know the reason why, even if you weren't here for the battle. I wasn't myself, but its memory is as fresh as if it were yesterday, instead of thirteen years ago."

"Orphans, yes," Illmuri repeated, looking at Mistislaus with a faint smile quirking at his lips, "but I regret to say I've caught you in a lie, Mistislaus. That lad in the russet hood is a girl."

"I didn't say he wasn't a girl," Mistislaus said. "You assumed for your own reasons it was a lad, and I saw no harm in allowing you to continue in your delusion."

"Why are you so intent on concealing the fact that this girl is a female?" Illmuri inquired silkily.

"The girl herself is the most interested in concealing it," Mistislaus said. "She's as wild as a moor pony. You couldn't get her into a gown and apron for anything. She'd rather live under a skarp and eat grass like a goat than go indoors. It's one of the problems with orphans. You never know, without a pedigree, what insanity you're likely to discover. It's most pathetic, as you can imagine."

Illmuri snorted softly, looking still toward the barn. When Mistislaus turned, he saw no sign of Skyla. "Is she a Skylding child, do you suppose, or an orphan of one of the common families who were defending Rangfara?"

Mistislaus drew himself up stiffly for his answer. "As far as I am able to answer truthfully, I say no, she does not belong to the Skylding clan. The Skyldings who were lords of Rangfara are all dead."

"But don't you think it possible some of those Skyldings may have hidden their children somehow, so a few young Skyldings would survive?"

"Yes, that might have happened," Mistislaus said with great interest. "But the problem is, once those children were found by the simple farming and fishing folk of Nordanfirth, who are mostly clan Landbunadur and clan Veidimadur, then those orphans will be raised as Landbunadur and Veidimadur children, and hence no longer would they be Skyldings. No, I would say to you, no, there are no Skylding orphans in Nordanfirth, because there are no Skylding parents to teach them their heritage."

"But blood is blood," Illmuri argued, forgetting completely about the fire.

"So it is, and messy when it's spilled, but without teaching, a child is no better off than a pup or a pony," Mistislaus replied. "I could say to you, for example, that you are a Skylding yourself, but that wouldn't make it so, because it's perfectly obvious that you've been born and bred a Dokkalfar—although which clan I'm unable to guess, except that I know the best of wizards come from the Galdur clan, or perhaps Prestur. I've seen no distinguishing marks of either clan, but as I was going to say, you've been taught to be what you are, as well as born into it, but if a person were to take a Dokkalfar child and raise him up in a Ljosalfar clan, I maintain he would be as much a Ljosalfar as any of them. Or it would be equally so in the opposite case, I should think."

"We may have to argue the point in greater depth later," Illmuri said with a slight bow. "It's been awhile since I've encountered a man of intellect such as yourself. Most Dokkalfar value the work of sword and lance above the working of the mind. We needn't be enemies, Mistislaus."

Mistislaus hoisted his bristling eyebrows in astonishment and couldn't resist casting a dolorous glance downward at the heaps of books around his feet. "I suppose you haven't really burned anything of value," he said. "That next stack is the best. If you burn those, I fear I really can't respect you as a man of knowledge and intellect."

"Why do you think I spared them, then?" Illmuri said. "I would like to read them myself, and I would like to talk more with you, Mistislaus. When I return the books I have borrowed, we shall sit by the fire and drink ale and argue. I shall supply the ale, and you the argument."

"That would be delightful, if you're as clever as I think you may be," Mistislaus said with a smile. "This will be sorcerous dueling that's much to my liking."

Illmuri beckoned to one of the Dokkalfar and pointed to the books. "Bundle these up carefully, you dolt, and carry them back to my rooms in Rangfara. If you damage those books in any way, I'll use your liver for bootblacking. Now bring my horse. It's time we went on."

With another half bow to Mistislaus, he mounted his horse and rode away at a contemptuous distance from the Dokkalfar.

Mistislaus hastened to tread upon the fire. Nothing of any lasting value had been burned, but he wondered if he would ever see the return of the precious volumes Illmuri had taken.

Chapter Three

It was after sundown, usually, when Illmuri arrived to visit, but the northern twilight cast the world in silvery shadow for hours at that season, making travel uneasy for dayfarers but most convenient for nightfarers. When the sun had gone down below the misty spine of Hvalness to the west, Skyla crept into the kitchen, taking care not to disturb the thralls nodding and dozing over their evening occupations. Quickly she scuttled down the dark hallway to the cavernous great hall, where a fire always burned on the days Illmuri came to visit and two old chairs were pulled up near the coals, with a screen to shelter Illmuri from the heat and light of the fire. The lumber and clutter and battle wreckage had all been cleared away by a most unwilling Guthrum to give the hall a more hospitable appearance, although why anyone would want to be hospitable was more than Guthrum could fathom—particularly if that hospitality was to be extended to one's worst enemies.

Suddenly a bright tendril of light swept into the dark hall from an opening above, and footsteps and the tapping of a staff came down the narrow stairway leading up to Mistislaus' private rooms. Skyla dived behind a chair and found a space where she could watch.

"Hrysi!" Mistislaus called. "Saddle the horse for Meistari Illmuri, won't you, like a good fellow?"

A muffled snort echoed from the direction of the kitchen, followed by some thrashing around in the straw and savage muttering, followed by the slamming of a door.

"He's not pleased," a second voice said, with a soft chuckle. "I should not have stayed so late again, Mistislaus, but you did have to tempt me with that terrible old Agrippa, didn't you? Where did you have it hidden when I sent those oafs in to throw your other books out for burning?"

In a voice of quiet glee Mistislaus replied, "Why, it was in plain view all the time, my dear friend, with all the other books on my table. To all but the most ignorant of minds, that is. I can't understand how the noble Othefur didn't see it."

"Ofarir, you mean. I'm afraid he's more than a bad smell, although I wish someone would take steps to remedy that. Herrad is even more tedious, with all his bloodthirsty ranting and cursing over past glories. You must come and have a look at him, Mistislaus. I dislike continually teasing you about it, but if you could work a cure on that rot in his leg, it could give you quite a feather in your cap."

"Not as far as my fellow Ljosalfar are concerned, I fear," Mistislaus answered with a deep sigh. "They're not the least bit forgiving of giving comfort to the enemy."

"Have I caused you trouble by coming here for our intellectual discussions?"

"Oh, a wee bit, perhaps. Nothing worth considering. There are a few folk who say I ought to be burned, but they seldom brought me their livestock for curing anyway, and when they did, they neglected to pay me something for it, so I don't truly regard myself as having lost any real friends. Those who wish to be healed come here regardless. Hah, you need one last pull of ale to warm your vitals before you go back to Rangfara in that beastly wind. If you were a Kryppling, I wouldn't complain so much about it, but it does get into an old wizard's joints terribly of a winter night. If Herrad would consider putting a cork in it, I might consider healing the disease in his leg, before it rots off up to his neck. If he waits that long, the only remedy will be decapitation."

They both laughed at that. Mistislaus was leading the way and making sure of every step on the stairway before he trod upon it. Once he had stepped on one of Skyla's accidentally conjured toads and it had given him a nasty tumble. Fortunately it was only six steps from the bottom, so nothing had been broken, and the toad had escaped unscathed, except for its wounded dignity.

Skyla's legs were getting cramped from crouching behind the chair. When she shifted, she bumped the table and an ale horn rocked noisily against the planks.

"Who's there?" Mistislaus shouted, firing up his alf-light with an alarming glare, revealing him standing poised at the foot of the stairs, tilting a little bit to port, then to starboard as he tried to trim his balance. His nose was a flaring red and his eyes twinkled with too much jollity and too much aged ale from Dokkalfar cellars.

Skyla froze. There was nothing she hated like notice from Illmuri. Trapped, she measured the distance to the doors, one blocked by Mistislaus and the other too far away. As she considered, the far door opened and Guthrum's hulking shape lumbered into the glaring light.

"Only me," the dwarf grunted, rolling one flashing eye in Illmuri's direction. "Have you seen our Skyla? Her night terrors are going to be starting if she's not brought to heel soon."

"We haven't seen her," Illmuri said. "By the bogs of Murad, Mistislaus, little Skyla is getting to be a fine creature, isn't she? If her eyes were ice-bolts, I know I would be dead by now."

"If your Dokkalfar ale was sea water," Guthrum said caustically, holding up a jug so it emptied itself on the floor, "we'd all be swimming in it up to our chins. Master, if you don't put a damper on that torchlight, you're going to melt your esteemed guest from Rangfara."

"No danger of that, I'm too quick for him," Illmuri said. "He's tried it several times, trying to make it look like a good-natured accident, but I'm sure he was trying to murder me nevertheless."

"Don't worry, Guthrum," Mistislaus said. "He never gets me drunk enough to find out anything really important. He knows that it would be a futile endeavor, besides."

Laughing, they both moved toward the kitchen. Guthrum glowered around in the hall a moment, then followed Mistislaus' staggering alf-light.

"Are you going to look at Herrad's rot, or whatever is troubling him?" Guthrum rumbled suspiciously.

"Ah," Mistislaus said, tapping the side of his nose with one finger. "I might, and I might not. He would have to make it very much worth my while, before a healer of cattle and horses would stoop to cure a Kryppling warlord. A pity the rot's not in that hump on his back, or he might end up looking like a normal Dokkalfar, like Meistari Illmuri."

It sent him off again, wheezing and cackling, and he resumed his lopsided progression toward the kitchen, listing heavily until he ran aground against the doorframe.

Skyla used the opportunity to slink toward the door, thinking to cut behind them and thence to the back of the house, where she nested in a tiny room up under the eaves in a small round tower that had once been storage for grain.

Illmuri heard her soft footstep and turned and looked back at

Skyla. She froze again, staring at him like a wild hare poised for flight.

"Here's your lass, Guthrum," Illmuri said quietly, so as not to spook her away. "When Mistislaus comes to Rangfara, you should come with him," he said to her. "You'd like to see the finery that the Dokkalfar women wear. We've a visiting clan of Slaemur women here for the spring giftings. You'd see a wealth of fine clothes if you came to one of the wedding feasts. You'd look like a different creature in a Slaemur gown, with an embroidered headdress and fur-lined cloak."

Skyla's gaze dropped to her toes, and she blushed fiery red for no reason she could think of. Her grass-stained boy's trousers and boots and long shirt had never embarrassed her before. Suddenly she dived into the shadows, making a dash for her aerie in the little tower.

"She doesn't care for fine clothing," Guthrum retorted. "No more than she cares for you. Why don't you stop trying to coax her into talking? She never will say anything to such as you."

"She's been kept away from people too much," Illmuri answered sharply. "You're doing her no favor by making her as wild and shy as a marsh fox."

"People don't like such as her," Guthrum said. "She's slow in the head."

"No more than you or I," Illmuri snapped. "Skyla is as quick as anyone. Quicker than some, I'll warrant."

"That she is," Mistislaus said, quickly opening the door and ushering Illmuri out, away from the glowering Guthrum. "A dear child she is, our Skyla, though it is a pity she chooses to shun human society most of the time. I fancy she would enjoy your story about the treasure hidden somewhere in Rangfara, and how everyone searches for it beneath every stone, but no one has ever found it." He raised his voice slightly and directed his speech toward the dark hallway where Skyla had fled. He was rewarded with a slight scuffing sound, and smiled to himself. He could almost see her, crouching there against the wall like a cat, listening to his every word. But she would not come out as long as Illmuri lingered on the premises.

"Come," Illmuri said. "Light my way for a short space. Even a Dokkalfar knows the difference between light and dark, and appreciates being able to see better."

Mistislaus went outside, with the wind blowing his alf-light away in dangerous swatches that snatched at the dry grass and moss. With hands that trembled with indignation, Guthrum lit a couple of whale-oil lamps, although the price of the oil was almost as dear as blood.

"What's this for?" Mistislaus demanded when he came stumping back from the kitchen, his alf-light smoking blackly and waning to a murky glow at the end of his staff. "Are we expecting company who needs to be impressed with our extravagance?"

"Illmuri is the only company we have who fits that description," Guthrum said bitingly. "I'm going to speak plainly and I need plenty of light to do it by. Why did you choose him as a friend, Mistislaus? Half the people who used to come for healings refuse to speak to you now."

"Illmuri makes up the difference in the gifts he brings to Thorborg's kitchen," Mistislaus replied contentedly. "We're not going to starve because old Felag Bag-nose doesn't fetch us to look at his scrawny cattle."

Guthrum replied, "Doesn't it trouble you that the eggs and grain and ale he brings to us are taken from Ljosalfar who desperately need them?"

"Truly, the curse of old age," Mistislaus grumbled as he sank into his chair with a windy grunt, "is listening to the scolding of well-meaning busybodies. No wonder a man grows deaf. It's merely a tactic to defend himself when his body is a disregarded, unappreciated, worthless old ruin."

"And you're telling outrageous lies," Guthrum said.

"Only because I know there's no danger of your believing them," Mistislaus replied with a heavy sigh, followed by a sudden suspicious sharpening tone. "I suppose you've had some quarrel with Thorborg again, haven't you? I warn you, I won't give up Illmuri's companionship, or the ale, or my experiments upstairs, however bad they smell. What is it this time? Illmuri? The smells?"

Guthrum rolled his red-rimmed eyes in exasperation, like a bull who is becoming seriously annoyed. He snatched Mistislaus' drinking horn away as the old man lifted it to sniff loudly inside it for one last drop.

"It's this, Mistislaus! You shouldn't drink such vile stuff," he admonished. "It's terrible. You'll be drooling on your own chin before long, or you'll go blind. Nothing is worse than Dokkalfar ale. Mark my words, he doesn't come pandering his poison around you for nothing. He wants something, and I'm afraid it has to do with Skyla."

Mistislaus' wandering attention was arrested. He cast a wary glanced toward the dark hallway. "Tell on," he said.

"I've heard it from plenty of sources," Guthrum went on in a fiery whisper. "Your friend Illmuri is certain the Skylding orphans know where the treasure is. He's combing the settlements all around Nordanfirth and Rangfara to find children who may be Skylding orphans."

Mistislaus snorted fiercely. "Impossible. How could such orphans reveal its hiding place, even if he did prove they were Skyldings? Illmuri's not got those sort of skills."

"They could, to a wizard with skills at reading others' carbuncle stones," Guthrum said darkly.

"It's nothing but Dokkalfar greed and Dokkalfar clan feuding," Mistislaus said with a disgusted flap of one hand. "Herrad wants that treasure more than he wants to be cured. For that reason alone Illmuri was brought to Rangfara—to find the treasure before someone else does. Since the Krypplingur took Rangfara, all their relations are moving in with them to share the bounty. There won't be a moment's peace until someone finds the Skylding treasure. Then there shall be a fierce battle, many Krypplingur and Slaemur and Ottalegur and Magknoa are going to be killed, then they'll divide the treasure sensibly among who's left and leave. Probably then Rangfara will be abandoned, and anyone who wants it can have it. However—" He raised one hand and glared again toward the shadows, where he still suspected Skyla might be lurking and listening. "As far as I know, the treasure is only a legend. No one alive has ever seen it. None of the captives the Krypplingur tortured ever revealed it. With each passing year, it grows in size and splendor. It's my belief that it does not truly exist."

"If there is treasure in Rangfara," Guthrum said, "that treasure doesn't belong to the Dokkalfar. It belongs to her—and any other Skylding orphans. It's her heritage, Master. You ought to take some steps to make certain she gets what's rightfully hers. You can't keep her here all her life, hidden away from the truth."

Mistislaus scowled, giving his staff a distracted rap upon the earthen floor. "I was afraid you'd take that point of view. Dvergar are bloodthirsty creatures, with noses for trouble. Nothing causes trouble like gold. Unless it's women, beautiful or otherwise. Does Illmuri know for certain that Skyla is a Skylding?" Mistislaus asked, his features drawing up worriedly.

"He's here, sniffing and snooping, isn't he?" demanded Guthrum. "He must have a strong suspicion. He must also have a strong suspicion that the Skylding treasure is indeed somewhere in Rangfara." A fierce light dawned in his deep-set eyes. "If we could get to it before they do, that would be the end of the

Krypplingur. We could raise an army, if we had the gold to buy the allegiance of good fighting men."

Mistislaus sighed heavily. "Gold and armies are not the sort of things I want to mess with," he said. "It's been my observation that an evil assortment like the Krypplingur never stay in one place for long before they find easier pickings elsewhere and move on."

"Or until someone drives them out," Guthrum persisted.

"Well, it won't be us," Mistislaus answered with a heavy sigh. "Although I'd do almost anything to get rid of that cursed wind, even humble myself and go look at Herrad's wretched leg—may it rot away and take his soul with it."

"Hah." Guthrum snorted, his eyes still glittering. "It's that treasure that fascinates you. And you've most likely got the best chance of finding it." He jerked his head in the direction of Skyla's little tower room in the granary. "If she's a true-blooded Skylding—and we know she is—she's got the knowledge of all her ancestors waiting to be found in that carbuncle of hers."

"Illmuri knows it, too, or he wouldn't keep coming around," Mistislaus said, pinching at his nether lip in an anxious manner. "He's like a fisherman, throwing out a baited hook and wafting it past my nose to see if I'll bite on it. I'm not going to swim up and snap at it right away. We must be slow and cautious, or before we know it we'll be hooked. I know a few things about fishing myself. Now then, are you satisfied?"

"No," Guthrum said. "We must go to Rangfara, and take Skyla back to the city of her ancestors."

Mistislaus furrowed up his lugubrious brow and pressed his thumbs into his eyes, rubbing them with slow, worried oscillations. "What if we lose her in a meaningless quest for treasure? No treasure is worth that price. She's happy as she is, Guthrum."

Guthrum snorted explosively, rendering all previous snorts into amateur status. "Do you truly believe she can remain happy and childlike, with all the voices of her ancestors crying out to her for justice and vengeance? The voices will get stronger, Master, as she gets older. She's already got peculiar powers, as you know, particularly for an untaught child of such tender years. She reads more truth in a leaf or a pebble than all your hoary scholars have written in all your dusty old books."

Mistislaus blinked, startled and affronted. "She may well have natural ability," he said, "but the rest of us have to plod along as well as we can, with our hoary old scholars and dusty old books. Skyla may well be a splendid flying dragon ship, but all she has for a rudder is me. Without a rudder, she'll likely run onto some vicious rocks that will wreck her. As I see it, Rangfara and that treasure are those rocks, waiting to destroy her."

"Better that you're there, then, to steer her among them," Guthrum said, "rather than waiting until she slips away alone to answer the call of her ancestors' blood."

"She's such a child yet," Mistislaus protested. "Barely thirteen summers, as near as I can guess."

"Take off your blinders," Guthrum said. "She's not that wee pink thing in a blanket any longer. She's not a child, Master. She hears the voices, and she knows."

Mistislaus did not sleep comfortably that night. The Kryppling wind moaned and gnawed around the old hall. Twice he arose and peered out the window toward the nested towers of Rangfara rising black against the moon-bright sky, like a crown of torturous thorns.

In the morning when Mistislaus finally crawled from his troubled bed, Skyla had vanished long before, unable to resist the call of the fells and moors much past first light. Sighing wearily, he set out in search of her, hoping she might want to be found. As he tramped along, he had the feeling she was watching him in smug merriment from the cover of the bracken and fern and thorny thickets that threatened to overpower the road. He finally came to a clearing where the choking undergrowth halted in a ring at a respectful distance around some crumbling stones standing in a drunken circle. Skyla sat on the velvety greensward cross-legged, like a princess waiting to entertain supplicants in her court.

Mistislaus sat down on a fallen stone with a windy grunt and mopped the back of his steaming neck. The circle was at the crest of a gentle hill, a hill that never kept the snow long in the winter. The ancient name for the place was Dogunknip, the Hill of the Dawn.

"You are past twelve years of age now, Skyla," he said. "You are coming into realizations of many things. You have—powers." He looked at her suddenly, his eyes red-rimmed and troubled. She paid him no heed; she was busy with a row of small dead or maimed animals and the crude clay people she manufactured from earth and spit, frowning over them with a petulant expression.

"Skyla, what are you doing?" Mistislaus whispered, more to himself than to her.

"I can fix them," Skyla said. "I come here to think about things and listen to the voices."

Mistislaus made a groaning, guttering sound somewhere deep

within and started rubbing his eyes again, which was what he always did when he was worried. "What sort of voices, Skyla? What do they say to you?"

She was already distracted by a fluff of milkweed that came sailing past on the breeze. "Look, Mistislaus, it's like a little man with wings," she said. "Why is it that men can't fly?"

"Because they aren't intended to, nor shall they ever," Mistislaus replied. "Now tell me about the voices, Skyla."

She shrugged her shoulders airily, as if testing them for evidence of wings sprouting there. "Everyone has voices," she said. "And men will fly one day."

Mistislaus sighed patiently. "Your voices tell you to do things. The little clay people you make, the stones you change to jewels and gold—"

"Making things is wrong?" she asked in surprise. The pebble she had been rolling between her fingers had changed to a perfect little rosebud. She pinched it and changed it to dust and tossed it away.

"No, but it is a gift evil people might covet. And the little creatures you keep killing—" He stopped and ran his hand through his hair, truly at a loss to explain her behavior. She had always been such a tenderhearted child, always bringing lost and wounded animals home to shelter. Her new bent disturbed him intensely. "You were born with powers, but you must keep your powers hidden for a while longer. I'm afraid for you, Skyla, particularly if I am to take you to Rangfara."

"Rangfara?" she repeated, her eyes growing wide and dark with excitement. "We're going to Rangfara? The voices told me that I would."

"But there are people in Rangfara who would do you harm if they saw the things you do," Mistislaus said warningly. "If you wish to continue making things and killing mice, you'll have to be sent away. There is no one here who can teach you what you need to know."

"Can't you?" Skyla asked. "I don't want to be sent away from Ulfgarth—and Rangfara." She turned to look at the gray crags of Rangfara rising from the green hills several miles away.

"I cannot," he said. "A woman of your own lineage must teach you. If you don't wish to make it necessary for me to send you away, you must keep your skills hidden when we go to Rangfara. It would be dangerous for you to tamper with your hidden powers alone. There could be grave consequences—besides alerting every Krypplingur in Rangfara to your abilities.. You would spend the rest of your life as a captive, or hiding from them, searching for the lost treasure of your Skylding ancestors. There are safe places I could send you, Skyla, and people who would care for you, although they would be strangers to you—"

"I won't go," Skyla said swiftly, her eyes wide with the horror of the vision Mistislaus had painted for her. "I must stay here. I'll keep my skills hidden, Mistislaus."

"Good. It will be better for you. Now we're at an end of our discussion, I hope. Tomorrow morning very early we shall start out."

Chapter Four

The city of Rangfara had been built by no earthbound people. Skyla looked around her and up, ever upward, at the spires and towers rising toward the sky in such an outpouring of exultation expressed in stone that she wanted to shout aloud. Rangfara soared skyward, a forest of pinnacles encrusted with knobs and spikes and crenellations, all crowding together as if to make use of every available inch of sacred ground. Each edifice competed with the last for the number of spires and details and graceful arches and buttresses, as if the builder of each hall had vowed to outdo the last in beauty and aspiration.

By comparison, Ljosalfar settlements were low, green-turved buildings with steeply pitched rooflines, longhouses made of turf sometimes gabled in stone and tall enough for loft rooms above. Wealthy landholders might have a great long hall with annexes built on either side of it and to the rear for kitchen and storage and room for thralls, relatives, retainers, visitors, and livestock and longboats. All the buildings were connected for convenience during the winter. Long dark hallways sometimes wound between the main hall and all its annexes, and stairways connected buildings on sloping ground. In the long dark months of winter when the unlucky stars of the Dokkalfar were riding high in the sky, the Ljosalfar attended their livestock and conducted their affairs indoors in the mazes of halls and longhouses and tunnels and stairways, all buried under thick blankets of snow. It was as much an underground existence as that of the Dokkalfar hiding from the rays of the sun in summer.

The great halls and observatories of Rangfara had no use for burial and protection. It was the sky and the stars they yearned toward, welcoming the light through open arches and windows, all carven around with the most cunning and dextrous of decoration.

Nor yet was it all intended to please the eye, although Skyla's eyes were certainly delighted by the graceful forms soaring over her head; the carvings held significance, she was certain.

Mistislaus strove to keep his attention on Illmuri ahead of them and the narrow, crowded throughway down which the cart was threading a path. While Skyla was admiring the spires, he was forced to contemplate the hovels of beggars built against the foundations of the soaring structures, acrid puddles, heaps of stinking rubbish, and knots of sinister, hooded people, with faces both covered and bare. They stared with unwholesome curiosity at the cart, at Skyla, at Mistislaus, and at Guthrum sulking darkly with his short thick legs dangling over the tailboard; but the presence of Illmuri held their interest the longest, and they looked quickly away when he watchfully turned his head in their direction. Once he had to stop and back the cart into an alleyway to allow several other conveyances to pass, and Skyla had her first look at the finery of the Slaemur clan of women. Filmy material floated in bright colors from their headdresses and shoulders, and their gowns glistened like fishscales. They wore their cloaks and shawls casually fastened with one large elaborate brooch, instead of two, as Ljosalfar women did. Instead of wrapping their faces and exposed hands in strips of sober black cloth, they wore elegant masks, formed to look like the faces of animals. Long fringed and beaded gauntlets covered their arms to the shoulder, and they wore gold and silver and bejeweled bracelets over the gauntlets. As they jolted by at a brisk trot, four carloads of flashing gems and floating fabric, the air was filled with their raucous chattering and shrill laughing, as if a large flock of noisy birds had lumbered by.

"There's a gifting party on the other side of the city," Illmuri offered by way of explanation. "The marriage season is almost over. You're lucky you got to see the Slaemur before they travel back home."

"Lucky indeed." Guthrum grunted, perched in the back of the cart with the rest of the luggage. "Chattering, gaudy magpies."

Skyla's eyes dropped a reluctant glance downward at her own simple attire. Thorborg had convinced her that she ought to wear a woman's gown and long white embroidered tunic. The gown was soft gray wool, belted with red, with a wide matching border at the hem. She wore leggings underneath and high wrapped boots, and her long white cloak woven of her own hair and lamb's wool covered her from head to heels. She wore a blue hood embroidered and pieced with red and yellow and green, with a long tail hanging down behind, with a pocket where small important objects could be carried. Skyla had thought she looked rather fine, judging from women's costumes she had seen at the autumn fairings, but after a view of the Slaemur clan, she looked like a sensible drab gray goose comparing herself to a flock of bright chattering finches.

"I wouldn't want to look like that anyway," she said in quiet pride to Mistislaus, and resumed her rapturous study of the spires of Rangfara.

The largest hall was occupied by Herrad and his Krypplingur warriors, a tall dark building that had fallen into serious ruin in eons past. All but one of its spired towers had collapsed, and the main part of it was roofless, leaving an open courtyard inside where grass had grown between and over the paving stones in thick tuffets, which offered forage for thick-necked, hairy-footed Krypplingur war-horses. Stables had been built along the walls long ago by previous occupants of Rangfara. Skyla looked up in awe at the remaining high walls, noting where floor timbers had rotted away, leaving rows of windows far above, where no one could gaze through except the pigeons strutting and puffing on the mossy sills. Skyla could not imagine the people who could live in such grandeur and build such structures. The knowledge had vanished with the people who had possessed it. Vanished and destroyed. Herrad's hall, she noted, showed signs of shattered rock and violent destruction, rather than the amiable neglect evidenced in the other structures.

A black-masked guard admitted them to the courtyard and motioned them across the lumpy green toward a pair of tall arched doors, where another guard waited. Illmuri dismounted and offered to lift Skyla down from the cart, which she reluctantly assented to, after considering an undignified flying leap over the muddy wheel or the tailboard in her gown and tunic.

"Women's clothes were a mistake," she said. "I shall never wear them again, particularly into strange circumstances."

Inside the tall doors, Illmuri led them through a maze of corridors, with Guthrum stumping along well to the rear with his hand upon the broad axe in his belt. Rooms had been added on at intervals, at different levels, in different styles, over centuries of time, making the entire effect one of crowded shadow and gloom. Kryppling warriors lurked about, huddling over small fires, or sleeping in niches in the wall in unexpected places, like leathery bats who had folded themselves up for the night in the first available spot.

Herrad's lying-up place was a barracks hall down three flights of crumbling stairs, near another hall that smelled of horses and smoke. Another Kryppling admitted them, and they found Herrad lying on a heap of old smelly troll skins on a reclining chair. Arrow slits in the walls admitted light in dim bars, though the slits nearest his couch were covered. A dark-cloaked figure standing near him turned as Illmuri approached, and on the other side of the pallet the hulking form of a watchful Kryppling warrior grounded his lance with a warning thunk, turning suspicious eyes upon the visitors.

Herrad was a shriveled stick of a man, like a twisted willow limb that has become dry and shredded. His hair dangled in matted strings around a mean, narrow face sprigged with splotches and clumps of hairs. Small eyes peered out with nasty cunning, like the weasel Skyla had caught in a trap last summer. A deathly smell surrounding him made Skyla retreat a few paces, feeling sick and hot. One of his legs was swollen and festering like a rotting carcass, oozing a black fluid onto the floor in slow drips.

"So here is the famous healer, Mistislaus," Herrad greeted them in a hoarse, cawing voice. "It took long enough to get you here. You drive a hard bargain, Wizard."

Mistislaus bowed slightly. "It was most kind of you to stop the wind," he said. "Your generosity touched my heart. I am most grateful for the opportunity of offering my humble assistance to you in your need."

Herrad darted Illmuri a quick look, his black brows knitting. "This fellow here hasn't been much good. Overpriced and inexperienced, and a rotten diviner."

The silent hooded figure standing beside Herrad offered a snort of affirmation.

"And you, Witch, you're nothing better!" Herrad spat, twisting around to look at her with venomous yellow eyes. "All I've spent upon magicians is wasted. You hover around to pick my carcass like vultures. Like my sons, waiting for me to die so they can quarrel over my possessions like wolves tearing up a kill. My only hope is that they turn against each other first, and none of them shall survive to take the chieftain's seat!"

He glared at the other dark figures lurking in the shadows beyond his cot. Ofarir stepped forward and grinned briefly in the shadow of his hood and licked his lips.

"Your disease has made its way to your brain," Ofarir said. "One day you must die, Pabbi, and I am the eldest son. There is much you could trust me with now."

"Silence, upstart!" Herrad roared. "You want nothing more than to see me dead! I wish the midwife had wrung your wretched neck when you were born. Others may come after me as chieftain of the Krypplingur, but none will be worthy successors to my name. Dogs and rats, all of you!"

"Dogs and rats we may well be," Ofarir snarled, "but at least we'll be alive and enjoying Rangfara's treasure, while your rotting carcass is feeding the Kjallari-folk in the charnel house."

"You won't have Rangfara's treasure!" Herrad whispered harshly. "The treasure is mine!"

"Rangfara hides its secret well. The treasure is no one's, yet," Illmuri said into a brittle silence wherein father and son glowered at each other, red-eyed with wrath. "Almost as well as the secret of your affliction. Or curse, if you care to believe it."

Herrad's face twisted into a mask of fury, and he gripped the sides of his couch with the yellowed claws of his wasted hands. "If it is a Skylding curse," he snarled, fixing his furious eyes upon Mistislaus, "then a Ljosalfar wizard ought to be able to destroy it before it destroys me. I'll find that Skylding treasure, curse or no curse. I'll kiss each piece of it, as if each one were a drop of Skylding blood. They're not going to defeat me, after I've defeated them. You'd better see to it that they don't, Wizard, or you'll join the Skyldings in Hel!"

"I shall do my best," Mistislaus said. "Now if you'll permit me to look at the offending leg—"

"No, Mistislaus! Let's go away from here!" Skyla exclaimed, seizing him by the arm and attempting to drag him toward the door behind them. Her ears roared and her heart pounded thickly with rage, and she could scarcely restrain herself from picking up a rock and leaping onto Herrad to pound his skull into a pulp. The impulse was almost too strong for her to resist.

"This is no place for a young girl," said the hooded figure of the much-maligned sorceress, gliding forward quickly. "Let me take her outside. She'll be all right with me. Come along, child. Let's leave the men to this nasty job." Her voice was husky and deep, and she held out one pale hand to coax Skyla to follow.

"It will be all right, Mistislaus," Illmuri said. "Alvara will not harm her." Skyla looked anxiously toward Mistislaus.

"Go along with her, Skyla," Mistislaus said, already preoccupied with the complex problem ahead of him. "I shall be here the entire night and I don't want any distractions. Take Guthrum with you and you'll be safe. I shall come for you in the morning when I am finished."

"I am Alvara. No harm will come to you in my company."

Skyla started to resist, but the slim cool hand reached out and touched her wrist in a quick reassuring gesture.

"Come along, lass," Guthrum said in a low growl. "This is no place for you. Anywhere else would be better."

She followed Alvara outside Herrad's quarters, where the air was musty-smelling from the earth, but much fresher. Guthrum inhaled a noisy breath and snorted like a horse, casting belligerent glances at the Kryppling guards posted along the way.

Alvara threw back her hood and strode along as if she, too, were glad to get out of Herrad's presence. Her hair was black, except for streaks of white at the temples, and it was pulled straight back into a severe braid at the back of her neck. Skyla couldn't help stealing glances at her as they walked, fascinated to find herself beside a Dokkalfar woman. Alvara was about as tall as she was, with sharp features etched on a marble-pale countenance, and as she talked her hands mimicked her words, punctuating and underlining them. Skyla watched from the corners of her eyes, but she did not speak in return.

"What a strange child," said Alvara to Guthrum. "I thought at first she was a mute, but I know she hears and can speak when she wishes."

"Skyla has her own ways," Guthrum said by way of curt explanation.

"I doubt if anyone is going to cure him," Alvara said to Guthrum, indicating Herrad with a quick gesture over one shoulder. "The Skyldings put a curse on him for conquering them. I can't see any way through it, and Illmuri's no good, either. A pity your Mistislaus had to become involved in this wretched business. Herrad's going to take it very poorly when he can't be cured, and Mistislaus seems such a pleasant old gentleman, but it's plain to see he's far beyond his depth when it comes to healing Herrad. It's not just an ordinary sickness or suppurating injury, which a simple healer could cure. Illmuri's done Mistislaus no favor, I'll warn you, by bringing him here—if he truly regards Mistislaus as a friend."

"Where are we going?" Guthrum asked suspiciously as Alvara paused to cover her face with a mask before starting to lead the way across the grassy courtyard toward the outer gate of Herrad's hall. A few Krypplingur stirred in the shadows of the mews, looking out at Alvara and the lumbering Dvergar, then disappearing again.

"To my tent," Alvara said. "I can't abide living within a building—especially these buildings. The Ljosalfar say the Rhbus built them, you know. But personally, I don't believe the Ljosalfar or anyone knows for certain. They're very old, that we know, but as old as the Rhbus? They've been gone for many hundreds of years, if indeed they ever existed. No one is even certain of that anymore."

Skyla looked upward again at the spires and shivered.

"The Rhbus existed," Guthrum said firmly, "and they were the most powerful, the most learned and just people ever known to inhabit Skarpsey. The Dvergar learned much of their secret knowledge from them."

Alvara cocked her head knowingly. "I can see Mistislaus likes to tell the old stories. I wish there were Rhbus left, myself. Perhaps their knowledge could solve the conflict between Ljosalfar and Dokkalfar. There is no reason for the bitter competition between light and dark."

"Except that neither can abide the way the other wishes to live," Guthrum said. "And Skarpsey is too small to contain both Ljosalfar and Dokkalfar, at least since the Dokkalfar decided they don't want to live underground."

"But we are not so different, you and I," Alvara answered. "Dvergar are also creatures of the dark. Don't you agree there must be a better way than this bitter rivalry between Ljosalfar and Dokkalfar, which must result in the destruction of one or the other side? Perhaps the barriers of hatred will break down one day."

"I don't think the Skyldings will ever forget what happened to them here," Guthrum said, shaking his head. "Herrad's curse is only one example of it."

"But the Skyldings are all gone, they say," Alvara said. "Nevertheless, I'm glad I'm not related in any way to the clan Krypplingur. I come from a small sept called Misjafn—the Unequal. We are sorceresses, but not well thought of by the Prestur, who are all-wise and all-powerful, especially according to their own opinion. So we are paid less for our services, which is the reason I am here. Herrad is too tightfisted to hire a reputable magician."

"Then Illmuri is not reputable?" Skyla asked.

"No indeed. He's barely out of apprenticeship and eager to prove his skills. He hoped to embarrass me when he first came here, but Rangfara and Herrad's curse have taken some of the wind out of his sails. And now he has turned to Mistislaus. It's quite a mystery to me what he sees in your friend. Not to offend you, of course."

"No offense taken," Guthrum said, prickling with the desire to defend Mistislaus' honor. "Mistislaus has a great many old books, which Illmuri has borrowed and read. They sit and argue for hours, and sound very learned."

"I daresay that is true," Alvara said, guiding Skyla around corners and down alleyways as they talked. "But noble as the experiment might be, I fear Illmuri isn't going to gain anything from his friendship with Mistislaus, and Mistislaus will lose in the end. I offer you this warning because I'm not embroiled in this Krypplingur conflict with Nordanfirth. You would be wise to leave Rangfara quickly and quietly. Why ever did Mistislaus bring this girl with him? It's perfectly obvious that she's a Skylding, and he's come to try his hand at finding the treasure."

"It is?" Guthrum glanced around with his suspicious gaze narrowing, seeing two Krypplingur gliding away down the dark alley among the shadowy archways of the tall buildings. They stopped and stood whispering, looking back with their secretive wrapped faces. One of them Guthrum recognized from Herrad's hall and his arrogant forays among the settlements. It was Ofarir turning and sauntering after them, beckoning his companion to follow.

"I believe it's that little wench from Ulfgarth," he called out too loudly to be ignored. "And that old fraud Mistislaus is now within our walls—as a prisoner soon, I hope. What are you going to do with her, Alvara? Not another virgin sacrifice, I hope?"

"So it might appear," Alvara retorted. "It wouldn't be worth a search for one in Rangfara, would it?"

"How do you suppose old Mistislaus came by this girl?" Ofarir continued, coming up alongside Skyla and leering into her face with his dusty wrappings only inches away.

Skyla made a squeak of alarm and ducked away, shuddering with hatred.

"Take yourself away, Kryppling," Guthrum said in a menacing growl, planting himself in the alleyway like a solid rock, his eyes glaring beneath bristling brows. The two Krypplingur at once drew their weapons. Catching Skyla's arm, Alvara attempted to draw her along as she strode toward the end of the alley, but Skyla twisted out of her grasp and stood facing the Krypplingur from behind the bulwark of Guthrum.

"Can't you find someone more challenging to frighten than a young girl?" Alvara demanded. "Or is that the level you've dropped to these days?"

"I'm just curious," Ofarir said in a nasty, wheedling tone of voice. "Just as curious as you are, Alvara. You think she's one of those white-haired, whey-faced Skylding orphans that Illmuri is hunting, don't you? You think she's going to tell you something about the treasure, I'll wager."

"You're a fool!" Alvara spat.

"Let's have a look under that hood she's wearing," Ofarir said suddenly. "Why do you suppose she's so bundled up in broad daylight? Dayfarers are supposed to like the feel of the sun's rays."

"Ofarir, if you dare touch her—" Alvara began, but Ofarir had already grabbed Skyla's hood, his clawing hand tearing it off backward and taking her hair combs with it. The hood fell down her back hanging by its strings and her hair tumbled around her shoulders, white as new-washed wool.

"What did I tell you?" Ofarir crowed. "All those Skyldings had white hair—until we heaped them up and burned them to ashes, men and women and children alike. But this one was spared somehow, wasn't she? But we got her father and her mother and her brothers and her sisters—"

"No, not all of them, you didn't!" Skyla shouted, with the sinister thundering loud in her ears. All around her the air blurred, and she glimpsed images of people, walking to and fro on ordinary business, images of corpses where they had fallen in battle, all with the stones of Rangfara visible through them. Skyla could scarcely see through the waves of hatred washing over her. She stepped around Guthrum, who was too slow and thick to stop her, knocking away Alvara's restraining hand as if it were a feather, and seized Ofarir by the throat. A quick shake and a snap would take care of him, she knew, like a dog with a rat, but she merely threw him back against the wall, where he slithered down to a stunned huddle in the muck of the alley. His companion backed away, his eyes staring incredulously through a slit in his wrappings. He paused long enough to lift the wrappings up a notch for a quick survey of Skyla, then he took to his heels. The moment he rounded the corner, they heard him shouting.

"Skyla! What have you done?" Guthrum gasped, as Alvara prodded at Ofarir to detect any signs of life. "Is he dead? Herrad's not going to like it if we've killed his son!"

"No, worse luck," Alvara said. "'She held herself back at the last moment, when she should have dashed his brains out or shattered his neck."

"A pity—but she is a Ljosalfar," Guthrum said dryly. "She wasn't raised to shed blood."

Skyla stood trembling, withdrawing a step backward. Her head turned quickly as if she were wondering how she could find Mistislaus in this maze of alleys and streets.

"There now, lass," Guthrum said soothingly, patting her shoulder gently with one massive, black-seamed paw. "Come away with me."

With a roar, a dark knot of Krypplingur burst into the other end of the alley, some of them on horseback. Guthrum drew his broad axe from his belt, grinning with delight.

"So it's merriment and games you want!" he greeted them in a deep bellow as he swung the axe.

"Follow me quickly, we'll lose them," Alvara whispered to Skyla.

Skyla hesitated, looking fearfully toward Guthrum.

"Go with her, lass, and I'll find you later," he said, "As soon as I've mopped the street with this scum!"

Obediently Skyla followed Alvara, through a doorway and across a paved courtyard, up a flight of stairs to a narrow walkway. From there Alvara made a short leap to the adjoining towers and catwalks of the next building, and Skyla hoisted up her unaccustomed, annoying skirts and leaped after her.

More Krypplingur came swarming into the streets at the sound of battle, shouting from the parapets to direct the others into the adjacent building. Alvara, unconcerned, led the chase higher into the towers, leaping from roof to roof, walking coolly across arched buttresses braced between buildings; and Skyla followed fearlessly, confident in the strength that sustained her and drummed in her ears.

Twice Alvara descended stairs to peer out onto the street, but the Krypplingur were not easily deceived. Back to the towers they ran, down a long parapet, up the stepping-stones of a high stone face, across the roof-tree, then across a buttress to a balcony. As Alvara landed lightly on the balcony, a clot of Krypplingur suddenly burst from the stairway, before Skyla could step off the buttress. Skyla pivoted and ran back lightly to the neighboring roof and ran along parallel to Alvara, whose masked face kept flashing in her direction.

The Krypplingur chose to follow Skyla. In a very few moments, Skyla realized that her roof was running out, and there was nothing near it to leap onto. Across the intervening chasm, Alvara scrambled up a step-gable end and ran onto a parapet, twenty feet away, with a dizzying fall to a dark, rubbly courtyard below. Skyla heard the Krypplingur shouting exultantly behind her, anticipating the capture of their prey. Heart hammering, she fixed her eyes upon Alvara, waving her arms on the parapet, summoned a burst of speed from her tiring muscles, and leaped into the void.

It seemed she hung there in midair for a long moment, hearing the shouts of the Krypplingur, seeing Alvara standing frozen, her arms outstretched in a helpless gesture, uttering a long wailing cry of enraged despair. Skyla's ears roared, and she knew she had pushed her powers again. The parapet came toward her in a rush, she landed on it with hands and feet grasping for a hold, then she leaped off it and down to the next balcony with astonishing grace, where the leftover speed of her descent nearly bowled Alvara over. Alvara crouched against the wall, staring at her in disbelief. The Krypplingur on the opposite roof had fallen silent, standing in wary poses as they gaped over the interval.

Skyla turned to taunt them, leaping up on the rail of the balcony to laugh, and the sound came out in a harsh squalling cry that startled her into a small leap backward. She lit on all fours again—which was curious. She darted through a window into the protective shadows of the next building, feeling strange and different when she moved. Although she was still aware of her own body, it seemed to be removed to a slight distance, looking down at her. She lifted one of her hands and looked at it, seeing not a hand but a large gray paw. Long sharp claws curled inward as she rolled her hand over to look at the palm of a cat's foot. Her arm was now a furry leg, and she could feel her hind legs crouch underneath for a powerful, startled spring when Alvara's image suddenly swung into view. Alvara did not seem threatening, so Skyla risked a quick glance alongside and behind her. She saw no trace of herself, only the wiry form of a gray snow lynx. The lynx was a rare, shy animal that she had glimpsed only once several winters ago, when one had come down from the fells. It was a tall and rangy cat with a short flag of a tail and a small alert head with black-tufted sharp ears.

Guthrum's stocky form lumbered onto the parapet, dropping back warily at the sight of the lynx still crouching lightly there. Instinctively he clapped his hand to his broad axe.

Skyla felt herself rising, as if on a swelling tide of voices and forces compelling her to action. With a despairing cry, she succumbed to the powerful pull welling up within her. Turning her back upon faithful old Guthrum, she leaped out again into the dark unknown, clearing the echoing chasm below her. She landed on a balcony on the far side while the savage, mournful cry of the lynx still echoed down the dark alleys of Rangfara. Without another glance behind her, she darted away into the deepening shadows to do what the voices bid her.

"What in the name of all that's fey have you done?" Guthrum choked in an astonished growl.

"It's Skyla!" Alvara gasped. "She's shifted shapes!"

"I didn't know she could do that," Guthrum muttered, his features wrinkling up in consternation.

"Come, we've got to get off this roof and follow her," Alvara snapped. "I can't believe she's done such a thing, and with the Krypplingur watching, too."

"They won't follow us now, Guthrum said with a dire chuckle. "There's nothing the Krypplingur fear like the snow lynx. Death in gray fur and long teeth."

Across the chasm, Skyla's cat form added a menacing yowl. The Krypplingur on the next roof still stared up and down, looking for her. They retreated warily toward the doorway, edging along the rooftop, peering in all directions with their weapons clutched in their hands. Unseen, Skyla shrieked at them, filling the dark chasms below with the blood-chilling scream of the snow lynx. The Dokkalfar plunged through the doorway and disappeared in a disorderly clamor. Skyla threw a few more terrifying wails and snarls into the echoing vaults of the spires.

"Skyla! Hush now!" Guthrum commanded. "You've certainly thrown the terror into them. Come back here now, like a good lass."

He strode to the edge of the roof. Above him, a gray form materialized in the gloom, looking down at him as if it were ready to spring. Eyes glowed like coals in the dark.

"Come away! She could kill you!" Alvara exclaimed in sudden warning, and the eyes and the shadowy form vanished.

"You frightened her," Guthrum growled.

"I daresay not," Alvara replied. "This is a snow lynx, not a frightened young girl any longer. In that form, she would tear your heart out and eat it as readily as anyone else's."

"Bah," Guthrum muttered in a gravelly growl, but he fell silent nonetheless, venturing a quick peep overhead where Skyla had vanished.

In the dark months of winter when the Ljosalfar and other dayfarers cowered in their shelters against the onslaught of chaos and Dokkalfar terrors, the snow lynx hunted the Dokkalfar. Its soft padded feet strode easily over the snow, where the Dokkalfar fylgur-wolves plowed through laboriously. Legends claimed that the snow lynx was the death goddess Hela's pet cat, who stalked through the dark night of winter in search of Hela's prey.

"Come," Alvara said. "We must attempt to follow her and call her back before something happens to her."

As he was long accustomed, when Skyla was out too near nightfall, Guthrum threw back his head and bawled in his dolorous Dvergar bellow, "Skyla! Come home!"

His voice awakened the echoes of Rangfara, more rewarding by far than those of the hills and crags of Ulfgarth. He stopped and listened appreciatively to his own mighty voice bellowing a dozen times down the streets and alleyways.

"She's never been a lynx before," Guthrum said, "but I'd wager my heart's blood she's still our little Skyla, somewhere inside that beast."

"You're going to need some help to get out of this, I believe," Alvara said. "She can't stay for long in the form of a snow lynx before Rangfara raises the alarm. What would Mistislaus think? He gives me the care of his precious idiot, and she turns herself to a lynx the first thing."

"Mistislaus!" Guthrum rumbled. "It would be better if the earth opened up and swallowed us!"

"We'll try to lure her to my tent. No one will dare follow us there. Then we shall try to shift her back."

They called as they walked, descending stairs into ruined courtyards and open weedy galleries that had once been splendid halls, dodging the clattering approach of the Krypplingur, likewise searching for the lynx. They shouted and cursed, scouring each dead-end alleyway.

"It gave them a start, I wager, seeing a snow lynx in broad daylight," Guthrum said with a dire chuckle as they watched six hulking Krypplingur searching a neighboring rooftop.

"Listen!" Alvara held up her hand. "Now call her!"

Guthrum cupped his hands around his mouth and again uttered his dolorous bellow, which was soon echoed by a crooning call from the lynx, the sort of nattering speech cats use among themselves.

"There she is!" Alvara pointed to a fleeting pale shadow coursing along the top of a crumbling wall. "She's following us! Keep calling!"

Guthrum obliged, and they slowly worked their way northward through the maze of ruins and inhabited hovels. Stopping to listen for her in the lee of a wall, they waited, hearing only the rising uproar of the market and drinking booths and, from somewhere, the distinct sounds of a battle being fought. Grumbling and tweaking the edge of his broad axe, Guthrum knit his brow and strained his ears.

"There's blood underfoot tonight for certain," he growled. "Listen at that. And our poor Skyla running footloose in the midst of such a foul and pestiferous place! She must be frightened out of her wits."

"She could not have picked a form that would be more alarming to Dokkalfar," Alvara said. "Last winter a female snow lynx killed one of our guards every other week all winter long. We think she was feeding a den of kittens in the crags below Rangfara. Nothing could touch her, and nothing could stop her from taking what she wanted."

"Where is she?" Guthrum growled, peering into the night shadows. "She's been gone a fair length of time—too long, I think. Skyla! Come home!"

The Krypplingur seemed suddenly to abandon their search for Skyla, vanishing abruptly into the maze of streets. Not long after, the meek yowling of the lynx drew the dwarf's attention to a high window in a tower, where a pair of red-gold eyes blinked down at them in hopeful contrition.

"Skyla!" Guthrum called sternly. "Come down from there at once! Enough of this haring about late at night! I daresay you'll have one of your bad dreams tonight, after this! What would the master say if he knew about this? A willow switch ought to be taken to your hinder portions, ought to have been done years ago. Shall we be having any more trouble out of you tonight?"

The lynx replied with a kitten's mew, and Skyla descended from the window, quite willing to follow along, keeping Guthrum's sturdy cloaked backside close in view. Alvara glanced back often to see the silvery shadow padding attentively from one hiding place to the next, and she shivered to think what an omen such an apparition might portend.

Taking care to stay out of sight of any Krypplingur, Alvara led the way through crumbling arches and down narrow corkscrew stairways and outside again to look into the street before dashing across into another building, then up again into the winding stairs and belfries and arched walks and catwalks and long galleries. Skyla trailed along in the shadows, her golden eyes gleaming warily. At last Alvara descended a heap of rubble into a roofless courtyard thick with green grass, with high walls rising on all sides and not a single door or window available for access. Beside the remains of a tall fountain, a hide tent had been pitched, and four shaggy horses grazed nearby, safely contained by the walls. The horses threw up their heads and sniffed uneasily at the smell of lynx.

"They won't dare follow us here," Alvara said, sweeping open the flap of the tent, and Guthrum entered. "Now we'll see what can be done for Skyla."

"You'd better do it quick," Guthrum said, "before Mistislaus discovers what she's done. You've not got much time before dawn."

A faint voice called from the darkness behind them. "Guthrum? What is this place? How did I come here?"

Chapter Five

Only a fortnight had passed, but it seemed to Skyla that she lived in Rangfara a great deal longer. Memories of Ulfgarth became faded and remote, and Athugashol, the moss-blackened old observatory at the crest of Gibbet Hill, seemed like home. Her room was a small one at the top of a narrow tower, designed to escape from the dreary murk of earth and shadow to catch the earliest rays of morning sun. A dizzying corkscrew climb up a cramped stairway led to it, very inconvenient for Mistislaus, but the nearer Skyla was to the wind and sky, the more content she would be.

At the bottom of the spiral stair was something far less to Skyla's liking. A stout door with the bar on the wrong side was closed upon her each night when Mistislaus went to work on Herrad's cure. Guthrum posted himself outside the house in the courtyard, watching her windows and watching the infrequent traffic in the street.

At first she pined for her freedom. Then she remembered her amusements from Ulfgarth. With dust and spittle and blood she fashioned small human shapes, whose antics kept her company until she banished the force that gave them life and they disintegrated once more into dust. On her daily walks in the courtyard she set traps for mice and rats and birds, and they, too, went to the tower room, hapless little sacrifices in Skyla's quest for knowledge. Pebbles, sticks, flowers, feathers, and bits of metals all collected in Skyla's room, where she studied and rearranged and reorganized the elements and forces that made them.

From her tower room, Skyla could see those who scuttled up or down the Street of a Thousand Steps that led to Gibbet Hill. She knew there were a few lingerers who stopped outside their gate and watched the old observatory with endless fascination, although there was nothing of interest to be seen. There was only Guthrum huffing and growling over the injustices of his life as he hauled firewood or peat or the market basket, or Mistislaus stationed in a high room reciting his endless droning iterations, or Skyla herself, peeping from one window or the other or taking her exercise in the walled court.

Rangfara was full of watchers, some of them very near. When Mistislaus consented to take her to the market, she felt them watching. When she idled and daydreamed in the ruined courtyard behind the observatory, she could feel their eyes dwelling upon her. Several times she thought she glimpsed a fleeting movement in the hollow windows of the Hall of Stars, the next building to the observatory. At night, when Mistislaus was gone, she heard strange crying calls echoing through the standing walls.

Life became well-nigh dull. Each day after Mistislaus awakened her in the morning, she hastily muttered a few of the iterations he assigned her in the hope of ordering her mind and thoughts, then she quickly made her escape. It was an unpleasant consequence of Mistislaus' acquaintance with Illmuri that Mistislaus now believed that she ought to be taught something. She could see no sense whatsoever in repeating an idea several hundred times in the hope that some result would be brought about by sheer mental exertion alone. Mistislaus droned away earnestly at his morning iterations for an hour or so in behalf of Herrad's disease, reverberating through the old mossy tower like the monotonous buzzing of a large, bumbling insect. Then he would send Guthrum to the marketplace. The dwarf would bring back a hot breakfast from the cooking stalls, growling all the while about the ignominity of a Dvergar carrying a market basket.

While Mistislaus was occupied, Skyla ran barefoot up the stairway and squeezed out a window. She crept out onto the rooftop, where she gazed around at the sight of Rangfara's crusty old black towers reluctantly greeting the light of dawn, rising through the musty murk of the streets toward the light, like strange convoluted plant sprouts made of stone. It was far different from the worn and peaceful green beauty of Ulfgarth, and it made her heart pound and her breath catch to look at the expanse of Rangfara. Four miles on a side, enclosed within a bristling wall, and exuding clouds of smoke and unclean vapors, Rangfara lurked in the mist like a dragon awaiting her acquaintance.

Below, from the direction of the horse stall, the reverberating snores of Guthrum assured her he was still asleep in the old stone horse trough he had chosen for his bed. She flitted along the tops of the walls, as if at last she had discovered a way of traveling without bothering to touch the earth, following a walkway around the courtyard where once rooftops had rested, where some broken roofs still clung tenaciously. With the dark visage of the Hall of Stars watching her, she did not go far.

Her white nightgown caught the red morning rays, and she shimmered like a butterfly with its wings unfurled and glowing, high up where the sun was, above the evil and the decay of the old hall below. Old Fegurd grazed there now on the velvety grass seaming the paving stones, where kings and earls and grand ladies had once trod in lofty pomp.

Below her, beside a choked fountain, in a patch of sun that somehow penetrated to the earth, a ragged figure sat cross-legged on a block of fallen stone. It was a very large boy, or very young man, several years older than herself, but old enough to carry a sword resting in a sling over one shoulder. His expression was devout and pained, his eyes were shut as he murmured a cadence over and over while his fingers dutifully counted off the repetitions on a greasy knotted string.

Skyla glanced back at the observatory, where Mistislaus was doing the same thing as part of his morning ritual for gathering power for the day. He had told her sternly to speak to no one, but this was an intruder in her own favorite territory. When she was allowed out, she came here. A dark pool welled up from the rubble, where some sucker-mouthed fish caromed around sluggishly when she threw pebbles at them. This was the most amusing sport she could find in the ruined and gloomy place.

Her attention returned to the young ruffian. His knees showed, dirty and scabbed, through the holes in his breeches, and his toes came through his boots, which were held together with not much more integrity than their lacings provided. The ragged cloak and tunic he wore were of the indistinguishable color always worn by beggars, thieves, and other people who lived off the land by their wits. He was tall, yet still skinny, as if he had reached the age to begin considering becoming a man one day soon, but not just yet.

He was a fascinating object. Skyla had seen few boys in her lifetime, and only at a safe distance. Mistislaus had taken her to the autumn fairings, and she had seen more people than she had dreamed existed, but he had watched over her like a suspicious old eagle with a single chick. He had taken care to keep her close to him, safe on the high seat of the cart. She had filled her eyes, ears, and memory with the fairings, with all the people and livestock and tents and booths, so she would have something to mull over in her mind during the dark months of winter, when she couldn't get outside much.

Boys and fairings were noisy, rumbustious, and dirty. One could not exist in its full excitement and glory without the other. Boys ran and tumbled and wrestled and shouted and chased sheep with sticks and sat in disreputable camaraderie on tops of walls, whistling and shouting insults at other boys who had the misfortune to be working or otherwise engaged in profitable ventures. Boys were an element of chaos in an orderly world, and Skyla shivered with the adventure of standing so near to one, particularly one who was in her own domain, and therefore her property.

The most interesting thing about him was his hair, glinting like pale fire in the dawn-light. Skyla felt drawn to it, not knowing that her own white hair glinted in a similar red-gold halo floating untidily around her head.

"Boy!" She called in her clear voice. "What are you doing here? You are trespassing, and I'm very weary of your watching of me every day."

The youth leaped to his feet, stuffing away the cord and jerking out his short sword. Even Skyla could tell it wasn't a very good sword, but he certainly looked willing enough to use it. He shaded his eyes and squinted up at her, his mouth falling open in a curious expression.

"Who are you?" he demanded. "A flaming salamander? No draug would shine so bright."

"I am Skyla," she replied, as if that were sufficient explanation for anyone. "What are you doing here and why do you spy upon me? This has been our place for more than a fortnight now."

"It's been my place for two years and more," he retorted. He scowled up at her. "You are the trespassers here, not me. I haven't been spying upon you. I've just watched to see when you would leave."

"You have white hair, the same as I do," Skyla added, further discomfiting him as he quickly covered up his head.

"You're the girl who stays in the small tower," the boy said. "We thought you were a prisoner of the wizard."

"Prisoner?" Skyla asked. "I am allowed to do whatever I wish, as long as Guthrum or Mistislaus is watching out for me. Rangfara is not a safe place."

"You sound like a prisoner to me," the youth said. "Do they know you're out now?"

"No indeed, and Mistislaus wouldn't like it if he did. He has told me to speak to no one. But your hair is the same color as mine. The voices told me I must speak to you. Who are you, boy, that the mist people are aware of you?"

The youth took a long, slow look around the courtyard of the observatory. "What mist people?" he asked warily.

"Oh," she said, "you don't see them, either. Well, they are all around us." Her voice took on a dreamy enchantment as she glanced about, pointing slightly with her chin or shoulder. "I've learned to see them only when I want to, however. It's strange to see a battle going on right over the stalls in the market and everyone going merrily about their business of buying and selling—and cheating one another, as Mistislaus says. And right here now, there's a grand feast going on right where old Fegurd is grazing. Everyone is wearing jewels and headdresses, and there's gowns and robes that drag on the ground for their heaviness with gold and silver embroidery. It's not what the real builders of Rangfara intended at all. I see them from time to time—quiet, gray people who studied the stars and wrote everything in books. You see the old fellow with the white beard? There, beside the well. I think he's one of the Rhbus—or the draug of one. He looks as if he doesn't approve of any of this."

As she talked, she turned and gazed at things the ragged boy could not see, and pointed out things invisible to his eyes.

"Who are you, besides Skyla?" he asked with a deeply perturbed frown. "And how old are you, and who were your parents?"

"I know nothing of my true age or parentage, except that I was carried to Mistislaus at Ulfgarth in the cold springtime, and Thorborg thought that I was about two months old. It was almost thirteen springtimes ago. Now you may tell me your name."

"Jafnar is what I am called—my real name is unknown," he said pridefully. "My father was a Skylding warrior when Rangfara was destroyed at the crest of midwinter, when Fantur the Rogue stood highest in the sky. Thirteen midwinters ago, this coming next one."

"Thorborg says my mother was a lady," Skyla said, sitting down and composing herself gracefully on the top of the wall, with one slim foot swinging over a bone-shattering drop to a heap of rubble below. "After the Krypplingur destroyed the Skyldings, she came to the hill shepherds, who are wild people now, and she was carrying me yet unborn. At home in Ulfgarth I have her clothing and the fine things she sent with me. She came from Rangfara with little besides her life and mine. Sometimes I see Rangfara through other eyes, and hear voices, but I am yet too young and inexperienced."

"Then you must be a Skylding, from one of the mother clans!" Jafnar said, his eyes shining suddenly with excitement. "We are kin, you and I! Cousins, at least! Our fathers were warrior Skyldings!"

"I know nothing, save Rangfara is mine," Skyla said, "and now that I have found you, you, too, are mine, my own brother-kin."

"I shall help you escape from Mistislaus," Jafnar said. "I helped my other brothers to escape from those that held them against their will."

"There are other Skyldings? I should like to see them," Skyla said.

Jafnar hesitated a moment, then whistled softly toward a black ruin adjoining the once-grand Hall of Stars, a magnificent structure still boasting its embossed diagrams of the heavens. A shaggy head appeared at a window, which was joined by another. In a few moments, the heads vanished, and four more ragged shapes came slinking across the mossy paving stones, darting from pillar to pile of rubble until they were quite close. Warily they peered out at Skyla and their leader standing below her lofty perch. The sun still shone in her hair like a red halo, and she looked down at them as if she were a queen surveying her subjects. There were seven of them, of various sizes and ages, all as dirty, shaggy, and ragged as Jafnar. Two of the youngest were twins, thin little lads about Skyla's age, with large, deep eyes that bespoke perpetual hunger and suspicion. They were all scruffy, small to be carrying the weapons they bore, and young to carry the scars they had earned in their battle for life.

"You don't need to hide," she called out.

"Jafnar, who's she?" one of the youths growled warily.

"A Skylding of the true blood," he replied.

"How can that be? The Skyldings were a male clan," the other said, still lurking behind his sheltering stump of pillar.

"But she's got the white hair, and that's the sign," another of the young vagabonds added, giving the first a shove so he could get a better look at Skyla.

"Rangfara is my own city, and I've always known it," Skyla said. "My lady mother was going to birth me here."

"I'll bet she didn't know you'd turn out to be a girl," another of the wild boys added with a lowering glare. "I expect it would have been a great disappointment to whoever your father was. Naturally he would have wanted a son to carry on his warrior tradition."

"Hush, Modga! Don't be rude!" Jafnar snapped.

"Disappointed?" Skyla repeated, turning her head on one side like a curious cat. "Warriors fight and perish, but the women carry the knowledge. My unknown father would have been very pleased to receive a daughter. I have looked often for his ghoul lingering in Rangfara when I go out with Mistislaus. I'm sure I would recognize him, but I haven't seen him yet."

The wild boys exchanged wondering glances, their eyes bright like fox eyes as they nudged each other and whispered. The lowering one shook his head in a violent negative.

"She can't be a Skylding!" Modga declared. "It's a clan for men only! Don't listen to her, Ordvar!"

The others shoved him rudely aside, ignoring him.

"If you are a true Skylding," said Ordvar, a tall youth with a steady, level gaze, "then you must know something about the treasure, which is our birthright as the last living Skyldings."

Skyla's eyes traveled past him, contemplating the ruins behind him, where old Fegurd was cropping mouthfuls of grass. A breath of cold air played over the gaping windows and broken parapets with a moaning sound. She climbed down the wall, using the barest of toe and finger holds.

"It is here," Skyla said, turning her wondering gaze upon the Skyldings. "Beneath our feet. Did you not know it?"

"Just here? Beneath our feet?" The Skyldings stared down at their feet, and the young twins hastily turned over a few stones.

"Didn't you know it always?" Skyla asked, shocked. "The dreams—the Kellarman—"

"Shh! Thogn will hear!" Jafnar said, pointing to the seventh of their number, and the others shook their heads frantically, but the dread word was out. Skyla had scarcely noticed him lurking on the far edge of the group. He was one of the older ones, with a strangely silent and distracted manner that marked him as an addled witling in the heartless world of Rangfara, and therefore regarded with suspicion, or even killed.

"Kellarman? Kellarman?" The youth moaned, dropping the smooth pebbles he was admiring beside the fish pond. Pure terror etched his wild and hunted face as he darted glances all around, like a rabbit caught in a gin. He made a short frantic dash forward, then shied aside as if he had seen something, and Jafnar and Ordvar and Modga grabbed him. He struggled with desperate strength, sobbing and moaning incoherently.

"No, Thogn," Jafnar said soothingly. "There's no Kellarman here. It's just a bad dream."

"You're all right," Ordvar said, patting his back. "You're wide awake now and nothing will happen to you."

"Prestur?" Thogn queried. "Where's Prestur?"

"He's dead," Modga said. "Long ago. The Krypplingur killed him. We're protecting you now, you great dummy."

Thogn quieted, and they forced him to sit down on a stone nearby, but still his head swiveled from side to side with fearful alertness.

Skyla reached out and gently patted Thogn's shaggy head, as if he were a large dog. He gazed at her wonderingly but didn't seem frightened.

"Good Thogn," she said. "Poor Thogn. What a hard life he's had."

Jafnar shrugged and his mouth twisted bitterly. "So have we all. Our fathers and mothers and kin were all slaughtered by the Krypplingur and we grew up like thralls. Ordvar, Modga, Thogn, and I were of an age to remember. You see what the memories and nightmares have done for poor Thogn. Einka, Lofa, and Lampi—" He pointed out the younger boys. "—were babes in arms, given away at the last moments to the Fiskimadur and the Landbunadur in the hopes of saving their lives. Einka belonged to a smith and had to pump his bellows all day and fetch monstrous loads of ore. Modga became the eyes for a thieving old beggar, who kept him chained up and barely fed. He finally fell into a ditch in the Skurdur and drowned. We stole Lampi and Lofa from a tanner, and Ordvar escaped from a farmer who came to sell sheep. And Thogn belonged to an old blind priest who tried to keep him hidden. Then one day the Krypplingur murdered the old priest and Thogn escaped to the Kjallari, where we found him. We don't ever mention that person you mentioned, or Thogn has bad dreams and fits like this one you just saw."

Each of the boys acknowledged this introduction with a wave, or a smile, or a wry bow, except Thogn. He crouched on the rock, his pale gray eyes still wide with dread. He stole sharp glances at Skyla and around the courtyard fearfully, as if he were hearing other voices speaking than Jafnar's and seeing other people than his brother-kin.

"And I am Jafnar," he concluded with evident pride. "I was captured and sold by Otkell the slave trader, but I escaped and made my way back to Rangfara. We are the last of Hoggvinn's clan of warriors and we have come to reclaim our birthright, our forefathers' city, and our treasure. One day we won't be afraid to show who we are."

Jafnar tore off his hood and shook his head in defiance. The other boys also tore off their hoods and caps, revealing a glistening crop of white hair in various pale tints of gold and silver. Jafnar's hair was as pale as Skyla's own, cropped roughly over his ears as if a goat had grazed it off. He had done it himself, she judged, with a knife. Perhaps the goat would have done the job more neatly. The others were trimmed off in the same inexpert style. Skyla shivered suddenly, looking at them, feeling somehow that she was looking at herself.

"One day we won't fear to be recognized. We'll be the feared ones," said Ordvar, the tall, quiet youth. "The Krypplingur hunt us like rats. They won't be satisfied until every Skylding is dead. This is our favorite place. We are safe here, because the Krypplingur are afraid of it. In better days, the Skyldings used to hold their rituals here, and some of that power still lingers to help us with our endeavor."

"What endeavor is that?" Skyla asked.

"The restoration of our birthright," Jafnar said, and the others echoed him.

"If you need help, you must speak to Mistislaus," Skyla said earnestly. "He is very wise."

"But he's helping Herrad," Einka said.

"And he's searching for our treasure," Modga threw in, "but he's never going to find it. We know Rangfara better than anyone else. If anyone finds it, we'll be the ones."

"He's also great friends with Illmuri," Ordvar said. "The one who follows and spies upon us."

"You are kept here like a prisoner," Jafnar said. "Don't you wonder why?"

"It's because of the treasure," Ordvar said. "They think they can use you to reveal it."

"Mistislaus has always been like a parent to me," Skyla said. "He doesn't care about any treasure. He's very fond of me and wants to protect me from the evil of Rangfara. Mistislaus is getting terribly old and fat. He likes eating and drinking and iterating and taking naps in the sun. He wouldn't have come here at all, except for Illmuri, who told Herrad about him being a healer. Mistislaus doesn't care much at all about what has happened to Rangfara."

"He doesn't?" Jafnar pursued, with a disappointed frown. "You've never seen him shift shapes, or read runes, or cast fortunes? Nothing at all like that?"

"Nothing at all," Skyla said. "But he's got a lot of old books. Older than the earth, I'm sure, covered with dust and cobwebs, and he has forbidden me to open them. I suppose they're books of spells and all the knowledge in the entire world."

Jafnar's face brightened at the mention of the books.

"One day I shall know how to read the runes," he said. "One day there will be Skyldings ruling again in Rangfara."

"Indeed!" Skyla said, with a questioning glance at the other six boys. "How can you seven take the fortress by yourselves and drive out the Krypplingur? You're not yet full-grown men, and the Krypplingur are so many."

"So we may be," Jafnar said, "but we are Skyldings. I was four years of age when the Krypplingur came. I can remember it as clearly as if it happened yesterday. My mother was one of the last Skylding defenders of Rangfara. Before she died, she took me to the common people sheltering in the walls of Rangfara and begged that I be protected. These others were likewise given over or found by the clans Fiskimadur and Landbunadur."

"And only we eight of the children of Rangfara survived?" Skyla said. "Why are there not more Skylding children scattered around Nordanfirth?"

"I have searched and found no others," Jafnar said. "The Krypplingur did their job well, finding all the survivors they possibly could and executing them. In the beginning, I was with Otkell the Slaver, who thought he was going to get a good price for me one day. If I hadn't escaped when I did, I might have gone into a Dokkalfar mine or warlord's fortress by now. I, too, felt the shadow of some great deed hanging over me, without knowing what it was the Three Sisters of Fate wanted me to do. I came to the realization, when I was twelve years old, that my destiny was the destruction of the Krypplingur, although I could see no way to do it. So I escaped and came to Rangfara and rescued my brothers from their lives of slavery, and now we're a clan of our own. But we are all doomed to go nameless forever, unless we manage one day to recover the genealogy scrolls of the Skyldings."

"If we could only find our true names written," Ordvar said, "it would prove our right to Rangfara. Our names must be written there, since we were born before the destruction."

"We don't need scrolls to kill Krypplingur," Modga said with a fiery snort of contempt. "We need swords, not names."

"Names are important," Skyla said. "My true name given me by my mother means 'duty'—or 'revenge.' The name Skyla, as Mistislaus calls me, means 'shield.' There is power in a name. You are right to search for your names in the genealogy scrolls of the Skyldings. I fear mine won't appear there, since I wasn't born in Rangfara. All I have is my mother's clothing, some of her jewelry, the little clothes she had made for her newborn child, and a great gold ring with the sign of the wolf."

"The ring and the clothing will help," Ordvar said. "Plenty of people survived Rangfara's destruction. After the Skyldings were all dead, the Fiskimadur and Landbunadur who had come to help them fight laid down their arms and surrendered. The common folk won't talk about it, but we've found one or two who are willing to tell me what they know. Like old Eyda, the blind beggar. The Krypplingur put out his eyes with hot irons and tortured him and threw him on the midden pile thinking he was dead. He lost his foot to a shattered ice-spell and lives in Othr Fidla's barn."

"Perhaps he would remember my mother," Skyla replied. "I know she was someone important, because of that gold ring with a wolf on it. They say the wolf was Hoggvinn's sign. She was the daughter of Hoggvinn, perhaps."

"I suppose if that were so, it would make you the chieftain of the Skyldings," Jafnar said. "I don't know if a female has ever held that position."

"The Skyldings are a warrior clan," Modga said in an arrogant tone. "They had no use for women, except to produce more warriors."

Jafnar gave Modga a whack that raised the dust in his hair. "Silence, you dolt, that's not true. My mother was a warrior and a Skylding. I remember her white hair falling down her back as she shot arrows down off the ramparts. When her bowstring broke, she wove a new one from her hair."

"You needn't boast about it," Modga said. "We've heard your story a hundred times. We are all equals until we find the scrolls and discover who's got the most Skylding blood. Skyldings were a warrior clan, and it's known to all of us who among us fights the best and likes it most. Einka is so fat and cowardly, I daresay he's barely a Skylding at all, and possibly his birth is not even recorded as legitimate."

"Don't you say that!" Einka raged suddenly, leaping on Modga like a panther and wrestling him down by dint of surprise and sheer weight. "I'm not a coward, and I'm as much a Skylding as you are!"

"And you're a glutton!" Modga added, spitting out a mouthful of grass. "You care more about food than anything!" They rolled over and over, puffing and growling and flailing.

"Stop that!" Jafnar commanded. Lofa and Lampi moved as one to separate the fighters, quelling any further hostilities by sitting on the combatants and grinding their faces into the soft turf as punishment. Jafnar signaled to let them up, and the wrestlers rose, their expressions sorry and sullen.

"No more fighting!" Jafnar glowered at the two miscreants. "We're family. Cousins. Even brothers. We're all that any of us have got left. If you don't stay faithful to our oath of fealty to each other, then we might just as well part company and go back to being beggars and thralls. Is that what you want?"

Modga muttered resentfully and dug his toes into the sward. Einka shook his head.

"Well then, I should think the future before us together is far better than our individual futures apart," Jafnar went on. "And don't any of you forget it, ever."

They all murmured in affirmation, and even Thogn appeared to be paying attention enough to nod his head.

"Let's get it in blood," Ordvar said. "Einka, bring out the rune stick, we're going to swear. I've got the knife."

"What about her?" Modga asked, waggling one shoulder suspiciously toward Skyla. "She's not really an orphan, if she's got a home and someone to look after her. Are we really going to let her in?"

"She'll have to swear fealty to the Skylding clan," Lofa said.

"With blood," Lampi added.

"I say yes," Einka said immediately. "You can tell by her hair that she's one of us."

Ordvar added, "Better that we make sure she knows who and what she is, before the Krypplingur discover her."

"Oh, yes, of course," everyone murmured with a sudden darkening of spirit, and Thogn nodded his head in silent agreement.

"They'd kill her," Lofa said, at the same time Lampi said, "They'll be looking for her."

"Form a circle, all of you," Ordvar commanded, taking the rune stick from Thogn. "Quiet now, we must concentrate on what we're doing."

"You will swear with us eternal kinship, won't you?" Jafnar said earnestly to Skyla as they knelt in a circle with Ordvar in the center. "It doesn't hurt much."

Nodding her head, Skyla briefly took her eyes off the long knife Ordvar was brandishing around with complete disregard for eyes, ears, noses, chins, or whatever might get in the way of his waving. All the while he was uttering a dolorous chant and flourishing the knife in what he hoped were significant gestures fit for attracting the attention of the powers that be. Thogn crouched with his eyes half shut, humming a peculiar cadence over and over to himself.

"Put out your thumbs," Jafnar commanded. His was the first to be nicked by Ordvar's knife, and the welling drop of blood was rubbed into the faint scratchings on the stick. Next was Einka, Thogn, Lofa, Lampi, Modga, and Ordvar himself, with rather a lot of wincing and holding of breath. Then it was Skyla's turn. She held out her thumb, and Ordvar pressed the knifepoint against her flesh, but his hand trembled so much that she was forced to take the knife and pierce her own finger. It didn't hurt much, and she diligently smeared her blood into the runes. She was accustomed to using her own blood for her experiments.

Then they all put their fingers on the rune stick and repeated in unison, "Now we are forever bound to each other by this blood. We are all brothers—and one of us is our sister," Jafnar added swiftly, and the rest echoed him. "Forever more we will defend our clan and the members of it until the last breath leaves our bodies, or until Rangfara and its treasure are once again ours. Long live the Skylding clan!"

Thogn hummed his own cadence along with the words of the others, lending the chant an eerie feeling that made Skyla shiver and look around the stone circle. It was a suitable place for oaths and rituals, and she did not doubt that a good many had taken place here during the long history of Rangfara.

A blast of wind suddenly buffeted at them, churning the surface of the quiet pool into a froth, then it charged away through the rooftops of Rangfara with a wild shriek. The young Skyldings winced at the peppering of dust and looked at each other a moment in frightened awe.

"What was that?" Ordvar murmured worriedly. "That's never happened before."

"It was nothing," Skyla said. "Just something old trapped in this place. Our swearing released it."

As part of the ritual, Jafnar took a half loaf of bread out of his pack and broke it up and passed it around.

"Don't wolf it," he said. "This is all the food we've got until tonight when we can steal more from the stalls. We only steal from nightfarers," he added by way of justification to Skyla.

She didn't appear to have heard him. She held her share of bread and looked at it as if she had never seen bread before. It was indeed far coarser and blacker than anything Thorborg ever made.

Slowly she began to pick it apart, humming softly under her breath, catching the pieces in the cradle of her nightdress.

"I think I can fix this," she said.

"She's as addled as Thogn!" Modga muttered in disgust, with a sharp poke of his elbow in Jafnar's ribs. "And you've told her all about us. What if she babbles to someone? This Mistislaus is working for Herrad. She'll tell him about us, and the Krypplingur will be here hunting us!"

"Silence," Jafnar snapped, watching Skyla worriedly. "She won't tell anyone. She's a Skylding."

"A looney one," Modga replied. "You have no way of guessing what she's going to do. She's just like Thogn."

"No, she's better," Jafnar said. "At least she can talk, and Thogn can't."

Skyla stood up, holding her nightdress to form an apron. She took a handful of crumbs in one hand, then proceeded to spread a small feast upon a smooth slab of fallen stone—fresh bread, berries, soft cheese, butter, tasty roots, seeds, and nuts. The wild boys all stood around and stared, except for Thogn, who handed her his own portion of the rank Dokkalfar bread and cheerfully helped himself to the berries.

"Secret powers!" Ordvar murmured, quickly making a sign to ward off evil. "How did she do that?"

"The mist people told me," she said. "All Alfar have these powers, but they are forgetting them in favor of the sword. That was the reason the Skyldings died."

"Mist people!" Modga snorted. "There's no such thing. She's got an evil force to do these things for her."

"It tastes pretty good, however she did it," Einka said, stuffing the soft new bread into his mouth and reaching for the cheese.

They all fell upon the food and devoured it so voraciously that Skyla broke more of the coarse bread and changed it into better fare. In too much awe to press her with questions, they simply watched, knowing perhaps that she was incapable of explaining how she did it.

"Now I must go back to Mistislaus," she said unexpectedly, and got to her feet, shaking the remaining breadcrumbs out of her lap. "He's done with his iterations. Good-bye."

"Skyla!" Jafnar hurried after her. "Don't go back to the tower. Now's your chance to escape!"

"I'm not a prisoner," Skyla said. "I can leave whenever I want. If I left, Mistislaus would be grieved."

"Don't let him deceive you," Jafnar said. "He knows who and

what you are. We've got to get the Krypplingur out of Rangfara. And there's the treasure to find, if the snow lynx doesn't eat our hearts first."

"The lynx!" The wild boys all hastily made signs to ward off evil, while Skyla looked on in polite amazement.

"What is the snow lynx?" she asked.

"A fortnight ago, six Krypplingur were killed and their hearts torn out and eaten by the beast," Einka said with great relish. "In broad daylight. Everyone in Rangfara is terrified of it and goes around with lynx amulets, lynx powders, lynx repellents, anything you can imagine."

"I don't want anything to do with that lynx," Modga said vehemently, casting a wary glance at Skyla. "Even for the treasure. We'll have to find it some other way."

"I must go," Skyla said. The distant vibrations of Guthrum's snoring had turned to coughs and sputters and irascible grunts and snorts. "Mistislaus will be frightened if he discovers I've been out here alone."

"Is there nothing we can do to help you escape?" Ordvar pleaded.

Skyla paused, cocking her head as if listening. "Yes, there is something. Mistislaus is old and fat. He will be grateful for the needful household duties. Wood and water and ashes carried away and such."

"Easy enough," Ordvar said, "though I don't see how it's going to help you get out of that tower."

"See that window there?" Jafnar pointed to the top of the Hall of Stars. "I'll hang a flag in it when we're at home. If you ever need our help, you must give this call, and we will come at once." He threw back his head and uttered a piercing howl.

"I've heard that before!" Skyla exclaimed. "At night, when Mistislaus is gone to Herradshol. I thought it was a draug, or a dog dying."

"It's the Skylding battle cry," Ordvar said. "One day it's going to curdle the blood of the Krypplingur."

"I must go," Skyla said again, hearing Guthrum growling and shuffling about in his quarters in the stable near the outer gate. "Guthrum is awake."

The wild boys leaped warily to their feet.

"The Dvergar!" Ordvar said. "We've met him before. He chases us with that axe of his."

"Don't forget," Jafnar said urgently. "If we don't find the treasure, Rangfara will never be Skylding again."

In a moment Guthrum came around the side of the house. He stopped and glared at the wild boys a moment. Then with his head well down, he came at them with surprising speed in a rushing charge like a short, snorting bull.

"Get out, you vermin!" he roared. "Didn't I tell you I'd split your livers and fry them if I ever caught you here again?"

The wild boys vanished over walls in a tide of flying rags and scuttling feet, with Guthrum harrowing up the air behind them with vicious swings of his axe. He charged past Skyla, intent on chasing away the wild boys. She climbed up the wall and scampered nimbly over the narrow and crumbling places and vanished through the narrow window. Looking back toward the Hall of Stars, she saw a hand hanging a ragged banner out one window. She sighed, suddenly warmed by the thought that at last she had found her kin.

Chapter Six

On the following day, Mistislaus discovered that someone had shoveled out Fegurd's stable. Also, the fallen stones that cluttered the paths and courtyards outside the tower gate had been pulled away and piled, so Skyla had paved walkways to walk upon during her outings. Mistislaus said nothing. Presently a wall began to be mended, all by the same invisible hands. The thorns and nettles disappeared from the Hall of Stars. Peat and kindling began to appear regularly upon the doorstep, along with jugs of fresh water. After a week, Mistislaus felt moved to make some comment.

"Well then," he murmured faintly. "Something is going on around here."

"Oh," Skyla said, "it's just the wild boys."

"We've got an infestation of wild boys, eh?" Mistislaus hoisted one craggy eyebrow suspiciously. "I suppose you've seen them?"

"Yes, and talked to them."

"But did I not tell you to speak to no one in Rangfara? Must I keep you always locked away in the small tower?"

"They're Skylding orphans, Mistislaus, the same as I. We've all sworn a blood oath of fealty. We're going to drive away the Krypplingur and find the Skylding treasure."

"I think I must see these wild boys," he said, passing one hand over his brow, where a sudden sheen of moisture had sprung from nowhere.

"They're afraid of you," Skyla said. "Because you're working for Herrad. If you try to find them, you might frighten them away, and then we'd have no one bringing us wood and peat and water. Guthrum would have to fetch it himself, and you know how he growls; or you'd have to hire that spotty pigman's boy to do it."

"I see," Mistislaus said carefully. "Where do these wild boys live?"

"In that old tower next to ours," Skyla said with a twitch of one shoulder in the appropriate direction. "The Hall of Stars. Mistislaus, I wish to find the treasure of Rangfara. It isn't right that you should be so poor. When Rangfara is mine, you shall have your choice of the fine halls here."

"Thank you, my dear, but a fine hall is not important to me. What I find important is your safety and discipline, and I fear you're at risk if you take up with a pack of wild boys who are treasure-seekers. You should be practicing your iterations even now, if you are ever to control your given powers."

"I don't need iterations, Mistislaus."

"Nonsense. Everyone needs iterations. It disciplines one's thoughts, and if one doesn't control one's thoughts, there is little else one can control. And you'd better forget about hunting that treasure. Rangfara has been plowed up from end to end by the Krypplingur and they haven't found it yet."

"Yet? Then it's still there," Skyla said.

"No, that's not what I meant at all. I meant to say that the treasure is not findable, by the Krypplingur or anyone, or it would have been found."

"But I am a Skylding," Skyla said, "and the treasure is a Skylding treasure. It will be found by a Skylding."

Mistislaus snorted gently. "Come along to your lessons, child. The day is wasting, and I shall have to go to Herrad sooner than we like."

"Must you go?"

"I'm sorry, child. I must."

"Must you always lock the door?"

"For you to be safe from harm, yes."

Mistislaus went to Herrodshol each night and Skyla was locked up inside her cramped little tower room at the top of the twisting narrow stair. The only company she had were her experiments and three cats, for which she was grateful, but she was locked in nonetheless. Presently she was reduced to two cats when she attempted to discover where life goes when released from its mortal bondage, and whether or not it can be called back. For some unknown and annoying reason, she was not able to duplicate the success she had once had with a rabbit, though with smaller creatures she was quite successful.

Guthrum was no company when he was left in charge of her; he posted himself outside the gate and menaced anyone who came by, like a savage old dog who knows the master is away. He was the bane of the wild boys, in particular, and seemed most earnest about his threat against the sanctity of their livers.

"When shall Herrad be cured, Mistislaus?"

"Very soon, I hope, but it's a nasty disease, and I suspect there's more to it than mere illness. Something to do with a spell, I shouldn't wonder. When he's cured, we shall scamper back to Ulfgarth, where it's green and peaceful, as fast as we can go."

"I hope it takes a great deal of time to cure him," Skyla said, her dreaming gaze turned outward and beyond the musty observatory.

Mistislaus glanced at her, sitting curled in a seat beside the window, resting her chin upon her fist and gazing out. As a precaution, he'd had a heavy grate installed over it, but it still didn't satisfy him.

"So you've become fond of Rangfara and the Krypplingur?" he asked.

"The Krypplingur will be here forever, as mist people, just as the Rhbus and Skyldings are," Skyla said, "tangled in the shadows with the shapes of all those who lived and died here. I hear their voices calling to me, but I don't know which way to go to answer them."

"Don't go anywhere," Mistislaus said hastily. "You don't know what those voices want. You're far too inexperienced yet to deal with the shadow realm."

"One day I shall be ready," she said with a sudden flare of resolve, "and then you mustn't try to keep me locked in, Mistislaus."

"I'm certain I shall know, far better than you, a mere child, when that day arrives," Mistislaus said. "Now come away from the window. Someone on the street may see you and get too curious."

The wild orphans continued their ministrations, done during Mistislaus' morning iterations. Skyla slipped out the window overlooking the courtyard of the Hall of Stars to watch them. From her days on the heath at Ulfgarth, she had learned to keep her distance from wild things until they were accustomed to her, and by gradual degrees she tamed them. Thogn, the wildest and most shy, had become trusting and curious of what she was doing with her experiments with clay and spittle and blood, so she showed him how to make things from dust. He sat beside her and listened and gazed upon the activities of the mist people, while the other orphans roistered around searching for the treasure.

After breakfast was eaten, Mistislaus would not be finished with his concentrating and humming and muttering until nearly noonday, which gave them quite a bit of time if they started at early light. Guthrum was not at his best during daylight hours, grumping and dozing watchfully from his comfortable bed in the horse trough in the reassuring gloom of the stable. While Mistislaus diligently iterated, trusting that she was doing the same, the wild boys audaciously hunted for the treasure among the ruins of the observatory while Skyla stood watch for Mistislaus and Guthrum.

Krypplingur had long ago thrown up the paving stones and chopped at the walls with the random, wasteful fury of a blind search. Skyla walked among the heaps of earth and refuse until her eye fell upon an undisturbed spot, perhaps with a few thistles growing on it. For a moment she would stand and gaze, and the wild boys watched her uneasily, knowing she was seeing something their eyes could not—an old woman, a duel to the death, ghouls walking and talking and acting out their former lives. When she turned away, they fell to digging feverishly.

Scarcely an hour into their digging one day, Lampi let out a sudden yelp. Skyla remembered her job and scanned the courtyard for signs of Mistislaus coming from the observatory, but the cause of the trouble was Modga. He had sat down to take a rest and decided to amuse himself by throwing clods of earth at his fellows. His next chosen target was Einka, and a clod exploded with a satisfying thwack right in the middle of his backside, nearly sending him tumbling off the wall. Angrily Einka turned and threw one back.

"You missed me," Modga jeered. "Missed by two miles. Would you like me to move closer so you'll have a better chance?"

Jafnar picked up a clod himself and threw it at Modga, and he didn't miss. Modga slapped away the dirt indignantly, turning a lowering glare of wounded pride upon Jafnar.

"I meant it only in fun," he said piously. "That wasn't fair, Jafnar."

"If you can't take your own jokes with good spirit, they aren't very good jokes," Jafnar said.

Modga climbed down from the wall and stalked away to find the water jug, still muttering about unfairness.

Skyla returned to her watching post atop a mossy boulder that gave her a perfect view of the path approaching the tower. Presently Skyla became conscious of a soft, rhythmic humming coming from the other side of a nearby thicket. She slipped down off the rock and came around the thicket, where she found Thogn kneeling near the path, working a small bit of clay in his fingers.

Thogn seldom spoke; when he did, it often wasn't sensible speech. Occasionally he seemed as clear in the head as anyone, but usually he was preoccupied with the unfinished conversations of the mist people around him. Jafnar had assigned Modga to watch Thogn to make certain he was never noticed by outsiders with his strange, disjointed talking or staring. Unfortunates like Thogn often roused the ire and superstitious fears of ignorant people, who never saw the flicker of quick cunning in his eye or imagined the invisible world Thogn could see all around him.

She squatted down beside him to watch as he rolled the bits of clay between his fingers. He moistened it with spittle, humming monotonously all the while and rocking slightly to and fro, completely absorbed. She could see that he was making little dolls from the clay, with a row of them lying on a flat stone before him. His large hand cradled a tiny body while his other fingers formed a small head. Skyla reached out one finger and gently touched one, and gave Thogn a brief and encouraging smile.

"That's very good," Skyla said. "They look just like little people."

Holding his breath, he put the head onto the clay body. They were both concentrating with such interest that they didn't see Modga, who had come slipping around a thicket the other way, probably trying to hide from the work or to play some hideous practical joke upon someone.

Modga scowled at Thogn and cast a swift scornful glance at Skyla. "You big lazy clot," he said to Thogn, "why aren't you out here helping us? You're glad enough for your share of the food, but you never work for it."

Skyla made a sign for silence, frowning at Modga. He was one she could speak to very little, always surrounded by a dark cloud of bad temper and impatience. One such as Modga would never see the mist people or hear their garbled, pleading voices.

Thogn did not hear him. He carefully placed the little clay figure on the stone beside the others and sat looking at them for a moment, his hands on his knees, as if pleased with his work.

"Thogn! You big dummy, you can hear me," Modga threatened, coming a few steps closer. "Get over here and help us with the digging, or I swear you won't eat tonight. I'm tired of pulling your weight for you."

"Modga, Thogn is busy," Skyla said. "Look at what he has made. If you don't feed him, then I will."

"Oh, you will?" Modga mocked. "You're good with dumb animals, aren't you? Well, Thogn's as dumb as an ox, so it's no wonder you like him so much, but you can stop your meddling with him, because he's my responsibility, not yours. Thogn, come on!"

Thogn bent down over the little clay figures and blew softly on them, as if to hasten their drying. Modga came up behind him and cuffed him on the ear, startling him. He looked up at Skyla, his soft eyes astonished and pained. Then he went back to blowing on the clay figures as if he had already forgotten the intrusion into his private realm.

"Modga, you are beginning to make me angry, and I'm not accustomed to being angry," Skyla said. "What Thogn is doing is very important. Go away, please. I don't like being provoked."

Modga stepped back, astonished, but his astonishment instantly boiled into fury. Clenching his fists, he crouched like a berserker, drawing quick shallow breaths. Thogn, who was oblivious of them both, kept on humming and droning over the little creatures.

"What could possibly be important to an idiot?" Modga snarled. "There's nothing in his head! Nothing he does or says makes any sense! He's a worthless lump! Now get out of my way, and I'll show you what has to be done with him to get him to do anything!"

"No, you won't!" Skyla retorted, standing up and bracing herself in his path. "Thogn does better work here than you with all your useless digging."

"You're a crazy person, too," he said in a low tone. "I've seen the nasty little things you do, like a Dokkalfar witch with her torturing and sacrificing. You're peculiar and unclean, and you're making Thogn worse than ever by teaching him your wickedness."

Skyla kept her eyes upon Modga, but she was also aware of what Thogn was doing. He was sitting back on his heels, smiling in gentle satisfaction, and watching something on the ground before him. Something was moving, small gray things the color of clay. Skyla turned her head to take a closer look, holding her breath. She had been teaching Thogn as diligently as she could, and now perhaps he was finally approaching the place where she stood in her own knowledge.

Modga strode past her, giving her an intentional jostle that threw her off balance.

"Thogn! No! You stop that at once!" Modga commanded, and he stomped upon the little figures almost before Skyla could get a good look at them. "Don't you know that's bad? You've got to quit these nasty little games of hers, or I swear we'll keep you chained up, like old Prestur Bolva did. How would you like that, you idiot?"

Giving no sign that he had understood, Thogn reeled back in horror, his face contorted by shock as he stared at the havoc Modga had wrought upon his creatures. His hands came trembling to his lips. Skyla gasped, feeling horror flooding over her as she stared at the little broken figures, struggling and twitching in death throes. Swiftly Thogn spread his hands over them, moaning something that might have been words, and at once the writhing halted and the figures became nothing but crushed clay.

Skyla felt a second wave of shock dash over her like a cold spray from the ocean, and her knees trembled with sudden weakness and a soft, deadly rumbling filled her ears.

"No! No!" she yelled, pulling herself back suddenly, and the muted thunder in her ears vanished.

"You're possessed!" Modga exclaimed.

"You're a coward! Murderer!" she bellowed at him in a fury, with hot tears streaking down her face.

"Witch! Sorceress!" he retorted as he stalked away.

She reached out one hand and seized Modga by the shoulder, effortlessly spinning him around to face her. Modga gasped and turned deathly pale, his breathing halting in his throat. He shuddered convulsively and his eyes rolled upward. Terrified, Skyla released her hold on him. He reeled on his feet a moment, drawing huge breaths of air, unable to speak.

"Are you all right?" she asked, giving his arm a small worried shake and looking into his stunned eyes. "I'm terribly sorry, Modga."

He jerked his arm away, his eyes blazing. "You witch," he snarled. "You tried to squeeze the life out of me, like you do to your mice and birds."

"You don't understand," she said. "I'm trying to help them."

"By helping them to die?" Modga sneered. "That's evil, killing just for the enjoyment of it. Why don't you practice your killing on the Krypplingur?"

Thogn clutched his face in his muddy hands and uttered a howl that lifted the hair on the back of her neck, a howl filled with such yearning and loss and despair that she felt herself being drawn to the very edge of the same dark pit that Thogn lived within. For a quick moment she glanced over the edge, then retreated, terrified at the awful attraction she felt pulling at her, yet elated, also, because she had discovered something unexpectedly inviting and familiar.

Modga leaped away and beat a hasty retreat, without looking back once. Skyla turned to Thogn, whose face was tear-streaked and smeared with clay. To her surprise, he smiled at her peacefully. Still seated on he ground, he reached out and patted her foot in a comforting gesture.

"I made them live, Skyla," he whispered.

Jafnar came bursting around the edge of a thicket, followed by Ordvar and Einka and the others, with Modga lurking in the rear with a sullen expression.

"What's all that shouting?" he demanded. "Guthrum's going to hear and come to see who's being killed!"

"Thogn was making those nasty little mud people again," Modga answered defiantly, glaring at Skyla. "Like she does. I stepped on them, and she attacked me like a demon. She worked some evil spell and stopped my breath and my heart. She would have killed me! She's possessed!"

"What rot," Ordvar said. "Skyla's not possessed! You're the one that's possessed by stupidity and a liar's tongue, Modga."

"I tell you, it's true!" Modga sputtered.

"Can't you just leave him alone?" Jafnar demanded. "He's just a child, Modga, with a child's mind!"

"Thogn's little clay people were alive," Skyla said. "That's not child's play, Jafnar. They were alive, like real people."

"But that's evil!" Modga cried furiously. "No one is supposed to make things alive! Necromancers do it with dead spirits, but it's unclean. What's she teaching him, Jafnar? What is she?"

All the Skylding orphans stood and gazed at Skyla and at Thogn.

"Skyla is a Skylding, and she belongs with us," Jafnar said belligerently. "Thogn's a Skylding the same as we are, and we've got to take care of him. And you, Modga, you don't help him one bit with your taunting. I've warned you before to leave him alone. The next time you do anything to him, I'm going to thrash you!"

Modga tossed his head, letting his hood fall away from his shock of silvery white hair. "He's disgusting," he said contemptuously. "He doesn't deserve to be a Skylding. And I'll swear upon the bones of all my Skylding ancestors, Skyla is possessed by something. I know it, and she knows it. Ask her if it's true!"

They all turned and looked at Skyla, faintly stirred by a thread of doubt. Someone coughed gently in the ensuing angry silence, and they all turned around as one, except Thogn. Mistislaus stood beside a heap of rubble, listening and leaning upon his staff, gazing around and puffing slightly from his hasty departure from the tower.

"A good thing Illmuri's not about," he said. "All that screaming would have made him very curious. Imagine his delight at discovering eight Skyldings right here, practically under his nose, having a great fight. Skyla, I presume these are the wild boys you've been feeding from our table, hoping that I wasn't noticing such a sudden and dramatic tripling of your appetite." He motioned with his hand to indicate the ring of startled and guilty young faces surrounding him. Gradually the circle was easing backward, away from the wizard.

"Yes, although they're not quite so wild now," Skyla said. "Except Modga. He's still a very unpleasant boy. He just trod upon Thogn's little clay people and so he is now a murderer."

"What sort of little clay people were they?" Mistislaus inquired, taping his staff gently on the ground.

"Alive people," Skyla said. "Thogn blew the life into them. I taught him how to do it. He is a very quick learner."

Mistislaus rolled his eyes and patted at his overheated forehead. "I'm pleased to hear it," he said. "But you must come in now and resume your iterations. As for you—" He let his eye wander genially up and down the line of ragged youths, all gazing at him in a frozen state of wonder and dread.

"Scat!" he roared explosively, brandishing his staff with a spew of sparks and smoke.

The Skyldings dispersed like rabbits into a warren, including Thogn, who silently vanished over a crumbling wall without being prompted by anyone.

"Come along, Skyla," Mistislaus said. "Your iterations are waiting."

"I don't want to do iterations," she said. "I felt real power, Mistislaus. It came from a place inside me where I felt there was a great blackness, like a pit. I want to know about this black place, Mistislaus. I want to make things—" She wavered, recalling how her anger had nearly squeezed the life from Modga. It was so tempting, so easy to use that side of her powers, while the creating side was so difficult. "I want things to come alive."

"Then you must learn control of the unseen things," Mistislaus said. "And before you do that, you must learn to control the seen things, including yourself. Now away with you. One hundred iterations before breakfast is the rule. I shall take you to the market with me tomorrow if you are diligent today."

"What are you going to do about the Skyldings, Mistislaus?"

"Why should I do anything about them?" he countered.

"Because you don't want the Krypplingur to find them," she said. "And you know Illmuri is looking for them, too, as well as the treasure. He would like to find the wild boys, wouldn't he? Why, Mistislaus? What would he do to them?"

"Nothing at all," Mistislaus said quickly, perceiving a shadow of fear behind her words. "I won't allow any of the Skylding orphans to become tools of the Krypplingur in their maddened search for that cursed treasure."

In the morning, Skyla went outside early to see if the wild boys would come back after their scare from Mistislaus. The red rag that flapped from the window of their tower still dangled as a sign to her that they were coming to visit, so she was satisfied. Jafnar, however, was the only one she found below in the courtyard, hiding rather apprehensively behind a heap of masonry.

"You needn't be afraid of Mistislaus," she said. "He wouldn't harm so much as a spider."

"I'm not a spider, though," he said with a scowl. "I've had plenty of people trying to step on me and smash me all my life, so you needn't worry about me. I'm of a size now that I can take care of myself and my brothers. I couldn't get the others to come back just yet, so I guess we won't be searching for the treasure today."

"It doesn't matter. It's not in the Hall of Stars or Athugashol anyway," Skyla said.

"I thought your mist people were telling you where we should dig," Jafnar said. "I thought you were helping us."

"I heard nothing. Weren't the voices telling you where to dig?" she asked, her eyes wide and astonished.

"No," Jafnar said with a short, sharp sigh. "Some of us don't hear voices. I don't know which are better off for it, either. I thought Mistislaus had moved into the observatory because he knew the treasure was here."

"Not in the least. Illmuri told him to stay here because the Krypplingur dread this place. I don't believe he ever thinks one way or the other about the treasure. Guthrum would like to find it, though."

"Well, he's not about to help us. We're not going to find it the way we've been going at it, either."

"We must ask our dead ancestors," Skyla said in a voice that made Jafnar turn and look at her, his skin undulating in a wave of gooseflesh. She was staring at nothing, watching the mist people visible to her strange sight. "We must go to the place of the dead—the Kjallari."

"The Krypplingur tired to search the Kjallari years ago," he said, his revulsion and unease increasing the more he thought about the crypts of Rangfara. "They said they ran into some very nasty things, and that is where Herrad's diseased leg came from. They said there were creatures down there: not trolls, not human. They haven't gone back down there, either. Perhaps it was the Kellarman the Krypplingur saw," he added with an ironic chuckle. "I used to believe the Kellarman lived in the Kjallari."

Skyla turned her clear, fathomless stare upon Jafnar. "He does live in the Kjallari, Jafnar."

"He's nothing but a childhood nightmare," Jafnar retorted roughly, tossing his hair out of his eyes. "Nothing but a tale to frighten children and give them bad dreams."

"That's not true," Skyla said heatedly. "He's real. I've seen him."

"You have? Where?" Jafnar demanded, crushing his own unease with heavy scorn.

"In my nightmares. I saw him, and I saw myself there, seeing him."

"It was only a dream, Skyla. He doesn't exist."

"You don't believe that. If you did, you wouldn't look away and clench your jaws like that."

Jafnar glared at her. "You're just like Thogn, sometimes," he said cuttingly. "Sometimes a mystic, and sometimes nothing but a foolish child. Maybe we're all foolish children for thinking we can find that treasure, after so many people have looked for it so many years. And what could we ever do to drive away the Krypplingur? I can't even think of a way for you to escape from Mistislaus. You may stay in that tower forever."

"You must help me escape, Jafnar. The time has come. Mistislaus has been my protector all my life, but if I don't get away, he's going to suffocate the life out of me."

"I don't know if I should do that," Jafnar said.

"I thought we were brother and sister Skyldings, sworn by blood to protect and defend one another."

"We are, but Mistislaus is a wizard, and there's nothing on earth more savage than old Guthrum, who watches beneath your windows each night, just yearning to find someone there to murder. You've grown up with people to protect you and be kind to you. You don't know how hard the real world is. You wouldn't know what to do if you did escape from Mistislaus, or how to defend yourself. I don't know if I want another Thogn on my hands."

Skyla turned her back on him and started toward the observatory, her head and spine held very stiffly. "Thogn is not the fool you suppose him, and neither am I. We are Skyldings and the birthright is ours. Even the Kellarman is our inheritance. He is real, and I will show you."

For two days she did not appear when he hung out the red rag in the upper tower of the Hall of Stars. During the next three nights, he dreamed his old terrible dreams of the Kellarman, chasing him through a dark and vaulted place that he knew must be the Kjallari. The other Skyldings also threshed and whimpered in their sleep, and once Einka awakened them all with a terrified shout.

On the morning of the third day, he went to his favorite spot for his morning iterations. Midway through, his concentration faltered and his eyes popped open to see Skyla standing before him, her hair red as fire in the first light of the sun rising over Rangfara's black towers.

"Hello, Jafnar," she said.

"You made us dream about the Kellarman," he said accusingly. "Is that how you think you're going to make us believe in him?"

"You caused yourselves to dream, not I," she replied. "The truth and the need are whispering to you, whether or not you hear the words."

"What must we do to make the dreams stop?"

"I cannot say, but choosing the right action could stop the problem."

"What should we do, then? Attack Guthrum and cut his throat? Get a battering ram for the front gate? Make a charge on the Kjallari? Lay siege to Herradshol?"

"The mist people told me what to do," Skyla said. "If I went away, Mistislaus would come searching. I must escape, but he mustn't know it, or he will see to it I can't escape again. They tell me that you must ask Mistislaus for a boon. He can't refuse it, now that you have done all this work."

"A boon? What shall I ask for?"

"For help in claiming our birthright. Wizards can never resist an appeal to their superior powers."

Jafnar shook his head dubiously. "Fancy me, a ragtag wild boy, hiring a wizard. What am I to pay him with?"

"A share of the treasure, once it is found. In the meantime, offer him your services. Mistislaus is old and fat. He needs wood carried, water brought, victuals fetched, stones cleared, and a thousand other things. You've done all that for him a long time now, and you've proven your usefulness. As a member of the household, you'll have privileges. You'll be trusted—once you prove yourself. And great good will come to the other wild boys—you'll be able to feed them all with the leavings from Mistislaus' table.

He's a great eater, but finicky. There's always lots left over. Think of the good it would do you if you learned a few simple powers by watching Mistislaus."

Jafnar backed away from the idea like a balky horse from a cart. "I'd be making myself his servant," he said suspiciously. "I couldn't come and go as I please. No doubt he'd make me sleep in a bed and eat off a table as well, and before you know it, he'd have a ring in my nose like a pig to tie me up by. No, I'll have nothing to do with asking boons of wizards."

Jafnar took a few steps away. From the crest of Gibbet Hill where the observatory sat, he had a view of all Rangfara, spreading out like a blackened stand of decaying toadstools around the central blight that was Herradshol. It had not always been thus, something whispered to him, and he whirled around suspiciously to see if Skyla's mist people had decided to reveal themselves to him.

All he saw was Skyla gazing at a bit of clay she was rolling between her fingers. He thought of the black coarse bread she had transformed to a feast and he thought of his horrible dreams of the Kellarman.

"We Skyldings have sworn to help one another," Jafnar said with grinding reluctance. "I may lose my freedom for Rangfara and my birthright, but I can see it is a thing that must be done. I don't wish to dream about the Kellarman every night."

"Very good, Jafnar" was all she said.

Jafnar waited for the opportunity to ask for his boon, working at currying favor with Mistislaus. The orphans abandoned their efforts to search the observatory and its grounds. By day, while Mistislaus was iterating or sleeping, Jafnar and the other wild boys helped clear out the mossy courtyard to make it slightly more habitable, blocked up holes in the courtyard wall so Fegurd wouldn't be so tempted to stray away, and fetched peat and wood and water. With seven of them working, the jobs were completed as if by magic.

Every evening, near twilight, Illmuri rapped on the swollen old black door in the mossy courtyard, and Mistislaus went away with him to Herradshol. The doors were securely locked from the outside, and Skyla was locked up in the narrow tower. Guthrum posted himself in the courtyard, usually, or remained in his dismal quarters in the horse byre. Skyla knew he was watching and she often heard the soft crunch of his feet as he prowled beneath the windows. Other feet than Guthrum's large booted ones often lingered in the street, not far below her windows, and when she looked out, she saw nothing.

Mistislaus was often gone the length of the night, which was quite short in the summer season, although the most crucial hour was the between-time hour of midnight. At dawn he released Skyla from her imprisonment and climbed to the top of the main tower for his morning ritual of greeting the sun and saying a few thousand iterations of joy and thankfulness. A necessary part of his ritual was rousting Skyla from her warm eider to say her first iterations on the frosty stones, preparatory to his morning breakfast foray into the Skurdur, with Guthrum following behind to carry baskets and glower fiercely at anyone who gave him a second glance.

For three consecutive nights Jafnar lay in wait outside in the dew watching for Mistislaus' alf-light to come laboring up Gibbet Hill on the Street of a Thousand Steps. Once Illmuri was with him, once Guthrum discovered Jafnar and chased him away, and on the third night a pack of wild dogs descended upon him and he had to flee for his life, barely making it over a wall in time. Rangfara at night was dangerous and thrilling in the company of his brother Skyldings, but to one alone, Rangfara was fraught with terror and peril.

To strengthen his resolve on the fourth night, Jafnar looked at Skyla's narrow prison. The light from her brazier of coals glowed red in the slits of windows, and he could hear her voice humming with the same disturbing monotony Thogn used. Standing in an unsavory street at night with his hand on his sword, twitching nervously at every sound, he wondered if his good sense of self-preservation had somehow deserted him at last.

At last, the white glow of the alf-light appeared below, coming out of Horse-thieves' Alley. Mistislaus came puffing and muttering up the Street of a Thousand Steps and turned in at the gate, jovial and weary as a large, rather tatty old tomcat who has just spent the night in mighty endeavors of romance and combat. Whistling breathlessly, he propped his flaring staff against the wall and felt about in various pockets and tied-up knots for the key to the gate.

Jafnar stepped out of the shadows the moment Mistislaus stooped to put the key into the lock. Mistislaus turned around with a sputtering blurt of alf-light.

"Well then! What will you have? My wallet is too thin to be of interest to anyone."

"Meistari," he said formally, "I wish to ask of you a boon. I have no money to pay you."

At the sound of his voice, Guthrum raised a roar from the stable and charged into the courtyard.

"I've got him this time!" he bellowed from the other side, giving the gate a ferocious blow that made it shudder. "Stand to one side, Master, and I'll halve him for you!"

"Never mind, Guthrum," he said. "It's all right. He's one of Skyla's wild boys. He's got the words out, and I'm bound to at least hear him."

Chapter Seven

Mistislaus turned the key and opened the gate, keeping one eye warily upon the wild and shaggy figure before him. He sternly motioned Guthrum away and beckoned Jafnar to enter.

Much disappointed, Guthrum growled, "Another of Skyla's wild creatures is becoming difficult to keep," and stumped away with a last vicious glower at Jafnar, as if to assure him that nothing had changed between them.

"So you are Jafnar, chieftain of the wild Skyldings," Mistislaus said, leading the way into the hall, where a fire burned in the hearth in the middle of the room. He rubbed his hands briskly, reveling in the heat.

"I am," Jafnar replied truculently, looking around warily. He saw no sign of Skyla. An archway led to a flight of stairs and a jumble of storage rooms. Another door led outside, and a smaller one stood securely locked and barred. This one, he suspected, gave access to the small tower that Skyla had identified as her prison.

"How long have you lived in Rangfara, the home of your ancestors?" Mistislaus queried, easing himself into a comfortable chair and hauling off his boots with a grunt.

"For always," Jafnar said suspiciously. "I remember being brought here to see my father before the Krypplingur, when I was too young to leave my mother clan. And after the Krypplingur, I lived here with wanderers, beggars, and thieves, until now. I'm out on my own, with my brother Skyldings."

"Do you ever have nightmares?" Mistislaus inquired.

Jafnar shivered suddenly, thinking of the dark, dreadful nightmares that had plagued his younger years, and even now the Kellarman and other monstrosities ambushed him occasionally for a night of torture.

"I may have," he said warily. "Doesn't everybody?"

Mistislaus nodded. "Who taught you how to iterate?"

Jafnar slapped his pocket where the knotted string dangled accusingly. "An old blind beggar," he said gruffly. "He taught me that I could accomplish good things with the power of my thoughts, but the Krypplingur suspected he might have been a Skylding and killed him."

"Well then," Mistislaus said, looking Jafnar up and down critically, as if he were considering buying a horse at the horse market. He inflated his cheeks with a contemplative gust and expelled it with a regretful sigh.

"I could use a lad around here to fix things," he said, "and to watch things. I know you must have sharp eyes, or you wouldn't have lived as long as you have. About fourteen seasons?"

"Sixteen. I was four years of age when the Krypplingur came," Jafnar replied. "The mother clans were all there to celebrate midwinter and the turning of Fantur. The Krypplingur must have known it and planned their attack for that time. None were spared. If not the arrows and ice-bolts, the fylgur-wolves and the cold killed the mothers and children who escaped. What nightmares could be the equal of our memories?"

"Very well. A wizard must grant a few boons now and then. You've certainly earned something, for all the work you've done. What is it you want from me?"

"I want you to help us find the Skylding treasure and to help us find a way to drive the Krypplingur out of Rangfara. You shall be rewarded when we have our hands upon the treasure, or should we fail, you may have the seven of us for any period of indenture that you like—if we survive."

Mistislaus rubbed his chin and ran his sharpening eye over Jafnar with a contemplative glint. He heaved a last long sigh, as if relinquishing a hard-fought battle, and reached down to pull on a pair of slippers.

"Sit down and make yourself comfortable," he said, waving vaguely at a chair lurking in the shadows on the other side of the fire. Jafnar looked at it suspiciously. Not having used much furniture during his lifetime, it seemed pretentious and unnatural to make such a to-do about sitting down, when there was plenty of earth to sit on.

Mistislaus gazed thoughtfully into the smoldering hearth, with his feet propped on a stool, his slippers on his feet, their long toes pointing ceilingward. Jafnar sat edgily upon a stool where he could keep his eyes upon him, curling his long legs underneath him as best he could.

"If we are to succeed in this boon you have required of me," Mistislaus said at last, "you shall have to be taught discipline, of both your visible and invisible selves. Discipline is the great secret of any endeavor. I suppose I've seen less likely apprentices. You're rather old for this kind of instruction. Ten years ago you would've been at your prime. Small and teachable and easily thrashed for misbehavior. But you have been iterating, and that's good. You know somewhat of believing. The secret of power—" Mistislaus cast his eyes upward contemplatively, his iterations and breakfast momentarily forgotten in the joy of revelation.

"The secret of power—" He stood up and paced the length of the room twice with his arms clasped behind his back, then arranged his chair nearer the fire and propped his feet on his footstool. "Bring me the jug and my cup," he said, pointing to a shelf.

Jafnar fetched them against his better judgment and watched Mistislaus guzzle down half a horn of the potent Dokkalfar ale before coming up snorting and gasping like a walrus, eyes watering and red.

"Now, where was I?" he demanded. His eye had taken on a frisky sheen. "I've forgotten what I was about to say."

"The secret of power," Jafnar prompted, watching him with feverish intensity and no small degree of impatience. "You were about to tell it to me."

"Oh yes, of course. I have a mind like a labyrinth, with hundreds of turns and paths and dead ends. I fear I went up one of them just now. The secret of power is the most beautifully simple of all concepts of magic and its practical applications. Simplicity is the hallmark of the most divine principles. Remember that, lad. Simplicity. The more simple a thing or idea is, the more difficult it is to explain. Somehow, simple things—just happen, regardless of what you do about them, like the sun rising or the change of the seasons. Very simple, but just try explaining to someone. Simple ideas often are the most befuddling, defying all attempts to describe them—"

"But the secret of power," Jafnar prompted. "Very simple, eh?"

"Of course. The secret of power—I wonder why everybody doesn't know it already. It's one of those ideas that is so divinely simple that no one will ever think of it on his own. If he did, he wouldn't believe it, and without true belief, there is no power. True belief, that's the cornerstone of every simple truth in existence, and without simple truths, you have no foundation for your power. True belief. Simplicity. There's your answer to every question." Mistislaus smiled contentedly.

"Not to mine," Jafnar said. "Just tell me, what is the secret to power?"

"Haven't you been listening?"

"I have, but you weren't talking about power."

"I certainly was. If you knew anything about belief, you wouldn't be pestering me now about power. You'd already have it. As I said, you must master belief first. Then you would have known what I was talking about."

"Just give me something to work on. Old Eyda taught me to iterate before he died, and I've worked on believing and iterating until I'm certain I believe everything I know and see and smell and feel."

Mistislaus shook his head and shut his eyes in sorrowful resignation. He took a large swallow of ale to steady himself, then spoke with great restraint. "It seems that the older I get, the more you young Alfar bellyache and want everything handed to you on a platter. All right, listen closely. I'll only tell you this once in such plain talk, and pray there's no hostile ears listening. The secret of power—" Gravely, with a portentous wattling of his jowls, he elevated one finger to underline and punctuate his words. "—is simply—to act—as if—you already—had it." With a wide and beautiful smile he nodded encouragingly at Jafnar. "Now do you understand it? That's what I mean by simplicity!"

Triumphantly Mistislaus drained his cup and poured another to celebrate making such a dazzling point. Jafnar dropped his face into his hands, hiding his crushed hopes and the growing conviction that Mistislaus was almost entirely mad, or at least maliciously taunting him with nonsensical advice.

"Do you mean to say," he asked cautiously, after a moment of gathering himself together again, "that all I have to do is pretend?"

"No, not pretend," Mistislaus said impatiently. "Pretending is only for fooling others. Yourself, you cannot fool. Be something. Do something. Reach out and seize the power. Believe you have the power, and it will come to you, as naturally as spring water finds its way to the surface and fills a waiting well. It's there, waiting for you to take it and use it, if only you have the sense to let it in." He raised his cup in salute and took a noisy gulp.

"But I won't have power, just because I tell everyone I do," Jafnar said in confusion.

"You needn't tell a soul," Mistislaus said. "Except yourself. And you must believe it, in order to get past the gateway. You have a gatekeeper in here—" He gave Jafnar's head several knocks with his knuckle. "—who tells you I'm a mad old fool full of a lot of strange blather, and nothing comes just from believing, am I right?"

Jafnar considered a moment, before answering warily, "What you say has a certain ring of truth."

"This gatekeeper is your worst enemy," Mistislaus went on in a conspiratorial tone. With the aid of the ale, he was warming to his subject. "He doesn't believe anything except what he sees or touches or tastes. He is like a rat living in a pottery bottle, denying the real world outside the bottle. Don't let yourself be held prisoner by a rat in a bottle, Jafnar. You can do all things, once you get past the gatekeeper."

"I thought magic was done with spells and powders and bits of animals and birds and things," Jafnar said. "Mirrors and spirits and summonings and runes and staffs and bloodlettings and trances and necromancy—"

"Oh, it can be," Mistislaus admitted with a great show of reluctance and another deep pull at his cup, "but all those trappings are unnecessary for the most part. They're just tools, and some wizards get too taken up with fancy methods and devices. It's nothing but a lack of confidence. A lack of belief. An inability to get around the gatekeeper to the treasure house that awaits you. It's in the stars, my boy, and in the earth under your feet, all around you in this noble earth and splendid sea. Every stone, tree, blade of grass, every creature, and every man, all have a jewel of truth in them, and this is the treasure the gatekeeper is protecting. All these secrets would be yours, if you can get around the rat in the bottle, m'lad."

"But it takes more than just believing in a thing to make it happen," Jafnar protested.

"Go into the treasure room, m'lad," Mistislaus said huskily, leaning forward at a dangerous cant. "It's all there, if you know how to get to it and use it. Powers beyond belief. Everything you ever knew, your parents ever knew, every person who was ever born ever knew. It's all there, along with the rat in the bottle, which is what you'll be unless you shut your eyes and start seeing, stop your ears and start hearing, quiet your thoughts and start thinking, still your tongue and start talking—"

He was heeling badly in the direction of the fire, his eyes glazed over, still spewing nonsense in ever-more convoluted phrases. Jafnar pushed him back gently into his chair and pried the empty cup out of his grasp.

"You've drunk too much," he said in disgust. "Just when I think

I'm going to find out something important from you, it all turns into a drunkard's babbling."

"I've never been more sane and lucid in my life," Mistislaus said with dignity, sliding down into a heap in the depths of the chair. "Cut out my tongue, and I'll sing you songs that will make you grow old and die in a day for yearning after their beauty. I've warned you about the rat in the bottle, m'lad. Keep your eyes upon him or he'll chew and chew until your brain pan is completely empty."

"Better empty than full of Dokkalfar ale!" Jafnar retorted. "I'm going outside to do something worthwhile—to shovel horse dung or stack up rocks!"

"No, you've got to listen," Mistislaus said. "I've got a poem for you. It's the Ballad of Eilifir the Eternal One, the warrior who tasted death a hundred times and was never killed. Or would you rather hear about Fulvissa, the master of all the elements, who built a ship on the shores of Kalinn-jardur, where no tree has ever grown, or Sigra, who made an army of clay men and called life into them—"

"No thanks," Jafnar snapped. "I'm tired of stories and songs. I'm tired to death of iterations. I want something I can do now that will make me a true Skylding, as I could and should have been. I want my birthright. My name. My inheritance!"

"The treasure," Mistislaus muttered from some distant shore of slumber. Lacing his hands over his paunch, he launched himself from that amiable shore with the beginnings of a sputtering snore to get himself well underway.

Jafnar shook his head and began to look around in growing alarm. The key to the courtyard door was somewhere on Mistislaus' person. All the windows were of the narrow sort designed for shooting arrows out. He could unbar either of the doors at the end of the hall, but that would put him at the mercy of Guthrum. When he approached the door and tentatively slid the bar a very little bit, a sinister sniffing and menacing rumbling assured him that Guthrum was indeed out there, waiting. He took his hand from the door and returned to the hearth to await daylight. He curled up on the stone flags and soon fell asleep.

The next thing he knew, sunlight was streaming in on him through an arrow slit and someone was treading upon him. Mistislaus, as bright-eyed and vigilant as an early-rising rooster, gave him another prod with his toe and said, "That's not the way to reclaim your birthright, my man. Sleep is a curse, a robber of precious moments. Today is a treasure, tomorrow the satisfaction of all your dreams, if only you have the fortitude to strive for them."

"I'm ready," Jafnar said. "What shall we do first? You're the nearest to Herrad, so you could easily slit his weasand whilst I guard the door."

"Killing Herrad will only give us that mad dog Ofarir to contend with," Mistislaus said. "Your chief duty, if you are to earn your bread and salt, will be watching out for Skyla. She's an innocent child and liable to get into trouble looking for this treasure. With you to protect her, she can have a little more freedom. Guthrum isn't fit company for her—or much of anyone, for that matter."

Jafnar nodded in heartfelt agreement. "I shall protect and defend my sister-Skylding to the last drop of blood in my body," he said, gripping his old sword.

"Good. But for now that won't be necessary. You must come with us to the Skurdur and carry the basket. It gets heavy, and Guthrum complains so savagely about carrying it. We mustn't forget to get some pickled lamb's feet. The old crone at the stall by Hangman's Bridge has them, but she hates to give them out unless there's a hanging so she can charge double the usual price. Nothing like a hanging to whet the appetite, she says. Herrad pays for everything, so we won't stint ourself on the delicacies. He's been feeding seven extra mouths for some time now, so he's not going to notice if we continue."

"Don't you think there are more important things than eating right now?" Jafnar demanded.

"That's a dangerous philosophy," Mistislaus said. "Food is what sustains all activity of the brain. Without constant nourishment, the brain ceases to function and becomes just a mass of inert flesh. And plumabrot for Skyla. The stickier the better. Now away with you to your iterations. Five hundred repetitions of 'Belief is the gateway to freedom and wealth, the staircase from illusion to substance.' I shall get Skyla started upon hers, and then we shall depart."

When their iterations were finished, rather more speedily than was usual, and with a regrettable lack of true intent, Jafnar and Skyla negotiated the path to the cooking stalls of the Skurdur, treading respectfully behind Mistislaus' broad backside.

"Why is this place called the Skurdur?" Skyla asked, with a graceful twist of her head to indicate the tattered tents and booths and carts heaped with merchandise and rubbish. Its apparent worthlessness did not seem to hamper the interest of the scavengers who endlessly pawed it over.

"Skurdur means 'ditch' in the old tongue," Jafnar said, with a negligent and knowing hitch of one shoulder, which he had seen old warriors and thief-takers do. "The lowest place for things to collect, and this is where everything gathers in Rangfara. It's the market street for Rangfara. Whatever there is to be bought or sold can be found here, from your breakfast to an assassin to kill your enemy. It's rather boring in the daytime. The worst characters are denned up where it's dark. The Krypplingur seldom show their noses in daylight hours, and there's no fights except among street urchins, and the Slaemur women wouldn't dream of risking a sunburn."

"Don't stop and talk to anyone," Mistislaus advised over one shoulder. "Rudeness is the only way to be polite in Rangfara, so if someone is friendly, you can be assured their intentions are evil."

"Don't you hate being crowded in here with all these horrid, stinking strangers?" Skyla asked, edging away from a knot of insistent beggars.

Jafnar kept glancing around self-consciously. He hoped no one would recognize him as the arrogant, thieving pirate he had once been, now respectably reduced to carrying market baskets for a fat old wizard and a slip of a girl.

He lifted his shoulders in a shrug. "It can't be helped," he said, addressing her question as well as his own revulsion, "if we are to reclaim what is our own."

Mistislaus showed the old crone at the Hangman's Bridge a token from Herrad, and they continued on their way through the market with the choicest of pickled lamb's feet and two baskets that gradually became laden and fragrant. Skyla kept glancing around, and three times she spied the same woman clad in a long black cloak and gown, with her face masked, always busy at some stall or another. Skyla stared at her directly, curious, and the woman kept glancing at her, trying all the while not to seem to be doing so.

"Who is that woman, Mistislaus?" Skyla inquired. "She's following us about and watching us."

Mistislaus turned and looked, and so did Jafnar, who opened his mouth to say something, but Mistislaus trod heavily upon his foot and briskly advised him to go buy some cheese.

"She's just some curious old hag," Mistislaus said. "One usually doesn't see a young girl from Ulfgarth in the Skurdur."

"I have never before felt so many eyes watching me," Skyla said with a shudder. "Rangfara is full of eyes."

Mistislaus threaded her hand protectively through his arm, towing her along past the fascinating and often repulsive sights of the Skurdur. Skyla could scarcely walk past the butchers' lane as she stared and stumbled, with the gore running in the gutters and heaps of meat and offal and dead animals lying about everywhere. Mistislaus gazed back over his shoulders often, briskly keeping up a running commentary on the merits of the food offered by the various cooking stalls they had passed. Jafnar, too, looked back, more narrowly, seeing a fleeting dark-cloaked shape always just darting out of sight.

Obviously too clean and foreign for Rangfara, Mistislaus and Skyla in her white cloak attracted many an unwelcome stare. Jafnar sweated and glowered ferociously until they were out of the noisy, smelly Skurdur and back to the quiet ruin of the old tower on Gibbet Hill, where Mistislaus fastidiously assembled their breakfast.

"The Skurdur hags cook almost as well as Thorborg," Mistislaus said critically, although it was perfectly obvious that it made no appreciable difference in his appetite, judging by the way the food disappeared. "The convenience is what I enjoy the most. Good food without Thorborg's endless nagging and nattering and cleaning up, and Guthrum's perpetual growling. Sit down to eat, Jafnar, don't run out the door with your food in your hands like a common thief. How long has it been since you've sat on a chair with your legs under a table?"

Jafnar sat down uneasily. "I don't know," he mumbled. "I can't remember the last time I ate off a plate."

"You'll get used to it," Skyla said encouragingly.

"I'd rather not," Jafnar said, "especially when my brothers are going without. I'd rather go to them."

"You can take them what you want," Mistislaus said. "It's all the same to Herrad. We should drink to Herrad's leg. It's the father of the feast, after all. We owe all this fine food and this elegant roof over our heads to a diseased leg."

After a suitable training interval, Mistislaus summoned Jafnar and directed him to fetch the day's victuals from the market unattended. Skyla was allowed to accompany him. All along the gloomy way into the Skurdur, Skyla danced on her toes at the unexpected treat of such freedom, while Jafnar paced along glowering suspiciously at anyone who glanced twice at Skyla. The weight of his responsibility caused every creature he saw to look even more sinister than usual. Constantly he nodded or beckoned to the other wild boys of his troupe who were following at wide and watchful intervals, marshalling his troops as if he were the captain of an army advancing into hostile territory.

Skyla gazed around at the forest of disused, blackened towers and high rooftops and walkways and balconies with new and adventurous eyes. Jafnar divided his attention between watching her and watching out for her with such ardent fervor that he tripped over crooked paving stones and stepped into stagnant puddles. Skyla snickered at him from the depths of her hood, but nothing could dampen her enthusiasm for what she was seeing. Every tower beckoned to her, begging to be explored, and every arched gateway yearned to lead her into a maze of fallen halls, courtyards, stables, and alleyways. Each noble establishment was guarded by a high wall with a tall archway that had once boasted a pair of wooden doors, although the wood had long since gone into fires to warm some rude intruder. Huts had been thrown together in doorways, angles of stairs, and against walls where roofs were gone, each ingeniously designed to take advantage of the remaining bits of useful architecture and rubble. Most of the archways still bore the symbols of the ancient former owner of the household: eagles, bears, boars, horses, and bulls, all protecting what had long ago been ravaged and allowed to fall into ruin around the uncaring ears of those who dwelt there.

"What is down there?" she asked, suddenly halting and turning in her tracks like a weathercock in an errant puff of wind. She pointed down a narrow, dark street winding between the buildings, ending at a dark ruined hall crouching behind a tall arched gateway. Blackened, mossy towers raked the sky, spewing clots of cawing ravens like airborne corruption.

"That's the Kjallari," Jafnar muttered. Firmly he towed a half-resisting Skyla along with him, giving her hardly any time for looking back.

"Kjallari. The cellar of Rangfara. Have you ever gone down there, Jafnar?" Her eyes glowed with danger and expectation.

He shook his head fiercely and pulled her along. "No one goes down there without a reason. You can see there's no room for barrow mounds in Rangfara. People have used that place for a charnel house since Rangfara was first built. That house was where bodies were taken for preparation. Down below are the rooms where the corpses of the nobility were buried. Common people and thralls are thrown down the pit. You don't go to the Kjallari, you don't ask questions about it, you don't even linger to look at it. The only ones who come here deliberately are those who are looking for death: assassins, duelists, and the diseased. Corpses from secret murders. I wouldn't even walk down this street, not even in daylight. Now are you quite satisfied?"

"I suppose. Thank you," she said, still looking over her shoulder. Then she added, "Jafnar, that is where the Kellarman lives."

"There is no Kellarman!" he retorted. "Now come along, or Mistislaus will be angry!"

Without further incident, they obtained their purchases and wound their way home again, with Skyla licking her sticky fingers after gorging on her favorite plumabrot. Mistislaus reproved Jafnar mildly for allowing her to spoil her appetite, so he became an even more stern guardian on subsequent Skurdur expeditions. Skyla's curiosity about Rangfara, however, proved irrepressible, and each voyage never failed to include an unexpected digression, much to the distress of Jafnar.

Skyla soon learned a rough map of Rangfara. Nearest its main gate, the desertion and ruin gave way to the squalid evidence of Dokkalfar habitation. The major Dokkalfar clans currently dwelling in Rangfara kept themselves suspiciously apart, Krypplingur taking the nearest to the gate and the best of the large halls. The others occupied smaller strongholds nearby, taking care not to get too close to anyone they might not like. All clan members packed themselves into the largest of the halls in smelly camaraderie, although a hundred other halls stood empty. Their horses and goats and sheep and quarreling thralls spilled over into adjoining houses, filling the air with their reek and noise.

"Rangfara is wonderful," Skyla observed, "but it was not built by clan people. Who could imagine one clan large enough to fill four square miles of great halls? How did such a great number of people find enough food? What did they all do here?"

"I don't know. Rangfara has always been ruins," Jafnar said with a shrug. "Even before the Skyldings. Old Eyda told me that a great deal of study and observation and magic went on here. You can see how these towers are designed to mark the passage of the seasons and the movements of the stars. Not a stone is wasted in Rangfara. Each has its purpose." His tone became suffused with awe and his eyes sparkled with longing and anticipation. "One day we'll know those purposes, Skyla, when we become true Skyldings."

Skyla divided her attention between what Jafnar was saying and the laggard knots of Dokkalfar plying their sordid trades by daylight, or hurrying quickly out of the sun into some dark recess to await nightfall. Livestock had to be cared for, dung had to be shoveled, and when it came to the washing and drying of clothing, there was no substitute for sunshine. Skyla pitied the Vaskur women; theirs was a traveling clan whose lot in life was to follow about the male clans, washing and bleaching and mending.

"Quickly, Skyla!" Jafnar suddenly drew her aside into an alcove, nodding toward an approaching procession of laborers following dispiritedly behind a cart laden with shovels and picks and prying bars and levers. Some of the workers were masked with rags, some were dayfarers who had no need to fear the sun. All were ragged, wretched, shambling creatures, scarred and crooked from fighting the unfair battles of life too long and against too great odds. Four masked Krypplingur herded the miserable procession along the street, hastening the laggards with prods and curses and the snapping of a whip.

"Who are they?" Skyla whispered, craning her neck to see. Jafnar pressed down on her head to keep her out of sight.

"Prisoners," he said. "You must stay down. The Krypplingur don't like curiosity. Not about their prisoners, or much of anything. They're used to dig for the treasure. Most of them dig until they die. Thirteen years and they have not found it yet."

"Nor will they," Skyla said. "It's for us to find."

"Not without the help of Mistislaus," Jafnar said. "Now try to behave, so I won't fall into disfavor. If I've got any luck at all, I shall become an apprentice one day. He said I might accompany him sometime to Herradshol to see how healing is done."

Skyla gazed at the wretched prisoners shambling along the gloomy street until they were gone.

"You won't like Herradshol at all," she warned him after they resumed their walk to the Skurdur. "I've been to see Herrad. He's disgusting. And Mistislaus' healing is nothing to see. It's just hours of sitting and droning iterations. We'd be better off plotting how I can get out of the tower and find the treasure."

"He said I might yet make an apprentice," Jafnar said. "I don't want to do anything to make him change his mind. We'll do exactly as he says, and no more."

"You're too wild to be an apprentice," Skyla said. "You wouldn't fancy spending hours indoors studying and meditating. You're much like I am. The wind and sky have gotten into your blood, and you can't abide constraints."

"I can't stay wild forever, can I?"

"I hope you can. I intend to."

Refusing to let her spirits be dampened by the misery of the passing train of prisoners, Skyla remained jubilant and hopeful, darting unexpectedly here and there with Jafnar at her heels, until she suddenly stopped in her tracks and seized his arm and pinched him.

"Look! There she is again!" she whispered urgently, pointing slightly with a twitch of one shoulder. "The sorceress! I remember her now! Alvara is her name!"

Jafnar turned and saw Alvara at the next stall, where a dealer in magical charms was trying to interest her in an assortment of severed heads, all of which were guaranteed to speak if the proper spell were applied. Alvara was paying no heed to the severed heads; she was gazing straight at Skyla. To Jafnar's alarm, she started to come toward them, raising one hand in a summoning gesture.

"She wishes to speak to me!" Skyla whispered.

"No, you mustn't. Mistislaus wouldn't like it," Jafnar protested, but Skyla slipped away from him like a silvery fish and stepped forward to meet Alvara.

"Skyla, my child, I've wanted to speak to you," Alvara said. "I'm so sorry for what happened that day, just as we were becoming acquainted. Are you quite all right now? You've had no more episodes?"

Skyla drew back, confused by the muted roaring in her ears. "I don't remember," she said, suddenly turning shy and tongue-tied. "For a moment I thought I knew you."

Alvara halted in her tracks. "Ah, now I see," she said. "I beg your pardon. I didn't mean to accost you so rudely. I was mistaken, of course. The sun is getting too bright and hot for me to see as well as I would like. I thought you were someone else."

"But you knew my name," Skyla said. "And I've seen you watching us almost every time we've come to the Skurdur for marketing. I saw you, so why are you attempting to lie to me just now?"

"You seemed frightened," Alvara said.

"Do you know me?"

"Yes, I do."

"Then why don't I know you, except by sight?"

Alvara sighed, darting wary glances at Jafnar who was lurking and glowering at her in helpless objection. "I fear I must bid you good day. I think your mentor Mistislaus would rather you did not speak to me," she said delicately, and turned slightly as if to leave.

"No, wait," Skyla said. "Don't go. There are questions I must ask. Mistislaus won't mind."

"I betrayed his trust once and something terrible happened," Alvara said. "It would have served us right if he had managed to leave Rangfara, but he was prevented. It was at the time the snow lynx killed six Krypplingur in the usual horrible fashion. You must recall it?"

Skyla looked away evasively. "Mistislaus never tells me of such things," she said.

In a low voice Alvara pressed, "Have you no recollection of coming to my tent with me by the Hestur-turn, the Tower of Horses?"

"Of course not," Skyla replied. "Mistislaus would never let me out of his sight in Rangfara."

"I see. Of course," Alvara said swiftly. She pressed her fingertips to her forehead. "I may have seen you in another time, coming to visit me. We sorceresses have that gift, you know, of seeing the past and the future, and sometimes it becomes confusing. Particularly in the heat of summer, as it is now. Perhaps it was your mother I saw. I see so many ghouls in Rangfara—"

"My mother! You might have seen my mother?" Skyla caught at Alvara's sleeve as the sorceress turned away, shaking her head and muttering at herself deprecatingly.

"Oh, it might have been," Alvara said. "One really never knows, with ghouls or with sorceresses. Come to the Horse-tower and we shall talk, one day."

"I shall, if I can," Skyla said eagerly. "I've seen the ghouls of Rangfara, also, but never the ones that might have been my parents. I've never seen their faces or heard their names, but I'm sure I'd know them."

"Ah, poor child, you're an orphan," Alvara said. "Perhaps I can help you. I think I can. But you must come to the Hestur-turn."

"No, Skyla, you mustn't," Jafnar said as Skyla stepped forward eagerly. "You know Mistislaus won't like it. Not to mention missing his breakfast."

"Some other day, then," Alvara said, and she glided away with a quick backward smile over one shoulder.

Jafnar did not breathe easily until they were proceeding homeward with the baskets filled and fragrant.

"Will you tell Mistislaus I spoke to Alvara?" Skyla asked when they came to the gate, and Guthrum was unfastening it from the other side.

"I must," Jafnar said.

"But if you do, Mistislaus won't trust us to go to the Skurdur without him," Skyla said. "He is so old and fearful of something happening to me."

Jafnar gnawed his thumb. "Yes. He doesn't want to lose you to the Krypplingur. And neither do I."

"But nothing will happen if I stay locked up in the tower," Skyla said.

"Yes, nothing," Jafnar agreed. "I suppose no harm was done by talking to Alvara. She's fallen out of favor with Herrad anyway. But Skyla, if I don't tell Mistislaus this time, will you promise to behave tomorrow and ever after when we go to the Skurdur?"

"I shall promise," Skyla said promptly.

Chapter Eight

Much to Skyla's satisfaction, Mistislaus no longer locked her in the tower during his nightly visitations to Herradshol. She was allowed to remain downstairs as long as she wished, with Jafnar to keep her company and ensure the doors remained securely locked. She usually amused herself with her peculiar spell-casting, while Jafnar tended the fire and warily kept his distance and watched, along with Mistislaus' cats. Sometimes she wished to hear about his life with Otkell the Slaver, a thrall, and as a wild boy of Rangfara, so she sat down and quizzed him about it. Sometimes she wished to be entirely alone, and went up to her chamber in the tower. When she no longer wanted his company, she informed him of her weariness, and Jafnar retired to the cot provided for him in a small storage alcove, leaving her to dream beside the hearth, wrapped in her own unfathomable thoughts.

Outside, the other six wild boys watched from the tops of the walls, having agreed upon a code of warning calls for Guthrum and other enemies.

With extreme reluctance Guthrum tolerated the presence of Jafnar, at a distance and at infrequent intervals. It was bitter gall in his cup that Jafnar audaciously sat down at the same table with Mistislaus, a familiarity to which Guthrum would never stoop. His temper was never reliable, so Jafnar wisely kept his distance, and Guthrum continued to menace the other wild boys whenever he saw them.

Three times a day, and often four or five, Jafnar was sent into the Skurdur to fetch something to tempt Mistislaus' appetite and thereby give his brain the necessary nutrients for the inspiration to cure Herrad's leg. Fortunately the Skurdur cooking stalls abounded in delicacies and oddities concocted to cater to the most bizarre of tastes, and Mistislaus was determined to try them all. And of course, Skyla required her favorite sticky plumabrot every day, baked fresh by a wizened little old hag who lived beside an old well. The plum tree that supplied the plums grew out of the well, its roots lost in some faraway corruption that nourished its innocent fruit.

When he was not eating or iterating, Mistislaus was poring over his books, one stiff, stained page at a time, searching for the key to the riddle of Kjallari fever. Jafnar's duty was to keep his eyes upon Skyla and to keep her amused and out of his way. Jafnar did not mind the responsibility; one day, he was certain, it would lead him to some information about his Skylding birthright, although after more than half the summer passed in this comfortable arrangement, this pathway to his ambitions was beginning to appear more circuitous than he had ever imagined.

When she was working with her clay people or transforming crumbs or dust into something else, Skyla was most particular about her privacy. Jafnar was allowed to stand watch for Mistislaus or Illmuri, as long as he kept his distance, which suited him fine. Watching her kill small animals and birds for the sake of her strange research into death made him tremble and sweat like a frightened horse, fascinated and repelled all at once.

Frequently Illmuri bestowed his presence upon the observatory, which called for Skyla's indignant retreat to the farthest end of the courtyard, or even into her tower room. With alarming frequency, as Jafnar stood watch at a distance while Skyla labored over her spells, he saw Illmuri gliding along through the courtyard with a feigned air of nonchalance, as if he were merely out taking the air. Watching from the Hall of Stars, the other wild boys made squalling cries like jackdaws to warn of Illmuri's approach. He glowered around at them vilely and hurried away after being detected.

Yet one afternoon, about a month after Jafnar's boon, for an unknown reason, Illmuri's surreptitious slinking escaped detection until it was too late for anything to be done about it. Jafnar had left Skyla in the courtyard a moment, despite Mistislaus' instructions never to take his eyes off her, and returned to the larder room to steal a loaf of bread required in Skyla's messing-about. Mistislaus was intermittently iterating and dozing up in the observation dome and not likely to notice much of anything until dusk, when his presence was required in Herradshol. As Jafnar stepped into the doorway, glancing about warily for signs of Guthrum, he was totally astonished to see Illmuri inside, with his back to him. The wizard was pawing quickly over the clothing hanging from pegs, most of it Skyla's things. Quick as a wink he selected and stuffed a long-tailed blue hood of Skyla's into his sleeve. Jafnar dived out of sight just as he turned. The boy ran lightly around the side of the house and doubled around the stable, glancing over his shoulder frequently to see if Illmuri had glimpsed him. The wizard sauntered into the courtyard, looked carefully around and toward the Hall of Stars, where no jackdaw voices greeted his appearance. Then he went back inside and climbed up to the observatory dome.

After a short while, as Jafnar watched, Illmuri and Mistislaus came down the stairs and into the narrow mossy dooryard against the street wall.

"Do join us for dinner," Mistislaus was urging Illmuri. "The old crone with the cooking stall across from Haggi the Butcher does the most wonderful meat pastries. She bakes them just after noonday and they're perfectly hot just now, not cold and soggy with grease yet. I'm not certain what sort of meat it is, but it's very tender. Jafnar can be there and back before you can spit in the corner."

"Thank you, I mustn't," Illmuri said. "I've got some urgent business to attend to before it gets quite dark."

"Very well. But you must come some other time," Mistislaus said. The heavy gate opened and closed with a rumbling grunt. Mistislaus' soft slippers pattered lightly over the paving stones as he came around to the garden.

Jafnar anticipated his request before he could even get his mouth open and said, "Meat pastries, I'm away. Skyla is beside the fish pool."

"And some plumabrot," Mistislaus called after Jafnar's retreating form.

Jafnar set off at a fast walk, keeping Illmuri's narrow dark shoulders in view.

Illmuri took the street leading toward the Skurdur. Jafnar moved behind him at a cautious trot, taking advantage of doorposts and gateways so he could spy out the course the wizard was taking.

Plenty of sinister-looking ne'er-do-wells still sauntered up and down in close companionship with yet-unwrapped Dokkalfar, glancing warily at the declining sun in the west. Krypplingur were easily recognized by their hunched shoulders, but there were others from other clans, some distinguished by the embroidery work on their greasy hats and some identified by the designs of their masks, denoting spiders, bats, skulls, or other disagreeable objects. All were armed, as if each regarded himself as a single-handed army, spoiling for a fight. Jafnar had quickly learned long ago to step off the path into the mucky street when any of them approached. When he was younger and smaller, it hadn't been uncommon for a pair of jocular warriors to grab him and toss him out of the way like the useless lumber they evidently considered him. Now they glared at him in red-eyed affront when he was slow to give them the high road through the muck and mire, and he put his hand to his sword as he insolently edged aside out of their way, as if to say that one day he, too, would demand the right-of-way. At present, however, he was content to find someone smaller and less experienced than himself to throw into the slop whenever he could.

Illmuri threaded his way among market stalls and cloth-merchants' booths and food and ale tents until he came to a less-tenanted section of ruins, where the small hovels of the lordless and clanless had been thrown up against the foundations of much nobler, crumbling structures. He paused outside one with a warning cough, waiting to be recognized. The ill-fitting door opened a slight crack, and Illmuri vanished within.

Jafnar crept closer until he could peer into the hovel through the crack in the door. Crouched over a crude table were Illmuri and a disreputable old Dokkalfar with one empty eye socket, clad in a threadbare cloak with a blackened cap tied on his head with greasy strings. It was old Hofud, who touted himself as something of a diviner for the poor folks who couldn't afford the luxury of a truly qualified seer of the future. Between them on the table was Skyla's blue hood, woven of her own soft pure hair and dyed the color of the sky by the loving hands of Thorborg. It was the only object in the hut untainted by the atmosphere of filth and secrecy that exuded from the old Dokkalfar and his wretched surroundings.

They were speaking in such low voices with their heads close together that all Jafnar could hear was a faint mumble. The old Dokkalfar picked up Skyla's hood and rubbed the fabric between his withered, black-seamed fingers. He closed his eyes and rocked slightly to and fro, his mouth slightly agape. Then he touched his tongue to the material, smelled it, and held the hood against his forehead, still rocking in the grip of the trance that held him. Illmuri listened intently, leaning forward on his elbows.

Suddenly the old Dokkalfar dropped the hood as if it had burned him and leaped up to dance around the hut like a mad thing. Spitting frantically, he rubbed his tongue on his greasy sleeve. Holding up his grimy claws with a hoarse screech of pain, he spewed out a torrent of abuse at Illmuri, who was edging toward the door. With a quick pounce, Illmuri made a snatch at the blue hood, but the old Dokkalfar seized a staff and took a vicious swipe at him, still babbling and sputtering, so he missed it.

Jafnar whipped into the concealment of a heap of refuse as Illmuri dodged out of the hut, without the hood. Still cursing, the old Dokkalfar hunched his cloak over his face and charged after Illmuri a few steps, brandishing the staff in a businesslike manner. Illmuri did not glance back; he hurried away, back the way he had come, as if he were returning to Herradshol. Jafnar shadowed him nimbly, dodging in and out of doorways, behind carts and booths. Instead of turning in at the guarded gate of Herradshol, however, Illmuri loitered around the corner a few moments, glancing right and left, then he darted into the Kjallari street.

Before following, Jafnar glanced around, to see if anyone had observed them, and saw only cloaked backsides and hooded faces turned away. In Rangfara, minding one's own business was risky enough, without getting involved in something else. With a shrug, Jafnar plunged into the perpetual musty shade of Kjallari street.

Illmuri moved along at a quick pace, stopping frequently to look behind him. The deepening mist shrouded the highest spires in darkness and clotted the mossy, dripping roofs and balconies with slowly curling tendrils. Jafnar crept from one heap of rubbish to the next, taking advantage of the gloom to draw nearer, hoping to see what Illmuri was going to do next.

With a sudden dive, Illmuri vanished under the arch leading straight into the Kjallari.

Jafnar came to a halt, his heart pounding, his eyes fixed upon the arch carving. It was a spotted cat figure—a lynx with long ear tufts, with its teeth bared in warning to all who dared pass below. The last time he had gone underneath that arch, he had been in search of Thogn, knowing he had gone to earth in the Kjallari like a terrified rabbit, with the Krypplingur hard on his heels. The Krypplingur had not gone down into it after him, but they waited outside for him. After two days, Jafnar had found him inside, huddled in a heap beside a dead carcass and an offering altar, staring and silent.

Jafnar turned away, his heart pounding and his legs feeling weak and sick. So many times he had dreamed of the Kjallari and the sign of the lynx over the gate, and of going down helplessly into the crypts to where the Kellarman waited, drawn by a voice whose call he could not resist. After backing away, hot with fear and shame, he turned and dashed back toward the reassuring brawling uproar of the Skurdur.

Suddenly remembering the meat pastries and plumabrot, he doubled back at a run toward the butchers' street and arrived at the stall in time to buy the last dozen for Mistislaus, and thence to the tree in the well for the plumabrot.

Breathless, he returned to the observatory and delivered his parcels, then signaled Skyla to follow him into the garden, where he told her all about Illmuri's stealing her blue hood.

"I looked for it!" she exclaimed. "That sneak thief! I wonder what he wants with it."

"He gave it to a scurvy old Dokkalfar skryer in the Skurdur," Jafnar said. "If he expects old Hofud to tell him any great secrets, he's going to be disappointed. Hofud's addicted to eitur when he can get it, and Dokkalfar ale when he can't, so his wits are pickled more often than not in the vilest of Dokkalfar poisons."

"My best hood," Skyla murmured. "Thorborg made it for me with her own hands from my own hair. Now it's in the hands of strangers!"

"Don't worry," Jafnar said, scarcely knowing what prompted him to say it. "I shall get it back for you. The next time Illmuri steals something, I'll go after him, even if it means going into the Kjallari."

Skyla still scowled, plucking at a tuffet of moss as if it were Illmuri's heartstrings. "Illmuri touching my hood is bad enough, but this Hofud creature is the worst. You must get my blue hood back from old Hofud. I can't bear the thoughts of one such as he touching anything that belongs to me."

"He's got a small reputation for being clever at discerning lost, forgotten, and hidden things," Jafnar said. "Perhaps Illmuri thinks he's going to find out something about the treasure by taking your hood to him. Maybe if we watch him, we'll find out, too."

"I don't care, I don't want him touching it," Skyla said with a shudder of indignation running through her. "I want my hood back. Thorborg spent hours making it for me. I don't want that old sniffing, grubbing little troll of a creature keeping a thing of mine close to him. It's made of my own hair, Jafnar. Won't you please get it away from him? I don't want one such as old Hofud to know the least thing about me."

"Old Hofud would tear my head off if he could get his hands on me," Jafnar said. "We boys have tormented him and stolen from him until he's a regular savage. But don't worry. I'll think of something."

"Well, hurry. It is most important we get my hood away from him. Illmuri was wrong to give my hood to someone else. Headgear is too important to just hand around so casually. We shall have to keep our eyes very closely upon Meistari Illmuri from now on."

As she spoke, she unwound her belt and hung it over a bush. Then she removed and draped her hood over a fallen stone.

"I'm fishing," she replied to Jafnar's unspoken question. "For an ugly, ungainly fish that hangs about here, stealing things he has no right to."

On the following day, she left a hood and a scarf draped carelessly on the seats beside the fire. When Illmuri came to visit, he had to move the hood before sitting down, but he didn't attempt to steal it.

On the next day, after the prerequisite iterating was done, Jafnar reported to the main room with the market basket for his orders.

"I think," Mistislaus mused ponderously, "I think I'd like a batch of those pickled pigs' trotters for breakfast. Jafnar, take your limber legs down to the old hag's stall and get us some. You're three times faster than old Guthrum, and he's in such a foul mood that I hesitate to ask him anything. Take Skyla with you," he added, catching the hopeful question in her glowing eyes before she could even voice it. She loved the Skurdur, with its boisterous, huckstering merchants, pickpockets, beggars, and travelers, all interspersed with the booths and stalls and carts that offered strange merchandise from far-flung places.

They had only gone a short way down the street of rope, string, and cloth merchants when Skyla seized Jafnar by the sleeve, drawing him to a sudden halt behind a shoulder of mortared stones.

"Look there, at that archway!" she hissed, pointing to the crumbling gateway leading to a deserted hall. "It's Illmuri, behind us!"

Jafnar peered around the corner warily. Indeed, it was Illmuri, pacing along slowly with his head up, his eyes sweeping the crowded marketplace.

"Maybe he's bitten on some of your bait left lying around," Jafnar said.

"We'll follow him and see where he goes."

Jafnar regretted her decision almost instantly as he recognized the street Illmuri had chosen. It narrowed between towering walls that loomed overhead without so much as a window to relieve the stern cliffs of black stone. The sky seemed impossibly far away, a narrow strip of light above sliced by towers. The harsh jeering of ravens stopped his blood in his veins and the smell of the Kjallari made his heart start to pound.

"We made a mistake," he said, halting in his tracks. Even his voice sounded strange and hoarse to his ears. "We can't go this way. It's a nasty, dirty place. I think we've lost him anyway."

Skyla nodded, just barely. It was true, the street was almost deserted, except for a few wretched beggars who were too sick and weak to even hold out their hands. Then, ahead, she spied Illmuri's black form dodging around a heap of fallen masonry.

"Come along, Jafnar, he's just ahead of us!" Skyla slipped past him easily.

"Skyla, no! You don't understand! It's the Kjallari!" He whispered the last word in a terrified squeak.

Skyla paid him no heed. He hurried after her, glancing right and left into dingy alcoves and niches where unsavory things lurked and watched with red-rimmed eyes. She scampered ahead, her soft boots scarcely making a sound on the mossy paving. She halted before the gateway to the Kjallari, standing open, its doors run aground in rubble, rotting where they stood festooned with moss.

"Look at the carving, Jafnar! It's a lynx! Perhaps it's the one who preys upon the Krypplingur."

Jafnar hurried after her, cringing with every instinct for self-preservation. He looked up a moment where she was pointing. His old friend the lynx grinned down at him invitingly, making his hair bristle.

"Don't stop here," Jafnar said gruffly, giving her a shouldering push as he seized her arm. "We must hurry, or Mistislaus will begin to worry, and we'll never be sent out without him again."

But she was still troubled with a powerful attraction to the place. She twisted around, looking back over her shoulder.

"The Kellarman lives here," Skyla whispered excitedly to Jafnar. "Can't you feel his eyes looking at you and smell the stink of his breath, with his long yellow teeth, ready to tear at you? Come with me to the Kjallari, Jafnar!"

"Skyla, no!"

"I was only teasing you, Jafnar."

"No one in Rangfara jokes about the Kjallari. Now come away, quickly."

"Whatever could he be doing down there, Jafnar?" Skyla demanded. "Especially if he's got something of mine?"

Jafnar shuddered and made some gestures to ward off evil. "I don't know, Skyla. I can't stand to think of it. And that's the man who is Mistislaus' particular friend. What would he be doing down in the Kjallari, with the dead and the Kjallari-folk, unless it be mischief? Skyla, be warned. I have instincts from a lifetime of staying alive. Illmuri's not what he seems. If he seems a friend, then he's a foe. If he seems kind, then he's plotting evil."

"Poor Mistislaus," Skyla said in a troubled tone. "You see how he needs us to look after him. He's like a trusting child. How fortunate I found you, Jafnar. I'm going to need a great deal of your help. Especially if we are to find that treasure. The lynx is a sign. The mist people told me. And there you saw it." She pointed back, indicating the gateway arch over the Kjallari entrance. "You will help me, won't you, Jafnar?"

"To the very last drop of my Skylding blood!"

"You said you'd go into the Kjallari after Illmuri."

"I know I did, but I can't very well take you down there with me, can I, if that's where the Kellarman lives. I've sworn to keep you safe, not to endanger your life."

"You must go after Illmuri," she said. "The very next time. I will see to it he has his opportunity."

They hurried to make their purchases and arrived back at the observatory breathless from their run up the Street of a Thousand Steps. Mistislaus said nothing, scarcely noticing that they had taken overlong in the Skurdur. He stabbed his knife toward a vacant place at the table, indicating that Jafnar was to sit there, despite his muffled objections.

"Now you're part of this household, you've got to learn to eat at the table," Mistislaus said. "I trust you can manage it?"

Jafnar nodded uneasily and sat down on the chair. He still felt peculiar sitting at a table. The wild boys usually ate squatting around a fire, or sitting on rocks. Mistislaus grunted with faint approval and tucked into his breakfast with his usual gusto.

"Tonight," he said when he was finished, "I must take my satchel, so don't let me forget it. Herrad insists upon me appearing with one, like a proper wizard, so I shall, though it's full of nothing but a lot of trash and rocks. It's mortally heavy, too."

"Might we not come along, also, Mistislaus, so Jafnar can see Herrad, too?" Skyla inquired hopefully. But Mistislaus shook his head until his wattley jowls quivered.

"No indeed," he said, still shaking his head. "You turned absolutely green last time and got no end of sick. I don't want to risk it again. Herradshol is no place for a weak stomach." He patted his own, which, if judged by its size, certainly appeared powerful enough to face sobering challenges that would have cowed lesser stomachs.

"I don't remember being ill," Skyla said with a petulant toss of her head. Jafnar did not like the look of the malicious sparkle in her eye. "I remember very little, except the dullness of Herradshol and the smell of Herrad. Was Alvara the sorceress there?"

Mistislaus gave a startled sputter, hemmed deeply, and took a swig of ale, scowling at the dregs swirling around in the bottom of his cup. "Yes, she was there," he said reluctantly. "You know her, do you?"

"I saw her in the Skurdur, and she most kindly asked if I was well again. I wonder why I don't remember her."

"You mustn't speak to her," Mistislaus said, hastily stuffing a wad of bread into his mouth. "She's not to be trusted. I forbid you to speak to her. It quite frightens me to think of her pouring her lies and tales into your willing and receptive ears. You're too much of a child, Skyla, to deal with a Dokkalfar sorceress."

Skyla's chin lifted and she gazed squarely at Mistislaus. "I shall decide that," she said calmly. "The same as when I decided you and Thorborg would no longer cut off my hair."

Mistislaus put down his cup and sighed, with a worried expression furrowing up his countenance. "I'm only trying to protect you," he protested, "and I shall go on protecting you until I think you're able to protect yourself. Is that such a bad thing?"

"It might be, if you go on too long," Skyla said.

"Well, it must go on for a little while longer, and for the present I forbid you to speak to Alvara. Your chance will come," Mistislaus added, seeing a stubborn darkening of Skyla's clear gaze. "I promise, you'll have your freedom one day, when I'm certain you can bear it. Now away with you to your iterations. Enough time has been wasted with this quarrel, and enough perturbation of our thoughts. Jafnar, Fegurd's stall needs attending to."

Jafnar went out to the stable, although he knew Guthrum would have attended to Fegurd's stall. The dwarf had one soft spot, and that was for any sort of horse. If Jafnar came anywhere near old Fegurd, Guthrum would likely cut off his arm. He took one quick look inside as he scuttled past the door of the stable and was rewarded with a snarl from Guthrum.

"The meistari sent me to shovel out the stall," he called over one shoulder hastily, "but I see you've attended to it already."

"He thinks I can't do it myself?" Guthrum blinked wrathfully in the gloom of the stable. "He thinks he needs a pack of wild boys to do his work for him? Useless nuisances, the lot of you! Surrounds himself with nuisances and enemies, he does!"

"You mean Illmuri," Jafnar said, standing his ground for once as Guthrum rattled his axe ominously, as if he were preparing himself for one of his berserker charges. "I'd like to do something about Illmuri. He's stolen some things from Skyla. One of them he took to a diviner, and the other I think went down the Kjallari."

Guthrum stopped his huffing and rattling and edged forward curiously, gazing at Jafnar with an incredulous squint. Although he was a head shorter than Jafnar, he was at least three times as broad across the shoulders, and his arms were longer and gnarled with fighting muscle. He glared at Jafnar eye to eye, as if daring the boy to take the first step backward, and then he would have him.

"If anything happens to that girl," Guthrum rumbled, giving himself a thump on the chest with his knotted fist that would have knocked Jafnar flying, "I shall take whoever did it and tear their limbs off as if they were flies' wings. If I ever see Illmuri taking the least hair of Skyla's head, I shall cut off his arm and feed it to him. Just tell me if he takes anything else and I'll finish him off for you."

Jafnar shivered in the hot blasts of Guthrum's fiery breathing. He was standing near enough to touch. His own temerity made him dizzy-headed.

"Skyla is my blood-kin," he said defiantly, "and I am blood-sworn to protect her, as if she were my own sister."

"With this paltry excuse for a weapon?" With astonishing speed and deftness Guthrum reached out, and Jafnar's sword seemed to appear in his hand as if it had leaped out of its poor sheath in all its chipped and pitted sorry glory.

"It frightens away enemies of similar quality," Jafnar said. "It has kept me alive four years."

Guthrum grunted, scowling at it from hilt to tip. In his hand, the old sword took on an unfamiliar sheen, as if the hand of the Dvergar caused the metal to remember better days.

"I shall fix it for you," the Dvergar said abruptly. "Send your lads around with the fuel, and I'll reforge it tomorrow night. You're going to need a decent weapon for the work ahead of you. And some training." His eye raked critically over Jafnar's wiry frame. "Now you're getting some proper fodder, you might come up to form."

"What are we to expect?" Jafnar questioned eagerly. "Attack by the Krypplingur? Illmuri's treachery? Or is it some unnamed thing from a place we don't suspect?"

"The threat is all of Rangfara," Guthrum growled. He tapped his huge beak of a nose and sniffed the air suspiciously. "And all of it that's unseen as well. Let them break their ice-bolts on my head as long as I survive, but while there's breath in this body, I shall stand and defend the girl and the meistari. What else is there for an old Dvergar like me to live for, with lord and hall and kin all nothing but dust, thanks to the Dokkalfar? You—" He stabbed one massive finger at Jafnar. "—and I will defend the little lass and help her to do what she's here for. It was an ill night and an ill wind that brought her to Ulfgarth. I saw the portents then of war and blood and evil, and I trembled. If you were not a Skylding, I would not give you any hope of survival at all."

Jafnar felt a chill creep into his spine then that did not desert him even after Guthrum reforged his sword, which turned out to be hot and sweaty work. A vast amount of fuel had to be stolen by Jafnar and the other orphans before Guthrum was satisfied. Amid much fiery puffing on the bellows, the labor for which Jafnar was employed to supply, heaps of scorching coals splashed the walls of the Hall of Stars with ruddy light, and smoke rolled out of the old stable as if it were in the midst of a conflagration. The wincing and ringing of the anvil and the sword under Guthrum's mighty pounding filled the night with the music of warfare, punctuated by ferocious hissing and steaming when the blade was plunged into water.

Skyla stood wrapped in her white cloak watching from a safe place where no flying sparks would find her, with the wild boys hovering around, keeping their distance from the fiery Dvergar.

"Now then!" Guthrum said when the work was finished and he held the sword aloft, sharp and gleaming and red with firelight that sparkled like blood. He made a short chirp of satisfaction and handed the sword to Jafnar. "You've got the sword to defend the maid; now it's up to you to prove you've got the courage."

On the following day, Guthrum began to show him how to use a sword to the trickiest of advantage, instead of winnowing around with it like a mad harvester in his own defense. In spite of the sweating and puffing, Jafnar still felt the cold place in his heart, and often at night his dreams tortured him with terrible images of death and murder. The terror of the Kjallari stalked him, with the Kellarman either grinning over his shoulder or calling him inexorably to his destruction.

No matter how hard he practiced with his thrust, parry, and cut, he felt something lacking, which made his heart cold. If Skyla required him to defend her one day, she would have in him only a second-rate swordsman, a half-reformed wild boy of Rangfara. It was a nasty, niggling little voice, but he couldn't ignore it telling him that he might be a Skylding born, but he was nowhere near being a true Skylding warrior yet, and there was not enough time for him to become one before the Kellarman that stalked his dreams was replaced by a genuine danger.

Not a day passed that Skyla did not remind him of his promise to retrieve her blue hood from old Hofud.

"You have an elegant sword now," she said one evening as they played at quoits, safe behind barred doors. The sounds of the Skurdur came in thinly through the narrow windows: shrieks, wild laughter, and the guttural brawling and clamor of short, fierce fighting. "You could demand my hood from Hofud at sword point, and he wouldn't dare laugh at you now."

"That's true," Jafnar said. "I'll do it the first thing tomorrow." Old Hofud would not put up much resistance, he suspected. He might not even recognize Jafnar at all.

"Tomorrow and tomorrow!" Skyla said in sudden temper. "That's all you ever say! Jafnar, if you don't get back my hood for me, I shall cease to regard you as a true brother!"

The next day, Jafnar went so far as to lurk guiltily about Hofud's hut, until Hofud came out and chased him away with a stick. Then a rival gang of wild boys took up the chase, and what with hiding and dodging for several hours, Jafnar was late getting back to Athugashol. Mistislaus scolded him for his lack of diligence, with Illmuri listening and smirking in the background.

"It's what you might expect of a wild boy," Illmuri said, with an unpleasant glint in his eye. "No training, no discipline. I could take him for you and teach him some lessons in responsibility. There's only one thing a young savage like him understands—punishment and constraint. You're far too kind to him, Mistislaus."

"I fear you may be somewhat right," Mistislaus said reluctantly. "You can't take the Skurdur out of a wild boy, it seems, no matter what you offer in return. And tormenting poor old Hofud besides, so I hear. What possessed you to behave so badly, Jafnar?"

Jafnar glowered hotly at Illmuri. It had been a trying enough day without listening to this insufferable abuse.

"I wouldn't have been there at all except for the blue hood that Skyla lost," Jafnar retorted pointedly, hoping to see Illmuri flinch or look guilty.

"Blue hood?" Mistislaus muttered. "That girl is always trailing her possessions about and losing them everywhere. I tell you, sometimes—"

Jafnar perceived himself as forgotten in the flow of Mistislaus' ensuing tirade, so he slipped away and retreated to the Hall of Stars to nurse his wounds. Besides having his sensibilities offended, the rival wild boys had gotten their hands on him more than once with the intent of wreaking grave havoc upon his person.

"It serves you right," Modga said by way of consolation, as he rummaged through the basket of leftovers from Mistislaus' table. "It's gone around that you've taken up with Mistislaus and that girl. Word has it you don't want to be a wild boy anymore. You want to fetch and carry and lick boots like a lapdog."

Jafnar knocked him down for his audacity. "I wouldn't do it except for the treasure," he snarled. "You wouldn't believe what I have to put up with from them! Always, from all sides, it's pick, pick, pick, and Jafnar do this, Jafnar do that. Do you think I like what I'm doing?"

"Then leave them," Ordvar said. "I'm getting tired of watching out for everyone all alone."

"But the treasure," Einka said, his eyes shining with visions of future wealth. "We can't find it by ourselves."

"Why not?" Modga demanded. "We don't need that old fat windbag from Ulfgarth. We're Skyldings, we'll find our own treasure without anyone's help."

"We haven't yet," Jafnar argued. "And I don't hear anyone complaining about the food. Nor does anyone seem to have any better ideas. Until something else comes up, I'll stay with Skyla and Mistislaus. And I don't want to hear any more complaining. Life isn't exactly easy for wizards' apprentices, either."

Regretfully he left them and went back to his quarters in the storage room of Athugashol. Fortunately, Skyla did not once mention her blue hood that evening, or he might have abandoned the entire treasure enterprise and gone back to the streets, wild and free.

Chapter Nine

For nearly two days Jafnar truly made an effort to do exactly as he was told. He earnestly practiced his iterations; he clung to Skyla as watchfully as old Guthrum himself would have done, with one hand never far from the hilt of his newly sharpened sword. With grave suspicion he viewed the Krypplingur sauntering past Athugashol, as if they had business on Gibbet Hill. When Skyla accompanied him to the Skurdur, he stoutly refused to be drawn into any exploratory side excursions. He saw Krypplingur and enemies everywhere, including Alvara and Illmuri. The wizard scarcely made a pretense of keeping out of sight as he shadowed them to and from the Skurdur.

It all seemed to be going very well, until Jafnar looked up from his yearning inspection of a weapons booth, and Skyla was nowhere to be seen. He tore away through the Skurdur, scanning the booths desperately. It was the longest moment of his life until he spied her beside a cloth-merchant's cart, talking to a woman in a black cloak. His heart leaped with relief, then plummeted like a stone down a well. It was Alvara.

"Skyla, come," Jafnar said. "You mustn't listen to her. We promised."

"What a rude wild boy," Alvara said. "This is the one who is afraid to get your hood back from old Hofud?"

"Skyla! Come away!"' Jafnar commanded. "You shouldn't talk to strangers. Didn't I tell you that?"

"But we're not strangers," Skyla said. "I'm remembering now. It was the first day we came to Rangfara. You brought me to Athugashol, while Mistislaus was looking at Herrad."

"Yes. You were very tired," Alvara said. "And you were wearing that blue hood then, I remember. How did old Hofud come to get his hands on it?"

"That slinking Illmuri stole it," Skyla said.

"We must be going," Jafnar said. "Mistislaus will be noticing we're late."

"For a wild boy, you're forgetful of your position in Rangfara," Alvara said.

"He's not so wild anymore," Skyla said. "We've been taming him."

"You're liable to regret it," Alvara said. "They can't be tamed, and they aren't to be trusted. Good day, Skyla. I'm sure we'll meet again."

Jafnar seized Skyla by the arm and propelled her away, glancing back frequently. Alvara seemed to vanish into the motley tapestry of market stalls and market patrons, but Jafnar knew with all his wild instincts that she was still stalking them.

"Jafnar, I want to stop at Hofud's and get back my hood," Skyla said, halting stubbornly in her tracks. "Alvara told me where he lives. It's not far, and I'm sure it would only take a moment."

"No!" Jafnar exclaimed. "He's a vicious old pig, and Glodar and his wild boys are over there. It's dangerous, Skyla, even for me. You saw what happened last time I tried. I was nearly torn to shreds!"

She sighed impatiently. "Do you have a better plan?"

"I'm working on it," Jafnar said evasively.

To his relief, she turned and started homeward. The cold, prickling feeling of being followed did not subside until they were safely within the walls of Athugashol. Warily he climbed up and peered over into the Street of a Thousand Steps, where the shadows were lengthening and the unsavory night mist was rising. Someone was there, he knew, watching and waiting for he knew not what.

"I can't bear this prison any longer!" Skyla suddenly flared that evening, after Mistislaus had gone, locking the doors and the gate securely after him. She darted from one narrow window to the next, like a swallow trapped in a barn. "I must get some air, some freedom! I can't bear all of you watching me all the time, staring and waiting! What are you watching me for? What have I done?"

"Nothing! I don't know," Jafnar protested. "Mistislaus says you need to be protected. I thought it was because you were precious to him, like an only child."

"It's because he doesn't trust me," Skyla said. "It's not love. I can't bear it, Jafnar. I just want to be alone for once." She pressed her fingers to her temples. "So many voices are in here, telling me things. Sometimes I want to listen, and sometimes I'm afraid. The burden of Rangfara and its memories and the treasure—I don't know if I can bear it. I just want to go back to Ulfgarth and run across the fells again with the wild ponies. Do you truly believe we'll ever find out who we are? Or the treasure, Jafnar?"

"Yes, of course we will," he said stoutly. "Why else were we spared? The Norns know we have an important destiny before us, and it must be to find the treasure and cleanse Rangfara of all Krypplingur!"

"Before you do all that, why can't you just get my blue hood back from old Hofud?" she demanded.

"Well, old Hofud is as mean as a wild sow," Jafnar said uneasily. "But I promise, I'll get the other Skyldings together tomorrow and we'll start working on a plan. I swear it, without fail."

Skyla sighed and composed herself on a stool beside the hearth. For a moment she studied the fire, lost in her own thoughts. Then she rose up and went to the shelf in the corner where leftover food was stored, out of the reach of the rats. After a bit of rustling around, she returned with a sticky slab of plumabrot in a wooden bowl.

"Have some, Jafnar," she offered. "I've taken too much. It'll keep me awake if I eat all this."

Jafnar eyed the gooey purple mess suspiciously. The winey smell of it alone made his mouth start watering. Plumabrot was Skyla's special treat, and none of it had ever been offered to Jafnar before. Not that he had been particularly tempted; it always looked rather revolting, with the plums oozing bluish syrup that saturated the cake around them. The old hag at the well baked plumabrot when the plums were in season and stored the cakes in casks in the cold well, wrapped in cloth and soaked with plum syrup and honey. They kept that way for a year, and the older the plumabrot, the better Skyla liked it, even if its cloth covering sported tufts of green fungus. Plumabrot was always made that way, Skyla explained, even by Thorborg, who stored it in the stone springhouse with the cheese.

"I think I won't," he said, reluctantly. "I've never eaten anything that rich and sweet before."

"Try a piece, Jafnar, just a small one. It would please me to share my favorite food with a good friend such as you are. Thorborg says it was the first food I would eat, as an infant," Skyla said around a mouthful. "I'm almost addicted to it. It's lucky for us Herrad feeds us what we want. Plumabrot is very dear at the market. This is the best I've tasted. I wonder what that old plum tree grows on, twisting out of that well the way it does. Go ahead and eat it, we'll get more at the Skurdur tomorrow."

Unable to resist, Jafnar sliced off a small helping with his belt knife and ate it slowly, savoring each sticky crumb and oozing purple drop of syrup.

"It's rather good," he said in surprise, after swallowing a couple of pieces. The initial taste was bitter, but it mellowed on the palate the more he ate of it, until he amended his opinion of it considerably.

Almost before he was finished licking off his fingers, his head was nodding and his eyes were falling shut. With a contented sigh, he propped himself against the wall near the cold draft coming under the door in a vain attempt to keep himself awake. His ears hummed with an enticing melodious singing that warmed and soothed until he felt that all things were good and everything was right. The room swam around comfortably, and he smiled peacefully at Skyla as she fastened her cloak around her shoulders and threw a hood over her head.

"I must go out, Jafnar," she said, as if from a great distance. Her eyes sparkled as if they had captured stars in their depths.

"No, Skyla, you mustn't," Jafnar mumbled, feeling a faint uneasy bubble of responsibility rising to the surface of his semiparalyzed contentment.

"I'm going to Hofud's to get back my blue hood. You don't need to worry. The mist people will protect me."

Jafnar nodded his head agreeably. The singing in his ears gradually took on the form of words.

"Skyla! You must come with me!" the voices purred. "We have many things to tell you and much to show you. Come away, the doors are opening before you. We shall lead you to everything you want to know."

"Can I bring Jafnar?" Skyla asked the voices.

"Not just yet," they trilled. "He is not ready."

Jafnar was only faintly aware of the sounds of Skyla's voice speaking to the metal elements of the locking mechanism. With a click, the lock turned. Skyla pushed the door open and slipped out, letting in a breath of cold air. With a contented sigh, he shut his eyes, giving himself up to the warm waves of oblivion rising around him.

Jafnar awakened from a half doze, fraught with uneasy dreams of the Kjallari. His joyous daze had vanished; it was nearly full morning, almost time for Mistislaus to return. He leaped to his feet, shaking the sleep out of his head. The door was unlocked and standing open, bringing back his memory with a sickening jolt. He whirled and raced up the narrow tower to her little room, but Skyla was gone. Half falling, he spiraled down again and into the courtyard. He whistled to the other boys, and they answered sleepily with owl-hoots from the Hall of Stars, reassuring him that all was well. Guthrum was snorting and rumbling around at the front gate in a sinister fashion, so Jafnar dashed around the corner.

Guthrum glowered at him, red-eyed.

"Guthrum, Skyla's missing," Jafnar said. "The locks are opened, and she's gone."

A pained expression came over Guthrum's features. He bared his teeth and gnashed them, as if yearning for the bones of his enemies to gnash. Snarling, he drove his massive fist into the door with a resounding crash, leaving a splintery dent and some skin thereon. Jafnar took the hint and scuttled back to the courtyard to begin a search for Skyla, in case she was mischievously hiding from him.

The mossy thunk of the front gate announced the return of Mistislaus from Herradshol. Jafnar cringed, hearing the bass rumble of Guthrum's voice delivering the news. Suddenly Mistislaus snatched open the back door and plunged into the courtyard, nearly trampling Jafnar in his rush.

"Where is she?" he demanded, his eyes glaring furiously beneath the white hedge of his eyebrows. He shook his ring of rusty keys threateningly in Jafnar's face. "Guthrum says he saw nothing and no one. He says he must have dozed off and when he awakened he found the gate unlocked and standing open. I possess the only keys to these doors. How did she escape?"

"It was the voices," Jafnar said, his wits suddenly thick and heavy. "She couldn't have—nobody could have—"

"She did, they did, she's gone!" Mistislaus shouted. "What did you say about voices? Human voices? Spirit voices? What sort of voices?"

"Not human, I think. I heard them, calling her to come out. She unlocked the door. Nothing harmful could happen to her. She was perfectly safe. I knew it, I felt it."

"Impossible! No one is safe in Rangfara!" Illmuri appeared in the doorway. "Particularly those who hear voices. She pulled a very clever deception on Jafnar and Guthrum. Have you thoroughly searched all of Athugashol?"

"It's no use, she's gone," Mistislaus said in a stricken tone. "We may never see her again!"

"The voices I heard will protect her," Jafnar said.

"I count voices for nothing," Illmuri snapped. "It was nothing but a clever trick of hers to fool you so she could get out."

Jafnar thought of the plumabrot, but decided not to mention it. The very thought made his skin itch.

"We'll search the Skurdur," Illmuri continued grimly. "She might have just wandered off on a lark to explore."

"She was talking about her blue hood, which is missing." Jafnar turned his gaze upon Illmuri. "It was taken from here and given to the diviner Hofud, and she's been upset about it for days. I believe she went to get it back, intending no evil, but when I was taken sick with indigestion, she saw her opportunity."

"A hood?" Mistislaus demanded incredulously.

"Yes, the blue one, made from her own hair," Jafnar replied with growing conviction. "She hated the idea of it falling into anyone else's hands. I followed Illmuri after he stole it, and she asked me to get it back, but I didn't, out of fear of old Hofud. I think she took the matter into her own hands."

Mistislaus slapped his brow. "Exactly! She would do that! Come, let's go after her! Does anyone know the way to this Hofud person?"

"Yes," Illmuri said tightly, darting Jafnar a venomous stare. "Both of us do. Follow me, and do be careful."

When they came to the row of huts built against the foundation of the buildings, the short northern night had reluctantly given way to dawn. The shiftless, cluttery huts all looked and smelled very similar to the lairs of mountain trolls.

"This is Hofud's," Illmuri said, nodding toward one of the seediest huts.

"He always hated us wild boys," Jafnar added.

Mistislaus stood in front of it and coughed and blew his nose and waited in vain to be admitted. At last he decided to be rude and knocked upon the door with the end of his staff.

"You won't be finding old Hofud that way," said a voice from a neighboring hut in a tone of offense, and a scruffy old woman came out to scowl on her disreputable stoop with her fists on her hips. She did not bother with any protection from the murky daylight, so she must have been a dayfarer. Whatever twisted path of bad choices had led her to such a nasty conclusion of her life was probably a tale as complicated and sordid as the creases and furrows of her wizened face.

"He's most likely still pickled like a herring in Dokkalfar ale," the woman continued with spiteful relish, her sharp eyes missing nothing of the proposed visitors. "You could knock until doomsday and he wouldn't hear."

"Thank you," Mistislaus said with a slight courtly bow. "I think we'll knock again. You didn't see anyone coming in here, did you, wearing a white cloak, perhaps?"

"White, you say? Not white, it wasn't. Who would wear such an unlucky color? Black I saw aplenty, but not white. Knock all you want, you won't rouse him this time of day. It's his drinking time," she retorted with an impatient shrug, lingering to watch, fists on hips.

Illmuri approached and gave the door a resounding thump. Then he shouldered it open.

"Halloa," Illmuri said softly as Hofud's door swung open wide, revealing a scene of carnage within. The table had been overturned, and Hofud lay with his feet toward the door. The room was spattered with blood, and his neck was a ragged ruin, nearly chewed through by some large beast. The final expression frozen on his face was one of unspeakable terror.

For a shocked moment they all stood and stared. Jafnar had seen a few grim scenes during his short and brutal life, but he couldn't help wincing away from this one with a muffled gasp. The old woman next door couldn't resist craning her head to see inside. Her eyes bulged like a strangled rabbit's, and she frantically signed with her hands to ward off the approach of evil.

"The lynx!" she gasped, going as white as a fish belly. "And my door the next to his!" She vanished into her hut and slapped shut the raggle-taggle door.

Illmuri swiftly shut the door. "We've only got a moment before the word is out," he whispered, his eyes darting around the murky interior. "Find the hood! Unless it's already been taken. Oh drat, oh misery! I should have known something like this might happen!"

"Then you shouldn't have risked Hofud's life by taking Skyla's hood to him," Jafnar retorted.

"You shouldn't risk yours by spying where you don't belong," Illmuri flared, his eyes murderous.

It did not take long to make a search of Hofud's meager possessions. Jafnar recovered quickly from his horror, but his flesh crawled the entire time, and he couldn't resist taking quick glances at poor old Hofud, lying stiff and silent on the ground. His heart thudded with increasing fervor when he thought of the creature that had done this.

"Drat!" Mistislaus muttered. "Where could he have put it? It might be on him, somewhere."

"I'm not touching him," Jafnar declared, shrinking back. "You look, if you dare."

Mistislaus searched the body, taking care not to get blood on his hands or clothing. Then he rolled the stiff carcass over and looked through Hofud's belt pouch.

"It's not here," Illmuri murmured in bitter exasperation.

"Perhaps Skyla was here," Mistislaus said, his voice tremulous. "Before he died. Or even shortly after. She might have taken it herself." Drops of moisture sprang out on his brow. "Perhaps—" He turned and looked at Hofud's body. "No, I can't bear to think of her being here, seeing this—this atrocity."

"She's probably back at the observatory, safe by now," Illmuri said quickly. "Perhaps she was never here. We might have passed her on the way. By now she knows the Skurdur almost as well as Jafnar does." He shot Jafnar an accusing glance. "Come, this is no place for lingering and chatting. The word will be out in moments that the lynx has struck again."

Guthrum was waiting anxiously for them at the street gate when they arrived at the observatory.

"She's back," he growled with a furious glower at Jafnar. "Safe and sound. So much for entrusting her to an untrained urchin who won't eat off a plate!"

"It wasn't Jafnar's fault entirely," Mistislaus said with a heavy sigh of relief, gazing toward Skyla's tower window. "I think Skyla is far more clever than we've yet imagined. We must all be more vigilant. Especially now that she's getting a mind of her own. Is she sleeping?"

"Yes. She came in not long after you left, merry as a lark from her adventuring," Guthrum replied, standing aside as they passed through the gate, his eyes upon the gloomy Street of a Thousand Steps. "I hope she doesn't develop a taste for being out at night. It isn't healthy."

They left the murky street and went inside. A fire was newly built in the main room, casting light around the walls. What arrested all their eyes was the sight of Skyla's long blue hood hanging neatly on its peg beside the door leading up to the tower.

"So she found it," Illmuri said.

"What luck," Jafnar said. "She was there just in time, before the lynx came. Or just after."

"This is a serious matter," Mistislaus said with a muffled groan. "It definitely calls for breakfast. Jafnar, back with you to the

Hangman's Bridge. Nothing but hot pastries is going to get us out of this one."

"Skyla's out of plumabrot," Jafnar said, suddenly remembering. "We finished off the lot of it last night."

His stomach gave a queasy twist at the mere mention of plumabrot, and all his itches demanded scratching.

"Then get her some, and whatever else might help," Mistislaus said, rubbing his eyes in a preoccupied manner.

By the time Jafnar returned with the basket, he had the feeling Mistislaus and Illmuri had discussed some very weighty topics without his listening ears on the premises. The only matter of importance remaining was the food. Mistislaus sawed off a slab of bread and took great comfort in pouring grease over his steaming pastry.

"Has Rangfara got the news of the lynx killing yet?" Illmuri inquired sharply of Jafnar. He only nibbled at his food unappreciatively.

"To be sure," Jafnar said grimly. "There's a rush of Skurdur people trying to get out the gate, but nobody's getting out except Krypplingur, Slaemur, and other highborns. It's peculiar this time because the lynx has killed a common Dokkalfar, instead of a Krypplingur."

Mistislaus and Illmuri greeted his statement with silence.

"If someone hadn't stolen her blue hood and taken it to Hofud, none of this would have happened," Jafnar continued directly to Illmuri with mounting wrath. "Skyla might have been there when that lynx decided to attack old Hofud. She might have been killed. What did you hope to accomplish by it? You're never going to find the treasure that way."

"You forget yourself, you young cur," Mistislaus sputtered. "One of your stature does not make such accusations! Illmuri is a wizard of respectable stature, not a sneak thief!"

Illmuri lifted one hand slightly. "It's true, I took Skyla's hood," he said. "Perhaps I was wrong not to mention it. I had hoped Hofud would be of help in discerning something about Skyla that might help her control these strange powers of hers. He was a quarrelsome old character, but I'm certain he would have told me something, had he not been prevented. If Hofud's death is on anyone's shoulders, I fear they are mine. As for you—" He turned his gaze upon Jafnar. "You'd better keep silent about this matter of the hood, or you might yet end up in the Kjallari with your throat sliced. Worse yet, the Krypplingur might get their hands on you, if they find out you're a Skylding and not just a gutter rat from the Skurdur. That wouldn't do any of us any good, would it?"

Jafnar shut his mouth with a dry click.

"Well, we've got Skyla and her hood back," Mistislaus said. "She doesn't seem to be any the worse for her experience. Rangfara has lost old Hofud, but I daresay there are others of his ilk to fill the hole he left."

Jafnar shadowed Mistislaus and Illmuri to the mossy front gate, where Illmuri made a curt farewell and disappeared down the narrow Street of a Thousand Steps. Mistislaus turned and bestowed a dark and thoughtful look upon Jafnar.

"I hope you've learned a lesson from this," he rumbled menacingly. "Not a word of what has happened must pass your lips, unless you want the Krypplingur here asking some very nasty questions. We have nothing to do with that lynx, save that old Hofud came embarrassingly close to us, thanks to Skyla's hood. Now away with you! One thousand iterations for penance this morning."

Suddenly a brown claw of a hand shot out and fastened itself on Mistislaus' sleeve. Jafnar hesitated, glowering and putting his hand on his old sword in a threatening manner.

"Stay a moment!" a voice croaked. Mistislaus turned and recognized the crone who lived in the hovel adjoining Hofud's. More than before, she looked like a human species of spider spinning her webs of deception in the dark alley.

"I've got some information for you," she said in a whisper. "If you've got a piece of gold for me, that is."

"Tell me what you know and I'll reward you if it's worthwhile," Mistislaus hedged.

The old woman's hand shot out at once. "Pay me now," she said. "You won't want to pay me for something you've already got."

"Is it regarding the death of Hofud?" Mistislaus asked.

"Yes. You and your apprentice are dayfarers, are you not?" she asked quickly, her eyes darting from Jafnar to Mistislaus as he nodded and fumbled with infuriating slowness with his belt pouch. "What have you got for me there, Wizard? Two bits of silver I could put in one eye and not be the worse for it afterward?"

"I'm not a wealthy man," Mistislaus said. "But if ever you need a cure for chilblains or boils, I can dissolve them in three days into perfect, healthy flesh. Would you take two pieces of silver and four chilblains and a boil?"

Mistislaus put two pieces of a coin into her blackened palm.

She tested the metal with her teeth and nodded in approval, before wrapping it up busily in a scrap of rag and stowing it away, like a spider who has captured a tasty insect in her web. The old woman folded her arms across her chest and cleared her throat. With her eyes half veiled, she said in a low, rapid voice, "It was early on last night when old Hofud died. I heard the hullabaloo but I was too afraid to go over there. Something worse than normal was going on and I knew it was too late to save him anyway, so I shut my door and watched and waited for daylight. I know who comes and goes along our side of the street. I saw who went into his hut before the hullabaloo, and how long she took to come out again."

"She!" Mistislaus murmured. "Do you mean to say it was a woman? In a white cloak, perhaps?"

"You keep going on about that white cloak, don't you? Well, it wasn't white, it was black."

"You saw no white cloak at all?"

"None at all, unless it was very quick. What I saw was Alvara, the sorceress. Isn't that good enough for you? That she-cat prowled around there spying upon the Illmuri wizard."

"Illmuri!" Mistislaus said. "But that's not possible; he was with me from sundown onward at Herradshol. He was a bit later than sundown, come to think of it. Was Hofud alive at the time Illmuri arrived?"

"He stayed inside quite a while to be talking with nothing but a dead carcass," she retorted.

"What about Alvara?"

"I can't say for certain if she found Hofud dead or if she left him that way. He didn't even have time to shriek, or I would have heard."

"Is that all you have?" Mistislaus asked. "Didn't you see the lynx itself?"

"Isn't that more than you had to start with?" she retorted, taking hold of Mistislaus' sleeve in a predatory manner. "Nobody sees the snow lynx unless it's his turn to die soon. One of those two murdered old Hofud by conjuring the snow lynx on him, or it was your white cloak. Now let me give you some free advice, Wizard. Don't go prowling around Rangfara looking for the Skylding treasure, or you're more likely to end up as maggot food. There's them that doesn't want it found, them that will kill to protect it."

"Maybe old Hofud knew something about it," Jafnar said.

"You see where it got him, if he did," the old woman muttered, shaking her matted head. "Oh, the young lads like you who have perished looking for it! Scores of them, just like you, all full of greed and ambition, and all full of maggots at the end, nothing but rubbish to be thrown down the Kjallari pits like so much offal, down to them that lives below Rangfara and takes what they wants from us above. Hear me, Wizard!" She tugged on his sleeve and shoved her beastly face near to his, her eyes bright like a rat's. "Rangfara is foul, but something even more foul walks here now, since the Krypplingur. The doors of the Kjallari are open, and I smell a stench that reeks to the skies. You're a decent sort and therefore something of a dolt, but you've got powers and wisdom. Unless something is done, Rangfara will be a hollow bone, chewn by the wind, and so will we all. Do you hear, Wizard?"

"Certainly I hear you," Mistislaus said mildly, gently tugging at his sleeve to extricate himself.

"You aren't too clean and removed to know what I mean? I daren't speak it for fear the name will call the thing."

"I know exactly what you mean," Mistislaus said, edging away and motioning Guthrum to shut the gate. "Now good-bye and thank you for your information."

Reluctantly the old woman allowed him to unwind himself from her grip, and Guthrum slammed shut the gate, leaving her on the far side of it still ranting about bones and maggots.

"A very pretty bit of information indeed." Mistislaus moaned. "Alvara and Illmuri and Skyla were all there, and Hofud died just before one of them left. Whatever am I to do with it?" He meandered into the house, murmuring to himself and pressing his fingertips into his temples in distraction.

The answer to every question in Mistislaus' mind was obtained through iterating or napping, so he speedily repaired to his favorite dozing spot in the observatory dome. Presently the gentle sawing of his snores grated mildly against the echoes of Athugashol.

At nightfall, Illmuri came to fetch Mistislaus to Herrad's hall.

"Herrad has heard the news," he said. "He's been flailing about like a mad beast all day. He thinks the lynx is stalking him and he thinks the Kjallari is working on him from the leg up. Worse than dying, he hates the idea of giving up the chieftaincy to Ofarir. You won't have an easy time of it tonight."

"I think," Mistislaus said, looking at Jafnar and Skyla as severely as he possibly could, "that we must make a different arrangement, after last night's debacle."

"I'd like another chance," Jafnar said, scowling. "Nothing like that will ever happen again."

"To be sure, it won't," Mistislaus said. "I'm locking the doors from the outside tonight and posting Guthrum on the doorstep. No one gets past Guthrum."

"She did it last night," Illmuri said in a low voice. "I think you should lock her in the tower, to be safe, and send this young ruffian back to the streets."

"I hate the tower," Skyla said. "I promise I won't go out. Now I've got my hood back, I'm perfectly content. If you send Jafnar away, I shall go looking for him."

"Don't threaten me, you vixen!" Mistislaus blustered. "A man has been killed, and the Krypplingur have their eyes upon us! If you don't do what you are told, Skyla, you must be restrained against your will." To Illmuri he added, "This is what comes of bringing up a child like a little pet of some sort. We all spoiled her hideously, instead of treating her with the firmness and discipline required for a child. I was thrashed on a daily basis as a child, and starved for disobedience, and you can see what a benefit it's been to me in my later life."

"I can scarcely remember what I did," Skyla said. "Perhaps the plumabrot made me feel a little giddy. Am I to be thrashed and starved then?"

"No, but you must learn to be obedient," Mistislaus said. "Rangfara is too dangerous for you to wander about in alone. I thought Jafnar could prevent just such a thing from happening."

"I will," Jafnar said, scowling ferociously. "If she gets away again, you may throw me out into the street and forget that you ever promised me a boon. I know now to avoid plumabrot. Haven't I done well in the past, going into the Skurdur and coming out safely? Is there anyone else who knows Rangfara like I do? I'm no newcomer here." He flashed Illmuri a defiant glare.

"That may be true," Mistislaus admitted. "But I am still holding you accountable for Skyla's safety. I suspect she was messing around with that bag of concoctions of hers. She's got just enough talent to get into trouble, which is probably what happened last night."

"No, it was not," Skyla said. "It was the plumabrot. I think it was getting a little too moldy."

Mistislaus' eye rolled about with excessive, fervid brilliance. He shook his finger angrily as he said, "If another episode like this happens again, Skyla goes back to the tower and Jafnar goes back to the street. And no more plumabrot."

Chapter Ten

Jafnar maintained his duties that day with grim vigilance. No wonder Guthrum was such a dour and suspicious creature, if he had devoted the last thirteen years of his life to protecting something as irresponsible and unpredictable as Skyla. By the end of the day, Jafnar was exhausted. He was ready to give it all up and go back to being a carefree wild boy, but he felt too tired to climb back up to the Hall of Stars.

When Mistislaus left that night, he locked the door after himself. In stricken silence, like wild hares, Jafnar and Skyla listened to the door being locked with a portentous click. When the wizard was gone, and Guthrum posted outside the door with no great pleasure at his duty, Jafnar glared around the confines of the room. It had seemed large enough at one time, but now that he couldn't get out, it seemed like a tomb. Distrustfully he glared at Skyla, combing her hair beside the fire until it stood up in a white nimbus around her head, catching the glow from the hearth.

"Would one Skylding thoroughly deceive another Skylding, just to get away for some secret business?" he demanded. "Did you know plumabrot would make me sick?"

"I wouldn't, Jafnar," she replied. "What happened to you was meant to happen. The voices of the mist people told me to go to Hofud for my hood. I knew I had to go at once, so I couldn't wait for you. I could see that you weren't feeling very well. Why is this so fearfully important to everyone?"

"If you had been a few moments later, the lynx might have got you," Jafnar said. "And Alvara was prowling around in the street last night. She might have kidnapped you or done something harmful."

"Oh," she said. "I don't think so."

Skyla pulled a ragged bag out from under a sleeping platform in her alcove and dumped out an assortment of objects on the table—bones, feathers, rocks, lumps of oddly shaped clay, and small woven boxes containing mice and insects, both dead and alive.

"Tonight we must practice our skills," she said.

"Skyla, you mustn't," Jafnar protested. "You promised Mistislaus. Besides, I'm no good at your magic."

"You must try harder, Jafnar," Skyla said, poking at the clay. "And I promised not to run away, not to stop practicing my spells. Here's the mouse," she said, holding up the stiff little carcass. "Breathe on him, Jafnar, and see if you can make him alive."

"Thogn's a more apt pupil for you," he said ruefully. He was getting accustomed to seeing poor wander-witted Thogn playing about with such strange and disgusting objects as dead things, but he still considered it a nasty, unnatural preoccupation, especially for a young girl.

"I can make it work, Jafnar, and so can you. I've even cut the tail off the mouse and healed it again. But only twice. Then I killed him yesterday and haven't been able to restore the life to him. I think it was something to do with the rat."

Jafnar shivered, his skin turning moist and pale as new curds at the memory of the rat. They had killed it, together, with what Skyla had said were the appropriate rituals. But the life they had restored to it was not the life of a rat. It was mad and savage, and escaped from them before they could separate it again from whatever force they had called into it.

"Skyla! Torturing these little creatures is wrong!" Jafnar burst out in angry disgust. "We've got to stop it before we get something far worse than the rat. Thogn kills things all the time now. I've seen him do it. He likes dead things, and that's crazy, unless you're a berserker, and he's not."

"He's practicing," Skyla said patiently. "He doesn't leave any of them dead or mutilated. They feel no pain."

"Practicing what?" Jafnar asked.

She ignored his question. "Imagine being able to call the life back into a dead person. Imagine healing wounds at a touch. Imagine being able to take this stone and turn it into a piece of bread or a piece of gold. Think what power you'd have. I know it's possible, because I've almost made all those things work."

Jafnar prodded the stiff, dried form of the dead mouse. "But what about this? He's dead, Skyla. You said you drove the life out of him with just words. Imagine what sort of power that would give a person. Terrible power. A man or a woman can't live with that sort of destruction available. Not without becoming completely evil."

"Evil is the destruction of the life force," Skyla said. "I don't seek to destroy life; I want the power to bring it back when it's gone. I wouldn't call that evil."

Jafnar was aghast. "You'd oppose the will of the three Norns, who spin men's fates and snip the threads when their lives are done?"

"They don't really exist," Skyla said. "I don't see any threads hanging about you."

"Skyla, don't mess about with casting life or death in or out," Jafnar pleaded. "It isn't natural."

"I don't call it messing," she said. "I call it a gift. If I've got that gift, and I think I may, I'm going to develop it. Now breathe on the mouse, Jafnar, and send out a call in your thoughts to bring him alive again."

Jafnar did as she told him. "There, you see, it didn't work," he said. "Dead is dead, and there's nothing—"

He broke off with a shout as the hitherto dead mouse suddenly started kicking and scratching in his hand. It bit his thumb, scuttled up his arm, and jumped off his shoulder.

"You see," Skyla said, "you can do it. I bet it had something to do with the plumabrot."

Jafnar put his bitten thumb in his mouth. "Don't mention that horrid concoction. I'll never see, smell, or taste it again. I'm still having trouble with knives." He held up his hand with his knife clinging to it. When he tried to pull it away, the knife clung to his other hand.

Skyla took the knife. "That's a very good sign your natural powers are coming to you, Jafnar. Now try the clay. Or transforming the dirt into something. You did very well with the mouse."

"I didn't do anything," he protested, but he obligingly formed a little doll from the clay, moistening it with spit and a few drops of blood from his mouse-bitten finger. When he breathed upon the inert little figure, calling it to take on the semblance of life, he had scant hope that anything would happen. But almost instantly the little malformed creature rubbed its eyes with its hands and stretched its blobby arms.

"Skyla! Skyla!" he gasped, not daring to move. "It's alive!"

"Very good, Jafnar. Now say the words to release it."

Fervently he said the words *"Fara af stad!"* and the clay creature became a lump of mud once again.

"No more," he said, panting slightly and sweating. "I don't know what's happening to me. I've never been able to work any kind of spells before. Will it wear off?"

"Do you want it to? You're a true Skylding now, Jafnar. Don't you want the powers you were born to inherit? Come now, try the transformation spell."

By the time she was done testing him with various spells and skills, it was evident that he had powers. He was trembling in every limb, as if Krypplingur had chased him from one end of Rangfara to the other. His dreams that night were lively and terrifying, with the Kellarman's hot, stinking breath at his back.

Early the next morning, while Skyla still slept and Mistislaus iterated, Jafnar summoned the other wild boys and handed out a basketful of leftovers from Mistislaus' overbounteous and adventurous table. Warily and reluctantly they came into the tower courtyard, spitting in their palms and making signs to ward off evil.

"Whatever is the matter with you?" Jafnar demanded. "There's no need for that sort of thing. What evil could possibly be here? Look at the plunder I've got for you."

"Jafnar," Ordvar said, "I think it would be best if we left this place. We've never been mixed up with wizards before, and we don't like it. Why don't we just move on to another place and forget about all this? It's stopped being fun now."

"And you've stopped being fun," Einka added. "Ever since you became a toady for Mistislaus."

Jafnar gave his ear a cuff for his disrespect, but he seemed preoccupied. "We're not leaving," he said. "There's more to this world than picking pockets and having fun. We've only been pretending to be real Skyldings and playing at searching for the treasure."

"Now it's getting real," Lampi said.

"And it's not fun anymore," Lofa added.

"It's better than fun," Jafnar said. "Can't you see that? If you can't now, you will later."

"I don't like this lynx business," growled Modga, who had been darkly and silently brooding. "It gives me a very bad feeling. There's a lot of talk in the Skurdur, too. Has anyone else noticed that the lynx didn't start appearing again until Mistislaus came into Rangfara? Mark my words, he's conjuring it. Look at what happened to poor old Hofud, and for no better reason than he had her hood. Hofud never hurt anyone, in spite of himself."

They all looked at Jafnar, waiting.

"Hofud's time to die arrived, that's all," Jafnar said. "Skurdur talk is as worthless as you are, Modga. I don't see how you could think Skyla or Mistislaus had the slightest thing to do with it. Now stop being a bunch of old women. It's time you stopped being children and grew up into men. We can't stay wild boys forever. We're Skyldings, and that treasure is waiting for us. If any of you is too afraid, you can go back to where you were before I found you."

"I say we stay," Ordvar said. "Jafnar is right. Besides, when have we eaten so well?"

"We'll let our bellies be our guides," Modga said.

The other boys hooted him down in derision and fell to eating. When Mistislaus came shuffling down the stairs, humming and contented from all his iterating, they scuttled away before he could catch sight of them, still too wild to bear his presence.

Jafnar told them nothing about the troublesome effects that clung to him since his bout with the plumabrot. The dreams faded over the next three nights, and so did his ability to perform Skyla's tests. By the fifth night since Hofud's death, Jafnar was as dull and useless as he had ever been before when it came to magic skills.

Mistislaus accompanied them to the Skurdur for three days before tiring of the exercise provided by the Street of a Thousand Steps and finally convincing himself of the sincerity of Skyla and Jafnar's contrite demeanor. Skyla trudged along at his heels, treading upon his cloak several times in her earnestness to stay cautiously near. Jafnar scouted along in the rear with his hand upon his sword, exuding a fiercely protective aura that caused several itinerant warriors of comparable stature to move out of his way.

Thus reassured, Mistislaus allowed Jafnar and Skyla to resume their expeditions to the Skurdur unattended. He also relented and took Guthrum off the doorstep. But he resolutely turned the key in the door lock every night when he departed to Herradshol.

On the first morning expedition to the Skurdur alone since Hofud's death, Skyla darted like a butterfly from booth to booth, from tent to tent, winding her way among carts, heaps of firewood, and small bands of sheep, goats, and cattle. Jafnar strode anxiously behind her, trying to shield her from the more determined hawkers, most of them little more than thieves in merchants' clothing, and steering her away from the places where evil was sold, such as the assassins' wall and wizards' stalls.

Skyla stared back at the scowling killers with their swords thrust into the earth before them to announce their profession, as well as their proclivities, while Jafnar tried to hurry her along.

She sniffed the air suddenly, stopping in her tracks.

"I smell blood," she said.

Jafnar glanced around nervously. Blood in Rangfara was common enough, but still not so common as to be welcome.

"Oh, it's only a butcher's stall," he said, nodding his head to one side. "Come along, it's nothing. The meistari wants a joint cut and taken to the old hag at the Hangman's Bridge to be roasted. He wants a cut from a tender young heifer, not some tough old bull that fell down of old age."

"How terrible," Skyla said as they approached the butchers' stalls, where freshly killed cattle and sheep were being cut up and sold piecemeal, as well as heaps of fish, whale meat and slabs of white blubber, ducks, geese, swans, and chickens. Jafnar selected a butcher's stall and stepped forward to request the front haunch of the carcass. The butcher was a jolly enough fellow, standing over the dead beast and swinging at it with an enormous curved axe, dripping blood all over him, unnoticed as a warm spring rain.

Shuddering, Skyla turned away. "Let's not buy any meat," she said, then her eyes fell upon the carcass of a horse, its head drooping limply out of the back of a cart.

"What happened to the horse?" she demanded, turning straight out of the grip Jafnar had on her elbow. She approached the cart and looked curiously at the dead creature. Addressing a ragged fellow lounging on the seat of the cart, she repeated her question more loudly, insisting upon being heard and answered.

The fellow bunched up his thin shoulders into a shrug. "I don't know, he just fell down dead in the shafts, like he'd been hit in the head with a hammer. Just this morning, and I thought the world of him. Raised him like my own son I did, and him not an old horse, either. Now he'll go for rich men's dogs' meat, or poor men's stew pots."

Skyla reached out and stroked the horse's neck. "Poor horse," she said, her voice vibrant with pity.

"Skyla, horses do die, it's nothing to worry over," Jafnar said, embarrassed. "Now come along, it isn't seemly to grieve over a beast. People will begin to stare at you."

Skyla turned obediently. "But you'd better get Mistislaus his joint of meat," she said. "He'll be unhappy without it. I shall wait for you over there. I don't like that butcher. He's a murderer, and much too cheerful about it to suit me."

Jafnar went back to have the appropriate joint of meat cut and wrapped in linen to keep the flies off. With the same unease he always felt, he showed the butcher Herrad's token and watched his blood-smeared cheer turn to a gloomy scowl.

"And that was the best quarter," he growled. "Gone and never to be paid for."

Jafnar took the joint of meat and hurried away, thinking himself a guiltier thief than he had ever felt while picking pockets.

Skyla was not in the agreed-upon spot when he returned to it. He threw a worried glare all around, wondering where she might have wandered away to, if some bright gewgaw had caught her eye, or if some clever trickster had lured her away. As he plunged off on a desperate search, he heard a sudden bawl of men's voices from the direction of the butcher's stall. Looking back, he saw Skyla's agile form dodging the thrashing hooves of a rearing horse. It was plunging from a cart, slipping and crashing against the sides in its haste to escape, all flying mane, flaring nostrils, white-ringed eyes, and waving hooves. The two horses drawing the cart weren't at all happy about such antics, so they were plunging and rearing in differing directions. In the midst of it all, Skyla darted around a knot of shouting men, including the bloodied butcher, all trying to catch hold of the horse somehow and avoid being trampled.

After knocking down a sausage stall and stampeding several bullocks waiting for slaughter, the horse broke free of the captors clinging to his nose and ears and mane and galloped away with his tail aloft, waving like a banner.

"Heading home, looks like," one of the men said, picking himself up off the ground.

"I swear he was dead!" the owner of the cart and horses declared in exasperation as he strove to quiet his animals. "Dogs' meat was all he was, and stiff as a stockfish besides!"

"He's lively enough now!" the butcher said.

"The sight of you put the life back into him," another joked, as the humor of the situation gradually began to tickle the gathering crowd. "He didn't fancy becoming dogs' meat just yet."

"Something put the life back into him," the horse's owner said, still in awe. "It was like he never knew me, that raised him from a colt. I'd say it wasn't my horse, from that glare in his eyes. Hi, what's that young lass doing here under the horses' hooves?" he added suddenly, catching sight of Skyla nearby. "She was nearly killed by that beast. Take her out of here before something worse happens."

Mutely Jafnar led Skyla away, her head still turned in the direction the horse had taken in his mad career homeward. Her smile was peculiar, and it raised the gooseflesh on his arms to remember how she had stroked the dead horse's neck, talking to it pityingly. He glanced at her sharply, sidewise.

"Skyla, what did you do to that horse?" he demanded. "I thought you promised Mistislaus you wouldn't do anything!"

Her eyes were already distracted by bright-colored birds in cages, singing their captive hearts out, and a cartload of the beautiful Slaemur women rolled by, cackling and chattering like the fascinating monkeys a far traveler showed for money in a tent.

"He was dead," Skyla said airily. "As dead as an empty house. I made him alive again. I called a horse back into him, but I don't think it was the right one. It won't matter, will it? The drover still has a horse, doesn't he, instead of a heap of dog meat?"

"I don't think he will mind," Jafnar said gruffly, looking about frantically to see if anyone was staring at them and perhaps overhearing. He saw many people he knew or at least recognized, friend and foe alike, from his friends the rag gatherer to the rat killer, and his enemies the Krypplingur. All seemed acutely aware of Skyla, even though they were pretending to be busy plying their own trades.

Then he saw Alvara slipping along behind a saddle-maker's booth, her face muffled, but he knew that long black cloak and hood from its alien clan markings. A cold trickle of sweat commenced its ticklish journey down his spine. He felt Alvara's eyes upon him. He gripped Skyla's arm and led her out of that street and into the cloth-maker's street, a safe shortcut to the Hangman's Bridge.

By the time he handed over the meat to the old woman to be cooked, he thought himself safe.

"Jafnar, you're forgetting the plumabrot," Skyla said, neatly disengaging his grip on her arm. "It will only take a few moments. You know I can't survive without it."

"I think you could if you had to," Jafnar said in exasperation. "I know I could. We've already been gone far too long, and Mistislaus will be beside himself. If we make him angry today, he might never allow us to come here alone again. He'll send Guthrum instead."

"Mistislaus must be humored," Skyla said with a sigh, "although this means I'll be without plumabrot until tomorrow."

For the rest of the day Skyla dawdled listlessly in the courtyard, too disinterested to throw pebbles at the fish, or to work with her dead mice and rats, or even her clay people. At last the droning of Mistislaus' endless iterations put her to sleep, curled up like a cat in the sun with her white cloak for a rug. Still inflamed with his resolve to protect her from all threats as well as her own folly, Jafnar stationed himself at a respectful distance to watch her until she awakened.

After a short while the brief patch of sunlight was obliterated by the dark murk rising from the tangled streets of Rangfara. Skyla awakened and stretched, then got up and went into the building, leaving her white cloak spread upon the grassy flagstones.

Jafnar waited for her to return and was just on the point of moving forward to pick up the cloak for her when Illmuri glided around the corner of the horse barn, where Guthrum was tossing soiled straw out a window onto the midden heap. Scarcely breaking stride, Illmuri snatched up the white cloak like a fox snatching the prize hen from the chicken yard and bundled it under one arm, smothering it quickly in his black habiliment. Then he got himself out by scrambling up a crumbling wall and dropping out of sight.

Outraged, Jafnar tore after him, going up the same wall and dropping down into the weedy courtyard of the Hall of Stars. He glimpsed Illmuri's dark cloak darting out the street gate. Jafnar followed, his heart pounding with dread as he recognized Illmuri's inevitable destination. He turned into the Kjallari street, not glancing back once.

Jafnar's footsteps slowed as he approached the gloomy gate, then involuntarily quickened, taking him past it in spite of himself. Mustering his courage, he turned around and faced it, feeling waves of dread and warning thrusting him backward toward safety. It was like one of his dreams, trying to force himself to move against an irresistible force. Then he thought of Skyla's distress at losing her treasured white cloak. If she had no fear of Hofud, she probably would have no fear of the Kjallari. She would slip away to search for her cloak, never to be seen again.

It was the impetus he needed. He forced one foot ahead, followed by the other, until he had entered the gate, passing under the sign of the lynx with a quick glance upward. Once inside the gateway, he found himself in virtual darkness, punctuated by a few flickering points of light coming from dark heaps of stone. Somewhere ahead, he heard the quick patter of Illmuri's soft-soled boots diminishing, as if he were going down a stairway.

Jafnar plunged after him, half blind in the gloom, stopping only when he tripped over something that clattered noisily, rolling away from his feet. When the thing came to rest, he recognized it as a human skull. He froze at once, staring at it and gradually expanding his attention to encompass the huge pillared hall around him.

The roof of the Kjallari house had not collapsed, and only faint slits of light in the high domed roof relieved the total gloom with twelve pallid bars upon the littered floor. To Jafnar's horror, as he gazed around he saw scattered skeletons and rags and heaps in various stages of decay that had once been people, probably street wretches who had lost all fear of anything and had crawled in here to die, or perhaps some of them had been murdered or had died in duels. Scattered among the corpses were cairns of heaped stone forming crude altars, where offerings had been left to the most implacable enemy of Ljosalfar or Dokkalfar. The small lights that he had seen were horn lamps blinking and sputtering in the drafty dark, illuminating someone's hopeful earthly inducement that death would pass him by—bowls of grain, seed, milk, cheese, bread, and the heads and feet of sheep and goats. The cairns and offerings encircled the opening in the floor, like a well, where the dead were cast away.

Jafnar skirted the circle of cairns and cautiously picked his way forward, each step coming more slowly than the last. As his eyes became accustomed to the gloom, he saw that the charnel pit had steps spiraling downward, around its walls. He hesitated. He had never gone down those steps, into that well of death and decay, but Thogn had, and now Thogn walked in a world of his own.

Jafnar crept closer, to the very edge, and looked down. A warm dry breath blew softly from the shaft, bearing the scent of dust and ancient decay. Below, a small light went bobbing downward, as if riding in someone's hand, then blinked out with a whisper of footsteps.

Chapter Eleven

Jafnar turned and obtained for himself one of the little horn lights burning on a cairn, then started down the steps. On a broad stone over the stairway, he saw the carved picture of the lynx again, with its left paw on the chest of a supine human figure. Its shadowy slanted eyes seemed to look straight at him, as if recognizing him for legitimate prey. Shivering slightly, Jafnar resumed his descent of the stairs.

At the bottom was another arch, also carved with the lynx. Beyond that, the tunnel branched into two ways. As Jafnar stood considering which way Illmuri might have gone, he felt his spine prickling with growing uneasiness, and he turned and looked back the way he had come. All he saw was the stone lynx gazing at him with steady intent, as if he were a hare and it was stalking him.

If only he had a grain of control over his natural Alfar powers, he would know which way Illmuri had taken. A thread of memory suddenly tightened. Mistislaus' words about power suddenly occurred to him with startling clarity. The way to gain it, Mistislaus had told him, was to act as if he already possessed it.

Jafnar drew a deep breath, quieting his clamoring fears. Looking first at one tunnel then the other, he tried to visualize himself choosing the right one. After a few moments of silent and unrewarding struggle, he strode ahead into the right-hand tunnel. He had not gone far when he discovered that there were crypts on both sides of the passage, small rooms carved into the earth with stone lintels like ordinary barrow mounds with the entrances blocked with mortared stones. The first crypts were ornamented with lynxes and runes and other symbols Jafnar did not understand, which probably signified the names and positions of the deceased persons within. Cautiously Jafnar tiptoed down the passage, pausing to look at the carvings, or peeking nervously into open crypts when he encountered them. With an awakening glow of greed, he thought of the walled-up ones and what might lie inside. It was Skylding gold, after all, and he certainly had a right to the treasure of his ancestors, since he was one of the last survivors of Rangfara.

At each turning of the way, he was certain he heard Illmuri's footsteps just ahead of him. When the passage opened into a circular area with a faint light filtering down from far above, he halted suddenly, realizing he had been following no one. The whisperers in his head told him he was alone here, the first to see this place in many years. Light came in from above through the arched openings that looked too regular not to be windows, which allowed pallid shafts of light to trickle down into the heart of the Kjallari.

Jafnar put down his lamp and let his eyes adjust to the pale light. He stepped silently into a large underground hall supported by carved columns of stone, more grand than any of the ruins he had prowled through in the ruined city above. Rangfara, the voices of his ancestors whispered, was built upon the ruins of a far more glorious civilization, like barnacles growing on the hull of a sunken ship. Faces of men and beasts looked down from the columns at Jafnar in amused derision, and the floor under his feet was all of squares of smoothly polished stone.

In the center of the hall stood a block of stone like a table, with a heap of something covering the center. Jafnar picked his way nearer carefully, noting stacks of stone tablets piled neatly around the shrine. They bore writing in the old language of runes.

The central altar or table was similarly covered with stacks of the stone tablets. The mound that had attracted Jafnar's curiosity turned out to be a heap of rotting cloth and human bones, lying undisturbed for many years. One skeletal hand still clutched a stylus, with the mallet lying nearby, where the skeleton's skull had detached and rolled away a short distance. Sparkling through the cloth and the bones of the man's rib cage was a golden-hilted daggar, with the remains of the other hand still gripping it. He had taken his own life, and died with his head upon his beloved records.

Jafnar felt no fear, only sad, tantalizing wisps of sweet memories that eluded him like handfuls of smoke. His head reeled as if a horse had kicked it. A strong wave of grief welled up from unknown depths, and his mouth burned with the agreeable sour sweetness of plumabrot.

"Skriftur! It's you!" he said aloud, knowing without knowing how that he had correctly spoken the man's name.

His heart pounded as he stood and gazed at the last genealogist of the Skylding clan, knowing with a poignant ache that those hands now reduced to dry and detached bone had once held each Skylding infant aloft and blessed it with a name and with a history. The dark and empty hall had once been a place of celebration and pride. Turning slowly, Jafnar saw the mist people gathered around in feasting and congratulation for the naming of a child, with old Skriftur standing in the center, cradling a new infant in his arms. On the table behind him, bathed in the light of horn lamps and the two great hearth fires, lay a bright new parchment inscribed with the child's name and parentage.

Jafnar stepped forward with the idea of reading the name on the parchment, his every hope and dream telling him it must be his own, but the instant he moved, the vision vanished, leaving him in the cold and gloom once more. The warmth of lamp and hearth gradually faded from his face. He gazed around the chamber hopefully, never having felt so bereft of family and kinship.

Moving randomly, he drifted around the hall among the orderly stacks of tablets until he came to a halt beside the ruins of old Skriftur, dead by his own hand, lest he be forced to reveal the location of this very place. A roaring grew inside his skull, thousands of voices all whispering to him like the relentless roar of the sea. It was as if he had just eaten plumabrot again; he felt hot and itchy all over, and the floor swayed beneath his feet.

"Stop! Stop!" he moaned, scarcely able to summon up his own voice. "I don't know who I am!"

At once the murmuring voices stilled, and Jafnar stood alone again in the ancient gloomy cavern. His eyes dropped from Skriftur's bones toward the floor, and he realized that the altar or table of stone was actually a vault, neatly lined with stacks of small wooden boxes, each marked with runes. Jafnar gasped; he had seen such boxes often, when the clan genealogists of the women's clans had come to Rangfara to set up their gifting tents and arrange the marriages for the coming year. Gold and birthrights changed hands during the gifting season, all recorded upon vellums that were rolled up and put away in ornate little boxes for safekeeping. Nothing was more valued than the proof of one's parentage and birthright when it came to dividing inheritances or passing along the essential skills of one's hereditary profession. From his Skylding father, Jafnar knew he had probably inherited warfare and leadership, but what had he inherited from his mother's clan?

And how was he to know which of the thousand little boxes contained his own name-scroll? There wasn't time to search. As he gazed at them, he felt a chill at the back of his neck, reminding him of Illmuri and the cloak. He felt that he had been told it was time to go, now that he had been shown what he needed to know.

Taking up his horn lamp again, he returned to the tunnels after one last glance back at Skriftur. It would be a happy place again someday, he told himself. Gazing around, he realized his fear of the Kjallari had been replaced by a comforting glow of encouragement. Nothing was trying to drive him away from this place.

As he walked away into the tunnels, however, the old feelings of threat and terror commenced gnawing at him. A soft and fetid breeze fanned his face, bringing with it the familiar terrible dusty smell of the Kjallari. Rounding a sharp corner, he suddenly saw a light ahead and heard the soft, purposeful padding of Illmuri's boots. He followed, tightening up his hold on all his old fears of the Kjallari as they came trampling back into his thoughts. This part of the Kjallari was sinister and damp, with Krypplingur-plundered tombs spilling rags and bones out underfoot.

The way narrowed, stuffy and scarcely shoulder-wide for an interminable distance, then it opened into another underground hall, lit from above by openings into the streets overhead. In the center stood a jagged heap of stones and lintels, where a shrine had collapsed. The rubble surrounding it was stone tablets, smashed beyond recognition. The Krypplingur had clearly had a grand heydey here, thinking they were destroying something priceless. Jafnar put down his lamp in a niche and watched as Illmuri prowled about the shrine with his lamp. He was reading the broken tablets and occasionally he pulled out a piece and set it aside on a pile, as if he found it significant. To Jafnar, it appeared as if Illmuri were trying to assemble and make sense of the shattered tablets, heaping them up in logical piles. He must have been working at it quite some time to have made such headway on the mountain of rubble.

To one side, on a large flat stone he had assembled a sinister collection of Skyla's belongings, including the white cloak made from her own hair. A pentacle had been scratched in the earth around it, and a small brazier was heaped with things ready to burn.

Jafnar crept closer, his progress softened by tuffets of moss and soft moist earth. Then he stepped suddenly upon two stones that grated sharply together. Illmuri whirled around and saw him as he made a belated dive behind a rock.

"You fool! What are you doing here?" the wizard snarled. "Come out from there at once, you slinking, spying thief, and explain yourself before I blast you to Niflheim!"

Jafnar came out of his concealment. "I came merely to regain what you stole from Skyla," he countered boldly, to cover his dread of Illmuri and his altar. "I saw you snatch her white cloak. It was brave of you, considering what happened to Hofud."

Illmuri scowled in the flickering light of a lamp thrust in a crevice. "I cannot decide whether to admire your courage for following me here, or whether to marvel at your stupidity."

"Skyla is my sister Skylding, and I am sworn by blood to protect her," Jafnar said. "Give me her cloak and I'll leave you to whatever unclean procedure you were beginning. Was it the Kellarman you were summoning to help you?"

Their whispers circled the chamber, hissing off the dripping stones. The word "Kellarman" in particular seemed to echo around the halls of stone.

"Quiet! Idiot!" Illmuri seized Jafnar by the shoulder and spun him around. "Now you've said his name! We've got to get out of here, fast! Hurry, before it's too late! The Kjallari-folk know when anyone comes down here. Why do you think so many Krypplingur died when Herrad searched this place for the treasure?"

Jafnar flung off Illmuri's hand indignantly. "Not without the cloak. You won't frighten me with those old tales," Jafnar said, with the hair beginning to rise on his neck. "I don't believe in the Kellarman and the Kjallari-folk. You'd like to keep me out of here, wouldn't you, away from the truth of my inheritance!"

His voice was not convincing, and the names seemed to stick in his throat. Nor could he avoid shooting a wary glance around the chamber, thinking the whispering echoes suspiciously loud.

"You're a fool and a poor liar!" Illmuri spat, and thrust him toward the stairway in spite of his struggles to free himself. "I would help you, if you had the sense to accept it, but you're nothing but a wild animal from the gutters of Rangfara!"

"You help only yourself!" Jafnar retorted. "You won't find out anything about the treasure from me!"

"*Fara af eftir!*" Illmuri said, and the words bound Jafnar helplessly to follow, his thoughts as paralyzed as his will, as if Illmuri had spoken to a part of him that had no need for decisions and doubting. He had no will except to follow the wizard.

It was only a short straight passageway to the spiral stair leading to the surface. Jafnar's senses reeled unsteadily. He had walked a long distance with many forks and turns, a lengthy period of time before he found Skriftur, and it was just as far to this place, and now here he was walking out of the Kjallari already. When they came to the steps they took them three at a time, but midway the spell began to lose its potency. Waves of terror thrust Jafnar up the stairs, stumbling, his strength sapped by fear. Countless times in his dreams he had staggered up these same stairs on faltering legs with that familiar old terror clawing at him, dragging him back into the bowels of the Kjallari. Always in his dreams he had wanted to look back but hadn't dared. Now Jafnar ventured to glance back, telling himself nothing would be there, no Kellarman raging after him, drooling jaws agape for him. He saw nothing but a wall of thick and earthy darkness, and heard nothing but his own frightened breath rasping in his throat and Illmuri cursing softly as he dragged him up the steps.

When they staggered out at the top, Illmuri gave Jafnar a shove toward the main gateway and commenced running as fast as he could through the cluttered hall. Jafnar had the good sense to follow, without any more glances backward. The evil and terror of the Kjallari seemed to impell him from the place as if he were borne on the current of a strong river, lending him sudden strength and spewing him through the doorway and down the stairs.

Illmuri seized him and threw him into the street, forcing him to walk at a normal rapid gait until they had left the Kjallari behind and the Street of a Thousand Steps was in view. Then Illmuri grabbed Jafnar by the neck and threw him backward against a mossy wall and glowered into his face with such an expression that Jafnar was frozen immobile.

"I saved your life today," Illmuri said. "I ought to have left you there for the Kellarman to have. It would have served you right, for meddling in things you know nothing about. And after all I've done for Mistislaus!"

"Mistislaus had nothing to do with it," Jafnar gasped, his face only inches away from the blazing fury of Illmuri's eyes. "I followed you because you had Skyla's cloak. You've got no right to take her things—"

Illmuri gave Jafnar another bounce against the wall. "You'll forget about the cloak," he whispered, his eyes only inches away. "You'll never mention it to Mistislaus or to anyone, or you'll have me to answer to! And don't ever go near the Kjallari again, or next time I'll tie you up and let the Kellarman have you!" With a final shake, he suddenly turned and strode away.

Jafnar peeled himself off the wall and started breathing again, but not without a certain degree of trembling in the knees. He thought of the wall of darkness he had seen at the foot of the stairs and felt cold and shaken. He had felt the life and soul of that darkness, knowing with a cold certainty that something had been there. It might have been trolls, who denned up in unsavory places like the Kjallari to prey upon humankind, but no one had ever really seen trolls slinking about there. Silence and unease prevailed when it came to anything associated with the Kjallari.

The day was well-nigh spent, and the uproar of the Skurdur was taking on its ugly, nighttime tone. Jafnar ran up the Street of a Thousand Steps and climbed over the wall to the observatory, hearing the welcoming owl calls of his brother Skyldings. Guthrum saw him come over the wall and groused about it, then resumed his watchful position by the gate. Jafnar waved to the tower of the Hall of Stars and saw Ordvar wave back from a window. As quietly as possible, he slipped into the observatory, hung his cloak on its customary peg, and mentioned nothing of his escapade. Mistislaus did not reprimand him for his absence, being occupied with his evening iterations. Skyla was working with her clay figures by the light of the hearth and looked up intently at his arrival.

"Where were you?" Skyla demanded. "You were gone half the afternoon and didn't say a word to anyone. Not even Ordvar knew where you'd gone."

"Illmuri stole your cloak, and I went after him," Jafnar whispered. "I was in the Kjallari. I saw amazing things, Skyla. I found the name-scrolls."

"You never!" she exclaimed. "And you didn't take me with you!"

"I couldn't. I didn't have time. And if I had, and Mistislaus had found out—" He made a throat-cutting gesture.

"You could have called to me," Skyla said.

"It happened so fast, I didn't even think," Jafnar said. "I wish you'd been there. It wasn't like I'd dreamed it, except at the last. I found the name-scrolls, and it was like coming home, as if the place were welcoming me in. It felt so good and so friendly."

"You must take me there," Skyla said.

"I don't know if I can find it again, unless the time is right," Jafnar said. "It was a long way, and parts of the Kjallari are still terribly dangerous."

"I'm not afraid," Skyla said. "Promise you'll take me there to see the name-scrolls."

"I can't," Jafnar said, "even if you're not afraid. What if something would happen to you? There is something down there. I've had the dreams and so have you. I think they're not dreams, Skyla; they're warnings."

When Illmuri came at dusk to escort Mistislaus to Herradshol, he glowered blackly at Jafnar but said nothing. Jafnar breathed a little easier when they were gone, but a gloomy presentiment assured him that Mistislaus would soon know all.

When Mistislaus returned at full dawn, Jafnar was awakened from his vivid and uneasy dreams by the mossy thump of the street gate. Quickly he dressed and braced himself for the expected scolding.

"You are a Skylding, never forget that," Skyla said, taking a stubborn stance beside him with the market basket in her hands.

Mistislaus was surprisingly cool about the entire matter. His hooded eyes flicked over Jafnar and Skyla and the market basket with a glimmer of anticipation.

"Well, Illmuri has told me about your escapade," Mistislaus said, turning a stern glance from Skyla to Jafnar, as if he were trying to forget about the promise of a breakfast of pastries and pigs' trotters. "I tell you, it won't do to have you haring off treasure-seeking, leaving Skyla to her own mischief."

"Treasure-seeking? Is that what Illmuri said?" Jafnar demanded. "That's not the truth! I followed him because he—" The words about Skyla's white cloak stuck in his throat. After only a momentary sputter he finished with, "Because he's a Dokkalfar, and not to be trusted!"

"Of course that would be your view, raised as a wild thing in Rangfara," Mistislaus said without so much as hoisting an eyelid. "But spying on Illmuri is not your responsibility. Fortunately, no harm has been done, and he got you out again before something happened to you."

"So you believe I'm lying?" Jafnar demanded. "I saw what he was doing down there. Illmuri is a Dokkalfar, which you seem to have forgotten. I at least am a dayfarer, the same as you."

Scowling, Mistislaus hemmed and cawed a moment to gather his wits, pretending something was roughening his throat.

"Illmuri may be a Dokkalfar," he said, "but his intentions are completely honorable. He has graciously consented to help me fulfill the boon you asked, since he knows more than I do about Rangfara and where the treasure might be. For all we know, your ill-conceived spying might have interrupted the very spell that would have revealed the treasure."

"Why haven't you gone down into the Kjallari, Mistislaus?" Skyla demanded. "Illmuri must think it's an important place. Jafnar said it wasn't so frightening. I'd much rather you were the one to find the Skylding treasure, instead of Illmuri."

Wounded from this attack from such an unexpected quarter, Mistislaus shot Jafnar an incredulous glower. "Jafnar is lucky to be alive," he said testily. "This will be your last opportunity, if you want to stay on around here. Skyla must not be left again. I hope you can be trusted a third time not to abandon her."

"I'm not a child," Skyla said sharply. "I'm almost of an age to begin making most of my own decisions. I'm glad Jafnar went into the Kjallari after Illmuri. Nothing terrible happened to me while he was gone. My only regret is that I didn't go with him."

"Perish the thought!" Mistislaus exclaimed, throwing up his hands in despair. "You might as well throw yourself on a Krypplingur sword point and be done with it! Summon up the Kellarman himself and his legions of Kjallari-folk, and tell them you're tired of the battle and simply wish to give yourself over to them to be devoured!"

Skyla turned pale. "I don't wish to be devoured," she said. "I want my own name-scroll. I want to know the names of my family and their histories. I hear their voices every day, but their names are in the Kjallari."

"All things come in their own good time, child," Mistislaus said, dismissing them with a wave of one hand and a heavy sigh. "Be patient awhile longer and you'll know all you want to know."

"Wait, Mistislaus," Skyla protested. "My cloak has come up missing. I believe Illmuri may have taken it down into the Kjallari. Down there where the unclean things are. Make Illmuri bring it back, Mistislaus."

"I shall speak to him," Mistislaus said rather dubiously. "In the meantime," he added, with a severe scowl at Skyla, "you must stop leaving your things laying carelessly about. You are not ever to leave the walls of Athugashol alone. I don't want you to suddenly decide to visit the Kjallari on your own. I daresay you'd find a much less hospitable host than poor old Hofud this time. And you," he said to Jafnar, "had better not even think of going into the Kjallari again. You were extremely lucky you found Illmuri, or you'd still be down there. Now then, away with you and fetch me my breakfast. And bring back a large flagon of dark ale from old Atvik's booth. This has already started out to be a very trying day."

Considering himself miraculously forgiven, Jafnar scuttled off with the market basket and Skyla at his heels, his spirits shifting from low ebb to exultant in a matter of moments.

"Well, I got out of that one!" he chortled.

"But Illmuri's still got my cloak," Skyla said softly, darting wary glances behind them. "You've got to get it back for me, Jafnar, truly you must."

"Then I shall," Jafnar said expansively, immediately forgetting his promise to Mistislaus.

"When?" she asked. "You wouldn't go after my hood when Hofud had it. I think you are afraid to go back down into the Kjallari."

"Afraid?" Jafnar snorted, slapping the hilt of his sword. "Not I!"

"Then tonight?"

"Well, I did promise Mistislaus—"

"But you are a Skylding and I am a Skylding. Our promises come first. You must get my cloak, Jafnar."

Jafnar made some evasive noises, feeling an uncomfortable reminder of the fear of the Kjallari, as if a chilly tendril of Kjallari breath had wound its way down the dank alleyways and found him in the middle of the crowded, noisy Skurdur, reminding him of things he wished he could forget.

"Mistislaus need never know, if you learn to be more careful," Skyla continued. "No one must see you this time."

"Rangfara has eyes everywhere," Jafnar said. "Someone is bound to see, even if I went at night."

"Are you or are you not a true Skylding?" she asked, looking directly at him with her clear, penetrating gaze.

"I am, of course," he answered fiercely. "It's just that—well, I'll get back the cloak, but not just now. I'll wait until Mistislaus has forgotten somewhat."

"Very well," she said, as if satisfied.

To Jafnar's relief, she made no more mention of the cloak that day. Every time he thought about it, the idea of going back down into the Kjallari made him sweat like a nervous horse. Skyla, however, had no intention of letting him forget his promise. Every day she reminded him, until a week had passed since Jafnar saw Illmuri snatch the cloak like a fox going over the henyard wall. Still Jafnar did not feel ready to brave the earthy darkness of the Kjallari again, although the smug and secretive face of Illmuri continued to taunt him each night when he came for Mistislaus, reminding him of his own shameful fears.

"I must have some plumabrot," Skyla said abruptly, not long after Mistislaus had departed and locked the doors. "Will you have some, Jafnar? It's a very good one this time. Not at all moldy."

"It looks like something that ought to be thrown out," Jafnar said with a churlish sniff as she held out a bowl of the stuff. "But I'll try it again," he added quickly, remembering the manners he was supposed to be learning. The tempting smell of the plumabrot filled the dank room with the sweet fragrance of plum blossoms in springtime and a hint of the greening earth's energy.

She carved off a large helping and served it to him in a wooden trencher. It tasted even better than the first time he had sampled it. He wolfed it down to the last crumb and sticky drop of syrup.

The plumabrot sat in Jafnar's stomach like a stone, sticky and indigestible as tar. He got up to pace around, hoping to walk off the heavy sensation, but it only made him feel sicker and hotter.

"I feel sick," Jafnar said uneasily. "I shouldn't have eaten all that rich cake. I'm not used to such fare."

"It's very healthy," Skyla said. "I could eat twice that much and feel fine. Maybe a breath of fresh air would help."

Jafnar shook his head heavily. It was pounding dully, like a belabored anvil. "I swore to Mistislaus that I would not open the door for any reason."

"Don't be absurd," Skyla said in consternation. "You're getting ill. One breath of air isn't going to hurt."

Jafnar's head reeled and his heart thudded sickly in his chest. All the edges of things around him took on a sudden suspicious clarity, and Skyla's voice sounded unnaturally loud in his ears. His skin felt hot and itchy, and glancing at the backs of his hands, he saw a delicate red rash spreading like a host of red pinpoints.

"Maybe just a breath—" He looked at the door and tried to push himself away from the table. His leg muscles quivered with peculiar and unreliable energy.

Suddenly, of its own accord, the stout bar shot back out of its pegs and the door burst open with a gust of icy wind that filled the room with dust and ash from the hearth. A roaring filled the room, threatening to burst Jafnar's eardrums with the pounding volume of a thousand voices speaking at once, as if the Skurdur's uproar had been magnified a dozen times and crammed inside his skull. The floor reeled and pitched underfoot, while the interior of the room whirled around him in a sickening, illogical way that threatened to rob him of his sanity. After leaping to his feet with the idea of shutting the door, he stumbled into a forest of people, crowded into the room so thick he felt as if he were lost and suffocating. They milled about, over and through each other with complete disregard, wearing unfamiliar clothes of different sorts, passing heedlessly over Jafnar, as insubstantial as shadows and breezes. With a frightened outcry he staggered backward, taking several of Mistislaus' chairs with him in his retreat, as if they weighed no more than dried leaves. He flung out one hand to protect himself, and a blast of wind shrieked around the interior of the tower, carrying away the mist people, clothing, bedding, ashes, and foodstuffs. Jafnar himself was flattened on the ground by the force of it, impelling him toward the open door. His fingers clawed at the flagstones, pulling one of them up and revealing a stairway below. Eyes glared up at him; teeth were bared in a grisly snarl of welcome, and the fetid breath of the Kjallari filled his nostrils with its stench. The Kellarman of his nightmares reached out a gory hand to grab him and pull him down. He rolled away, his ears hammering with the thousand voices. The Kellarman and the staircase to the Kjallari vanished, and for a moment he lay gasping and wheezing, struggling to draw enough air into his flaming lungs.

He was burning up, starting from a point just above his breast bone, beside his pounding heart. All around him the room shimmered behind a wall of flames. Whatever he looked at suddenly ignited in a burst of fire and smoke. His hand clutching a chair leg smoked as the wood charred in his grip, but he felt no pain. Rising unsteadily to his feet, he realized that the fire was illusion only, and the searing heat he felt did not wither or burn his skin.

"The realization of the illusion is the secret to controlling it," one of the thousand voices in his head said, as distinctly as if the speaker were in the room.

A warm glow of recognition spread over him. "Samtal!" his mouth blurted unexpectedly. "Is it you? Where have you been?"

"Where have you been, little brodur?" came the response. "I've been waiting for you to find me. We've all been afraid for you, left alone after the Devastation."

A chorus of murmuring voices assured Jafnar that Samtal was not alone.

"Who are you?" he demanded.

"I'm your brother, you infant. Don't tell me you've forgotten us. We're here with you always, if only you have the wit to see and hear us."

Memories flooded Jafnar, of his mother and father, his older half-brothers and sisters, and their memories also were his, as well as the memories of grandparents, aunts, uncles, and cousins, until he was trapped in a web of history, rolling out before him like an unfamiliar landscape, waiting to be explored. He burned to explore the thousand paths of memory and lives now freed from the constraints of mortal, perishable flesh. All were known to him, a thousand faces, a thousand names, glittering like the facets of a carved stone. He could lose himself in memories, in the history of his Skylding ancestors.

Gently he pushed them away, swimming again to the surface of his consciousness, returning to the lower room in the observatory. For a long moment he sat still, huddled under the table. He would never be completely alone again. The voices in his head were quiet now and orderly. He pointed his finger, and whatever he pointed at lifted itself and came to him, or flew away as if catapulted, according to his whim. Fire, wind, water, whatever illusion he desired surrounded him, and he did not fear even to evoke the dread apparition of the Kellarman, knowing he could dispell it with a flick of his hand.

This was power; whether a dream or a nightmare he wasn't certain. He dug up a handful of dirt from between the stones, as he had seen Skyla do. Concentrating mightily, he was knocked over backward when the earth suddenly exploded in a shower of fine particles that numbed his hand and peppered his face.

"Skyla!" he called, suddenly remembering his duty. He was half delirious from the pounding his senses were taking, swimming through a high, relentless surf of interfering thoughts and visions. "Skyla, where are you?"

Through the shifting curtains of illusion and genuine effects, he felt a cool breeze coming from the direction of the open door. Skyla made no answer.

Chapter Twelve

Alarmed, Jafnar began struggling to extricate himself from his hiding place under the table. He quickly discovered that his legs were completely insubstantial, and his head ached and buzzed with a sickening motion. A terrible thundering sound pounded in his head, as if sky giants were smashing at the tower with their fists.

"Go away!" he yelled, and the power of his own voice nearly took off the top of his skull.

"What happened here? Where's Skyla?" a piercing voice demanded, and a looming face swam into view, peering under the table at him.

Jafnar cringed back from the face. It was a multitude of faces, one shifting after the other to leer out at him, all elemental and demonic in nature. Never had he seen anything so horrible in all his life. "Get away! Get away!" he yelled, and his words summoned a torrent of wind that screamed through the tower. Mercifully, it seemed to take the face away with it.

While he floundered, a brilliant light suddenly illuminated the room, and the illusions all vanished. Mistislaus stepped into the room with his alf-light flaring, sweeping the chaos with an astounded stare. Illmuri gazed over his shoulder, clearly astonished.

"What has happened here?" Mistislaus demanded. "Where's Skyla?"

Jafnar could not persuade his tongue to move in the intelligent manner required for speech, and when he tried to rise, all he could manage was an undignified sprawl at Mistislaus' feet.

"Great Hod!" Mistislaus exclaimed. "What earthly sort of mischief is this! No, don't touch him!"

The warning was half a breath too late. Illmuri stepped forward to examine Jafnar, but the instant his hand touched him, a great crackling blue spark hurtled Illmuri backward against the wall. Muttering and shaking his hand, he leaped to his feet, glaring from Jafnar to Mistislaus.

"Check the tower room for Skyla," Mistislaus said, drifting his hand softly back and forth. "The atmosphere in here is incredible. Look at that."

He pointed his staff, showing a cluster of metal objects ranging from buttons, cloak brooches, and rings, to knives and cups slowly revolving in midair over their heads, like a new constellation. Occasionally an errant object shot from its place on the floor into the air or against the wall with a clamor. Mistislaus' light fell upon Jafnar, still gasping and twitching like a freshly hooked fish, revealing several knives and cups clinging to him.

"What is the meaning of this?" Illmuri demanded. He dashed up the winding stairs to Skyla's chamber and down again in moments. "She's gone," he reported, making a careful detour around Jafnar on the floor.

Struggling, Jafnar managed to sit up, cradling his face in his hands. "Gone!" he muttered. "Skyla?"

"Yes, she's gone," Mistislaus said, giving him a cautious poke with the end of his staff. "What were you doing here to stir up such a force?"

"Nothing," Jafnar said thickly. "We ate plumabrot, and I felt sick."

"I shouldn't wonder," Mistislaus said, surveying the scorched and shattered contents of the room. "It's revolting stuff."

"Lightning must have struck the tower. The door came open, and all sorts of strange things started happening," Jafnar went on, gathering himself into a sitting position. "I saw a hideous face, a demon, or a draug, or something even more evil."

"Lightning! Demons! Very likely!" Illmuri snorted. "A convenient explanation for all this havoc! Mark my words, Mistislaus, these young rapscallions were into your books."

"We weren't, either," Jafnar retorted. He rubbed the back of one hand, where the red dots glowed an itchy red. He felt itchy all over, on his neck, face, and back.

"What are those spots?" Illmuri inquired, his sharp eyes missing nothing.

Mistislaus bent over to look more closely, bringing the hissing alf-light dangerously near. "Skyla gets those same spots from time to time," he said, "and she's particularly volatile when she gets them. Dear me, it does follow. Both of them are Skyldings. An inherited disease, perhaps. This combined with that other—" He raked one hand through his hair, which was standing on its ends with faint crackling sounds. "It's almost too much to bear!"

"We've got to find Skyla," Jafnar croaked, gathering himself and rising to his feet, trembling and unsteady. "She must have been frightened. It was quite a show. Do you have any idea what caused it, Mistislaus?"

"Yes," Mistislaus said, touching one finger to Jafnar's shoulder and eliciting a crackling spark. "You. Whatever you've done, you've stirred up tremendous forces. Maybe lightning had something to do with it. Maybe you had something to do with the lightning. Do you hear voices now? Do you know their names? What about mist people?"

Jafnar was about to nod, but a sudden wariness silenced him. Talking about such things was not wise, his inner voices advised him.

"That face!" he blurted out unexpectedly. "I think it was Alvara."

"Alvara does a lot of creeping about Gibbet Hill," Illmuri admitted with a bleak scowl. "And following in the Skurdur. The woman has an abnormal amount of curiosity, especially when it comes to Skyla."

Mistislaus ceased his useless pacing and swung around to look a moment at Illmuri in silent communication. Then he turned upon Jafnar, almost knocking him off his shaky legs. His eyes glazed inches away from Jafnar's face.

"Once again, you have failed," he rumbled, his wattley jowls trembling with menace. "Thanks to your unwarranted tramping around in the Kjallari, I don't doubt that's where she's gone, looking for her cloak."

"It wasn't I who stole it and took it there," Jafnar replied. "It was Illmuri who took it, him I followed, and he refused to return it. If anyone is guilty, it's him, not me. He could have brought it back before this."

Illmuri and Mistislaus exchanged a taut glance. The Dokkalfar wizard coughed gently and looked away, not deigning to reply to Jafnar's accusations.

"Well then," Mistislaus said. "We'll have to go down there after her. She obviously believed this wild tale of yours. And you, sir, shall stay here in case she comes back while we're gone."

Mistislaus turned the key upon a scowling, glowering Jafnar and reluctantly returned to the streets of Rangfara.

"An absurd accusation, of course," he said to Illmuri. "No doubt to cover his own misconduct. I'm coming to fear that you were right about taming a wild boy. Skylding though he may be, his upbringing leaves much to be desired. As if I would even suspect you had a reason for taking Skyla's cloak. As if I would accuse you of some devious spell to reveal the treasure, perhaps."

"Indeed," Illmuri sniffed.

Outside in the streets, dayfarers and nightfarers alike scuttled across their way frantically, like frightened rats, all heading for one gate or the other in an attempt to escape Rangfara. From an old woman taking refuge under an overturned cart they learned that the snow lynx had been seen in the Skurdur the previous night. Bold as brass, she had stalked along the rooftops, in plain view to the human dregs of the Skurdur who had crawled out of their dark lie-ups for a night of gambling and murdering. It was interpreted as a sign of Rangfara's inevitable destruction.

Not long after, news of the savage slaughter of Herrad's last watch before dawn spread throughout Rangfara in a tide of hysteria. Their replacements had found them scattered, all five hideously mauled, their hearts torn out and presumed eaten.

"It threw the proper fear into the Krypplingur." She cackled with a nasty wink of one baggy eyelid. "It's their evil hearts the beastie wants, and I hope she gets them. I hope the lynx spawns a whole brood of lynxes with a taste for Krypplingur heart-meat, or them that's evil, and I hope to see their blood running down the gutters of the Skurdur, ankle deep. Like it was on the day the Skyldings lost Rangfara." She grabbed Mistislaus' sleeve and drew herself nearer and nearer, her voice hissing away to an impassioned squeak. "We'll see blood running in the streets again, mark my words, and it will belong to the Krypplingur and them that serves the Krypplingur." She grinned broadly, showing an assortment of broken and missing teeth.

Mistislaus disengaged her grip from his sleeve and edged away. The blood was drained from his face and he gripped his staff, white-knuckled, as he and Illmuri hurried onward toward the Skurdur and the Kjallari beyond.

A most unpleasant scene of looting and burning and fighting awaited them in the Skurdur. Every Krypplingur in Rangfara had been summoned to Herradshol, a not-unwelcome circumstance to those who hated the Krypplingur. Left to themselves, the denizens of the Skurdur took advantage of the situation and did as they pleased, beginning with burning the Krypplingur guard outpost and proceeding to the the attacking of certain merchants considered overly friendly to the Krypplingur.

Their circuitous course took them past Herradshol, where the

Kjallari cart with its blind horse had just loaded up the carcasses of the dead Krypplingur. Creaking and jolting over the cobblestones, the cart was making its way toward the Kjallari, scattering the street traffic almost as effectively as if it were bearing plague victims.

"It's no use," Illmuri said. "We can't get anywhere near the Kjallari now. Perhaps she's gone home."

They took the long way around the back of the hill, since Mistislaus was too winded to tackle the Street of a Thousand Steps. As they came into their street, they saw a knot of dark-cloaked Krypplingur clumped around the gate.

Mistislaus plunged into the tower and found everything in a state of upheaval, and several hulking Krypplingur crouched warily on the stairs, holding off Guthrum below with his broad axe. Jafnar pranced about with his sword in a state of unholy defiance, daring the Krypplingur to come closer. The burly warriors ignored him entirely, keeping their eyes upon the redoubtable Guthrum. Ofarir strutted officiously around the edges of the standoff, brandishing a short ugly Krypplingur axe.

"Skyla!" Mistislaus roared, plunging through the doorway among the Krypplingur. There was no answer, and he suddenly turned a wrathful glare upon Ofarir, who stopped his supercilious smirking and actually quailed a moment. "Where is she, you vermin?"

"We saw nothing of the girl," Ofarir said. "Your dwarf and this young horsefly of a wild boy refused us one step over the threshold. If the girl is missing, we know nothing about it."

"I'm sure she's safe within," Illmuri said. "What's your business here, Ofarir? State it and be on your way."

"After this last incident with the lynx," Ofarir said, "we deemed it wise to search the house."

"You came to search our house?" Mistislaus repeated, slowly turning his outraged eye upon Ofarir. "You broke in, attacked my protector Guthrum, you frightened Skyla, and all for what? I hope your reasons are convincing."

Ofarir licked his lips. "Five Krypplingur have been savaged by the snow lynx. It has been reported to me that one of my guards saw that one—" He pointed to Jafnar. "—going into and coming out of the Kjallari. We all know the connection of the Kjallari and the snow lynx. Did you send him there? Was there any sign of the lynx then? What were you doing down there, boy?"

Defiantly Jafnar shrugged his shoulders, retreating into the sly-eyed silence of the wild boys of Rangfara, poised for dodging a blow or for flight. Mistislaus sighed and rubbed his hand over his brow in pained distress.

"It was just youthful curiosity," he said with an air of preoccupied dismissal. "The lad went and did some snooping on his own, probably looking for that treasure. No harm was done, and he saw no sign of the lynx."

"You've found nothing to accuse anyone with, so why don't you take your leave now?" Illmuri said. "You've done much harm to the peace of mind of our guests. A great deal rests upon the ability of Mistislaus to cure your father Herrad. Nothing must interfere with his occupation."

Ofarir grinned, a nervous, nasty reaction that was a grim parody of true amusement. "Yes, it would be dreadful if Mistislaus was too upset to work his cure—if that is all he is here to do."

Ofarir took a leisurely turn up and down the narrow street courtyard, gazing about on all sides as if he expected to see some subtle, tiny clue that would hang them all, at once, on the spot.

"The last time anyone tried to stay in Athugashol for long, something terrible happened," he said, turning to face them suddenly, his small eyes raking them for a sign of fear or concealment. "After we broke down the door, we found nothing but rags and bones, and the stink of the Kjallari. Rangfara is a peculiar place, where peculiar things happen."

"More peculiar indeed, since the Krypplingur came," a sharp voice added, and Alvara strode into the courtyard of Athugashol, insinuating herself between two Krypplingur guards as neatly as a cat. "What are you doing here, Ofarir? Did you come simply to menace your father's physician, or was there some purpose to this visitation?"

Her eyes traveled significantly over Guthrum bristling on the doorstep, at Mistislaus and Illmuri blocked from entering the house, and at Jafnar still blustering with an excess of zeal.

Ofarir's dark brows beetled together in wrath.

"It didn't take you long to get yourself here, either," he retorted. "You've done more lurking around Athugashol than seems appropriate, considering that Mistislaus has taken the job you were fetched to do."

"I feel no professional rivalry toward my esteemed fellow," Alvara said with a haughty toss of her head. "If he has the talent to cure Herrad, then I say by all means let him. I don't understand this harassment of yours in the least. It's almost as if you don't want your father cured of his disease." Without waiting for Ofarir's response, she turned to Mistislaus and continued, "I hope you'll forgive Ofarir's overvigilant intrusion. Is Skyla quite all right, or did all this frighten her?"

"Skyla is fine," Illmuri said shortly. "You needn't have troubled yourself, Alvara."

"What would you blundering fools know of a girl-child with such a sensitive nature as hers?" Alvara retorted. "I was helpful once before, on your first day here when she was frightened by the Krypplingur. Where is she? Hiding up in the tower room, perhaps?"

"Yes, she's hiding," Illmuri said, before Mistislaus could speak. "Now take yourself away from here. We've got trouble enough without you underfoot."

"We shall see." With a grim little smile Alvara darted around him and vanished up the stairway before even Guthrum could intervene. Illmuri gave no sign of alarm, but Mistislaus' jaw dropped and his choleric red countenance drained to ashy white.

"Are you finished then with your business?" Illmuri inquired of Ofarir, whose narrow darting eyes missed nothing.

"Finished? Not likely, until this matter of the lynx is resolved," Ofarir replied. "And by the way, my father Herrad wants to see you immediately, old man," he added over one craggy shoulder, almost as an afterthought. "He's got it in his head that the lynx is coming for him and that you are the only one who can save him."

Mistislaus stifled an angry sigh. "Very well, I shall be there at once."

"But Mistislaus!" Jafnar sputtered indignantly, thinking of Skyla alone and frightened in the Kjallari, searching for her cloak and possibly lost in a maze of dark tunnels. He was instantly silenced by a brushy scowl from Mistislaus and a venomous glower from Illmuri.

"Well then, come along," Ofarir said. "I was sent to escort you safely to Herradshol. Rangfara is in something of an upheaval, thanks to the lynx."

Alvara descended from Skyla's tower. Jafnar's eyes were dragged helplessly toward her, knowing that she knew the room above was empty. Only a faint hint of a smile curled her thin lips.

Suddenly the eerie wail of the hunting lynx pierced the dwindling dark. The Krypplingur froze to listen.

"Snow lynx!" Jafnar gasped, dashing from the street door to crane his neck around for a look down the road, in case he might catch a glimpse of the fabled creature. Remotely he noticed Alvara taking advantage of the excitement to glide out the rear courtyard door and disappear into the murk outside.

Illmuri seized him by the back of his neck and thrust him back inside. "Do you want her eating your vitals for her breakfast?" he snarled. "Get away and get the door barred! Keep it barred until Mistislaus and I come back. For once, try to do as you are told, wild boy, or you might find yourself back on the street like an unwanted cat."

The Krypplingur recovered from their fright and marched away with Mistislaus between two of them. Ofarir and Illmuri kept their distance as they followed behind, darting watchful glances at each other.

Jafnar closed the door and locked it from inside. From a high window he watched Mistislaus being escorted away by the Krypplingur. A gray presentiment of doom settled heavily on Jafnar's shoulders, and suddenly the loneliness of Athugashol was too much for him to bear a moment longer.

Mistislaus had not taken time to lock the door with his key. The moment Mistislaus and Illmuri were out of sight, Jafnar was out the back door. Turning after stealthily closing the door, he nearly collided with the swarthy bulk of Guthrum, standing like a wall of axe and armor and scowl. Jafnar froze, wondering if his last moments had arrived.

"You'd better be going after Skyla," the dwarf rumbled with a steely glimmer of his teeth. "I'd go myself, but I'm bound to watch hearth and hall for the master, even in this chaotic place. Find the girl, wild boy, or don't show your face around me again. I'll use your guts for garters if you don't bring her back."

"I'll find her," Jafnar said, venturing to edge away a step. Guthrum gave a faint nod, sending Jafnar dashing across the courtyard toward the Hall of Stars. He scrambled up a ruined wall and raced across a roof to another wall. Scaling that, he dropped down into a roofless room into the midst of his old companions. They sat huddled around a small fire, cooking sausages on sticks.

"Look at this, Jafnar!" Modga greeted him, pointing to a heap of sausages and two large joints of meat. "Everyone was so petrified about the snow lynx, we were able to steal almost anything we wanted!"

"Have a sausage, Jafnar," Einka urged amiably.

Jafnar shook his head. "Skyla's escaped," he panted. "I've got to go after her and bring her back, or old Guthrum's going to string me up by my own heartstrings. We've got to go after her before she comes to harm. Other people are trying to use her to get what belongs to us. Now who's going with me into the Kjallari to save her?"

"She's been nothing but trouble since she came here," Modga said. "Let the Kellarman have her, I say."

For an answer, Jafnar knocked him down and sat on him.

"Now listen," he said. "I think Skyla's gone down into the Kjallari after the cloak Illmuri stole. I know there's secrets down there. I saw the place where our names must be. Now hush and listen to me!" He almost had to shout over their excited chatter. "Nothing is any different. We still don't have names and we don't know anything about the treasure. All we've got for a link is Skyla. Now who's coming with me?"

The wild boys greeted his challenge with dead silence and suspicious stares.

"I'm not going into the Kjallari," Modga said, and the others were not long in adding their refusal.

"Jafnar," Ordvar said with a pleading note in his voice, "don't go down there again. You know you can't. We all have the same nightmares of the Kjallari."

"I have to," Jafnar replied. "Our ancestors' bones are down there. Our treasure is down there. And our names. Now I'll only ask one more time. Who's going with me?"

No one moved a muscle. No one would meet or hold his gaze.

"Jafnar," Ordvar said, "you've got to choose between us or them in Athugashol."

"What's happened?" Jafnar demanded. "It used to be all of us against the Krypplingur, in everything. Now when I need you the most, you all turn away."

Ordvar spoke quietly, keeping his eyes averted. "It's that girl, Skyla. Since you've taken up with her and that wizard, you're not the same, Jafnar. It's like you're not a wild boy any more at all. They've got you tamed, running errands for them like a servant. And now look—you're more worried about her than anything—even the treasure."

"You don't understand how important she is!" Jafnar raged. "We've got to find her before the Krypplingur do! She needs our help!"

"Your help, not our help," Modga said. "She's been nothing but trouble for us all since she got here."

"Who do you choose, Jafnar?" Ordvar asked. "Us and the old way things were, or her?"

With an agonized groan, Jafnar turned his back on them and scrambled down to the street from the Hall of Stars. He paused and looked back, stricken with a sudden pang of loss, seeing his own doom written on the blank and empty faces of the ruined houses. Furtive figures scuttled from shadow to shadow, carrying their possessions on their backs, intent on nothing but finding a way out of Rangfara. It was the sort of soggy and gray day that he hated most, with a nasty, jeering wind that snapped at his cloak. Never in all his life as a homeless, unwanted wanderer had he felt so desolate, so thoroughly dissatisfied with himself and his lot.

"Where has she gone? Where has she gone?" he heard himself repeating over and over. The habit of iterating and repetitions was hard to avoid, once it had been cultivated. Pressing his fists to his temples, he received a strong picture of the rotting façade of the Kjallari in his mind. A wave of revulsion swept over him from some dark knot of ever-present nightmare in the back of his mind, warning him not to approach.

Nevertheless, he raced away at a dead run in the direction of the Kjallari, threading the familiar maze of streets and ruined halls. As he ran, he iterated Skyla's name in time to the pounding of his ragged boots on the uneven stones. Everything flashing by him had the sickening familiarity of one of his nightmares.

The cadence slowed to a cautious walk as he turned into that gloomy aperture between the towering hulks of ruined halls and towers. At a slowing rate he approached the mossy, broken steps of the Kjallari, struggling against the powerful urge to turn around and run in the opposite direction. When he reached the archway, his footsteps quickened, carrying him right past the entrance, and by the time he reached the end of the street, he was almost running. He pulled himself up angrily and with difficulty, as if he were a runaway horse, and turned around. Muttering about fifty iterations to encourage himself, he started back toward the Kjallari.

His footsteps lagged against waves of doubt and fear. This time, he stopped at the steps, still chanting softly, and climbed up six steps before suddenly whirling around and racing to the top of the street in a burst of wild panic.

Resting his head against the cool stone of a wall, he drew some deep breaths and tried to calm the furious pounding of his heart. It felt as if it would burst from sheer terror, and his knees quivered like a new lamb's. The Kjallari was pushing him away; it did not want him here.

Summoning up his courage, he reiterated encouraging words until the panting and quivering stopped. Firmly he marched into the Kjallari street at a measured pace. Slowly he drew himself up the steps and into the gloomy court where the altars stood with their gifts of food and lighted lamps.

I can do it, he thought in elation as he moved toward the stairwell. I'm not afraid.

At once the fear he had felt was banished, and he felt almost as bold and cocky as he had the last time he had come into the Kjallari, following Illmuri. He took a lamp, one with plenty of oil still in it, and soundlessly descended the spiral stairs. In the flickering light of the horn lamp he passed the burial niches, feeling the soft and sepulchral breath of the Kjallari fanning his face. He heard no sound of the Kjallari-folk—nor of Skyla either. For a moment he wondered if his own fears had tricked him into thinking she was here. Perhaps she had wandered down into the Skurdur to look into merchants' stalls at their amazing assortment of gewgaws and glittering jewelry and fine clothes.

Feeling more confident moment by moment, he strode along past the tombs, pausing occasionally to peer into an interesting tunnel or burial vault. An arresting carving of horses and cats caught his small pool of light cast by the horn Kjallari lamp and he stopped. When he thrust his lamp into the tomb, a pale face within seemed to leap out at him. A cloaked and hooded figure stirred and plunged forward to escape into the tunnel, almost knocking him off his feet as he scrambled backward with a choking yell. By some stroke of fortune, not quite all of the oil in his lamp spilled, and the grass wick continued to sputter. The apparition stopped and turned to look at him again. From the beardless outline of cheek and chin, he knew it was female.

"Jafnar, is that you?" a small and wary voice asked.

"Skyla?" he called eagerly.

"Jafnar! I knew you'd come! Now take me to my cloak and let's get out of here."

"Skyla, we've got to get out of here before they find us. Listen to that! We can't go back the way I've come!"

Skyla cocked her head, listening to the rustling sounds of the Kjallari-folk. "They won't find us if we hurry. Where's my cloak, Jafnar? What sort of place was it?"

"A great chamber with a shrine of some sort in it, and piles of records made on stone tablets, only they were all smashed. You go down the broad stairs straight to it. No turnings on the way in."

"The main room. I know how to find it."

"You do? How?"

"There's a map chiseled into the wall by the stairs coming down. Didn't you see it?" Jafnar shook his head vigorously. He'd never had the time or inclination to look around much when he was in the Kjallari.

"What you must do," Skyla continued, "is feel on the corners where the tunnels meet, and you'll find rows of notches. Wherever you find three notches, you take that way to the main court, two and two notches together leads you to Skriftur's court—"

"You found Skriftur? Did you find the scrolls? Did you find out anything about our true names, or our parentage—anything that will help us?"

"Yes. But not the names yet. I might have, if you hadn't come bungling along just now, upsetting the Kjallari-folk. It's wonderful, Jafnar. You should have brought me here much sooner."

"Well, I've got to bring you out or Mistislaus and Illmuri are going to nail my hide to the wall. I was supposed to keep you from doing something like this again. You tricked me, Skyla. With that poisonous plumabrot."

"I didn't mean to," she said. "One Skylding would never trick another Skylding. It was your fault you ate so much of it, when you're not used to it. It makes me feel a bit giddy sometimes, too."

"Giddy!" Jafnar remembered the chaos he had caused at Athugashol. "Your giddiness has brought us both into the middle of the Kjallari, with the Kellarman and the Kjallari-folk looking for us for their dinner. And it all goes back to the plumabrot. Skyla, don't eat that stuff ever again."

"Don't be absurd, Jafnar," she replied. "It's my favorite food, and completely harmless."

She drew him along as they talked, whispering among the dry echoes, proceeding rapidly down the corridor of tombs until they reached the main room. Skyla paused, crouching behind a heap of broken tablets. Peering warily over the top, they could see that her cloak lay spread upon a slab of fallen stone like an altar, with the braziers standing ready on the points of a pentacle scratched in the rubbly earth.

"There it is," Jafnar whispered, shivering with uncomprehending dread. "Just like I saw it before. I don't know what he's doing with it, but it can't be anything good for us."

"Illmuri wants to control every bit of power he possibly can," Skyla said. "Including mine. Come on, Jafnar, let's grab it and get out of here."

As they stepped forward to claim the cloak, a dark figure suddenly rose up from behind the altar with a threatening billowing of a black cloak. It was Illmuri confronting them, and he swooped forward and gripped Skyla's arm as if she were a recalcitrant child.

"What are you doing here?" he demanded in furious, hissing tones, addressing first Jafnar then Skyla with his blazing eyes. His voice set off the echoes, bounding and rebounding with rage and indignation. "Don't you know how dangerous and foolish it is to bring this girl into the Kjallari?"

"Jafnar didn't bring me here!" Skyla snapped, making an effort to twist away from the iron grip around her wrist. "The voices of the mist people led me! I came here myself to get back my white cloak that you stole! Wait until I tell Mistislaus that he's been harboring a thief under his roof!"

"I needn't explain anything to either of you," Illmuri said. "And you won't disturb Mistislaus with this bit of nonsense. He's got far weightier things to think about."

"Such as the murder of old Hofud," Jafnar said.

For a brittle moment Illmuri turned his cold eyes upon Jafnar. "Is that an accusation?" he demanded.

Jafnar stiffened his shoulders and put his hand on his sword hilt, glowering back into the teeth of Illmuri's scorn. Although he had no doubt of Illmuri's duplicity and the possibility he had murdered Hofud, prudence and the instinct for self-preservation made him hold his tongue. Years of knocking about had taught him how to measure a foe accurately, and he knew he didn't adequately measure up to this one.

In the accusing silence, footsteps pattered softly toward them through the main archway of the hall. Illmuri motioned for silence, pointing to a pile of stones for shelter, and took a defensive stance.

"Halloa! Who goes there?" he challenged the shadows.

Alvara swept into the chamber, undaunted by his menacing aspect, her eyes darting over the cloak and Skyla's possessions with practiced disdain.

"Did I hear Hofud's name mentioned? Was there an accusation about to be made? I'm not afraid to say it," she said, her eyes flashing defiance as she took a protective stance beside Skyla and Jafnar. "I think you murdered Hofud, hoping to get the blue hood. Anyone can see you've been awaiting a chance to get your hands upon something of Skyla's. Find the missing link to her Skylding memory and you'll find the treasure, isn't that what you've been planning all along?"

"It well may be," Illmuri answered. "But you were there at Hofud's, too, so the same suspicion is cast upon you. And you are here, following and spying and trying to insinuate yourself where you're not wanted."

"I have as much right as you to be here," Alvara flashed back at him. "Possibly more. Didn't I stand beside the child on her first day in Rangfara? Haven't I stayed true to our pact since? And I've stood guard many a night at Athugashol, while you've gone with Mistislaus."

"Only in the hope of your personal gain," Illmuri replied. "Why else would you trouble yourself?"

Alvara turned her back on him and shifted her gaze to the stacks of broken tablets. She poked at one with her toe, upsetting its precarious balance with a sharp clatter.

"What have you been doing here? You've certainly been busy quite some time to have done all this. Robbing barrows, perhaps? A very poor substitute for the treasure, I'd say, but if that's the best you can manage, with your limited skills—"

"Get out!" Illmuri commanded.

"I won't," Alvara said. "She came for her cloak and she must have it back. You won't find what you're seeking. There's no clue of the treasure to be found in Skyla or her possessions or in these useless bits of stones. There's nothing here but trash and confusion."

"So it may seem to one of your limited capacity," Illmuri retorted.

"It's not gold I'm searching for," Alvara answered. "I care more for knowledge and skills than gold. There's a secret room of records somewhere, I've heard, which nobody has found yet. That's the place where Skyla will find out who she is and the names of her powers. If we could pull the right thread of Skyla's memory, the secrets of the Skyldings' powers could be ours."

Jafnar opened his mouth, feeling a thrill from his head to his toes, but something made him shut it up again without making a sound, except for a strangled gurgle.

"No one is going to find Skriftur's cave," Illmuri continued with lofty arrogance. "You least of all, Witch." This time Jafnar jumped visibly, like a fish on a gaff. He would have looked pale in normal light, but the Kjallari light made everyone look as sick as he suddenly felt. He had been there, but he'd had no idea of what it was he had found.

"No one including you," Alvara retorted. "Now let the girl go and take yourself out of our way, you sham."

"That I won't do," Illmuri said. "I want all of you out of this place, and if you have any good sense, you'll never come back, at least not until the Kjallari-folk are gone. Your greed for gold has truly brought you to the depths, Alvara, when you employ innocents as your tools."

"You're merely envious," Alvara said. "I've seen you oiling your way around Mistislaus, hoping for just such an opportunity. But what have you done in return? Have you sought to give them the information they want? Not in the slightest. I will find out what they want to know."

"In the hope that you will find out the secret of the treasure from them," Illmuri added caustically. "But it won't work, Alvara. They can't tell you where the treasure is hidden."

"Forget the treasure," Alvara snapped. "It's knowledge I seek."

"I can well imagine," Illmuri said sarcastically. "Your clan is most pitifully endowed when it comes to true knowledge and real truths."

"Liar!" Alvara spat, her cloak swelling around her like the bristling fur of an angry cat.

"Listen! Listen!" Skyla shouted suddenly, setting the echoes roaring and rebounding, repeating the word "Listen!" a hundred times. "Doesn't anyone care about my reasons for coming down here? You're both too busy fighting over a treasure that no one has ever seen to listen to what I want. I want to find out who I am, and who Jafnar is. I am a Skylding, but which Skylding? What is my real name? Who were my people? What is my past? With no name or clan, we have no future and no family. Isn't that more important than any treasure?"

Alvara and Illmuri glared at each other a moment, not quite ready yet to end their quarreling. Muttering angrily, Illmuri stalked over to his altar of Skyla's possessions. He bundled up the cloak and several scarves and mittens and gave them to her.

"Thank you," she said quietly, and fastened the cloak around her shoulders. "You will all get what you are so earnestly working for. I only hope you enjoy what you receive. If we all worked together with such energy, we would all be satisfied much sooner."

"She's right," Alvara said in a sour voice. "Are you ready to reveal all and cooperate, Wizard?"

Illmuri hunched his shoulders huffily. "I don't know. I'd like to hope it were possible to be so trusting."

Jafnar opened his mouth again, almost ready to reveal the fact that he had seen Skriftur's cave, but in the moments of silence, they all heard the not-too distant scuttering of the Kjallari-folk, approaching with a sound like the rustling of drifting dry leaves. The sounds came from all around them, down each of the branching tunnels. With a clatter of hobnailed boots on the stone floors, a desperate figure burst into the main court. Looking around wildly a moment, he plunged toward them. It was Ofarir, his eyes bulging with terror, panting as if his lungs were about to burst. His sword was gone and his cloak hung in tatters.

"Kjallari-folk!" he gasped, staggering as he gained the dubious protection of the genealogy shrine. "We'll never make it out! We're completely surrounded!"

Chapter Thirteen

"Now you've done it!" Illmuri said to Alvara over the rumbling of echoes and the insidious chittering of the Kjallari-folk. "Krypplingur and Kjallari-folk followed you right to us!"

Ofarir nodded fervidly, still breathless and trembling. "Yes, I followed, with two Krypplingur warriors. They're dead now, both of them. What are you going to do, Wizard? You've got some way of holding them off, haven't you?"

Illmuri pointed to an aperture in the fallen stones. "We can stand them off from there. Quickly, everyone inside."

"You're going to fight them all, alone?" Alvara sneered. "Are we to believe that you're the best defense we've got?"

"There's another far better," Illmuri said shortly. "Get inside the niche, unless you want to hold them at bay yourself."

Alvara guided Skyla ahead of her, and Jafnar followed, with Ofarir at his heels, swearing and sweating and smelling worse than a freshly scalded hog. They knelt in the rubble of the shrine, grinding small scraps of broken tablets under their feet—knowledge forever lost.

Skyla patted Jafnar's shoulder lightly, her hair standing out in an unruly cloud around her pale face.

"I want to see them," she said, her voice as taut as her posture. "They're my nightmares, too."

She trembled as she pushed ahead of him so she could see the Kjallari-folk. Jafnar heard their claws clicking on the paving stones as the courtyard filled with dark forms, glimpsed around the figure of Illmuri blocking the aperture. He had a sudden horrible vision of his own face staring blankly out of a niche in the wall. Then it was Skyla's face. This was how it was going to end, he realized.

"Stop it! Stop it!" he commanded himself.

Skyla watched the foul creatures of her nightmares slowly surrounding the genealogy shrine, slinking closer and closer, their eyes burning hotly with blood-lust. The air became almost too thick to breathe with oppressing evil.

"Who am I? Who am I?" Skyla heard herself muttering, pressing her fists to her temples as if she could squeeze the knowledge out of her skull somehow. Her ears roared with unbearable pressure. The sheltering niche among the slabs suddenly pressed down on her as if it were a barrow, not a protection. She couldn't breathe; she couldn't move, with Jafnar leaning against her shoulder so he could peer out at the Kjallari-folk. His pounding heartbeats were her own, his fear hers—his rescue her responsibility.

Unable to resist his first good look at the Kjallari-folk, Jafnar pressed close to Illmuri to stare at them. They were everything he had dreamed of rolled into one heaving, snarling, chattering mass of hatred and sheer, drooling vileness. The creatures of his dreams had been tall and hairy like bears one night, short and full of teeth the next, or sinuous like snakes, or a dozen other horrible images. The true Kjallari folk were no two alike, even uglier and more strange than his dreams, stooped creatures that reminded him of pale and hairless trolls, or the strange colorless crabs that scuttled around in the dark waters of the firths. Their heads were large and misshapen, too large for their leathery, spindling bodies that loped along on two legs or all fours. Some had ridged spines or skulls that rose in crests, some were horned, some had great claws that clicked and rattled as they advanced warily across the courtyard. Some had tails, ropy, kinked, fringed, or scaly, and some did not. All had gleaming eyes that were fixed upon their prey huddling in the ruins of the genealogy shrine.

With a defiant yell, Skyla scrambled to her feet and leaped into the middle of Illmuri's obstructing backside. He fell forward and she leaped outside to freedom, to face the ancestral foes of all Skyldings. She opened her mouth for a word that would banish them, but the word would not come. Illmuri lunged from the niche toward her, hands reaching out, pale in the Kjallari-light. Skyla turned and scrambled to the top of the heaped-up rubble that had been the genealogy shrine.

Jafnar screeched a wordless sound of horror and scrambled after her. Emboldened by the sudden disorganization of their quarry, six of the beastly creatures surged forward and attacked Illmuri. He laid about with his staff for a moment, then it was knocked away. They carried him down with a ripping and rending sound of cloth. Jafnar seized the staff and leaped to Illmuri's defense, bawling wordless curses at the top of his lungs. He slashed at the dark figures but they seemed to melt away like dream-images, too fast for his cumbrous attacks.

Suddenly one of them came at him, its piglike head held low, mouth foaming as it champed its jaws with rage. Jafnar swung at it with the staff, but it gripped the staff in one shriveled fist and hurled it away contemptuously, scarcely slowing its fierce rush. He scrambled backward, climbing up the heap of the shrine where Skyla had taken refuge. She grabbed him by his cloak to pull him up farther, nearly choking him, but the creature made a scrambling leap and caught his foot in its mouth. He felt its jaws crushing his foot and its fangs penetrate his flesh with a burst of dull pain. With savage little grunts the beast dragged him downward, and he dragged Skyla with him, still attached to his cloak and choking him.

Then she let go and leaped down the pile in three long jumps, shouting a war cry of savage defiance. She dared them to attack her, whirling and shouting even while the Kjallari-folk abandoned Illmuri and reached for her with greedy black claws and gaping fanged mouths, like spiders going for a helpless fly. Her form blurred. Jafnar shook his head and the blurring resolved. A compact gray figure crouched on a rock, small feline head with long tufted ears, long of leg, lean of body. The sharp wailing cry of an angry cat welled up in the echoing vault of the chamber. It was the snow lynx, so close he could see its long whiskers quivering, see the darker spots on her sleek, silvery coat. One paw lashed out, carving a gaping black welt across the taut hide of the beast gripping his foot.

The Kjallari creature released him with a sharp cry, falling over onto its back helplessly, writhing in death throes. Jafnar scarcely glanced at it, not with the snow lynx standing so close that he could have reached out and touched the ridge of bristling fur from ears to tail. A wave of recognition broke over him, almost drowning him in amazement.

"Skyla!" he gasped. Green-golden eyes flashed him one quick glance as she turned, head still low, mouth still ajar with the wailing call.

"The girl! It was her!" Ofarir lurched out of hiding, his eyes glued on the snow lynx as he attempted a stumbling escape from the shrine. A ragged Illmuri snatched at his cloak in passing, spinning him around. For a moment they glared in mutual menace, locked eye to eye.

"Your secret is mine!" Ofarir rasped with a rat's grin splitting his narrow visage.

"Make it yours, too, or I swear you'll die of it," Illmuri growled.

"I plan to live well by it," Ofarir replied. "Very well indeed!"

Skyla made a sudden charge forward, uttering another chilling shriek. Ofarir broke away from Illmuri, turning tail and running with uncharacterisic Krypplingur cowardice. The Kjallari-folk before him scattered in a burst of terror, allowing him to gain the main corridor. The others retreated with a show of reluctance, their rearmost ranks filtering away more quickly into nearby tunnels. The snow lynx stalked around the shrine, facing them all down as they backed away with a resentful, fearful muttering. Quick feints with clawed paws put the audacious lingerers to undignified flight. A last piercing shriek sent the hardiest of the Kjallari-folk into retreat, and the gray form of the lynx loped after them, disappearing into the dark maw of a tunnel.

"Skyla! No! Come back!" Jafnar roared, snapping out of his dazzlement in a burst of outrage that was greatly augmented by the throbbing agony of his bitten foot. He floundered after her, wallowing through the boggy area that oozed from one of the tunnels, not heeding the warning cries of Illmuri behind him. Headlong, lightless, he charged into the tunnel where she had vanished, ignoring his pain, ignoring the walls he collided sickeningly with, until he gave his skull a good, sound knock and sank down befuddled, while lights popped and whirled behind his cyclids.

"Jafnar! You stupid fool!" Illmuri's voice said. Hands shook him roughly to reassemble his stunned wits. "Come, we've got to get out while we can."

"Skyla's the lynx," Jafnar said thickly. "They've got her with them now."

"I've known it since the first day she was here," Alvara snapped, leaning over Illmuri's shoulder. "'You poor dunderhead. She'll come to no harm as long as she's in that form. They're terrified of her. They worship the snow lynx as a sort of goddess of death."

"Skyla killed Hofud—and those others?" Jafnar croaked.

"Yes, I fear so," Illmuri said. "She doesn't remember what happens to her under the spell, luckily. I don't think she could bear the knowledge of her fylgja-self."

"But she's a Skylding," Jafnar said, in almost a whimper of protest. "How could this happen to her?"

Alvara's shoulders lifted in a quick shrug. "No one knows for certain. Offhand, I'd say she was born with the curse."

"Or she's been messing about with powers that she shouldn't be," Illmuri mused.

"We've got to get out of here," Alvara said, cocking her head and listening to a distant muttering uproar from the Kjallari-folk. "Can you walk?"

Jafnar rose and hobbled a few steps, nearly sinking to his knees with the pain. His foot was swollen already from the envenomed bite, with the bindings of his boots cutting into it murderously.

"Go on," he said, gritting his teeth. "You've got to save yourselves. Find Skyla and get her out of here. I'm no good to Skyla dead or alive."

"Don't be stupid!" Illmuri spat. "I'm not going to leave you to them. Get hold of him, Witch."

Illmuri summoned a dull glow to the end of his staff to light the way. Alvara and Illmuri seized Jafnar by the arms and half dragged him along, up the tunnel where the water ran out. The stones were slimy with moss and other foul-smelling stuff that seeped its way in through the open sewers above. It certainly had the familiar dreadful smells of the Skurdur. When they stopped to rest and catch their breath, they could hear sounds of battle from the direction of the stairs.

"Ofarir, I'll warrant, having difficulty getting out," Illmuri said with an amused quirk of his lips.

"We can't get out that way either then," pointed out Jafnar, whose pain was making him impatient.

"No matter," Illmuri said. "There's more than one way into or out of the Kjallari. Wait here, I'm going ahead to scout around a bit. I'll be back for you when it's safe."

Jafnar welcomed the opportunity to sink down on the ground, although he would rather have died than admit it. Alvara paced to and fro restlessly, listening to every sound that passed them by in adjoining tunnels. A knot of six Kjallari-folk loped silently out of the main tunnel and passed their little niche, heads erect and alert, scenting their foes.

"I think he's left us to die here!" Alvara declared. "A convenient way to get rid of his competition. Come, we've got to get moving or they'll find us!"

Alvara hustled Jafnar into the wet tunnel, where he was reduced to slipping and crawling along awkwardly. Alvara pulled and tugged at him with frantic exhortations to hurry, but each footstep came more slowly. Then Alvara was dragging him into a sluggish stream of water.

"Come on, we've got to cross!" she panted, shoving him toward the far side with no regard for his injured foot or even common courtesy. Jafnar sprawled in the smelly mud and crawled out on the bank.

"We're safe," Alvara gasped. "They can't cross running water. You'll be safe enough here for a time."

"What, you're leaving?" Jafnar demanded.

"I'm going for help. I've got a sister-clan here in Rangfara, and I'll bring someone back to help carry you out. You'll be all right here, as long as they're on the far side of the water. Perhaps I'll find Skyla."

"Yes, find Skyla. When she shifts shapes, she'll be frightened and lost."

Resigned and exhausted, Jafnar lay back against the cold mossy rocks and listened to Alvara's footsteps dwindling into the darkness. Then he was alone and lightless in the Kjallari.

He must have fallen into an uneasy doze; he awakened suddenly with a startled jolt, his heart thudding with alarm. Although the tunnel seemed quiet, it was the quiet of watching menace. He knew he had to get up and move. His foot didn't hurt as much now, it was as numb as wood. Feeling his way to the junction of tunnels, his hands explored the corners until he found rows of notches. Three notches; but he didn't want to return to the main court. Then he found two and two—the way to Skriftur's court, where he knew he would be safe.

The way seemed longer than he remembered, with more turns in the path. Before, it had seemed that he pursued a fairly short, quick path to Skriftur's hall in the heart of the Kjallari. He hadn't been wounded then, he reminded himself.

When he finally stepped into the dimly lit chamber where the light came down upon the shrine, he could see stone tablets that had been thrown down and smashed, carven pillars pushed over, and the scroll boxes crushed and trampled underfoot until nothing remained but rags and splinters. With a small choking cry Jafnar stumbled forward, approaching the long table where Skriftur's remains lay huddled over his last record.

The pitiful heap of fragile bones moved. Jafnar staggered back a pace. The horned head of an unfamiliar beast lifted stealthily, slowly, gazing at him with burning red eyes. In an instant his blood chilled, and the old fears from his childhood nightmares pressed at him, crushing the air and will from his body. The beast gathered itself and stood up on two legs like a man, but its shoulders were massive and hairy, its sides and belly bloated and bristling with coarse hair, with arms and legs almost spindly in comparison, obscene in their caricature of human proportions. A rumbling snarl grated through the echoing chamber, and sharp curling tusks like a boar's gleamed in the faint light. The snarl preceded a deafening, roaring scream that tore through the delicate echoes of that holy place of wisdom and repose. After dropping to a lumbering four-legged stance, the creature glided sinuously down the jumbled blocks and vanished into a shadowy aperture in the wall.

"Kellarman!" The word burned in his brain.

Jafnar stood still, utterly frozen. The Kellarman had looked straight at him, and he felt intimations of his own death fluttering hotly in his ears with each laboring beat of his heart.

What was he doing here? Where was he? The moment he began to doubt, he began to fear. The room was different now; there were no smashed boxes, no Skriftur, no pillars or stone tablets. He was back alongside the sludgy stream where Alvara had left him—at least it smelled the same, and the earth was as slimy with moss and scum. A trick had been played upon his outward seeing self, a trick no less real to that inner part of him that knew the Kellarman. He halted his aimless staggering, still feeling the hot red eyes of the Kellarman staring at him from the shadows as if they had left a permanent brand upon him. In his ears, pounding a frantic tattoo with terrified beats of his heart, he thought he heard the soft and deadly padding of remorseless paws and cloven hooves coming after him.

Halting suddenly, he looked back and listened. A rattling, hissing, clicking sound approached from all directions, cutting off his retreat. The Kjallari-folk were coming to get him. It was like all his nightmares as a child, only this time he was awake. The Kellarman was coming to get him and his legs turned to stone, pinning him to the spot while their terrible teeth and claws drew nearer.

With a great effort, he formulated an iteration in his head. After twenty repetitions, he suddenly broke free from the terror that had rooted him to the ground. Thanking old Eyda for his perseverance, he returned to a junction where six other tunnels beckoned to him. Feeling for the notches in the stone, his fingers discerned nothing to guide him. Perhaps that had been part of his dream also.

As he stood, swaying slightly, a faint sound came to his ears, vibrating down the maw of a nearby tunnel and amplifying into a voice. He strained his ears, listening, wondering if it was his imagination again. The call repeated itself several times, and by the fourth repetition he was certain someone was calling his name. After a long moment of consideration, he groped his way into the tunnel with the voice. The earth became more wet underfoot, and somewhere he could hear the faint sound of running water. A small stream trickled along darkly beside him and sank away among the flagstones lining the floor. He stopped several times to listen, testing himself to make certain he was awake and not dreaming. His foot hurt enough to convince him he was truly wide awake.

The tunnel sloped downward and the footing became treacherous, but the voice still called, distant but discernible. Suddenly Jafnar slipped, plunging downhill at a breakneck rate, skittering down flights of crumbled steps and along broken balconies overlooking a vast pit of darkness before clawing to a stop. Far above, tiny apertures allowed a faint semblance of light to filter down, lightening the blackness to a thick gloom. Sensing more than seeing that dark imposing silence waiting below, Jafnar could feel no opposite side, no bottom, only the broken stairway winding farther down into its depths.

As he crouched listening and trying not to puff, he heard the voice calling his name on the far side of the pit. It sounded like Skyla.

"Skyla!" he shouted, and immediately recoiled from the hundred mocking echoes. When the echoes died away, he thought he heard a thread of faraway laughter.

His wandering gaze suddenly touched upon a niche a foot or so from his face. The mocking grin of a human skull leaped out at him. He shrank back with a shudder, then noted that the wall he was leaning against was pockmarked with niches, all containing skulls. The hair rose on his neck as he slowly moved along, scanning the grisly collection. Rounding a corner, he found more skulls, then suddenly a face peered out at him with wide furious eyes and a livid grimace. It was the severed head of a Dokkalfar, and fairly recent. With a yelp Jafnar staggered back and pushed himself away from the place. The somber light from above revealed other freshly dismembered heads in niches, with the old skulls lying crushed underfoot. One was old Hofud, and the five most recent victims of the lynx.

Jafnar groaned softly and hitched himself farther away from the heads, not liking the mocking look in their slack expressions and dull eyes. He fancied they felt some sort of sympathetic brotherhood with him, as one who was now alive but shortly would join them in violent and most reluctant death.

Behind him, faint scuttling, chittering sounds gradually insisted upon his attention. Painfully he hobbled onward, winding ever downward, with only a rotting balustrade to offer scant protection from missed footing that would plunge him into the inky oblivion of the charnel pit below. Pausing, he listened to the low and evil hubbub approaching. A leap into the black void was the only escape from certain miserable torture and horrible death. He crept a step nearer the edge, but hurled himself back in terror when the rocks beneath his feet buckled and fell away into the cavern. Far below, he heard a splash.

As he stood gasping and trembling at his near escape, he heard a voice calling from above.

"Jafnar! Jafnar!" It sounded more like Skyla's voice.

He stood transfixed, listening a long moment, wondering if his imagination were playing tricks upon him. He felt as if he had fallen into one of his old nightmares as a child, pursued by hideous beings who would destroy him. Sometimes he was too paralyzed to run, and other times were like now, when he heard a voice luring him in the dark, perhaps to death, perhaps to salvation. In his dreams, the voice had led him to terrible death as often as it had taken him to safety.

"Skyla! Is that you?" he called back, as he knew he would from long experience with his dreams.

At once the bustling advance of the Kjallari-folk took on a nasty triumphant note, as if they had located him from the sound of the voice. Jafnar looked backward and upward and saw their eyes glowing, a hundred of them at least, like a drift of stars hovering above and looking down at him.

"Jafnar! Come! This way!" the voice commanded, coming from a point somewhere ahead and above him. He hesitated no longer.

"I'm coming," he answered through clenched teeth. His foot had reawakened with a vengeance, pounding and throbbing pure agony.

He discovered a narrow mossy set of stairs ascending and he crawled upward toward the voice, which urged him along encouragingly. When he reached the top of the perilous stairs, he found nothing and he heard no more. Stunned and disappointed, he crouched down in a crevice to rest, listening to the clatter of claws and nails on the rocks above him, coming closer by the moment.

He closed his eyes, wishing himself away to almost anywhere else. Immediately he was back in the courtyard of Athugashol, with Skyla sitting above him on the sun warmed wall, swinging one slim foot.

Something scratched his face and he awoke with a snort and a sputter. In the dim light filtering in from high above, he saw a dark shadow standing between him and the light, a shadow with long sharp ears, tufted at the tips. His ears rang with the dying echoes of an eerie wailing scream. He heard no trace of the Kjallari-folk.

"Skyla!" he whispered. "You came back for me!"

The lynx's rough tongue again scraped his cheek, awakening the faint suspicion that she might be tasting him, preparatory to a feast of death. Then she turned away, her image swirling, until the old Skyla form stood before him, wrapped in the long white cloak.

"What are you doing here?" she demanded. "Don't you know this is the favorite hiding place for the Kjallari-folk? It used to be a well, before it became a charnel pit. Rangfara could stand siege for years with this much water. How did you walk so far on that foot? It's hot and festering." She touched it with one hand, and he jerked his foot away with a muffled yelp.

"I thought I heard you—or someone—ahead, calling to me," he said gruffly. "I didn't have a light, so I followed the sound."

"Whoever it was, they did a terrible job of leading you," Skyla said. "Unless they wanted to lead you to your doom. Have the others gotten out? Illmuri? Alvara? Ofarir?"

"I don't know," Jafnar said, gritting his teeth. "And I really don't care. I just want out of here."

"Lean on me then. I'll help you. Once we get away from the well, we're not far from a place to get out."

"You seem quite at home here," Jafnar said accusingly. "I suppose you might well ought to be, since you're the snow lynx."

"A snow lynx, not the snow lynx," she said in a tone of quiet wonder. "Were you so foolish as to think there is only one of them? I thought it was only a strange dream before, those other times, but this time I remembered, and it was real. I truly am a snow lynx in my fylgja-form."

"Skyla, you killed people! Krypplingur, anyway, and old Hofud. Don't you remember anything?"

"Not killing people," she answered. "I don't believe that part. I want to heal life, not destroy it."

"Aren't you frightened?"

"Frightened of what? That the Krypplingur will kill me? Yes, I am. But mostly I'm afraid for Mistislaus and you and the other wild boys. Ofarir knows my secret. I feel a deep foreboding that everything will change, very soon."

She tugged him along, pressing farther into the dark in spite of his protests that he couldn't see where he was going. Assuring him that she could see in the dark as well as a cat, she pushed him and half carried him until a small circle of light appeared ahead. When they came nearer, Jafnar could see a grate made of bars covering the opening. The smell was immeasurably worse, until he could hardly breathe. He had no doubt that the effluvium pouring into the Kjallari was coming from the tanner's building at the far end of the Skurdur, where its smell added to the usual bouquet of stenches issuing from that chosen area.

Skyla crawled up the drain and pushed the grate off and climbed out, reaching back to help Jafnar crawl out, where he lay on the fetid earth feeling thankful to be there.

"The grate must be replaced," he said anxiously. "Look at it, there's nothing to hold those creatures back from coming right up and grabbing anyone they choose."

"That's the way it has always been," Skyla said with a shrug as she kicked the rusty grate back into place. "The Kjallari-folk have been here at least as long as our Skylding ancestors—maybe longer."

Jafnar clenched his teeth. His foot was beginning to throb in dead earnest. It was swollen to twice its normal size, and the bindings of his boot had all but disappeared in the puffy flesh.

Jafnar realized they had been in the Kjallari for much longer than it had seemed. The nightlife of the Skurdur was slinking away into deeper darkness as the sky lightened, and the day market was in full flower, blaring quarrelsomely from shabby carts and roistrous ale booths and ragged tents. The terror of the lynx killings of the previous day was seemingly forgotten already, although many charred reminders of the lawless hours that had followed still remained. Jafnar's appearance attracted no undue attention, although the reek of him caused a few well-clad warriors in their best regalia to step off the path hastily, making a wide margin for his dripping clothes. Leaning heavily on Skyla, his progress became slower and slower until he insisted upon stopping for a rest.

A black shadow darted out of an alleyway the moment he sat down. Jafnar reached weakly for his sword.

"It's Alvara!" Skyla declared.

"I've found you!" Alvar exclaimed, adding an oath of gratitude in an unfamiliar language. "And you're safe! Why did you leave? I was back in only moments with a close way out. You should have waited."

"You left me to die," Jafnar said through clenched teeth. "And someone was trying to trick me into falling into the charnel pit by calling me in Skyla's voice. Was it you, Alvara?"

"Anyone can imitate a voice," Alvara said, clucking her tongue reprovingly. "Why should I be more desirous of ridding the world of you than anyone else? Illmuri, for instance, or Ofarir, now that he knows our secret. Or Mistislaus."

"As if I would distrust Mistislaus for an instant!" Jafnar retorted with a grimace of pain.

Alvara glanced around, seeing that Skyla's attention was momentarily diverted by an advancing group of roisterers. "Or perhaps even Skyla herself," she whispered, leaning close to Jafnar's face.

"You lie," Jafnar snarled in helpless revulsion. "Get away, I don't want your help—"

"Jafnar," Skyla said reprovingly, "you're not being reasonable. Alvara will help us get home."

"Yes, but in a moment," Alvara said rapidly. "Now that Ofarir knows about Skyla's secret, there's going to be trouble for anyone else who knows." Her voice dropped to a whisper, and she tossed a suspicious glance over her shoulder. "You must warn Mistislaus not to trust Ofarir under any circumstances. Ofarir's got a scheme to kill his father, and it involves Skyla."

"Me!" Skyla gasped.

"The snow lynx," Alvara said softly. "Then no one can accuse Ofarir of killing his father for the chieftain's seat. It will seem like a natural accident."

"I refuse to be any part of Ofarir's schemes," Skyla said. "He's a vile creature to plot against his father. And for what? Rangfara will fall from Krypplingur hands, and very soon."

"You must let me help you," Alvara said in a conspiratorial hiss. "You don't have a chance against him otherwise. He's more clever than you can imagine. I should know, I was there trying to cure Herrad. When someone starts having a little success—as I did—Ofarir gets worried. He doesn't want his father cured. This is why you must warn Mistislaus to watch Ofarir with all his might."

"I shall," Skyla said, her wide eyes fastened upon Alvara, like a bird hypnotized by a snake.

"Very good," Alvara said. "Now let's get this lump home and look at his foot." With a shrill whistle between her teeth, Alvara summoned a tilt cart drawn by a scrawny pony and loaded Jafnar into it with little resistance. For the duration of the jolting ride to Athugashol, Jafnar swam in and out of a vague consciousness on a sea of fiery pain shooting up his leg.

When the lurching over the potholed streets ceased, he heard the familiar challenging roar of Guthrum.

"I must not be seen here," Alvara said quickly, pulling up her hood over her head. "Ofarir would wring my neck like a cat's. Remember me, if ever you get into trouble and there's no one to help. Don't trust Illmuri for a moment. Come to me at the Horsetower."

Scarcely acknowledging Skyla's whispered thanks, Alvara hurried away before the gate opened.

"Guthrum! It's me, and Jafnar!" Skyla's voice called, like a clear bell ringing through the gathering buzz in his head. "Open up the gate! Jafnar's been injured!"

Jafnar was barely conscious when Guthrum carried him into the house and deposited him on his cot in the storage room. He knew he was there by the ancient smell of smoked fish that clung to the room. With a sigh, he sank down in unconsciousness as if it were a soft and welcoming mattress, taking him away from the terrible pain in his foot.

Much later, he awakened reluctantly. For a few moments, he thought the fiery pain was gone. The closer he approached the surface of consciousness, the worse the pain became. He opened his eyes. A massive blurred face suddenly blocked his wavering vision as someone peered down at him.

Chapter Fourteen

"You needn't tell me where you've been," the voice of Mistislaus said. "Illmuri came with the news. You've been bitten by one of the Kjallari-folk, but you needn't die from it. You've got a long and difficult cure ahead of you, though."

"Mistislaus," Jafnar whispered, mustering up his strength to deliver his message. "The white cloak—Illmuri took it. Kjallari-folk were there and Skyla—Skyla is the lynx. Ofarir knows, Mistislaus. He saw it all."

"Yes, yes, I know all the bad news. Illmuri told me all. Hush now and settle your brains to begin your cure. Good lad, you did well. You found Skyla and brought her home safe."

In the background, Skyla's voice murmured protestingly, "If I hadn't found him when I did, he'd be in a thousand different bellies by now, Mistislaus. I was the one who rescued him."

"Mistislaus," Jafnar croaked in feeble reproach, "Skyla is the snow lynx. Why didn't you warn me? Couldn't you trust me with your secret?"

"It would have done no good to tell you," Mistislaus said with a deep sigh. "Nothing can hold her when she decides to shift shapes and go. You are but a youth, and now you must bear the awful burden of this secret—which it won't be for long, now that Ofarir knows."

"I got back my cloak, at least," Skyla said. "I'm not afraid of Ofarir. He's afraid of me."

"Mistislaus," Jafnar whispered. "Am I going to die, rotting away like Herrad?"

"It's possible you may go mad first and then die," Mistislaus said. "Or you may linger for years, like Herrad, with the poison slowly working its way toward your vitals. A lot depends upon you. But first of all, you need a good scouring, so it's out to the bathhouse with you, sir. A good steaming will work wonders. Skyla, fetch Guthrum. This will be one bath Jafnar won't get out of taking. We'll get rid of this atmosphere of Kjallari he's been carrying around for the last day and a half."

"Mistislaus, this is no time to think of bathing," Jafnar cried. Mistislaus had an unnatural addiction to taking baths, as many as one a week. "Ofarir knows she's the lynx. You're in danger every moment you stay here. You've got to take her and get out of Rangfara."

"Don't worry about us," Mistislaus said. "Think only healing thoughts. Banish all worry and doubt. Guthrum, carry this wretched object to the bathhouse and give him a bath. Be careful of the foot, though."

When he was done with his cleansing in the bathhouse, Guthrum hauled Jafnar back to his fishy-smelling room. His foot and ankle were hideously swollen and empurpled, throbbing with vivid spurts of pain. His head was beginning to lurch around in a sickening manner. He didn't know whether to blame his weakness on his injury or upon the effects of unaccustomed bathing. Mistislaus sat down on a stool beside his cot and examined his foot. His expression was grave.

"It looks to me as if it's spreading already," Skyla said anxiously, hovering over his shoulder. "Can't you do something to stop it?"

"Am I going to die?" Jafnar inquired dolefully.

"It depends upon you," Mistislaus said. "The nature of Kjallari disease is induced to a large degree by your own mind. You must use your skills of iteration to drive the Kjallari out of your foot, or it will spread throughout your body."

"Iteration? It's going to take more than iteration," Jafnar moaned. "Just look at it, after a day and a half! It's a mess already! I can imagine what it's going to look like tomorrow! Why haven't you done something?"

Mistislaus hitched one eyebrow higher. "I have. I let you sleep the healing sleep. And I said a thousand iterations in your behalf."

"Iterations? Is that all?"

"You don't believe in the powers of iteration?" Mistislaus asked in a tone of quiet horror.

Jafnar sighed. His head was whirling. "I haven't been trained enough. I learned something of it from old Eyda, but not enough, and I've only been with you for a short while. You said yourself I was almost too old to learn much as an apprentice. Can't you do something to help it, like you do for Herrad?"

"I shall do everything within my powers to assist you in your healing process. You are a Skylding. Remember that. Now you should begin with six hundred iterations for your own health. The thoughts of your heart are the most powerful tools you possess."

Mistislaus went out and shut the door. The fishy-smelling room was dimly lit by a small grate high in one wall. He was almost a prisoner here. In despair, Jafnar's thoughts revolved in angry, self-pitying spirals. Yet of what possible use were six hundred repetitions of the same word or phrase? Mistislaus could blissfully bury himself to the neck in useless words and iterations. If Herrad was being cured, it must have been out of sheer dread of Mistislaus' endless, droning babble.

"Don't worry, Jafnar," Skyla said soothingly. "I know how to heal you."

He heard her leave the room a moment, and then she was back. Immediately he recognized the stealthy sounds of her forbidden bag of magical spells.

"No, Skyla," he murmured, opening his eyes in alarm. "I don't think your spells are going to work."

"And why not? Didn't I heal the small creatures? What makes you think you're so different? Now hush and quit fighting it, or it's not going to work."

He felt her cool narrow hand on his forehead. The coolness seemed to spread gradually down the length of his body, bringing welcome relief to the raging fury of his foot. The moment the pain subsided, he fell asleep.

Much later he was awakened by Illmuri's boots grating on the paving stones outside. The wizard coughed politely by the crumbling gatepost, waiting to be admitted.

"Well, at least you got her back," Illmuri's voice said. "A pity about the boy, though. Just as he was beginning to be a bit civilized. It was a near thing, I can tell you. If Skyla hadn't driven off the Kjallari-folk, they would've had us all."

"Yes, well, I haven't given up on Jafnar yet."

"You should," Illmuri said. "There's no cure."

"Is there any more ah—news?"

"I fear so. I've been outlawed for intruding upon the secrets of the Kjallari. Ofarir himself has placed a price upon my head. Two hundred marks in silver."

"Alas, my friend, I feel responsible. I wish I'd never brought poor Skyla here. Nothing but misfortune has attended our footsteps since the moment we arrived here."

"I can get you out of Rangfara," Illmuri said. "I think you

ought to go, before the situation worsens. It's not safe for you or Skyla here, with Ofarir knowing her secret."

"And somewhere else would be safer, with Skyla's shape-shifting? How is she ever going to learn to control her powers anywhere, if not here in the dust of her own ancestors? And learn she must. We can't attempt to stand in the way of the purpose for which she was formed by her parents. Whatever duty lies ahead of her, the keys to that knowledge lie in her bone and blood. Her destiny lies here, in Rangfara. Who am I to try to halt its inevitable course?"

"Destiny is not so inevitable, if you run head-on into a more powerful destiny than your own," Illmuri observed. "She can't take on the entire Krypplingur clan alone."

"Nor shall she. She's got her clan."

"What, the wild boys? Surely you're joking. Except for Jafnar, they're a pretty useless lot. Who knows for certain if they're true Skyldings? And what difference would it make? I wish you'd just leave Rangfara, before something terrible happens."

"Well, for tonight Herrad is expecting me. I dread leaving her alone tonight, even with Guthrum standing watch. He's death to anyone who comes up with a sword or axe, but thick-witted as an ox to magical deceptions. Skyla gets past him as if no one were there."

"Let me watch tonight. Take Guthrum with you to guard you to Herradshol. I have an ominous presentiment about tonight, Mistislaus. The meshes of a great net are all about us."

"I fear that won't be safe for you, my friend. The Krypplingur will not leave a stone of Rangfara unturned until your head is on a pike. This is a place they will be watching."

"I have a great many more dangerous enemies than the Krypplingur," Illmuri said. "My worst fears are from within, not from without. Don't worry about us, Meistari. We have the snow lynx to protect us here, but you are in jeopardy the moment you leave."

"Tush, who would want my worthless carcass?" Mistislaus snorted. "But if it will make you feel better, I'll take Guthrum."

Illmuri stationed himself beside the hearth, using the red glow of the coals to see the pages of one of Mistislaus' ancient books. Frequently he left off reading to raise his head and listen intently to the wind muttering under the eaves. Skyla descended from her tower room and glided past him into Jafnar's storage room without sparing him a glance, leaving behind an icy wake of disapproval.

"Jafnar, you must eat," she greeted him, and sat down officiously at his bedside with a bowl and spoon. "Thorborg would never hear of a sick person starving merely because they didn't feel like eating. How do you think you're ever going to get better if you don't eat?"

Jafnar opened his eyes, grateful for the intrusion of a substantial influence in his torrent of delirium. Her cool touch had worn off, and his foot felt as if it were thrust into the fire again.

"Iteration and meditation," he said dolefully.

"And plumabrot," Skyla said firmly, aiming a spoonful at his mouth. He was too weak to resist, and the bittersweet syrupy mess seemed to ease the pounding in his head. A soothing softness spread outward from his belly and cushioned the pain, removing it to a faraway place where he didn't have to live with it.

"Now then, you'll be all right," Skyla said, rising to her feet. "If you're not much better by tomorrow, I shall use my powers. Mistislaus says tomorrow will be the crisis. You'll either pass off the fever, or you'll go mad and shortly die. But don't worry, Jafnar. You're my Skylding brother and I don't intend to let you die."

Skyla left the storage room and swept disdainfully upstairs, pausing only to scratch some runes on her door. Then she closed the door and locked it from within.

The plumabrot induced a peculiar state of relaxed wakefulness. Jafnar lay motionless, content to watch the flickering of the fire on the hearth and the subtle movements of Illmuri sitting in his chair reading. He felt no worry or menace, only a healing peace that stilled his thoughts, his laboring heartbeat, and slowed his breath. All his earthly worries seemed far behind and beneath his notice now as he contemplated his own stillness. There was a separation, he realized, between his busy self that worried each day about food and shelter and continued survival, and an inner self that he had not suspected before. As he lay and gazed at the fire without blinking, his inner self tugged gently for freedom, and he heard a faint rustle of voices calling to him.

"I'm coming," he heard himself say, although his lips did not move. His viewpoint of Illmuri and the room beyond changed. He was seeing the entire room and every object in it, not the narrow glimpse afforded by his own blurring eyes past the half-closed door. He felt like laughing, as if he were a flying bird soaring over the drab landscape. At the autumn fairing, one of the herdsmen clans bounced people aloft on a large hide, which was the closest Jafnar had ever come to truly flying. This sensation, however, was under better control. He could see everything, even the words on the page as Illmuri read them, and he could hear Illmuri's inner self reading aloud to him, though Illmuri's lips never moved.

Suddenly Illmuri slapped shut the book and looked around suspiciously. Without his hood covering his head, he looked considerably younger than Jafnar had imagined him. He wore his dark hair long, pulled back to a knot behind his neck. As the wizard stood gazing around and listening, Jafnar could feel the danger creeping into the room and swelling silently into a dark hooded figure that stood directly behind Illmuri, unnoticed. Illmuri's head turned slowly, surveying the entire room without seeing the entity that stood there.

Jafnar wanted to shout to warn him, but the speaking part of him was too far away to reach, lying like a corpse on the cot in the storage room. The dark figure slowly raised its hands, reaching for Illmuri's throat. With a quick pounce, the thing engulfed the wizard. Illmuri gasped and struggled, clutching at his throat as he was inexorably borne to the ground. With a final shuddering spasm, he lolled lifelessly on the stone flags, his sightless eyes staring outward from a face convulsed with pure horror.

Jafnar watched as the black shadow creature hung a moment over Illmuri's body, as if trying to discern any traces of life lingering. Then it glided toward Skyla's door, reaching out one pale hand toward the latch. A sharp spark leaped out of the metal, and the runes that Skyla had carved with her eating knife suddenly glowed as if they were etched in living coals. The creature flowed backward, turning toward the storage room. Jafnar felt a faint anxiety as the thing halted at his own bedside for a long moment. It held out one hand over the body huddled there as if testing it for warmth. The body never moved or blinked its open and staring eyes. With an indifferent twitch, the creature turned away and immediately began to dissipate, leaving behind two lifeless carcasses.

In his floating state, Jafnar had no idea how time passed, or even if it did. A great many comforting voices surrounded him, people he dimly recognized, urging him to come forward, farther away from his old pain-wracked body. Samtal, his brother, was there, a tall young warrior, whose face he could not see for the light shining through him.

"Are you ready to stay with us?" he asked Jafnar. "If you wish to stay, come with us to the place of light."

"I want to stay with you," Jafnar answered, floating peacefully toward them, as carefree as a leaf on the wind.

"No, Jafnar, you cannot stay," another voice said, and suddenly Skyla came into view, fire-bright as she had been the first morning he had seen her on the wall. "You've got too much that needs to be done. Your ancestors will manage without you for a while longer. I have come to fetch you home. Come with me."

"No, I don't want to go back," Jafnar answered. "I've done all I can do for you, Skyla. What does it matter, in this place? It all seems so useless and far away, Rangfara and all that mess with the snow lynx and the treasure."

"Not to those of us who have to stay and fight with the Krypplingur," Skyla said. "We must have you, Jafnar."

"But my foot. I don't want to go back to all that pain. It might go on for years. I might go crazy."

"Don't worry. It will be healed. I promise."

"Samtal!" he called. "I can't stay. I have to go back and finish what I have begun."

"Then you may go back," Samtal's voice answered. "We will meet again sometime."

The light and feeling of peace faded away, and Jafnar felt wind rushing past his ears, as if he were falling down a well.

As if from a great distance, he saw the small figure of Mistislaus burst into the room, breathless and steaming from an anxious hurry home.

In one sweeping glance he took in Illmuri's stiffening body. He lifted Illmuri's hand briefly and let it fall.

"Skyla!" he called up the stairway, and received no answer. Next he plunged into the storage room and inspected Jafnar's body lying there, passing one hand back and forth in the same gesture as the shadow creature had done. Surveying the room with a bewildered glance, he pressed his fingers to his temples and sank down in his chair.

"I knew something was wrong!" he murmured in anguish.

A cloud of mist gathered around him, blurring his image as if it were a tallow figure melting in the fire. Then he stood up again, a younger, much slimmer Mistislaus, lean of cheek and jowl, with long pale hair and beard that bristled around his head in a crackling mane that glowed in the ember-light. He left the massive hulk of old Mistislaus propped limply in the chair and strode to the center of the room with his staff blazing alf-light. Turning a flashing eye briefly around the room, he spoke firmly and quietly in a voice of powerful attraction.

"Skyla, Jafnar, come to me at once."

Jafnar felt himself immediately drawn toward the young Mistislaus. He looked down at his own form and perceived himself gathered into the form of young manhood several years beyond the place where he was now. He was taller, a weedy youth no longer.

Skyla was a young woman, tall and straight with a haughty tilt to her chin as she turned to face Mistislaus.

"Mistislaus!" she said. "Have no fear. Jafnar and I are in no danger."

"Yes, you are in danger," Mistislaus answered. "Where you've gone, you don't belong without guidance. You could get lost, unable to find the way back. There are creatures who could follow you, looking for an opening."

"I know the way, Mistislaus," Skyla replied. "I have studied and listened to the voices that have always guided me. They won't lead me astray. We're going to fetch back Illmuri." As she spoke, she sketched a pentacle in the air around the place where they stood.

At once the lines of the pentacle flared upward in a wall of fire. Athugashol vanished, and Jafnar beheld a desolate landscape surrounding them, dark and littered with the broken remains of houses and fortresses and great halls. With his new eyes Jafnar sensed that the ruins were limitless, and moving among them were the shadow-shapes of once-were people. They crowded around the fire of the pentacle hungrily, reaching out for Jafnar and Skyla within.

Skyla etched Algiz, the rune-sign of protection, into the air where it hung glowing, and the shadow people backed away. Beginning a chant, Skyla sketched more runes in the air, awakening an answering murmuring chant among the waiting shadow people. One figure among them came forward and paused at the edge of the fiery pentacle, the flickering light playing upon the impassive features of Illmuri.

"Illmuri, I bid you return at once and resume your duties," Skyla commanded. "Let not one other trespass or intrude in the mortal form of Illmuri, and let all others who may be present immediately depart. I command it in the names of the Four Powers."

The shadow figure of Illmuri stepped forward into the wall of fire, passed through it without harm, and instantly faded from sight. The world of the shadow people began to fade and the walls of Athugashol came back into view. Before long, the once-lifeless form of Illmuri began to groan and twitch with unmistakable signs of returning to life. The burning pentacle dwindled away as Illmuri gained strength and struggled to sit up. He gaped around a moment, seeing Mistislaus slumped in his chair as if he were drunk. He apparently did not see the spirit form of Mistislaus hovering over the body, clinging fearfully close and peering into the shadow realm beyond.

"Go back now, Jafnar," Skyla said, pointing toward Jafnar's own carcass, still staring vacantly outward from the cot in the storage room. "You're not ready yet for journeys such as these, and there's a great deal of living for you to do before you make your last journey."

Scarcely had Skyla spoken the words and pointed, when Jafnar found himself back in his cot gazing into the room beyond. He blinked his eyes. The spirit form of Mistislaus had vanished, and the same old fat Mistislaus was helping Illmuri to his feet and guiding him to a chair. Skyla was hurrying up the stairs to her tower room, glancing over her shoulder at Illmuri. Her eyes met Jafnar's for an instant, then she was gone.

"What you need is a good restorative," Mistislaus was saying, and he poured something out of a small dark bottle hidden in a niche in the wall.

With trembling hands Illmuri took the cup and drained it. The color returned to his sallow features, and he raised one hand to touch his throat.

"I don't know what happened," he said weakly, his voice a little hoarse. "I thought I felt something—and then I couldn't breathe. It felt as if a hand were squeezing my heart until it stopped."

"A nasty turn," Mistislaus said. "You've been worrying far too much about Skyla and her problem. But you're fine now, I should think."

"Don't suppose that I'm a fool, Mistislaus," Illmuri snapped in a sudden flare of temper. "You know as well as I what sort of attack this was. Only an ignorant barbarian attacks flesh and bone. A skilled sorcerer goes for the spirit. And a more skilled sorcerer—or sorceress—knows how to retrieve the spirit when it has been taken. I know what she did, Mistislaus. You forget, I was there, too, against my will and in bondage, but I was there and I recognized Skyla. She's a natural retriever, coming and going through the shadow realm and fetching back whomever she pleases."

Mistislaus hemmed and scowled a moment. "Talk of this sort is best never repeated around common folk. I don't know which one of us would be the more suspect of madness. No one else sees beyond the burden of this corruptible flesh, you know." He slapped his own corpulent belly and heaved a weary sigh as he sank into a chair and propped up his feet on a stool. "Oh, my poor Skyla. Would that I were free of it, but it seems I've got more work to do now than when I was a youth. You'd think that a man's life could be more efficiently spent, wouldn't you?"

"She was brought to you for a reason," Illmuri said. "Without your training of her mind with iteration and meditation, she would not be what she is. I'd give much to know who and what you really are, Mistislaus."

"You see before you nothing but the sad remnant of something that used to be far better," Mistislaus growled, reaching for a flagon under the chair and pouring out a generous dose of ale into a horn. "What you see before you is the ruins of a once-noble edifice. Such as it is, it's all I've got to defend Skyla with, so I wish you'd leave it alone awhile longer until she can fend for herself. The time will come when I'll be glad to be freed of this world, but not just yet."

"Aye, not just yet." Illmuri also helped himself to the ale and gazed toward Skyla's tower room. "I'm not saying anything to anyone about this. I must find the one who tried to send me to Niflheim. Perhaps she will help me."

"You were unprotected. Very careless of you."

"Who would have dreamed anyone with those powers was in Rangfara? Walking in the shadow land is not a common skill. I daresay there are perhaps only two with such talent of you among the number of people in Rangfara who would like to kill me. There are three of us who came to heal Herrad, and we are united in the knowledge of a terrible secret."

"You think it was Alvara, then?" Mistislaus questioned in a low voice, his forehead puckering with dismay.

"Certainly. Only the three of us know Skyla's secret. You and I stand between her and Skyla and that treasure. She'll do all she can to get rid of us."

"I dislike being distrustful," Mistislaus said. "It's a mean and narrow mind that can't trust someone until they prove themselves otherwise than trustworthy."

"Call me mean and narrow, then," Illmuri said, rubbing his throat. "At least I am still alive. Thanks to Skyla, of course. I wish you weren't so peaceable, Mistislaus. We're up against a very powerful and devious enemy."

"My dear fellow, Alvara doesn't worry me in the least. Harming me would be very upsetting for Skyla, and we all know what happens when she gets upset. Alvara wouldn't want to jeopardize her in any way. We're all walking a very fine line here. We must be civil to one another, now that the Krypplingur have discovered Skyla's secret."

Illmuri shook his head. "I don't think it's possible to be civil to Alvara after what she tried to do. And what about Ofarir? He saw Skyla change shapes. Every time you're at Herradshol he hangs around, watching you with those ferret eyes. He's most disappointed when his father makes some progress. Beware of him, Mistislaus. He cares for nothing more than that chieftain's seat—unless it is the opportunity to get his paws on that treasure."

"Ofarir, yes," Mistislaus said with a sigh. "He's not exactly the dutiful son, I fear."

"You don't think he knows anything about spirits and the shadow realm, do you?" Illmuri asked.

"Krypplingur are not ordinarily noted for their advanced powers of sorcery," Mistislaus said judiciously, as if he were observing the behavior of some sort of bird species.

"But they are capable of hiring someone," Illmuri said thoughtfully. "If they can ever overcome their distrust. Ofarir and Alvara might be working together."

"Won't you stay for breakfast?" Mistislaus inquired, his expression brightening suddenly with the happy thought. "I feel absolutely famished. It's high time for breakfast, you know."

"I think not," Illmuri said stiffly. He wrapped his cloak around him and pulled up his hood. "I must be going. I have a great deal to think about. One is not nearly murdered, then invited to breakfast."

With a black glower and a swirl of his cloak, Illmuri let himself out the door. The front gate signaled his departure with a muffled thump and a throaty growl from Guthrum, who was guarding it.

Mistislaus peered into the storage room at Jafnar, who was listening for all he was worth. Knitting his brows together menacingly, Mistislaus pointed one finger at Jafnar.

"Did you understand anything of that?" he demanded.

"Yes," Jafnar said. "Alvara wants to kill Illmuri. The shadow stalker would have killed me, too, if I hadn't already been wandering. I'm starting to think Rangfara is getting to be an unhealthy place for me."

"None of this would have happened if you'd all stayed out of the Kjallari," Mistislaus retorted severely. "Speaking of which, how is your foot?"

"Much better, I think," Jafnar said, cautiously flexing his bitten foot. He felt stiffness, but little pain.

"A walk in the shadow world often works a miraculous cure. And do you feel right in the brain? No sensations of madness or violence?"

"No, none. I think I'm cured, almost, except for a headache from plumabrot. But I have a lot of questions." He opened his mouth, but Mistislaus waved his hand, halting him.

"Don't ask them. I won't answer any. Try to forget what happened. And stay away from plumabrot."

"But Mistislaus, Skyla came and brought me back to this world. I saw you separate yourself from your body. You were young and—"

"Tut-tut! Your brain was delirious and possibly still deranged from the bite of that Kjallari creature. Now be still and rest."

"Is that what it is like to die? It was so peaceful. Where did Skyla learn how to go between realms of life and death that way?"

"You must be silent, Jafnar. Tell no one what you have seen—or imagined you have seen—unless you wish to get Skyla and me into some deep trouble. Wherever there are powers and talents, you will also find searing jealousy. Long ago I became sickened of all that and went into retirement—until I came to Rangfara. Now you must seal your lips and forget these unfortunate circumstances. Sleep well and complete your healing."

That was all Jafnar was able to get out of Mistislaus. Mistislaus made a sign in the air, and Jafnar suddenly became too sleepy to ask questions. He fell into a doze that lasted until midafternoon, then awakened to find Skyla laying out her ominous collection of rune sticks and bones.

"There's no need for all that," he said hastily. "I'm cured. Look at my foot and see for yourself. You promised me it would be healed. When you came into the shadow realm to fetch me back."

"I recall nothing of the sort, and neither do you," she said primly. The foot was indeed healthy and pink, instead of blackening and streaked with lurid colors. "It was the plumabrot that cured you. I knew it was a healthy food."

"If it truly is, that's the only healthy thing around here," Jafnar said with a shiver of uneasiness. "Skyla, life and death is a stranger business than anyone knows."

Skyla looked at him with her most disconcertingly direct stare. "Now you are feeling what I have always felt. Your death voyage was a good experience for you. It opened your eyes a bit."

"Skyla, I saw that thing try to kill Illmuri. It would have, too, if you hadn't saved him." He stared at her accusingly, waiting for an explanation.

She shrugged. "Illmuri is not what he seems" was all she would say.

"You can't possibly think any good of Illmuri, not after he stole your things. Skyla, someone is trying to kill us. In the Kjallari, someone led me to that pit, using your voice so I would think I was following you. And Illmuri was nearly murdered, right here behind our locked doors. Mark my words, something will happen to Mistislaus next."

"I am nothing but a source of misfortune to all who know me," Skyla murmured, her shoulders drooping.

"It's not really your fault. Well, it is and it isn't. Krypplingur getting their hearts torn out and eaten is a terrible insult to them. They have no experience in being the hunted prey. Skyla, did you really kill all those Krypplingur?"

Skyla swept her possessions into her bag, pausing only to retort "I've killed no Krypplingur. If I had, I'm sure I'd remember it. I'm not a killer. I'm a healer. There's a great differencc between the two."

"Skyla, do you know how to make those shadow things? Like the one that tried to kill Illmuri?" Jafnar shivered, thinking of her experiments with killing small animals.

"I know what you're thinking. I didn't try to kill Illmuri. It wasn't just a lark. Someone really tried to kill him. I hate how you all look at me. Everyone thinks I'm a murderer!" With a last wounded flash of her eyes, she turned and sped out of the room and up to her aerie at the top of the stairs.

Chapter Fifteen

In the ensuing silence, Jafnar could hear Mistislaus up on the roof contentedly iterating away in a monotonous droning murmur like a dovecote on a hot sleepy morning. Outside, Guthrum was grousing around in the stable, talking soothingly to the old horse. There was not another living being whom the dwarf valued a fraction as well as he did old Fegurd.

Jafnar crept out of his cot and proceeded shakily to fashion himself a crutch from a length of thicket wood. Then he hobbled across the main room to Skyla's door at the bottom of her stairs and knocked on it. There was no answer, but he knew she was listening.

"Come down, Skyla," he called out. "There's no use in quarreling. We are clan, and we can't lock each other out."

"I'm busy," her voice replied, icy even through the thick panels of the door. "Planning my next attack upon the Krypplingur. Suddenly I have a great craving for a nice juicy Krypplingur heart. Or maybe a liver."

"I am sorry," he said. "I don't doubt you for a moment, if you say you didn't do it."

"I think you're a pig," she retorted.

"Well, I don't mean to be, but since I sort of raised myself, perhaps I haven't learned some of the finer manners that parents sometimes teach their children. At least I can manage to eat at a table now."

"That's not what I mean. You slip away and go into the Kjallari and find Skriftur and other marvelous things and you get bitten and go to the shadow realm and come back. Plumabrot makes your natural powers go wild. All I ever get to do is sit here locked away like a criminal because everyone thinks I'm the snow lynx.

It's not much fun. Even you think I killed those Krypplingur and old Hofud."

"No. I can't imagine it. But I think you knew the plumabrot would do something to me the night you sneaked out to Hofud's for your blue hood."

"I was hoping you'd come with me," she said. "Plumabrot always makes me feel more alert. But you fell into a drunken stupor, so you weren't of any use at all. Sometimes I wonder what's the sense in having kinsmen at all if they're nothing but a pack of wild boys. How are we ever going to find our heritage, Jafnar? Everywhere, it's nothing but barriers and people who are problems. Every day I spend locked up and watched over, I think how pleasant it would be if I was just a dull and ordinary person without any mission in life except to live from one day to the next."

"But think how boring it would be," Jafnar said earnestly. He had worked for a long time to instill a sense of pride and destiny in his six clansmen. "Not to be a Skylding. Not to have any pride in your ancestors. Not to have any hope for the future. That's what it means to be ordinary. I don't think you'd like it, Skyla."

Mistislaus came shuffling into the room, blinking and scowling. "It's frightfully difficult to concentrate with people shouting all over the place," he huffed. "You're feeling better, I see," he added, running his eye over Jafnar in some surprise.

"Much better," Jafnar said. "I thought I'd run to the Skurdur for you and spare Guthrum the indignity."

"Guthrum thrives on indignity," Mistislaus said. "It gives him something to fester over. I won't hear of your going to the Skurdur yet. Besides, there's still the matter of your haring off to the Kjallari the moment our backs were turned. Didn't I warn you? Didn't I tell you to stay here?"

"I guess I've used up all my chances," Jafnar said.

"Yes, you have."

"So I'm sacked?"

"No, I need you too desperately to sack you. I'm beset on all sides by enemies, and I've got to protect Skyla as well as heal Herrad and avoid suspicion until—for as long as possible, anyway."

"Speaking of enemies, couldn't you do without Illmuri poking around and stealing Skyla's things to take to the Kjallari? Don't you suspect he's up to something?"

"Hush. I shan't justify myself to a mere young ragged savage such as yourself. I can manage quite well without your advice. Everything will be revealed in its own time, my disobedient young friend. What I need for you to do is to be an extra set of eyes for me. Watch over Skyla while I'm gone. If something peculiar happens, run and tell me as fast as you can, instead of trying to figure it out yourself. If you'd come for me, you would've avoided a great deal of pain and distress." His eye fell significantly upon Jafnar's bitten foot.

Abashed, Jafnar scowled and muttered, "I just get carried away by the moment. I'll truly try harder next time."

Before Mistislaus could answer, the door shook under several strong wallops and Guthrum announced curtly, "Someone here to see you, Master. That Ofarir person, and two thralls with large baskets. Should I let him in?"

"Yes, of course," Mistislaus snapped, opening the door.

Slowly, as if it were much against his better judgment, Guthrum returned to the street gate and stood back as Ofarir strode through, followed by two thralls carrying baskets.

"I bid you greetings," Ofarir said with a respectful half bow, his voice muffled behind a black mask. "I thought it was likely you hadn't gone out to the market today with your boy injured, so I brought you a few things to save you the trip. My father Herrad doesn't want you inconvenienced in the least way."

"How gracious of him," Mistislaus murmured, opening one of the baskets. "Ah! Pickled eggs!"

The two thralls commenced unloading a tempting feast from the baskets, ranging from roasted goose, head cheese, pickled trotters, soups thick and thin, various dainties concocted to tempt the most recalcitrant palate, a flagon of Mistislaus' favorite dark ale, and last of all, an entire round of plumabrot, soaking in its own purple syrup.

Ofarir's eyes narrowed behind his mask as he turned to contemplate Jafnar. "So you escaped from the Kjallari after all. You're looking quite restored from your ordeal." He turned to Mistislaus and added, "A pity my unfortunate parent can't be cured so quickly of his injury."

"It could have been, if the injury weren't over a dozen years old," Mistislaus replied. "If you'd called me when it happened, he'd be as spry as this lad now, instead of suppurating away like a rotten apple."

"What a stroke of fortune," Ofarir replied with the slightest hint of a sneer curling his lip. "But at least we're rid of that interfering wizard Illmuri now. I've outlawed him for his misdeeds. Do you have any idea what he was doing with that white cloak?"

"None at all. No one can penetrate the depths of the sorcerous mind. Are you sure he deserved to be outlawed?"

"He's a charlatan and a rogue. I disliked him from the start. When I saw what he was doing with those old records in the Kjallari, I knew he was up to no good. No one would go to all that work for as long as he's been at it unless they were plotting something against the Krypplingur. There are those who wish us gone from Rangfara."

"Hard to fathom why, isn't it?" Mistislaus murmured.

"And then there's the matter of that cloak he stole from Skyla," Ofarir continued pompously. "We don't tolerate that sort of petty pilfering in Rangfara. Is it very valuable?"

"Of course," Mistislaus said. "Her grandmother saved up Skyla's hair all her life and made it for her."

"I see," Ofarir said, but Mistislaus doubted it. "You're better off without him. He was thinking of nothing but his own gain. The treasure, you know," he added in a low voice. "Fortunately Skyla returned home and your wild boy looks as if he will recover, so no real damage was done. But Illmuri must pay for the trouble he caused my guests."

"It isn't ended yet," Jafnar replied, eyeing Ofarir suspiciously. "Someone made a very clumsy attempt to lead me into the charnel pit with a trick voice, but it was a wasted effort, as you can see. I'm still alive and still determined to protect Skyla as long as there's a breath in my body."

"Voices? It sounds like something Illmuri or that sorceress Alvara would do," Ofarir said. "Disgruntlement from their failures to cure my father, no doubt. Now they'll do anything to discomfit their replacement."

"Is there no one we can trust in Rangfara?" Mistislaus asked with a grieved sigh, preparatory to sinking his teeth into a wing of cold roast fowl.

"Only me," Ofarir said with a truly fulsome grin.

Skyla came down the stairs to take possession of the plumabrot, not deigning to notice anything else Ofarir had brought.

"Splendid, isn't it? Bought from old Migda by the well, just as you like it," Ofarir said with an ingratiating grin. "This is the best she made, by her own admission. Very rich and very special. And something else," he added, reaching back into one of the baskets. "Something found in Rangfara almost never. Something more rare and beautiful than jewels—like the little lass herself."

He held out a posy of fresh-picked flowers, sweetly pathetic in those massive, seamed hands. With a small glad cry Skyla seized the flowers and buried her nose in them, inhaling the earthy fragrance of fresher, purer places.

"These remind me of Ulfgarth!" she said, spinning away across the room to a pillar of sunlight where she sat down to look at the flowers. "Oh, Mistislaus, will we ever see Ulfgarth again?"

"Of course we will," Mistislaus said, knitting his brow in puzzlement. "Why should we not? Ofarir, this was very decent of you. You've picked all our favorite things, even down to flowers and goose livers for Skyla. You must have been watching us very closely indeed when we went to the Skurdur."

"Yes, and all so cleverly that you never knew I was there," Ofarir said with a narrow grin. "What with the recent turn of events, I didn't think you'd be eager to venture out just yet. I'm afraid you have powerful enemies in Rangfara."

"You are very kind," Mistislaus said around a mouthful of fresh bread with currants.

Ofarir banished the thralls, but he was not ready to leave yet. His eyes kept wandering nervously toward Skyla, still basking in her sunbeam as she arranged the flowers in a bowl of water.

"You'd never know such an innocent creature could possess such a dark side," he said in a lower voice, as if she could not hear. "I wouldn't believe it myself if I hadn't seen her shift shapes with my own eyes."

"She won't harm you, or anyone," Mistislaus said anxiously. "I daresay it still may be some other lynx doing the killing—the same one from last winter, perhaps. If she has done anything wrong, it was only because she was frightened."

"Or hungry," Jafnar muttered out of the corner of his mouth, just loud enough for the Krypplingur to hear.

"I wish only to make peace with the lynx," Ofarir said. "Many times I have looked death in the face, but all those times were as nothing when I faced the Kjallari-creatures. I realized then that I must change my ways. She controls them, Mistislaus. Can you imagine the power she could wield? All our enemies will be as naught. Whatever she wants will be laid at her feet."

"Skyla is not interested in subjugating enemies or in wealth," Mistislaus said. "She has no delusions of power. She is just a simple girl struggling to come to grips with the strange powers she was born with."

Ofarir continued, "If there is something she wants, she needs only to ask. If only the killings would stop, she can have anything in Rangfara she wants. What would she like? Fine clothing? Jewels? A horse?"

He turned to Skyla, who sat and stared at him open-mouthed as her brain whirled at such offers.

"I have everything I need," Skyla said.

"What else can I provide for your comfort?" Ofarir went on, sizing up the meager furnishings of gloomy old Athugashol. "Some rugs, perhaps. Some furniture. Perhaps you ought to take different quarters, nearer to Herrad. The Street of a Thousand Steps is an ordeal to climb. We can outfit you with splendid rooms in Herradshol."

"No, no, we're quite fine here," Mistislaus said. "The upper rooms get the first sun of the day and the last of it at night. Very important to iterations, sunlight. Thanking you all the same, we wouldn't trouble you for anything more."

"You have only to speak and I shall fetch you whatever you require from Herrad's own kitchen," Ofarir said. "My father hasn't thought of anyone else's comforts except his own since this disease started spreading. I wish to change all that. Your stay in Rangfara must be unforgettable. You're certain you wouldn't come to Herradshol, where you can be more comfortable—as well as safe from the rough characters of Rangfara?"

"No indeed, Athugashol is more suited to our needs," Mistislaus said. "And safe enough, thanks to the thousand steps required to get up here."

"You pass through the most unsavory section of Rangfara both coming from and going to Herradshol. If you won't come to stay at Herradshol, the least I can do is escort you safely when you must pass through that area near the Kjallari," Ofarir said, with another sidelong glance at Skyla. He ignored Jafnar's defiant glaring, as if he were nothing more than a dog on the end of a chain.

"I hate to be such a bother to anyone of your stature," Mistislaus said. "In the past, Illmuri has gotten me safely by the Kjallari and the wretches surrounding it."

"Illmuri! That charlatan! If ever trouble arose, he'd doubtless turn his back and leave you to face it alone. Besides—" Ofarir grinned a little wider and squared his shoulders as if he were preening himself on a weighty accomplishment. "Illmuri's been outlawed in Rangfara. I doubt if you'll be seeing him again."

Mistislaus replied, "Well then, if we've seen the last of Illmuri, then I shall gladly accept your offer for safe conduct to Herradshol."

"And will they be staying each night to guard the gate?" Skyla twitched one shoulder toward a narrow window, through which could be seen two Krypplingur warriors lurking about the gate, held at bay by a glowering Guthrum.

"I think not," Ofarir said a bit too hastily. "They've got better things to do with their time."

"Or their lives," Jafnar muttered.

"I must take my leave now, but I shall return the moment the sun is out of sight," Ofarir said. "Please, enjoy my gifts. Tomorrow there will be more. Good day, Meistari Mistislaus. Good day, little Skyla—or should I call you Madame Lynx?" He made a fulsome bow in Skyla's direction, as much as his bulky armor would allow, grinning ingratiatingly. Without his helmet, he looked like a particularly squat, anxious badger showing its teeth in a revolting and menacing smile.

"No, I don't like that name," Skyla said after considering him for a level-eyed moment. "When you come again, bring some skyr with berries. And more bread."

"No meat?" Ofarir asked, with a sheen of perspiration gleaming on his features. "Nothing . . . raw, possibly?"

"Certainly not," Skyla said. "We always have our meat cooked by the one-legged man at the Hanging Bridge. They say he cut off and cooked and ate his own leg during the siege of Rangfara. And you'd better bring more of everything next time. We feed the leftovers to the other wild boys."

Ofarir backed away with another bow. "Skyr and berries and bread. And something for the wild boys. Well and good. You shall have the best in Rangfara. Remember, I shall return at sundown."

With that, he was gone, with the surly Kryppling lumbering at his heels, darting last menacing glances back at Guthrum, savoring his threats for the next encounter. Jafnar flung himself and his crutch across the room to peer out the crack of the door, then the narrow window.

"Taking my job!" he snarled. "We'll see who does the marketing for Athugashol! I wouldn't eat anything he's touched! How do we know it isn't all poisoned? Why should he suddenly decide to be so kind? I don't like it at all, Mistislaus. What do you make of this sudden change?"

Mistislaus scarcely paid him any heed, digging into the food as he was. He carved off a leg of roast goose, poured out some ale, and helped himself to the squash soup.

"Come and eat," he urged. "Your brain is in dire need of nourishment, Jafnar. Skyla, this goose is the best thing you'll ever taste. It's stuffed with nuts and all manner of good things. And look, there's rhubarb soup, too."

"Is food all you ever think about?" Jafnar exploded. "Mistislaus! Ofarir's plotting something as surely as we're all standing here, or you may take me out and cut off my head!"

"It would be a good way to get some quiet around here," Mistislaus growled. "Of course I know Ofarir's up to something, but that has nothing to do with enjoying this meal at this moment. If it were our last meal in this world, why then, wouldn't we be virtually obligated to sit down and savor it and enjoy it the most of all?"

Jafnar could think of no reason, but it still didn't help him enjoy the feast Ofarir had brought.

When Mistislaus was done eating, he had another two horns of ale and settled down for a short nap, as was his habit. When he awakened, it was almost sundown. Instead of climbing up to his observatory tower to iterate as the sun went down, he clasped his hands behind his back and solemnly strode up and down the length of the room.

"Now I shall worry about Illmuri," he said.

"Can I take the leavings out to my brothers?" Jafnar inquired, indicating the remains of the meal.

Mistislaus nodded, preoccupied, and unlocked the door.

"Why are you so worried about Illmuri?" Jafnar asked. "We're well rid of him, I think."

"It might be better if you didn't try to think," Mistislaus replied testily.

Jafnar limped out to the courtyard with Skyla at his heels carrying the basket. Almost before they came to the usual place beside the pool, Lampa and Lofa came scrambling over the wall, hurrying toward them.

"Jafnar! You're hurt? What happened?" they demanded, darting wary glances at Skyla, who sat down cross-legged to contemplate the carp in the pool.

"It's nothing to be concerned about," Jafnar said. "I was bitten by one of the Kjallari-creatures when I went down to find Skyla. It was a good thing none of you came to help me. It was far too dangerous."

"Tell us! Tell us all of it!" Lampa and Lofa demanded, leaping around and bumping against him like wolf cubs.

"Well, if I must," Jafnar said. "But if you don't call the others, they'll be upset at hearing it secondhand from you. Everyone had his chance," he added severely, "and no one had the courage to come with me. It would serve you all right if I didn't tell you my story."

Lofa whistled sharply for the others. Chiming in at regular intervals, they both said, "It wasn't our fault we didn't come. We would've, but Ordvar is getting so bossy without you around. He's such an old woman when it comes to doing anything. Modga is worse than ever. We don't dare open our mouths, hardly. When are you coming back, Jafnar? We miss you."

To cover his conflicting feelings, Jafnar gave each of them a halfhearted buffet on the ear and tried to scowl. "I've got important things to do and I can't be worrying about you little boys. You do just what Ordvar says while I'm gone. Before long we'll be together again, and I'll teach Modga a lesson he won't forget."

"Have you found the treasure yet?" the twins demanded.

"No, not quite," Jafnar said, with a glance toward Skyla, sitting on the edge of the pool feeding the great ancient carp. "But I think we're closer to finding out our real names."

"What good are names? We already have names," Lampa and Lofa said.

"Not the ones our true parents gave us," Jafnar said. "You're being stupid. I'll explain it to you later."

The other boys came dropping over the wall into the courtyard and fell gladly upon the food and Jafnar, eager to hear about the Kjallari and most fascinated when he showed them the toothmarks in his foot. By their attitude he knew they were anxious to be forgiven for their cowardice in not going with him, so he told them all the tale of the Kjallari, with a great many descriptions of the Kjallari-folk. Only silent Thogn seemed unimpressed; he sat on his heels and gazed away inattentively into nothing, lost in his own inner visions. Jafnar lowered his voice when he mentioned the Kellarman, out of consideration for Thogn and the difficulty of settling him down again when he got frightened.

"We would've come," Ordvar said earnestly when he was finished, "but what would we have done with Thogn? And Lofa and Lampa are too young for something like that. And Einka is so fat and succulent, the Kjallari-folk wouldn't have rested until they got him and ate him."

"It's well and good for you to run off and have an adventure without us," Modga said, "but some of us have responsibilities, you know."

"I know," Jafnar said, silencing Einka's protests by sitting on him. "I'm glad you weren't there. It was more real than I cared for at times. Especially when someone was calling me into the charnel pit."

"Who was it, do you think?" Ordvar asked. "Illmuri? Alvara? Kjallari-folk?"

"Or her?" Modga added, with a nod toward Skyla.

"It wasn't Skyla," Jafnar retorted.

"You said it sounded like her," Modga said. "What if it was?"

"It wasn't. I don't know who it was. We've got to go in. Mistislaus is about to leave for Herradshol." Jafnar stood up, suddenly unwilling to talk any more, particularly about Skyla and her secret. He didn't dare tell the wild boys that she was a snow lynx, or they would probably abandon him and her in unthinking terror.

"There's something I want you to do," he continued. "With Illmuri outlawed, Ofarir's coming for Mistislaus. I want some of you to follow them and make sure Mistislaus is all right. If ever you see any sign of Ofarir doing anything to threaten or harm Mistislaus, or any unusual numbers of Krypplingur hanging around Gibbet Hill, I want to know about it. Ofarir's got plans for the chieftancy of Rangfara, and Herrad is all that stands in his way."

"But Herrad is his father!" Ordvar said. "He wouldn't do anything to his own father, would he?"

"Yes. Krypplingur are different. I don't know what Ofarir's got in mind, and Mistislaus is so unsuspicious."

"Spying on Ofarir, we've got it," Ordvar said.

"And another thing," Jafnar continued, "go see if Illmuri's still in his lie-up in the Bone-tower, or if he's gotten out of Rangfara somehow."

"Hst! It's the Dvergar!" Modga warned. "Looking for you and the little sorceress!"

"Remember who we are," Jafnar said. "Skyldings, and Rangfara is our birthright!"

Hastily they bundled up the last of their feast of leftovers and scuttled over the wall as Guthrum approached.

"It's time you were coming in," the Dvergar rumbled quietly. "Shall we try to have a quiet night for once, without any alarms or excursions?"

As they returned to the hall at Guthrum's heels, Ofarir signaled his appearance at the street gate with the tramping of several pair of hobnailed boots and an officious rapping on the panels with his axe. Guthrum took his time in letting him in, then stood watching sourly as Mistislaus went out and into the darkening street to join the Krypplingur escort. Jafnar also stood and watched, hearing the warning whistles and chirps of the wild boys following.

"At least we're rid of Illmuri," Jafnar said glumly. "But I don't like the sight of this at all. Sometimes I wish I could just go back to being a wild boy. It was such a simple life, distrusting everyone. I hate trying to figure out who is honest or not."

"You had the right idea before." Guthrum grunted, grounding his Dvergar axe with a clank. "Don't trust any of 'em. Now away with you inside, as the master ordered. We'll not have any more adventures into that charnel pit chasing wizards, will we?"

Jafnar knew better than to stay and argue. He scuttled into Athugashol and listened as the doors were locked after him for the night's imprisonment. He went from one arrow slit to the next, looking out and seeing Krypplingur surrounding Athugashol, lounging around corners, casually posted where they could keep the old hall under guard.

"What am I doing here?" he asked himself out loud, giving himself a whack alongside his head. "This is a death trap!"

His heart sank even further when Skyla came down from her tower and commenced opening up her bag of spells and charms, mostly small dead creatures, and spreading them out upon the table. Last of all she unwrapped a wedge of plumabrot, oozing its tempting purple juice and perfuming the air with its tantalizing sweet fragrance.

She folded her arms on the table and looked across at him intently, like a cook about to pluck and dismember a chicken.

"Jafnar, it has come to me that the plumabrot is the key to your powers," she said. "Tonight we shall experiment to see how much it takes to get you up to your best strength without getting completely drunk."

"No," Jafnar said without hesitation, shutting his lips firmly and trying not to look at the tempting, deadly stuff.

"You must learn to trust me," Skyla said. "Did I not bring you back from the shadow realm? Did I not rescue you from the grasp of death?"

"Yes, but—"

"You will be perfectly safe. Now take one bite and we'll carefully note any changes."

"No, I—"

"Believe me, I know what's best for you. One bite, Jafnar. Surely you're not afraid, are you?"

Remembering past experiences, Jafnar had no trouble in privately agreeing with her. He shook his head disdainfully and replied, "Of course not!"

"Wouldn't you like to be free again, Jafnar?" she asked in a softer voice. "To go flying along the walls of Rangfara once again, heedless of all the cares of everyone toiling and moiling down below? Free as the wind, where no one can stop you and make you sit down and be quiet or lock you up in a dusty old pile of stone or make you do anything you don't want to do. Free again!"

She spun around the room like a captive sparrow and came to rest sitting on the back of Mistislaus' chair with her feet on the seat. The brief exertion made her face radiant, her eyes deep and sparkling, as if she had just returned from a run on the fell with the wild ponies. The wind seemed to lurk just beneath the surface of her, lifting her hair and rumpling her gown and tunic.

Jafnar felt the dark, dank walls of Athugashol closing around him like the walls of a barrow, as if he had been buried prematurely. He missed the danger and bustling activity of the Skurdur, the thrill of the chase after he had stolen something, the rollicking camaraderie of his wild brothers. He reached out and broke off a large lump of the plumabrot and stuffed it in his mouth.

"To freedom!" he said, licking off his fingers.

"Yes, to freedom!" Skyla gazed at him expectantly.

After a few moments he began to itch and his skin felt hot. "Skyla, you won't leave me, will you? Like you did when you went for your blue hood?"

"No, I'll be watching you every moment. Hah, it's starting to work."

In the morning, he could remember nothing from that point onward, except feeling slightly sick and totally exhilarated. Athugashol was left far behind, wherever they went, and all the cares that beset them were forgotten.

When Mistislaus came whistling in at dawn, he reported to Guthrum that two more Krypplingur had fallen prey to the lynx. Jafnar awakened in his bed in the storage room, not remembering putting himself there.

"Didn't even have time to draw their swords," Mistislaus declared. "I tell you, Herrad is frightened almost to death and Ofarir is gnashing his teeth. Happened right down here at the bottom of Gibbet Hill, not a stone's throw from the Thousand Steps. You didn't see anything? No one happened to . . . escape?"

"It wasn't Skyla," Guthrum replied. "I sat here with my eyes on this door all night long. No one came or went. It was perfectly quiet."

Skyla came down the stairs in her long nightdress, yawning and stretching. The sunlight found her, beaming down a ray through a gap in the stones high above.

"Good morning," she said cheerily. Then she noted the long

gloomy faces of Mistislaus and Guthrum. "Whatever happened? You look as if someone died."

"Two Krypplingur," Mistislaus said. "Found by the lynx."

"It wasn't I," Skyla said. "You can ask Jafnar. Myself, I think it is the winter lynx and her young kits doing the killing. It might be four or five different lynxes, for all we know."

"A real lynx and not a fylgja?" Mistislaus murmured. "Would that the truth could indeed be so simple."

Then Guthrum growlingly admitted Herrad's thralls with the basket for breakfast, distracting Mistislaus from his gruesome tale. Jafnar felt like crawling back into bed. His head pounded and his mouth was as dry as dust. Skyla was already skipping around on the tops of the walls outside, greeting the early-morning sun with the happy fascination of a moth caroming around a candle flame.

"And how did your night pass?" Mistislaus inquired, looking up to see Jafnar with his head propped up between his hands, elbows on the table. "Uneventfully, I hope?"

The slight tone of anxiety snagged in Jafnar's consciousness like a fishhook. Horror dawned upon him by gradual degrees. Two dead Krypplingur—plumabrot—he and Skyla and her bag of spells.

After tottering to his feet, he stumbled toward the door leading to the courtyard behind Athugashol.

"I shall fetch Skyla for breakfast," he mumbled, feeling his face and neck flushing a hot and guilty red.

"Skyla!" he called, coming up to her where she sat on the top of the wall, watching something on the other side. She dangled one ankle casually, as comfortable atop the wall as a cat taking a sunbath.

"Good morning, Jafnar," she answered. "You're looking fit today. I told you plumabrot would agree with you."

"I don't think it agreed with two Krypplingur last night," he said in a low voice. "Two of them were lynx-killed right at the bottom of the Thousand Steps."

"Yes, I know," she said, looking back on the other side of the wall. "They're cleaning the mess up right now."

"Skyla, did you leave me last night?"

"No, of course not. I said I wouldn't, didn't I?"

"Skyla, I think it was you and I who killed them," he went on, his voice shaking with fear and revulsion. "We are both Skyldings, are we not? So are we not both snow lynxes?"

"I suspected that all Skyldings may indeed share the same

fylgja-form," she said, nodding her head. "And I suspected that plumabrot was the key to your shape-shifting."

"And did I—was I—a snow lynx, also?"

"Yes, of course, just as I suspected," she said on a note of triumph.

"And then what happened, Skyla?" he demanded.

"Well—there's the problem," she replied reluctantly. "I don't really remember what happens when I shift shapes."

"So we might have gone out and killed those Krypplingur?"

"No. Never say that, Jafnar. I am not a destroyer of life, I am a healer. I could never bring myself to end a human life—even a stinking Krypplingur. Destruction is from the dark side of nature. We must do all we can to resist its temptation. Do you . . . remember anything?"

Jafnar groaned. "No, not a thing. But I certainly have a terrible feeling about it."

"Why can't I remember? Why don't I know these things?" Skyla exclaimed, leaping to her feet and facing the morning sky. "I am a Skylding, but I'd just as well be a Dvergar living underground, for all I truly know about powers and life and everything going on around me. I feel as if I'm blind and stupid. If only I had the knowledge—if only I had the keys to unlock the mysteries!"

She held out her arms hopelessly, addressing the blackened and impassive walls of Rangfara rising around them, fringed with dead gray grasses and sprouting unwholesome tuffets of moss.

"I think sometimes ignorance is the safest course," Jafnar said, with a shiver of apprehension. "It's not a comfortable feeling to know your fylgja-form is a snow lynx and maybe you've just killed two Krypplingur. Even if they are our enemies. If ever we were found out—" He made a slashing motion across his throat and some gagging sounds.

"Then no one ever will find out," Skyla said. "Don't be so afraid, Jafnar. Your fear will mark you and lead your enemies to your door. You are a Skylding and Rangfara is your home. One day we will find our heritage and our names, and Rangfara will be ours."

"I'm not so sure," Jafnar said bitterly, looking toward the nearest knot of Krypplingur. "If they only knew our secret, our lives wouldn't be worth a straw. I wish I could go back to the days when we thought we were going to find the treasure by digging holes and poking around under rocks. It was much more fun then."

"Ah yes, the innocence of youth," Skyla said, nodding her head as if she were an old woman in a shawl. "Well, you can't go backward now. Knowledge is a treacherous gift sometimes."

"Could it really have been us who killed those Krypplingur?" he demanded again, clenching and unclenching his hands. "Many times I've yearned to kill Krypplingur, to tear their throats out, just like that, or to frighten them with just my appearance. But not to even remember anything about it—I don't like it, Skyla. I want to know what I've been doing."

"I shall find the keys to our past and our heritage," Skyla said with a fierce toss of her hair. "Let the Krypplingur beware if they think to stand in the way of our destiny."

Chapter Sixteen

Three more days passed in much the same fashion. Each day two thralls arrived with baskets from Herradshol stuffed with the gastronomical artistry of Herrad's cooks. At sundown Ofarir and several lumbering guards halted at the street gate and waited for Mistislaus to come out. Ofarir had shed his battle armor in favor of the plain clothing of an ordinary person, hoping perhaps to mitigate his savage appearance. To Skyla he was unfailingly polite, when she deigned to notice him, and he brought her a fresh nosegay of flowers every day, picked from the tops of old walls that rose above the murk and grue of Rangfara.

Without his armor, Ofarir seemed to Jafnar like a turtle without its shell. The sight of him coming and going from Athugashol was not something Jafnar could readily accept, hating Krypplingur as he did. The other wild boys kept a sharp lookout, informing Jafnar that there were more Krypplingur than usual lurking about Gibbet Hill, turning away anyone who wanted to wander up that way. Of Illmuri they saw no sign, unless he had disguised himself among the number of ragpickers and scavengers driven away by the Krypplingur.

The confinement of Athugashol became oppressive with the sensation of Krypplingur eyes watching and Krypplingur ears listening, and Krypplingur guards tramping past the gate at all hours. Jafnar desperately missed the freedom to walk through the streets to the Skurdur for even the humble task of doing the marketing.

On the morning of the fourth day when Ofarir and the Krypplingur guards returned, Mistislaus invited Ofarir into the hall, where Jafnar had just kindled a fire to take away the night's damp. Guthrum lurked in the background, dividing his attention between Ofarir grinning on the hearthstone and the Krypplingur warriors lowering at the gate. Skyla gazed at Ofarir with distaste and stopped brushing her hair, pointedly gathering up her hair combs and pins and things for a quick retreat to her tower room. She did not leave so much as an errant hair behind.

"So kind of you to share your breakfast with me," Ofarir murmured, speaking to Mistislaus but watching Skyla narrowly and licking his lips.

"It was you who provided it," Mistislaus said, unloading the delectables from the basket with the reverential attitude of a high priest on the most solemn of ritual occasions. "Is this a blueberry tart or does my nose deceive me?" He inhaled deeply, shutting his eyes and exhaling a blissful sigh.

"Meistari Mistislaus," Ofarir began with cringing, cunning servility, "we ought to speak upon the matter of your little Skyla. Certain people won't take it at all well that she has a habit of shifting shapes and eating Krypplingur gizzards."

"Actually, birds are the only species who have gizzards, if it's any comfort to you," Mistislaus said. "Dragons are reputed to have gizzards, but I wouldn't know that for certain without closer examination. I wouldn't expect much cooperation from a dragon and I confess I'm not too curious as to whether or not dragons have gizzards—although I have heard marvelous stories of the powers of dragon gizzard-stones. Just look at this head cheese, will you? Who could resist, I ask you?"

"Meistari," Ofarir persisted, "I think you should bring Skyla to Herradshol where it is safer—and less likely for her to get out and go hunting for her . . . ah, favorite type of sustenance."

"Plumabrot?" Mistislaus sniffed a wrapped bundle covered with warts of green mold. "We keep her well supplied. She has no need to go hunting it."

"No, no, I meant her—well, you know she kills Krypplingur," Ofarir said nervously, darting a glance toward the tower stair.

"I've never seen any evidence to prove she does," Mistislaus replied rather more sharply than Jafnar had ever heard him. A menacing flash penetrated the amiable film over his eyes, but it was quickly gone the moment he uncorked a small bottle and smelled it. "Currant wine? This is my favorite."

"Come, Mistislaus, why don't you leave this wretched old place?" Ofarir said, rubbing his hands together in a miserly fashion before the fire's warmth. "We're most eager to see you safely established in your new rooms at Herradshol—more comfortable quarters, and far more safe from the vermin of Rangfara. My father Herrad is most eager for you to join him there. Henceforth, you shall spend no more nights in this wretched ruin, virtually unprotected."

"We don't need to renew this argument every day, do we?" Mistislaus inquired gently. "Our minds are made up to stay in Athugashol until Herrad is cured. Your hospitality is not being spurned or disdained. We simply like it here."

"Very well," Ofarir said, with a hint of an ugly expression flickering quickly over his countenance before smoothing away to an obliging smile. "If there's nothing I can do to change you mind, then I suppose I shall just leave it alone."

"Jafnar is healed nicely now," Mistislaus said. "I think he can manage to fetch our baskets now from the Skurdur and thereby save you a great deal of trouble."

"No, no, allow me to continue this kindness. Krypplingur thrive upon trouble," Ofarir said with a hint of fierce pride.

"It certainly follows wherever you go," Mistislaus said.

"We don't mind bringing your food at all," Ofarir went on. "It gives us an opportunity to get better acquainted. You're doing such a splendid job with my father's healing that I wish to do something in my own small way to repay you. I should have done something long ago to spare you the necessity of obtaining a wild boy to do your work. Shifty little rascals, for the most part, who grow up into the ugliest of characters. They always turn upon their masters eventually. If I were you," he leaned forward and confided, "I would get rid of that one there and quit feeding those others who hang around here."

"Thank you for your advice," Mistislaus said courteously.

On the fifth day, Mistislaus did not return at dawn. Nor did the baskets of food arrive. Jafnar scaled the walls and watched apprehensively, but there was no sign of the old wizard. There were more Krypplingur than usual skulking about, picking fights and bullying passersby. He had no chance of sneaking out to the Skurdur. Fortunately they had a few scraps of food left over from the previous day, in case Mistislaus felt the need to nourish his brain cells at odd moments, so they did not go without sustenance. Jafnar sent the wild boys through the Krypplingur line to spy out Herradshol and see if they could overhear any gossip about Mistislaus, but there was no word on the streets.

At dusk Ofarir marched up to the outer gate and thumped on it with his axe. Guthrum escorted him inside, barring the gate behind them in the faces of five Krypplingur.

"We have Mistislaus at Herradshol," Ofarir announced upon stepping into the room, with a fulsome grin at Skyla. "If you want to see him again, alive, you'd best pack your things and come with me now."

"You're holding him prisoner?" Guthrum rumbled, hefting his axe menacingly.

"Prisoner? No, not exactly, I wouldn't say," Ofarir said. "But he's most anxious that you comply with my wishes and come to Herradshol at once."

"I need time to think about changes," Skyla said. "I'm not a sudden person. You must recall, I am known to be daft. The idea of unexpected changes makes me very excitable, and you know that dreadful things can happen to me when I become frightened or excited. I'm not responsible for what might happen." Her eyes flashed around the room in a very excitable manner and her breathing came deep and quick.

"Skyla, no! Don't shift shapes!" Jafnar said in utmost alarm.

Ofarir took a hasty step backward. "Very well then, my lady, don't do anything I would regret. Don't change yourself into the lynx. I shall leave you to become accustomed to this idea. But I warn you, don't take overlong, and don't attempt to escape. Not unless you wish to see Mistislaus hung off the main gate of Rangfara," he added as if by afterthought, as he nimbly dodged around Guthrum through the door.

Skyla kept her eyes on him as long as he was in sight, racing from window to window and up the stairs like a mad thing to the high windows above.

She returned, rushing by Jafnar in a burst of cool wind, then halting suddenly by a slit window to gaze out.

"Skyla! What is it? Has something happened to Mistislaus already?" Jafnar demanded.

"Not yet, something hasn't," she answered, distractedly plucking at her hair tumbling untidily out of its fastenings. "But he doesn't have much time. I don't want to go with Ofarir. I shall never trust him."

"What shall we do?" Jafnar asked.

"We shall not go to Herradshol," Skyla said, scarcely paying him any heed as she wrestled with the decision. "This is what Mistislaus wants. We shall stay here and defend Mistislaus' valuable possessions. We have Guthrum to protect us, and all the wild boys."

"But we can't hold off the Krypplingur army forever," Jafnar said. "And they might hurt Mistislaus."

Her chin jutted out as she scowled and thought about it, with her arms crossed. Finally she said, "Surely they wouldn't hurt

Mistislaus. He's no threat to anything. Besides, he is the tool they hope to use to get us and the treasure."

"He's no threat to anything except Ofarir's becoming chieftain of Rangfara," Jafnar said. "If Herrad is cured, Ofarir won't be chieftain. And that is a terrible threat to Ofarir. He knows you're the snow lynx, Skyla. He wants to use those powers against his own father, and anyone else who opposes him. Without some such advantage, his chances of holding the chieftain's seat very long are very slim."

"He won't harm Mistislaus as long as I stay away," Skyla said in a low voice. "When he has me captured, he'll have no use for Mistislaus any longer."

Jafnar called a conference of the wild boys. Then he sent them into the Skurdur to steal some food and listen around the flaps of the ale booths. When they returned, they came into the house with trepidations, as if expecting Mistislaus or Guthrum to materialize at any moment and chase them away. Jafnar assured them they were safe from Guthrum, who was guarding the front gate against the Krypplingur stationed outside it. Gradually their fears eased, soothed perhaps by the succulent roast lamb they had snatched right off the baker's spit. They tore it apart with their fingers and devoured it, stuffing their mouths and quarreling good-naturedly and trying to talk all at once, relating all the news and gossip of the Skurdur. Jafnar realized how desperately he missed the rumors and lies that filtered down from Herradshol, the scrapes with the merchants and the Krypplingur.

"We've not seen anything of Illmuri," Ordvar said. "We've looked and looked. He must have a new lie-up we haven't found yet. Or maybe he's left Rangfara. Or he's dead."

"We hope he's dead," Modga added.

"And you'll never guess who's been outlawed," Einka added, swelling with importance.

"Alvara," Lofa said, stealing his thunder and earning a greasy swat from Einka.

"Alvara!" Jafnar repeated, glancing at Skyla, who had graciously bestowed the feast on the wild boys and retreated to a safe distance to nibble on her portion. They weren't nice eaters, and enforced manners inhibited their enjoyment.

"It seems to me," Modga whispered, leaning forward so that he almost sputtered right in Jafnar's face, "that everyone who comes in contact with that little witch ends up in a very bad way. If not dead. Illmuri and Alvara are outlawed, and Mistislaus is being held prisoner by the Krypplingur. You're next, Jafnar. Or we all are."

"I hope you choke, Modga," Jafnar said. "Let me give you a bone to help do it." He wiped off the grease and went to tell Skyla the news about Alvara.

"And I never did get to speak to her about what she knows of my ancestors," Skyla said regretfully. "I suppose I'll never see her again now."

"Not that I would go to her and ask her for help," Jafnar said with a scowl. "But sometimes it does seem we're running out of friends in Rangfara, doesn't it?"

On the following day Ofarir presented himself at the gate, which Guthrum barred with his axe.

"You're not coming in again, unless it's by force," he growled, an inviting sparkle in his eye. To his disappointment, Ofarir retreated a few paces.

"I only came to deliver a message from Mistislaus," he said, holding out a vellum in Mistislaus' own unmistakable writing. Jafnar carried it to Skyla to read. She broke the wax seal and studied it a moment before reading it aloud. Very clearly it instructed Skyla and Jafnar to pack up his valuables and to accompany Ofarir to Herradshol.

"You see," Ofarir said, "even Mistislaus knows it is futile to resist. I shall bring some thralls and a cart for your possessions. Tonight, after the second night watch, at midnight, you will surrender."

"I learned my distrust from my ancestors," Skyla said. "Such things take time to overcome."

"Of course," Ofarir said with a slight bow. "Until midnight then. Mistislaus is most anxious to see you again, and the worry is interfering with Herrad's cure. Wild boys and a surly old dwarf are not protection enough for you in this wretched old place. I'm sure I feel an evil influence whenever I'm here."

"So do I," Jafnar muttered.

"Time is getting short," Ofarir added, as if it were an afterthought. "As short as Krypplingur patience. I don't want to keep trotting back and forth between Athugashol and Herradshol. If this matter isn't satisfactorily settled by midnight tonight, you can expect something terrible to happen to Mistislaus by dawn."

When he was gone, Skyla began putting Mistislaus' things into boxes and baskets.

"Skyla, you can't go to Herradshol," Jafnar protested. "The Krypplingur will put your talents to evil uses. Once Herrad is dead, Ofarir will have no use for Mistislaus. And there's no way we can go anywhere near there. You'll never see us again."

"But you're my brother-kin," Skyla protested. "You must come and help me, all of you. And what about Mistislaus? We can't just abandon him."

"No, of course not. But I can't risk the entire Skylding clan in any crazy ventures rescuing Mistislaus. And I can't let you go there alone. Life was never this complicated when I was a wild boy. We stole to live, we ate what we stole, we hid afterward. It was nothing but a game."

"You must go away from here while you can, Jafnar," she said. "We know what the Krypplingur would do to wild boys."

"But that would be cowardly," he said. "We can't just go off and leave you to the Krypplingur."

"What shall we do then, Jafnar?" she asked.

He kneaded his temples with his fists. "I don't know. I shall think of something."

They worked until noonday, making a heap of books and crocks and boxes and baskets in the middle of the floor. At noon, Rangfara was at its quietest; nightfarers shunned the high sun, sleeping soundly in their daytime lie-ups; and the dayfarers were dozing in preparation for another night defending themselves from the nightfarers.

Jafnar followed his old habits and looked for a shady spot for a nap the moment the midday meal was finished—some scanty pickings stolen from the Skurdur. The Krypplingur had everyone on edge, knowing something was about to happen.

Just as he had settled himself in a cool windowsill overlooking the courtyard and the Hall of Stars, he heard a faint, urgent tapping at the street door. Looking down, he saw a ragged figure hunched on the stoop, knocking at the panels. One of the beggars or wanderers had gotten past Ofarir. Mistislaus had earned a reputation for feeding anyone who came and asked and was not put off by Guthrum's unfailingly hostile welcome. A noonday visitor was bound to put him into a fearful humor, disturbing him at the least desirable hour of the day. Jafnar heard him grousing in the gatekeeper's hut, like a bear disturbed in its den.

With a sigh, Jafnar hurried downstairs and opened the gate himself to admit the scruffy creature, wondering how the Krypplingur had overlooked this one.

"I know, you've come for something to eat," Jafnar said. "I've heard all the hard-luck tales there are to hear, so you can spare me yours."

"Jafnar, it's me, Alvara," the beggar whispered, pushing aside the ragged hood slightly to reveal her face. "Inside, quickly, before the Krypplingur get suspicious."

"What are you doing here?" Jafnar demanded, once they were inside with the door barred. "Twenty Krypplingur are surrounding Gibbet Hill. You're outlawed. They'll kill you on sight."

"I must see Skyla," Alvara said, turning as Skyla came down the stairs from her tower room. "There's not much time. For an outlaw, each day may be the last—even each moment. So much I could have told you, if only you'd trusted me when you had the chance. Now I fear there are things you'll never find out."

"Sit down," Skyla said. "Tell me what you can."

"I can't stay more than an instant," Alvara said, shaking her head. "I can hardly stand still a moment before I'm spied again. This much I can tell you, though—don't trust Ofarir for a moment. Rumor has it he's taken Mistislaus prisoner, and you're next. You must not go to Herradshol. I can help you escape, if we act swiftly."

"But I can't just go off and leave all his books and possessions for the Krypplingur," Skyla said. "The knowledge and skills here must be preserved. Mistislaus sent me this message instructing me to pack up everything and send it to him at Herradshol. He also says I must come in order to save his life. Ofarir said something terrible will happen to Mistislaus at dawn if I don't surrender."

"Don't do it!" Alvara said, taking the vellum and studying it first one way, then another. "It's only a trick to waste time and to ensnare you. Look at this, my child. See the first letters of all the lines. One unskilled in the perusal of runes would not notice, but the letters spell out the word 'Beware.' "

Skyla snatched the vellum and studied it. Her face blanched even more, and she let it fall out of her fingers unnoticed as her gaze shifted away and became unfocused.

"You've got only a few hours to make your escape," Alvara said. "Come to the Horse-tower tonight. Be there when the Krypplingur ring the gong to change the last day watch at dusk. So little time, and so much to be done!"

"Can't you tell me anything at all, right now?" Skyla demanded. "My parents' names, at least? If I knew my heritage, I could help Mistislaus. I could command the walls that held him to turn to dust, so he could walk through them. It's the last and most difficult of the four powers—the power of destruction—and I can't do it without more knowledge, or I will become a destroyer myself, forever dark and doomed."

"I daren't speak yet," Alvara whispered, her eyes darting back and forth. "You must come to my safe place. Then you will have the knowledge you seek. Mistislaus and his books will be saved. There are eyes and ears everywhere in Rangfara, glad to see or hear for a piece of gold. And not only Krypplingur would gladly see me die. I may have already sealed my doom in coming here. Be careful, be canny. Watch for Krypplingur following you. Don't take the direct way. I shall be watching for you."

"I'll be there," Skyla said.

"Skyla!" Jafnar said warningly.

"It's our only hope of saving Mistislaus," Skyla said. "If I have knowledge, I will meet Ofarir with weapons to fight him."

Jafnar let Alvara out the back door and watched her glide across the courtyard and scramble up the wall. In moments she had vanished into the ruins beyond the Hall of Stars, escaping even the watchful eyes of the wild boys.

Skyla's eyes glowed; she scarcely heard him. "Think what I might find out, Jafnar! Names! Ancestry! Tomorrow at this time, I may know exactly who I am and what I am supposed to do with these powers!"

"You are a Skylding and you're supposed to reclaim Rangfara for our clan," Jafnar said with a nasty twinge of envy. "How do you know Alvara can be trusted to tell you the truth, if she does know something?"

"I shall know the truth when I find it," Skyla said. "I won't leave any opportunity without trying."

The last Krypplingur day watch signaled its conclusion at dusk with a brassy wallop of an ancient weathered gong that hung in the courtyard of Herradshol. Its resonating tones served as the timekeeping method for all of Rangfara. In years past, less warlike hands had signified the passing quarters of the day to regulate the hours of the inhabitants. The Krypplingur adopted its use as an efficient method of changing the ever-present guards posted around Herradshol and other significant locations.

When the gong sounded, Jafnar and Skyla took advantage of the momentary confusion of the Krypplingur tramping to and fro changing guards. In a matter of moments, they were over the wall and into the maze of alleyways of Rangfara. Shortly they were crouching behind a heap of rubble, looking down into the courtyard of the Horse-tower. Alvara's packhorses were gone and there was no light in the tent. Enough daylight remained in the sky to show the details of the courtyard and the tent. They waited for some sign of her presence, while the bats overhead swooped above the ruins in twittering pursuit of invisible prey and the muted uproar of the Skurdur took on its ugly nighttime overtones.

"She can't show any sign," Skyla whispered. "She's an outlaw, and the Krypplingur are looking for her. Don't be such an old woman, Jafnar, always so suspicious."

"It's how I've kept myself alive," Jafnar said quietly. "Old women are very clever. It doesn't feel right here. It might be a trap. The Horse-tower has a bad reputation for evil spirits."

"I can handle evil spirits," Skyla said, sketching a rune in the air. "Now come on. I must talk to her."

They crossed the courtyard quickly, moving from one shadow to the next, until a short dash brought them up to the tent. Skyla froze with a hissed warning. Everything from inside the tent had been thrown out, trampled, and smashed. The small animal cages were crushed and some of the little creatures lay strewn about, dead. The stones of Alvara's altar were cast away and dishonored with urine. The evil presence of those who had done the deed still hung in the air like a bad smell that made Jafnar's skin prickle.

After a stunned moment, Jafnar reached out to grip Skyla's arm to draw her away to safety, but she twisted out of his grasp like an eel and hurried straight toward the tent. Jafnar floundered after her, gasping in the lingering atmosphere of death-wreaking.

She halted suddenly, stooping over a pile of ragged clothing, pulling it aside and revealing the marble-white countenance of Alvara, staring sightlessly into the night sky. Jafnar felt the breath squeezed out of him. He grasped Skyla's arm to pull her away and felt a peculiar dizzy sensation pass from her into him, as if he had just eaten a large portion of plumabrot. Helplessly he stood back and watched Skyla kneel down beside Alvara, her deft fingers searching around Alvara's throat. She found a wire, almost imbedded in Alvara's flesh. With a few quick words under her breath, Skyla severed the wire. Jafnar saw a small pinpoint of red light, then the wire snapped. Skyla continued to chant softly. Alvara gasped weakly for air, or it may have been a final death spasm. Then her eyes closed and blinked, fastening upon Skyla and Jafnar in a flash of recognition.

"Skyla!" she whispered. "Get away from here! Now!"

"But you promised—"

"No time! Just go! And stay away from Ofarir! Don't believe a word he tells you!" the tortured voice hissed. Alvara's eyes blazed and she fastened one hand on Skyla's shoulder to give her a shake. "They'll be watching for you! You mustn't let them capture you! Now away!"

Jafnar seized Skyla's arm and dragged her away, back toward the safety of Rangfara's maze of streets, running as if pursued over the uneven mossy stones. After plunging into the last archway before the street beyond, they halted, both suddenly struck by the thought there was no safety for them to run to, no protection at Athugashol except Guthrum, and no deliverance in sight.

As they crouched there, gasping for breath, a narrow shadow suddenly swooped forward, blocking their escape to the Skurdur. Jafnar fell back and drew his sword to defend Skyla. He wasn't schooled, but he knew he was skillful enough to put up a good defense.

"Run, Skyla!" he commanded. "Ordvar will help you!"

"What are you doing here?" a harsh voice spat. "Put away that sword, Jafnar! Don't you think you've been foolish enough for one night? At least I caught up with you before you did anything fatal!"

It was the voice of Illmuri, and the faint sordid gleam from an ale tent revealed half his face, lowering out at them from the gloom.

"You followed us?" Jafnar demanded. "Spying on us?"

"Only to make certain nothing happened to you. It was the height of idiocy following Alvara into her little trap. I'm amazed to see that you actually escaped from her."

"She was nearly dead when we got there," Jafnar said. "Someone destroyed her tent and her things and tried to kill her. I wouldn't be at all surprised it you knew something about that."

Illmuri glanced quickly back toward Alvara's tent, then thrust Jafnar and Skyla ahead of him away from the doorway, down the narrow street and into another dark niche in the wall. Warily he scanned the alleyway.

"I've got enough to do to keep myself alive," Illmuri said. "Let alone the time to murder Alvara, however much she deserves it. You're lucky someone else got to her before she ensnared you in some holding spell or some such to extract the secret of that treasure out of you."

"She said she had something I was searching for," Skyla said. "The names of my parents and my ancestry."

"Bah! She hasn't got it," Illmuri snorted. "The only one who knows for certain is old Skriftur, wherever he lies. And if anyone could find him, it would be me, as much time as I've spent looking for him."

"But you're not a Skylding," Skyla said. "You'll never find him."

"No Skylding ever will if there aren't any Skyldings left alive!" Illmuri retorted. "Now that Ofarir's got Mistislaus, it makes my job far more difficult. We've got to get you out of Rangfara for a while. My clan will be willing to defend you. I can get you out if you'll do exactly as I tell you and ask no questions."

"We'll defend ourselves," Jafnar answered.

"And we're not leaving Rangfara if Mistislaus is a prisoner," Skyla said.

"If you'll let me help you out of Rangfara, I'll come back for Mistislaus," Illmuri said.

"Out of Rangfara and into what?" Jafnar asked. "Rangfara belongs to the Skyldings, and we'll stay here until we make it ours once again."

"Against Ofarir? Against the entire Krypplingur clan and all their unsavory cousins?" Illmuri hissed. "How do you think you can do that, with just a handful of raggedy wild boys and a young untrained girl?"

"It's the right thing, and it will happen," Skyla said. "And I'm not completely unskilled. If you're finished talking, we'll be on our way now, if you don't mind."

"Where are you going?" Illmuri demanded.

"Back to Athugashol, of course," Skyla said. "I've got all of Mistislaus' books and spells and things to protect."

In spite of their objections, Illmuri shadowed them to Athugashol on the pretext of protecting them. Guthrum was waiting when they came over the wall in the courtyard, down from the rooftop ways Jafnar knew so well, where a pack of wild boys could cross most of Rangfara without touching the earth once. Even Illmuri was a bit shaky after some of the harrowing traverses of narrow walls and buttresses offering a thin and crumbling walkway over a heart-clutching drop into darkness below.

Guthrum growled and muttered over their absence as he escorted them to the hall, darting crusty glances at Illmuri all the while.

"It's been more than should be expected of me to watch over these younglings and all of the master's stuff," he grumbled. "Especially what with them haring off and not telling me, and what with the master gone unannounced. We could do with someone else around here to watch things."

"I'm doing my best to watch out for all of you," Illmuri said. "It's not easy being outlawed in Rangfara when the gates are shut. I want to get you all out of here and safely into the hands of clan Galdur, until we can free Mistislaus from Herradshol."

Guthrum grunted and shook his head. "I shall stay here until the master comes back. Or I shall go and get him. But I won't leave him in Rangfara as long as he or I draw breath in this world. A Dvergar is not a slacker once he has assigned himself the protection of a master."

Inside the hall, Illmuri looked at the untidy piles and heaps of Mistislaus' prized possessions.

"Ofarir is sending a cart for it at midnight," Skyla said. "We were trying to pack it up, but we only made the mess worse, I'm afraid."

"Something will have to be done about this," Illmuri said. "There's a cartload here, and no place for a cart where we'll be going. We can't allow these things to fall into the hands of the Krypplingur. I know several people in Rangfara who'll be glad to hide some stuff for a while. Here, we'll begin by putting some of the smaller things into his satchel."

Illmuri opened Mistislaus' satchel, releasing a cloud of dust. With unabashed curiosity he peered into the bag, then felt around inside it with his hand.

"Empty!" he said. "What sort of wizard has an empty satchel? Either a charlatan or an expert. I don't yet know which Mistislaus is. Jafnar, begin by putting in those little bags. We've not much time, but perhaps we can save a few of the most valuable things."

Jafnar obligingly tucked the bags into the satchel, then some little boxes, a few vials, then a small book or two, and the bag showed scarcely a bulge. Lost as he was in his own worried thoughts about the future, he continued loading things into the satchel, scarcely aware of what he was doing until he shoved in something rather large that ought to have taken up all the room, but it didn't. The satchel was still limp, and when he looked inside, it was completely empty. With a wave of gooseflesh, he dropped it and leaped across the room like a startled deer.

Illmuri examined the bag and began to chuckle. "It's one of the oldest and best ways to carry things around," he said. "Wizards were the first to discover that there is a certain necessity to carrying around possessions. Right after them came traveling trash merchants. Whatever you put into this satchel simply becomes much smaller and easier to carry around."

"I don't see a thing in there," Jafnar declared. "It's completely empty."

"You aren't able to see it because it's organized into a far more compact form. Virtually invisible. Only Mistislaus knows how to pull it out again. Or sometimes, it's like dropping the things down a chute, and they come out someplace else. For all we know," Illmuri said as he shoved several books into the satchel, "we're dropping this stuff on someone's head at a considerable distance from here. I had an old uncle, a wizard, in my clan who was always receiving strange things from an unknown source. Any time of the night or day he could expect to be showered with the worst assortment of junk. Contrary to what you might think, wizardry can be a very funny occupation."

"Even when you kill each other?" Skyla asked.

"Even then, most especially," Illmuri said with an amused half smile. "Retrievers of spirits can spin some fascinating yarns, too. The mixups they get into, and the trouble—" As if suddenly recalling himself, Illmuri gave his shoulders a shake and scowled grimly, more like his usual self. "Enough idle chatter. We've got to get this done and get ourselves gone before Ofarir gets here."

"We haven't agreed to any help from you," Jafnar said, bristling contentiously.

"You needn't agree to anything," Illmuri said. "I'm taking you out of Rangfara whether you like it or not."

"In this way you think to force us to help you find the treasure?" Jafnar demanded. "Well, it won't work."

"Silence, upstart, before I cuff your ear," Illmuri retorted. "I'd like to see my old masters in the clan teach you some manners. It would be a sight that would cheer me to the bottom of my heart. You know nothing of respect and discipline. The only way they are learned at your age is through a great deal of pain and misery. Now then, are we done here?" He surveyed the room a moment. Nothing remained except a clutter of old furniture.

"Not quite," Skyla said, turning and running lightly up the stairs to her little room, adding over her shoulder something about not leaving until she had what she had come for.

Illmuri started after her then hesitated, hearing Guthrum sound a challenge at the street gate.

"Curse him, he's here early!" Illmuri muttered.

"What are we going to do? Fight? Hide? If we get out the back before they see us, we can get into the Hall of Stars and across the roofs—Skyla!" Jafnar dashed up the steps to her tower. "Skyla, we've got to get out of here! Ofarir's here already! Skyla?"

The little room was empty, except for a small rush lamp still burning in a niche in the rocky wall and Skyla's narrow straw bed. Several items of clothing were neatly folded, as if waiting to be packed in the basket of her possessions lying on the floor. Also on the bed was her hateful bag of spells. The lamp fluttered slightly in the breath coming in through the tiny window. Jafnar crossed to it in one stride. Too small for a girl to slip through, but ample space for the supple form of a cat. A few silvery hairs still clung to the rough stones.

Jafnar flew down the stairs. Guthrum was bawling threats outside, while the Krypplingur rammed at the gate with their shoulders, cursing and snarling. Illmuri waited with Mistislaus' satchel slung over one shoulder.

"She's gone! Shifted shapes!" Jafnar said tersely.

Illmuri slapped his brow and his eyes darted around the room. "Where could she have gone?"

"Alvara," Jafnar said with a groan. "Alvara said she knew Skyla's ancestry and all the secrets she needs to master the last of the four powers."

"She'll be heading for the Horse-tower then," Illmuri said swiftly. "Well, at least she's safe. Now show me the way out of this place before we both find our hides nailed to the wall. Enriching some bloody-fisted Krypplingur with my head-price is not my idea of living a productive life."

Guthrum sounded a furious bellow as the gate parted with a splintering crash. Jafnar and Illmuri dived toward the arrow slits in the front of the house to witness the Krypplingur pouring into the narrow courtyard.

"Now then!" Guthrum roared in delight, with a furious swirling of his axe, like a mad harvester getting ready to scythe a few acres of ripe wheat.

The Krypplingur charged forward, jostling and entangling with each other in their eagerness to engage in battle with the surly old dwarf. The insults of the past four days burned in their memories, raising a terrific thirst for vengeance. Guthrum took a defensive stance in the gatekeeper's niche, bellowing a stream of encouraging epithets and colorful insults. Ofarir strode past them toward the front stoop.

"Too late!" Jafnar cried, throwing down Mistislaus' satchel with a dusty thump. "We're trapped!"

"Well, that's it," Illmuri muttered, looking around distractedly. "I can hold them off awhile from Skyla's room. There's only room for one of them at a time on that stairway."

They were halfway up the stairs when the chilling squall of the lynx pierced the nasty din of the fighting in the courtyard below. At once there was silence. Then with a clangor of arms and weapons the Krypplingur charged for the gate leading back to the street, jamming shoulders in the narrow archway and swearing at each other in their rush to escape.

"Skyla!" Jafnar whispered, and dashed down the stairs. He fumbled with Mistislaus' complicated locks and bolts a moment then charged into the darkness with Illmuri at his heels.

Chapter Seventeen

A muffled, choking cry was followed by a sputtering and gurgling sound, as if some creature were drowning. Then the gruff questioning calls of the Krypplingur guards penetrated the silence. Jafnar heard the sounds of them taking up positions outside the gate and along the street wall.

"Skyla!" Jafnar whispered hoarsely. "Where are you, Skyla? Answer me!"

The narrow courtyard was as dark as a well. He saw nothing of Ofarir or Skyla until he nearly tripped over the girl crouching on the path leading to the doorstep. Behind, Illmuri flung the door open wide, revealing the spectacle of Skyla leaning over Ofarir, his throat spurting a black gout of blood as he sputtered and struggled in his death throes.

"Great Hod!" Illmuri muttered. "Ofarir's murdered, right here on our doorstep! The Krypplingur are going to take this very badly!"

"Halloa! Ofarir! What's going on in there?" came the wary shout from the street, which elicted an answering barrage of curses from Guthrum.

"You get rid of the Krypplingur," Jafnar whispered rapidly. "I'll fetch the horse. We've got to get rid of him before the Krypplingur think Skyla did it. We'll dump him down the Kjallari and no one will ever know."

"Jafnar," Skyla said. "He's not quite dead. I know I can save him. I want to try."

Jafnar looked at Ofarir choking on his own blood and clawing feebly at his neck with his hands.

"But why?" Jafnar demanded, shaking his head and shuddering. He looked away from Skyla, fearing and hating to look at her.

"He's our enemy! He's got Mistislaus! Why would you want to save him? Didn't you try to kill him?"

"No, I did not!" Skyla retorted, turning to him with such a blaze in her eyes that he took a step back, fearing a lynx transformation on the spot. It could bode ill for anyone she was angry at. "I found him like this. I was going to find Alvara, but I changed my mind and came back. Someone had just done it. Now keep those Krypplingur out of here. I'm going to call him back. He's trying to pull away, but the body has still got too much strength."

"I'd suggest doing something about the body then," Illmuri said half to himself.

"Can't you see it?" Skyla breathed in awe, still hovering in morbid fascination, as if he were one of her small animal experiments. "His spirit is hanging over him, not quite free, like a butterfly escaping its cocoon. I can easily retrieve him."

"Skyla! This is no place for experiments!" Jafnar sputtered. To his own astounded eyes, a cloud indeed hovered over Ofarir's body, glowing with a faint light.

"The shadow world is not to be trifled with by an amateur," Illmuri said. "Let's drag him inside, at least, where we can hold off those Krypplingur. When they smell the blood they're going to know something's amiss."

Together they dragged Ofarir toward the doorway, still twitching and flailing weakly, leaving a wide and incriminating trail of fresh blood behind them. The Kryppling was far heavier than he looked, and they had to stop on the doorstep, puffing and trembling.

Outside the gate, the Krypplingur bawled in fury now, as if they had caught a whiff of Ofarir's blood.

Jafnar and Illmuri each seized a leg and dragged Ofarir inside the hall. Skyla sat gazing down into the twisted features of the dying man, evidently fascinated by the blood that had poured out of the wound. She hummed and whispered to herself, as daft as poor Thogn.

"Skyla! Come away from that!" Jafnar implored. "You heard Illmuri. The shadow realm is not for amateurs. Leave him alone to die in peace!"

Skyla ignored him and went on with her humming, tracing the line of the gash with one finger, paying no heed to the blood that soiled her hands and her gown.

Ofarir threshed about, shoving Skyla away from him with surprising strength and rising to a sitting position. He looked down at the blood plastering most of his clothing and pooling on the ground. Instead of the black and gaping wound in his throat, bubbling air and sluggish blood, there was nothing now but a great deal of sticky, drying gore.

"Illmuri!" Jafnar cried, his blood turning cold. He felt as if every hair on his body suddenly stood on end, quivering. "Something's happening!"

Illmuri lit his staff with a brilliant white light that turned the room to shifting shadows and merciless glare. He passed the staff over Ofarir's body.

"Ofarir, are you dead or are you alive?" Illmuri demanded. "Speak if you live, or give some sign."

Ofarir's hands traveled up and down his form, feeling the black beads of the healed wound across his throat. "I'm alive," he said hoarsely, holding up his hands, which trembled and jerked in peculiar spasms, "but what has that witling done to me?"

At that moment, the Krypplingur charged the door of the hall with a furious bellow. On the third charge, the door came down in pieces and the Krypplingur surged into the room in one concerted spurt of destructive energy, with Guthrum snipping at their heels with his broadsword. The sight of Illmuri and his flaring staff brought them up short immediately. Guthrum chuckled dourly from the rear.

The armored Krypplingur edged suspiciously around the light, glancing about them nervously. Their leader squinted at Ofarir and Skyla through the eye-holes of a helmet fashioned to look like a skull.

"What has happened to you?" he demanded.

"The lynx has struck again!" a Krypplingur said in a voice of horror, and the other Krypplingur bristled and snarled, sniffing at the blood as if they were facing mortal combat. All six Krypplingur sweated like war-horses, gripping their axes as they gazed from Illmuri clutching his flaring staff to the bloodied form of Ofarir.

"Fools!" Ofarir gasped, rising ponderously, swaying to his feet. "Do I look dead to you? Has the lynx ever only wounded anyone before? Has she ever let anyone survive? It was no animal that did this. It was human hands that tore my flesh."

The heavy-footed Krypplingur all skittered backward a few steps, making signs to ward off the walking dead.

"Beware, he's walking!" one of the Krypplingur said, and they all retreated further.

"Alive! Alive again, back to mortal form. A face, hands, a body, all mine again." Ofarir cackled wheezily and turned a crazed stare upon the gaping Krypplingur. Then he staggered, almost falling, shaking his head with a sharp cry of agony. "No, no! Get out! Go away, all of you! Get out and leave me alone!"

"He's mad!" one of the Krypplingur declared.

"No! Idiot!" Ofarir shouted, pulling himself up sharply. With uneven, jerky motions he walked a few paces up and down the length of the room. "Do I look mad to you, Ofus? Is it not I, your chieftain Ofarir, speaking to you?"

Ofus squinted through his skull-shape helmet. "I don't know," he rumbled suspiciously, taking a step backward as Ofarir approached. The Krypplingur all shrank back at his approach, hissing and muttering among themselves and making signs behind their backs to ward off evil.

"You're nothing but ignorant hackers and slashers and killers of small children," Ofarir retorted, his voice deep and rough, growing stronger by the moment. His features also shifted to a dark and lowering expression, with only a few glimpses of his own weasel face in between. The threatening glower and the harsh voice prevailed.

"It was human hands that did this, or you may boil my head for a pike." He touched the ragged mark on his neck. Slowly his dull eyes turned, causing the Krypplingur all to quail before his unblinking stare. Then his gaze fixed upon Skyla, who was gazing at him with an increasingly troubled expression. "But it was the girl who healed the body and retrieved the spirit from the dark void of Niflheim. Just a girl, a young and seemingly innocent girl. A Skylding girl, when the last of the Skyldings were supposed to be dead thirteen years ago. How do you account for this oversight?" He uttered a raucous, snarling laugh so chilling that even the hardened Krypplingur flinched and looked at one another apprehensively. "The Skyldings are supposed to be dead, long before the first signs commence. The girl knows how to open the gates and go through, but she does not know how to close them behind her. You'd better not trifle with things you haven't mastered, my pretty pet."

Skyla blanched pale. "You're a vile thing. You don't belong here."

"Oh yes, I do belong here," he answered. "I must protect what is mine, before you stumble onto it. You're dangerously close, my dear, dangerously close."

"He's befuddled as a bot fly," one of the Krypplingur muttered.

"Something has gone wrong," Illmuri said. "You've got the wrong spirit into him, Skyla! Do you know anything about casting out?"

"Casting out? Casting out?" Ofarir boomed with a thunderous scowl.

"Yes! Help me!" choked the old voice of Ofarir, half strangled, as if it were being tortured and squeezed.

"Silence!" Ofarir snarled to himself in reply. "You're nothing but an idiot! Stay out of my way or I shall make it very painful for you!"

"Oh no," Skyla said in dismay. "It's gone wrong again. I thought I was over that. There are so many disembodied ones trying to get back into a living form of any kind, all pushing and shoving. This one got past me."

"You're nothing but a bungling novice," the spirit growled with a savage grin. "You don't have the strength of a master retriever."

"Who are you, spirit?" Illmuri demanded, fanning his staff's end gently, creating a blue mist. "Why do you return to annoy the living? Tell us your name and your business."

"Mistislaus would know who I am," the voice spat with venom. "He's the one who sent me here—and now, thanks to his little pet, I have come back." The creature laughed, a burst of uproarious, mirthless cackling. "Mistislaus thought to get rid of me, but now I'm back to finish the job we started so long ago. The living realm thought it had seen the last of me when I was put to death. How I laughed to see all the haughty Skyldings joining me in the shadow realm, those who thought I was not worthy to engender the foretold clan of the wizard warrior! All those who scoffed at me are now nothing but shadows, while I, Kraftugur, am a real, living, breathing being once more! This time there are no self-righteous Skyldings to stand in the way. And very shortly, there will be no Mistislaus either!"

Ofarir's voice burst in, rushing desperately. "No! They mustn't be harmed! Mistislaus! Skyla! You've got to help me! You Krypplingur, you know my voice! Don't listen to him! Ofus, you know my voice. I command you to bring the girl safely to Herrad's hall, if you have any regard for me at all—" He ended with a scream, pawing at his head as if a swarm of bees had attacked him.

"It is Ofarir's voice," said Ofus, of the skull-shaped helmet. He stepped forward boldly. "We will take our orders only from Ofarir. We don't know who you are, but you have no right to be here."

Like lightning, Ofarir's hand shot out and struck Ofus a staggering blow that sent him reeling. Gasping, he struggled to rise, half stunned. Felling a Kryppling at one blow was no mean accomplishment.

"I am your master now," Ofarir's new voice growled. Eyes like those of a mad and ravening wolf glared out of Ofarir's weasel face. "Do as I tell you, or you will all perish." He held up his hand and squeezed something invisible in it, and Ofus uttered a terrible howl of agony, clutching his chest as if he were mortally wounded.

"But you'll find I am a reasonable master," Ofarir said, dropping his hand and releasing Ofus, leaving him gasping and astonished to find himself alive. "If you are obedient."

The Krypplingur guards cringed away anxiously. Ofarir's body swayed as if pulled in several directions at once.

"Get out! Leave me alone!" Ofarir's voice whimpered.

"Silence!" the new voice roared, and Ofarir's voice yelped and whimpered.

Illmuri raised his staff and pointed. "I command you to depart at once from the sphere of living. Go back to the place of the dead where you belong!"

"You won't get rid of Kraftugur that easily," the creature said with an evil chuckle. "None of you. You don't have the power, my friend." His leaden eyes suddenly flared, and he made a gesture, sending Illmuri staggering backward, gasping. Another gesture and Illmuri fell back against the wall, his knees buckling as his eyes rolled upward. Insensible, he sagged and collapsed into a motionless heap.

"And you, dolt—" Ofarir's voice uttered a tormented, muffled shriek. "I don't want to hear from you again. Now the girl has talent. She has the retriever's gift—inexpert, perhaps, but promising." He leaned closer to gaze into Skyla's eyes with his flat dead stare, and she recoiled, her breaths quick and uneven. "A pity she is a Skylding and must therefore die before Samhain. But before then, she can be useful. The legions in Hel waiting for deliverance are the new masters of Rangfara."

"Never!" Skyla replied. "You are completely evil! There is no light in you at all, only darkness and the desire for destruction!"

"Yes, of course," Kraftugur purred. "Destruction is the only way to deal with one's enemies. Now enough of this chatter. I wish to see my dear old friend and associate Mistislaus. Once the two of us held the future of Rangfara in the palms of our hands. Now we hold its final destruction." His fingers closed like claws, squeezing the life out of an invisible foe in a death grip. "Bring her to Herradshol. I can hardly wait to see my dear old friend Herrad once more. How I've yearned to see him join me in the shadow realm. And that one—" He spun around suddenly in Jafnar's direction like a hound scenting a rabbit. His lips parted in a sly grin. "Bring me that one, also. He's a Skylding, and I'm going to extract beads of truth from him like rubies from a toad."

The Krypplingur growled in astonishment and surged forward to grab him.

"Run, Jafnar!" Skyla screamed.

"Skyla, come on! Change! Let's get out of here!" Jafnar gasped, dodging the Krypplingur.

"No, I'm going to be with Mistislaus! Go, Jafnar!" She spoke some words rapidly, gesturing in his direction.

"Skyla!" He heard his own voice turn to a high-pitched wailing cry, felt his hands and feet turn to paws on the floor. His viewpoint dropped nearly to the ground and the Krypplingur loomed over him in a blurred ring of gaping, screaming mouths and wildly bulging eyes.

"Snow lynx!" someone bellowed, and the room exploded into a roaring cacophony of trampling, crashing, and shouting. They fought among themselves to get away like drowning rats fighting over a splinter.

Jafnar looked at Skyla again, pleading silently.

"Go, Jafnar!" she commanded.

With a floating leap he gained the vantage of the stairs to her room, and from thence through the window and out onto the rooftops.

Ofarir uttered a guttural roar of rage and frustration. Clenching Illmuri's staff, he laid it about the heads and shoulders of the Krypplingur until he had their fears subdued.

"The lynx is gone," he said in a soothing voice bordering on a snarl. "All Skyldings are lynxes. Do you wonder they linger still, eating your vitals for revenge? Yes, there are yet Skyldings among you, but I have returned to ferret them out. This little child, with her innocent eyes and pale skin like fine silk—"

"Guard the girl, you idiots!" Ofarir's own voice burst forth. "Don't let him hurt her! She's the one who brought me back to life! She's the only one who can save me from this curse! Don't let anyone harm her—" He was cut off with a strangled squawk.

"Be silent, you weakling," the harsh voice said. "I shall decide who lives and dies around here—you included."

The Krypplingur eyed Ofarir uneasily. They were still breathing raggedly from their confrontation with the dreaded snow lynx. Ofarir's body shivered in the grip of a powerful convulsion. His eyes glazed and rolled around, and he bared his teeth in a speechless roar of uncontrollable rage. The Krypplingur flinched and shuffled uneasily, some forward and some toward the gate.

"What should we do, Ofus?" several of them murmured in consternation.

Ofus raised his shoulders as he drew in a deep breath.

"Do as he says," he answered. He stepped forward and gingerly laid one paw on Skyla's shoulder. "Come with us, girl, and don't attempt to escape or a little thing like you may be unintentionally harmed."

"Don't worry, Ofus," Skyla said in a voice of supreme control and authority. "I have no intention of escaping. Now if you'll be so kind, please take me to Mistislaus in Herradshol at once."

Ofarir uttered a chilling laugh. "You shall see your precious Mistislaus soon enough. You buffoons begin a search immediately for the rest of those cursed orphans. These white-haired, whey-faced Skyldings will show us where the treasure lies. You'd like that, wouldn't you, my Kryppling friends? When we find it, there's a share for all of you, more gold and jewels than you've seen in your entire lives! Bring me the Skylding orphans alive, and you'll be rewarded with a hundred marks in gold for each one!"

It was the right key to turn in the minds of the Krypplingur. Their eyes behind their helmets immediately lighted up with avarice.

Jafnar invited them to come after him with a shrill wail, pleased to see them fall into disarray once more. Only the harsh bellowing of Ofarir kept them from fleeing. His words and powers lashed among the Krypplingur like a whip, bringing them up short into sweating, trembling ranks.

"Now then, you cowards," Ofarir growled when he had them subdued, "you shall know what it is like to have a real master. What clan Krypplingur needs is discipline and a strong leader. What a lucky day this is for you, if you only knew it."

Jafnar watched from a high rooftop as the Krypplingur marched. His lynx eyes had no trouble discerning the slight, disdainful figure of Skyla walking in the midst of them. The possessed form of Ofarir lurched along with a rolling gait, dragging one leg slightly. Jafnar shivered, feeling the fur on his back standing on end, and a low wailing cat cry welled up inside him. The Krypplingur heard it and stopped dead, craning their necks to listen.

"Skyla! Get away!" he yelled, but the words were a shrill feline shriek. If she understood him, she had no intention of obeying. She spared him not a glance and stayed with the Krypplingur as they hurried away, their weapons bristling with readiness, craning their necks around to watch every shadow.

Jafnar stalked them from the tops of walls and rooftops all the way to Herradshol. Ofarir gazed around intently each time a lynx cry shattered the restless night.

"Cursed Skyldings," the voice that possessed him growled, in a tone of dire hatred. "I wish all their carcasses had rotted in heaps, picked by the carrion eaters. Long I slept, thinking all was secure. And then came this girl into Hel's gate, with her hair white as the moon and those great eyes like owls' eyes, looking you through and through—Skylding eyes if ever I saw them. I knew then I had to return and finish the work I started."

He glowered at Skyla, who shrank back in the grip of the Kryppling who held her arm.

"I've done nothing to deserve your hatred," she said. "I was not even born when Rangfara was destroyed by the Krypplingur. I don't know what threat you think I am to you. But I do know that you don't belong here, and you are not Ofarir."

He hissed at her furiously, his face a knotted grimace. "Silence, you white-haired demoness! All the Skyldings must be dead by Samhain! Have you not seen the signs already, you fools? Has the snow lynx not stalked you as prey? Has not one of the old wise ones returned to the halls of Rangfara? Doesn't anyone remember any of the old prophecies? Shame, shame on all of you! You don't deserve the chieftain's seat of Rangfara!"

"He's mad," one of the Krypplingur muttered, once they were inside the safe walls of Herradshol.

"Believe it if you will," Ofarir replied with a harsh cackle. "Take me to Herrad, Ofus. You can't imagine how anxious I am to see him again. And bring the Skylding girl with you."

Ofus blinked behind his skull helmet as he took Skyla by the arm and led the way down the dank passageway to Herrad's quarters. He glanced over his shoulder often at Ofarir treading at his heels. Ofarir lurched along at an uncharacteristically clumsy gait, even for a Krypplingur, one leg dragging slightly. Even for a drunken Krypplingur, Ofarir moved strangely and talked nonsense like a witling. Ofus shook his shoulders and muttered a few words under his breath to ward off evil as they approached the doors to Herrad's quarters.

"You may go," Ofarir said to Ofus. To the guard at the door he said, "Open up, or I'll have you gutted and hung before dawn." He reached one hand out to grab Skyla, but she darted in through the doors before they were half open, toward the dim welcome of a smoldering light in the room beyond.

"Mistislaus!" she exclaimed, seeing his familiar figure reposing in a chair beside Herrad's couch. She crossed the room in one streak and buried herself against his vast and comforting belly, wrapping her arms around him like the tendrils of a young vine.

"What's this? What are you doing here?" he exclaimed.

"I've done something terrible," she murmured, turning her head toward Ofarir, who came inexorably forward at his dragging pace, grinning a death's head welcome.

"I brought your pet to you," he said in his unfamiliar cawing voice, leering at Mistislaus and giving him a conspicuous wink.

"Ofarir? What happened?" Mistislaus sputtered, not taking his eyes off him.

"Nothing worth mentioning. Good evening, Father. I trust you are feeling well tonight?"

Herrad craned his neck forward, narrowing his eyes in utmost suspicion. "I'm not dead yet, as you can plainly see. I know that's a great disappointment to you, but I intend to live a few more years yet. What have you been drinking? Some foreign brew?"

"Ever hasty with your evil opinions of me, aren't you? It was always thus, was it not? Particularly back in the early days of our sojourn in Rangfara. If it hadn't been for me, you would have accomplished nothing—just as you have accomplished nothing since the last Skylding throat was cut. Or the throat you thought to be the last Skylding throat. They yet live, you rotting old fool. While you were searching the crypts for treasure, Skyldings were living in your midst, treasuring up their thirst for revenge. That seat you sit upon, your so-called chieftain's chair, is going to be stolen from you by a Skylding, and if a Skylding sits upon that seat when the sky signs come, then all will be lost from the Oskiptur mountains in the south to the frozen tundras of the north. You let Skyldings live, you useless piece of offal, and this girl standing before you is one, and *she* will take the chieftain's seat from you, if she is permitted to live."

Herrad struggled to sit himself more upright, his wizened features twisting into an astonished snarl. "You forget yourself, you traitorous dog! I'll have your tongue cut out and boiled for your last meal. Is that the truth?" he snapped at Mistislaus. "Is this orphan girl of yours truly a Skylding?"

Mistislaus did not appear to have heard him. His eyes were fastened upon Ofarir and his jaw hung slightly ajar, slack with disbelief.

"I don't believe it," he murmured faintly. "Skyla, I warned you not to do this sort of thing."

"Ofarir was dying on our doorstep," Skyla said in a muffled voice, peering out at Herrad and Ofarir from the safely of Mistislaus' imposing bulwark. "I thought I would be accused of being the lynx and killing him, so I brought him back. I know I left something out. I left a gate open that I should have closed, and something escaped when Ofarir returned."

"Something indeed," Mistislaus said. "And I think I know what—or who—it may be."

"Do you? Do you indeed?" Ofarir snarled. "Then make it your best-kept secret. You have troubles enough of your own. What about this Skylding girl you have brought into our midst, like a viper in a gifting box? You never seemed so devious, but I know in your heart you want to see a Skylding on the chieftain's seat. Pious, pious Mistislaus, pretending to heal our unfortunate and ailing chieftain Herrad, all the while nurturing the seeds of his destruction in your own bosom."

"What seeds? What destruction?" Herrad demanded, looking back and forth from Mistislaus to Ofarir. "Will you talk straight, you idiot?"

"It was not intentional," Mistislaus said, "but if our fate is bigger than our own plans, then we are powerless to stand in the way of the larger machinations of fate."

"Then you admit your own treason and conspiracy!" Ofarir pounced with a triumphant grin. "You have sealed your own death warrant!"

"We are all so born under a death warrant," Mistislaus said with a shrug. "If it be, then so be it, but I was brought here for the purpose of healing Herrad of the Kjallari curse, and if I had intended to kill him, I could have done it easily a thousand times. And what makes you think that a young orphan girl could claim a chieftain's seat even if she had the inclination? She has no family but me, no clan, no warriors, no one to hold and claim such a perilous seat."

"But there are other ways of holding," Ofarir said. "You know as well as I about the unbending bonds of prophecy. If no Skyldings remained, then Nordanfirth all would fall to the Dokkalfar. But someone failed to do his duty." He turned a smoldering glare upon Herrad. "Rangfara is riddled with Skyldings, all waiting for revenge. Those wretched wild boys that make themselves such a nuisance in the Skurdur all are Skyldings. This monstrous stinking pile of refuse did not finish the job he was sent to do thirteen years ago. The cleansing of Rangfara was not complete and the threat to all of Fairholm—or what he arrogantly and temporarily calls Herradsrike—still lives and breathes and will one day rise up and take the chieftain's seat and strike the Kryppling clan right off the face of the land."

He lurched closer to Herrad, stooping down to put his face on a level with his father's, continuing in a rising voice that led to a frenzied shout.

Herrad snatched his sword out from under his bed clothes and made some menacing thrusts with it at Ofarir.

"You sniveling dog!" he seethed through clenched teeth, his features livid with empurpled blotches. "You back stabbing, treacherous, vile embodiment of evil! I should have cut your throat when your nurse showed you to me, a weak, puking fistful of human deceit and vanity. Cut your throat and thrown you in the river, or on the dung heap for the wild pigs to find. I know what you want. You won't kill me easily. You don't deserve a chieftain's seat, and you never will if your wits are as addled as I think they are. What's this nonsense about Skyldings? Didn't we purge Rangfara of every man, woman, and child, until the paving stones were awash with their blood? Perhaps a few infants survived, what of it? You're afraid of this white-faced slip of a girl, just because she once threw you against a wall with evil powers? It seems a mighty long row to hoe just to soothe your own personal pride." He dismissed the argument with a derisive snort and a flap of one withered hand.

"You don't remember?" Ofarir cried. "The words of the prophet? The greatest prophet ever to set foot in Rangfara?"

"Prophet? In Rangfara? I never knew of any such thing," Herrad said.

"It's Kraftugur," Mistislaus said. "You remember how he always pored over those old books. Old prophecies in old books that should have been burned centuries ago. The dust of those ancient pages went to his brain, and he fancied himself a prophet. Those foretellings are nothing but the raving of a deranged mind grasping where it can for aggrandizement. The Skyldings refusing to sell him a birthright to any of their mother clans was the final straw, I fear, when he realized that neither he nor his own progeny would be the foretold and fabled chieftain who would one day rule all of what we once knew as Fairholm."

"Kraftugur?" Herrad retorted with a wrathful snort. "He wasn't any prophet. He was a jinx, a maniac, the one who sent me down into the Kjallari with the hope that I would be killed."

The creature possessing Ofarir flung back his head and roared with a mirthless bellow.

"Yes! Yes! It is I, returned with more prophecies!" He whirled around, capering with awful glee. "You will all die! Rangfara will be crushed to dust. The darkness of the Dokkalfar rule will extend from Oskiptur to the southlands, and no light will ever touch the earth again. Chaos will be absolute and complete and the hearts of men will be as cold as ice."

"Mistislaus!" Skyla whimpered, cowering close to the wizard. "What have I done? Who is this monster? Is he truly a prophet?"

"Don't be frightened," Mistislaus said. "I shall deal with him. He was insane when I knew him, and his visions of the future were nothing but the mindless spasms of a brain stewed in too many Dokkalfar poison eiturs. Ofarir should be chained to a wall someplace until we can drive Kraftugur back to Hel where he belongs."

"Kraftugur? Is it really Kraftugur?" Herrad demanded, his eyes flickering with a dangerous gleam. "You're the one who told me the treasure was in the Kjallari, so I'd go down there and get killed by those creatures. You wanted the chieftain's seat for yourself, didn't you? You just wanted to use the clan Krypplingur to clean out Rangfara for you, so you could move right in, didn't you? I've had nothing but time to think of your treacheries, Kraftugur. If you think coming back with my son as a vehicle is going to be any protection for you, don't plan on staying here long. I've yearned for a good excuse to kill him since he was born. Thanks to the indoctrinations of his mother's clan, since he was three years of age he's plotted to kill me to take my place as chieftain of the Krypplingur. I know what it is to live with treachery. I'm not afraid of you, Kraftugur. You didn't get my chair then, and you're not going to get it now. The whole clan will rise up against you when they know who you are!"

"Silence!" the voice of Kraftugur bellowed. "Keep your silence or I shall take you off the face of this earth!"

"No, I won't!" Mistislaus shouted, plunging forward, his cloak billowing and swirling with astonishing gusts of power. "I saw the horror you created once before. You won't get another chance to wreak such havoc."

"Havoc and horror are my lifeblood," Kraftugur purred. "Chaos and terror are my heart and soul. I could not rest knowing one Skylding is alive and drawing breath. All of you will rue this day to the end of your lives."

"Faugh! Get away!" Herrad growled. "You're nothing but an imposter, a crazy person!"

Kraftugur uttered an ugly laugh. "Being a Krypplingur, you have about as much understanding of the unseen elements of this world and the spiritual aethers as a lump of mud. You are little more than dung beneath my feet. This time you're going to suffer and squirm while I grind you beneath my heel. For every moment I've writhed in Hel's torments, you will suffer the same, old friend."

"Mistislaus!" Skyla gasped, drawing back in terror and awe. "What have I done?"

"Have no fear, I'm going to get rid of him," Mistislaus said.

"Are you indeed?" the voice of Kraftugur sneered. "Try casting me out and see where it gets you. Your friend Illmuri tried it. I don't think he'll be so rash again, if he survives the attempt, which is doubtful. Keep your mouth shut, Mistislaus, and you will live awhile. If you wish to die, I shall be forced to shut it for you."

"Kraftugur, I command you to return to Hel's kingdom where you belong," Mistislaus said.

"It won't be that easy," Kraftugur said with an evil leer. "I'm once dead now. A journey to Hel's realm teaches a spirit strength and skill. You can't get the better of me, you old wretch. For the past thirteen years, I've had the very best of teachers. And now I shall have my revenge."

"You tried to kill me," Herrad cried. "But I got you for sending me into the Kjallari. What are you thinking of, walking right into the fortress of your bitterest enemy? Who do you think I've thought about all these years, lying here festering and rotting? The only satisfaction I've had was in treasuring the memory of driving my sword straight through your throat. Hah, what a great joke it was, summoning you to help cure me of the disease you inflicted upon me. I knew your intentions then. You never expected to see me come out of the Kjallari. Then there was the pleasure of watching you die on the floor, like a crushed snake. I'm almost glad for the opportunity to kill you again, Kraftugur, mad prophet of Rangfara!"

"And I, too, will relish a chance to finish what I so rightly began thirteen years ago," Kraftugur replied. "As if a Kryppling were worthy of any chieftain's seat, let alone Rangfara, the jewel of the southlands. The haughty Skyldings who were too good to sell me a birthright were all humbled to the dust by the crude Kryppling, who now defiles the chieftain's seat of Nordanfirth. All will be purged to make way for the final chieftain to rule in the light of another planet in the sky—the final and chosen one who will be the master of all, the servant of none."

"Mistislaus!" Herrad turned to the wizard. "Cast him out and be quick about it!"

"Ever the traitor still, aren't you, Mistislaus?" Ofarir turned upon Mistislaus, his face a snarling mask. "I once offered you a share of what I planned to take, but you chose to be a fool. I should have killed you then."

"It wasn't enough to discredit me in the eyes of the Skyldings?" Mistislaus queried gently. "It wasn't enough to destroy the least scrap of my reputation? If I had been killed, someone might have remembered me with fondness. What you did was far worse. You lied."

"No matter now," Kraftugur purred. "Everyone who knew you is now dead. Was it a bitter pill, watching all your faithless friends destroyed? Knowing you almost saved them?"

"Great Hodur," Herrad muttered, glowering apprehensively at Mistislaus, then at Ofarir. "I trusted you to heal me? A Skylding wizard?"

"You never had anything to fear from me," Mistislaus said. "What is one feeble wizard against all the clan Kryppling?"

"But if that wizard is one of the old wise ones," the voice of Kraftugur said, "and if there's nothing more he wants than to sit upon the chieftain's seat, then anyone there before him is in deadly peril. He is evil and greedy and seeking to steal that which does not belong to him. He must be stopped, or he will stop at nothing."

"This is a lot of nonsense," Mistislaus began, taking a step forward.

Ofarir swiftly drew his sword. "Wretched traitor," his voice grated. "You should never have returned to Rangfara."

"Neither should you," Mistislaus retorted. "Kraftugur, I command you to depart at once."

Kraftugur replied with a screaming bellow, and Ofarir's body reeled forward a few steps. "No! No!" he screeched in a voice of terror.

"Depart, you unclean creature!" Mistislaus stepped forward, raising his staff aloft with a plume of vapor.

"No! Never! Not until the seat is mine!" Raising his sword in a wild, flailing motion, Ofarir plunged it straight into Mistislaus' breast.

Chapter Eighteen

Skyla screamed, trying, to hold Mistislaus as he swayed on his feet a moment, a startled, even glad expression crossing over his face. Herrad tried to gather his puny legs under him, his eyes nearly starting out of his shrunken head as he frantically clutched his sword in a half-forgotten defensive posture.

"I command you to depart," Kraftugur's ugly voice said, adding a wild laugh.

"No! Mistislaus!" Skyla pleaded. "I can heal you!"

Mistislaus shook his head slightly, not taking his eyes off Ofarir. "Not again," he gasped. "Never use those spells again, my child. Do not be afraid, I'm not going far from you. It is all right, believe me. He doesn't know—he couldn't realize what he has done."

So saying, he sank slowly to the floor, and the life went out of him with a gentle sigh. With a desperate wail, Skyla dropped down on her knees beside him in an abject heap.

"What did you do that for?" Herrad gasped, fearfully hitching backward on his couch. "There was no more harm in him than in an old woman."

"Then you don't know old women," the voice of Kraftugur retorted with an elated cackle. Ofarir's form took on a more sprightly demeanor, striding up and down without a trace of a limp, and the dull eyes and slack expression were vitalized with the savage gleam of blood-lust.

"This is not the sniveling son I thought I knew," Herrad said, a sly, admiring grin crossing his sweating countenance for an instant. "Ofarir was never so clever. The experience of death was definitely an improvement for him. I should hope we'll be able to come to some sort of agreement about how things should be divided up between us, however we decide is most equitable and fair."

"Equitable? I'm not interested in being equitable or fair. I want what is rightfully mine, and anyone else who stands in the way is going to go the same way that one did." Ofarir nodded toward Mistislaus' inert form as he wiped the blood from his sword on one of Herrad's tapestries.

"There's no need to do anything hasty," Herrad said quickly. "We'll let bygones be bygones. No harm was done, after all, when you sent me into the Kjallari. Nor when I had you killed, eh? You're back again, better and stronger than before. You should perhaps thank me for the privilege of sending you to Hel's kingdom, where you learned so much." He added a nervous laugh.

Ofarir shot him a dark look. "Maybe I should, but I won't. I don't need to thank anyone for anything." He crossed the room to the door and opened it. To the Kryppling outside he said, "Get another man and a cart. We've got a load to go to the Kjallari."

"No! Not the Kjallari!" Skyla exclaimed, her face startled and tear-streaked. "He would hate it there, in the dark with all those creatures. He should be burned on a pyre, on a hilltop, next to the sky."

Kraftugur's voice laughed nastily. "That would be very nice, wouldn't it, but we don't do nice things for our enemies in Rangfara."

"What are you going to do with the girl?" Herrad asked, his eyes darting nervously as Ofarir turned and moved toward him across the room.

"I shall kill her presently," Kraftugur said, as he whipped the sword back and forth, eyeing it appreciatively. "When I'm feeling the need for more life force. To shed Skylding blood again will give me the strength of a dozen men."

Skyla stepped back as a couple of Krypplingur trod heavily into the room and dragged away the body of Mistislaus, leaving a smear of blood trailing after him. Quickly she knelt and touched the blood with one finger then placed a mark upon her forehead with it.

"As I live, I will not forget what you have done," she said in a low voice, casting her eyes sidewise at Ofarir. "I have marked myself for vengeance. I promise that you will live to rue this day."

"Begone with you until you're needed," Kraftugur's voice said contemptuously. "I am the master of Rangfara now, in all but a few small details that I shall shortly attend to." He rolled his eyes toward Herrad, who was listening attentively from his couch and glistening with a faint sheen of desperate apprehension.

"Put her in a safe place," Kraftugur continued, beckoning to the

Kryppling lurking unwillingly outside the door. "Make certain there are no openings big enough for a cat to escape. A good stout chain would be a good idea, too, perhaps."

"She's only a girl," Herrad ventured to protest.

"And double all the guards at the gates," Kraftugur commanded.

"You needn't worry," Skyla said, sidestepping the heavy paw of her captor. "I have no intention of leaving Rangfara." With a sudden glimmering and a swirl of the white cloak, she transformed herself into a snow lynx, crouching and hissing, one paw upraised to strike.

"Catch her!" Kraftugur bellowed.

The Kryppling warriors at the doorway leaped back with a startled yell. Skyla bestowed a last glare upon Kraftugur and leaped through the door with no interference from anyone.

Kraftugur ordered a search of Rangfara, which lasted until dawn, with no result except to excite the city to a newer pitch of excitement and dread.

"Cursed Skyldings," Kraftugur muttered, striding up and down Herrad's room with his dragging gait. "When will their curse be erased from the earth? Ever arrogant and haughty, Skyldings live only to plague me."

"Unlike the Krypplingur," Herrad said with a fulsome smile not unlike that of the Ofarir of old. "We are always ready to welcome anyone into our ranks and treat him as an equal—if not better," he added hastily.

"That's because Krypplingur are scum," Kraftugur said. "The only people who would wish for their society are those who are unfit for anyone else." He scowled broodingly. "Would it have hurt them so much to grant one birthright to an extraordinary man—a prophet, even—of slightly less than orthodox ancestry? Would you think that I would be such a blot upon their spotless pedigree?"

"Their conceit is utterly contemptible," Herrad agreed eagerly. "If you were a Dokkalfar of some obscure clan who kept no marriage and birth records, marriaging and mating with no thought or design until there was scarcely a name to call yourself by, why, then I could understand it, I suppose, but no one really is so disregardful of the common proprieties as that, I should think."

"You have described my heritage exactly," Kraftugur said in a sinister growl. "The only thing you have omitted is the strong suspicion that somewhere in my family tree lurks more than a few individuals thought to be trolls. If you had remembered that small detail, your insult would have been complete. As it is, I shall let you live awhile longer."

"Thank you!" Herrad gasped, blinking as the sweat trickled down into his eyes. "Is there anything else you wish attended to at the moment? If there's not, I think I shall retire to my inner chambers and rest awhile."

"I wish only to attend to the last of the Skyldings still treading the stones of Rangfara's streets," Kraftugur said. "Seven Skyldings remain, and while they live, I cannot rest. Take your rest while you can, my dear father. When I am done hunting, I shall return and probably kill you. In the meantime, you may refer to me as your dear son, and remember, my esteemed parent, if you so much as breathe the name Kraftugur to anyone, I shall let the breath out of you with a thousand punctures from your own eating knife."

Jafnar lingered outside Herradshol after Skyla had disappeared inside. He stalked along the walls yowling, until the place suddenly exploded with activity as bands of Krypplingur set forth with purposeful haste, armed to the teeth and jittery as fledgling warriors on their first foray into battle. Jafnar terrorized them with a few lynx screams, but a strong sensation of anxiety precluded his enjoyment of the game, so he turned back toward Athugashol. He knew better than to present himself to his Skylding brothers in his present form and he wasn't going to be much help to Mistislaus and Skyla as a lynx. He didn't know how long the fylgja-spell was going to last, so he decided there was nothing to do but wait it out.

He knew he had nothing to fear as he padded through the broken gate, the shattered door, and into the house. It seemed to be forgotten in the furious searching of the Krypplingur. No one would bother him, and if he chose he could simply leap to the top of a wall and bound away. He found Guthrum slowly poking through the ruins of the house, muttering to himself.

"Useless dwarf," he was growling. "Couldn't save the master, couldn't save the house. Might was well be a lump of rock in the road, an affliction to every foot, hoof, and wheel that passes."

He prodded the inert form of Illmuri lightly and shook his head when there was no discernible result. Discovering Mistislaus' satchel, he picked it up and sat down in Mistislaus' chair with a rumbling groan, clutching the satchel to his chest, staring unseeingly at the clammy wall before him as he went on with his self-beration.

Jafnar sat down on a windowsill and stared at him, waiting impatiently for the effects of the fylgja-spell to start wearing off. He wondered uneasily if only Skyla could release him, since she had said the words that had shifted his shape. The loneliness of his position was steadily becoming intolerable. Skyla and Mistislaus were both captive now in Herradshol. He finally padded forward from his shadowy hiding place, looking up at Guthrum warily and uttering a questioning, "Miaow?"

"Skyla!" the dwarf exclaimed with a joyous illumination of his craggy features. He dropped the satchel unheedingly to the floor. "You've escaped and come back! A pity you're still in that wretched cat form. Why don't you be a good lass now and shift yourself back to a human? You know I can't abide cats."

Jafnar would have shrugged if he could, so he did the next best thing by sitting down and licking one paw. It was an odd experience for the human part of him. Then he sauntered over and sniffed at the inert form of Illmuri.

"He's dead as a turnip," Guthrum said, shaking his head. "And the master is gone, I fear forever, and I was able to do nothing about it, nothing at all."

Guthrum had his hand over his eyes, mournfully scouring his eye sockets with thumb and forefinger, preparatory to launching himself into a Dvergar lament. There were no words recognizable to Jafnar, but the dolorous song conveyed all the grief of a vanquished and disappearing people. Jafnar's fur bristled at the impressions that the lament created in his mind. While Guthrum was thus distracted, he crept over to the satchel and gave the handle an experimental tug with his teeth. If he could somehow get it to Mistislaus, perhaps there was something in it which he could use to engineer his escape.

"Don't grieve yet," a faint voice said. "I'm not entirely dead. Finish me off and then sing your song."

On the floor, Illmuri stirred his limbs faintly, gasping and wincing.

"Alive then, are we?" Guthrum rumbled with a gathering scowl. "Didn't know when you were well off, you poor fool. This world is nothing but a lot of bother."

Slowly the wizard struggled to gather himself together, with faint twitchings and moans. Illmuri's feeble gaze next settled upon the gray form of the lynx, sitting on its haunches and watching him intently.

"Sorry, my heart and liver are already spoken for," the wizard said, looking into the round-eyed unblinking stare of the lynx. "Kraftugur can have them if I'm not wizard enough to destroy him before he destroys Mistislaus and Skyla."

"As if you cared whether they live or not!" The words came out in a savage cat yowl. Jafnar leaped across the room in a bound and sharpened his claws viciously on the doorpost to demonstrate his emotions regarding Kraftugur. It was a wonderful feeling of power, ripping out slivers of wood with his own deadly, efficient fighting hooks attached to each finger.

Illmuri flattened himself against the wall, eyeing Guthrum apprehensively. "It's anyone's guess whose power she's under in that form," he said in a low voice.

"Faugh," Guthrum said. "I hate magic as much as I hate cats in the house. Skyla! Come out of that now. We've had enough of your tricks."

"Fools! If you cared, you'd go after Skyla and rescue her!" Jafnar exclaimed, startling himself with his own voice. The fylgja-spell fell off him like a cloak of mist and he was himself again.

"You!" Guthrum gasped.

Illmuri groaned aloud. "Jafnar! How did you do this? Have you been shifting shapes, too?"

"No, this is only the second time," Jafnar said, shaking his head, which was reeling dizzily. His body felt huge and heavy and clumsy after the light and silky form of the lynx. "Skyla and her bag of tricks did it."

"The whole clan must share the same fylgja-form," Illmuri said rapidly, his rapt gaze wandering off to the unknown aethers. "The sign of the lynx. That's why we see it everywhere. I thought it was a death-worshipping cult."

"So it hasn't been Skyla murdering these Krypplingur," Guthrum said, a wide grin overspreading his ugly countenance. "It's been these sneaking, slinking wild boys."

"I wish it were," Jafnar said wholeheartedly, "but it's not. Skyla just showed me how to shift shapes, using plumabrot."

"Plumabrot?" Guthrum's eyes narrowed and nearly vanished, except for two tiny knife points.

"The vile concoction definitely affects him strangely," Illmuri said. "I've seen decisive evidence of it with my own two eyes. An inherited susceptibility to something in the plumabrot enables them to experience unusual magical effects. Certain wizard clans use substances to enhance their contact with their abilities, but I never suspected it of the Skyldings. I wonder why they didn't use this knowledge in their final hour to save themselves from destruction. Perhaps not all of them are susceptible to plumabrot. Perhaps only a few—perhaps they were trying to create their ultimate wizard warrior, who could weave magic as well as fight, who would one day save Rangfara and the surrounding domain of Fairholm from the incursion of the Dokkalfar. Mistislaus told me somewhat of those days, when the Skyldings were at the peak of their powers, so near the discoveries of the greatest secrets of creation and destruction. He was a minor wizard in an arcana of power. Then the Krypplingur turned against the Skyldings—and the genealogy records all were destroyed. If only I had Skriftur here to talk to me for an hour!" He slapped his forehead viciously, as if stung by a horsefly.

Skriftur. Jafnar's hair prickled at the thoughts of going back down into the Kjallari. His eyes came to rest upon Mistislaus' satchel. Jafnar casually picked it up and took a few slithering steps toward the door, awakening Guthrum's suspicions immediately.

"Where do you think you're going with that?" he demanded with a surly clouding of his knotted brow.

"To take it to Mistislaus," Jafnar answered. "Someone's got to help him escape, instead of singing dirges. And certain others have been scant help in the past." He bestowed a withering scowl upon Illmuri.

"It's not as if they're helpless, after all," Illmuri said. "You don't need to risk yourself trying to get into Herradshol. Skyla can escape whenever she wants to by shifting shapes and going out a window. And Mistislaus has his own rules, however inscrutable. I, at least, was never able to figure out how much power he's actually got."

"Good for Mistislaus," Jafnar said.

"I think you and that satchel had better stay here," Illmuri went on. "I don't want either of you to fall into the hands of Kraftugur—that beast! As if we didn't have troubles enough. I shall have to deal with him later. Besides, I want to keep an eye on you for a while. Who knows what other effects that plumabrot might have on you? And you could be very useful in getting Mistislaus back, if we can get your shape to shift to the lynx again when we want it to. You know he probably won't do anything to help himself, lest he be guilty of tampering with his own exorable fate, so we'll have to do it for him."

"No, I don't want to do that," Jafnar said. "What do you care about Mistislaus? You've done nothing but sneak and slink and spy around him. You're a Dokkalfar—our natural enemy. Why don't you just forget about Mistislaus and go back to wherever it was you came from?"

"I've got commitments here," Illmuri said, gripping Jafnar by the back of his neck suddenly. "To Mistislaus and Skyla and even you. I don't want you out of my sight. I might not be able to get you back when I want you."

Jafnar writhed under Illmuri's grip on his neck. "Let me go," he growled. "I've had all of you I can stand! I want to go find my clan brothers!"

"I don't think that's such a good idea, just yet," Illmuri said. "The Krypplingur will be looking for you. Remember Kraftugur's reward? I think you'll be safer if I keep an eye on you."

Jafnar spun around to bolt for the back door, but Illmuri grabbed him and shoved him against the wall.

"Let me go!" Jafnar growled, struggling fiercely.

"Be still! *Thegja!*"

Jafnar was silenced as if a hand had gripped his gullet and shut it off.

"Are you going to be reasonable, or shall I leave you muzzled?" Jafnar nodded his head and Illmuri removed the spell with a flick of his hand. "We must talk, you and I, if we are going to do anything about this situation. Now be careful what you say, or I'll silence you again."

Jafnar nodded his head.

"Very good," Illmuri said. "For a wild boy, you learn quickly."

"I don't want anything else to do with wizards or sorceresses!" Jafnar said the moment the spell was removed. "I don't need your help. I was meant to be wild and, after I rescue Mistislaus and Skyla, that's what I'm going to be for the rest of my life!"

"Indeed!" Illmuri said. "It's an overcrowded profession. Skarpsey already has far too many wild men and scraelings howling in the cliffs. No, my lad, you have a great career ahead of you, if only you knew it, and I'm going to see to it that you get into it properly. You will be a Skylding and Rangfara will be your inheritance, whether you like it or not."

"Being a Skylding is a nuisance," Jafnar said fiercely. "From now on, I'm not a Skylding. I'm wild, and I'm going to eat raw meat and never speak to people again."

"The trouble with you," Illmuri said, "is the fact that you've got no discipline whatsoever. If you're ever going to realize the potential of your birthright, you've got to have some training by someone experienced with recalcitrant young nitwits. Growing up like a wild animal is not the proper upbringing for the future rulers of Rangfara. Before Mistislaus was taken, he told me to take care of Skyla and you wild boys, so I guess that duty falls to me."

"It's too late for that," Jafnar retorted. "I don't want any of your help or your advice. Look where it's gotten Mistislaus. And Skyla. Couldn't you have done something to have stopped all this?"

"This is hardly the time for recriminations," Illmuri snapped. "What's gone is gone, I fear. You've been precious little help so far. But I've got a plan that will change all that."

"I'm not interested," Jafnar said bitterly, turning away. "I've got no faith in wizards any longer."

"You will come with me," Illmuri said. "And you will lead me to the hiding place of your Skylding brothers."

"That's what you think," Jafnar said. "I'd rather be killed than betray my fellow Skyldings."

"Well, don't give the Krypplingur that notion," Illmuri said, extending one hand in a commanding gesture. "*Fara af eftir!* And don't forget the satchel. Nor will you be needing that sword any longer, so hand it over."

Helpless to resist and fuming inwardly, Jafnar gave up his sword. Then he picked up the satchel, but Guthrum snatched it out of his grip and protectively tucked it under one arm. "It's the master's things," he growled, "and I'm sworn to protect them wherever they go. Now that I haven't got the master himself to protect, this satchel is all I've got left of him."

"Well, come along then," Illmuri said impatiently.

Illmuri lit a dull glow on the end of his staff and led Jafnar into the street outside Athugashol. Guthrum followed, grumbling and growling and peering around suspiciously on all sides. Dawn colored the sky a lowering red, and the nightfarers were scuttling for cover after a harrowing night of torment from the Krypplingur. Intermittent irate clashes with the awakening dayfarers lent an ugly tone to the birth of the new day. And worse, the word of Mistislaus' demise was on nearly every tongue.

"Can it be true?" Guthrum asked in a hushed voice. All his fierce posturing sloughed off him suddenly. His square sturdy shoulders sagged and his scowling features fell into lines of utter gloom.

"I don't know," Illmuri snapped. "I can't believe it, but yet that Kraftugur creature would do such a thing. I can't understand why anyone would want to kill Mistislaus."

"If it's not true, why else would everyone be talking about it?" Jafnar asked dolefully.

"Well, it changes nothing in my plans," Illmuri said, giving his shoulders a shake. "Come along, let's go."

Illmuri's new lie-up was far from the Kjallari and the Skurdur. By the time they got there, the following spell was beginning to wear off Jafnar, and he was able to put up a fair amount of resistance when Illmuri shoved him through a trapdoor into the cellar. Jafnar raged around, yelling and howling to no avail.

"This is for your own good," Illmuri said. "One day you'll thank me for it."

"I'd rather do something else than thank you!" Jafnar roared back. "Let me get my hands on your throat and I'll show you!"

"A nasty-tempered little brute, isn't he?" Guthrum rumbled, looking down at Jafnar with a faint gleam of approval in his eye. He still had the satchel under one arm, and he sat down beside the trapdoor with a great sigh. It occurred to Jafnar that the dwarf was indeed protecting his master's possessions, both satchel and wild boy.

"I'll get out of here and then it will go very badly for anyone who tries to stop me," Jafnar snarled, and commenced fuming and raging and breathing dire threats from his cellar until Illmuri summarily shut the door on him, leaving him in near-total darkness.

"Don't say anything you'll have cause to regret later," Illmuri called through the door. "One day you'll thank me for this."

"Before or after you hand me over to the Krypplingur for Kraftugur's reward?" Jafnar shouted back furiously.

He couldn't reach the door, situated in the floor above his head. After exhausting himself with futile leaps and gymnastic antics to reach it, he sat down gasping for air and trying to discern somewhat of his surroundings. As a wild boy, his senses had been acute enough that he could see in the dark almost as well as a cat, but his comfortable living at Athugashol had nearly robbed him of many of his talents. Straining the limits of his abilities, he peered around, willing himself to see. It was harder work than jumping at the door, but gradually dim forms began to take shape. Some beams, a heap of rocks, the earthy walls, and the door locked above him were all that he found to look at. A small amount of firelight seeped in around the cracks in the door above, just enough to offer him the least bit of illumination.

Illmuri opened the door a cautious crack some time later, after Jafnar was done with his temper.

"Are you ready to listen to reason?" the wizard asked.

"I doubt I'll hear it from you," Jafnar replied.

"Very well, you can stay down there," Illmuri said. He dropped down an eider and a wrapped bundle that proved to be food. Jafnar draped the eider around his shoulders and ate the food ravenously. Thus contented, he began to yawn and feel quite comfortable, so he curled up and went to sleep.

The creaking crash of the door opening and a splash of light awakened him. Illmuri and another looked down at him.

"Yes, I see what you mean," the other said. "I think I can get you a fair price for him. There's no shortage of stray lads to be taken up and sold on the market for thralls, thanks to the Dokkalfar marauders."

"The younger ones are so apt to die before they reach the size of this one," Illmuri said.

"But he is a wild boy," the slaver said. "They're harder to train."

"Only if you overfeed them," Illmuri said, and they both laughed callously.

For a moment Jafnar was too stunned to move or protest. He knew that voice and that scratchy, bearded face that peered with a speculative grin down into the cellar, although that evil face was considerably older now and more scarred and weather-scoured than ever. Waves of old horrors washed over him, turning his knees to water and his tongue to ashes. It was Otkell the Slaver, the first of many who had taught him that life was a perilous, merciless occupation for a nameless lad of no parentage.

After the fall of Rangfara, when he was about three years of age, a kindly family of fisherfolk had raised him for a few years, and then the father of the household had perished at sea. His foster mother had gone to live with kinfolk who let it be known that only her natural children were welcome to be adopted. Jafnar, at ten years of age, took to the wandering life of the itinerant beggar. Shortly after, Jafnar had his first experience with Otkell the Slaver, who traded in wretched human beings of all ages. Unwanted children, criminals, wanderers, the unlucky: Anyone who fell into his net was his legitimate prey and sold as slaves to the mines or the chapmen to man the oars, or any other occupation where human life was of scant value.

"No!" Jafnar sputtered, tearing his gaze away from that familiar leering face. "Not again!"

He made a desperate attempt to claw his way out of the cellar, but they thrust him back into the hole, slammed shut the door, and locked it again. This time he wasted no energy. He sat down with his eider over his shoulders and tried to force his scuttling brain to think. When they captured and sold him before, he was only ten years old, and sold to a farmer as a bird-boy to scare the birds away from the newly planted fields. Older thralls showed him scant mercy; he never had enough to eat, and the dogs had a warmer place to sleep. When he wasn't scaring birds, he had to pick rocks out of the fields. Now he was of a size to send to the mines. Once there, hardly anyone ever escaped. Repeatedly he thought of his Skylding brothers, wishing powerfully that he were with them, that he had never stopped to talk to Skyla that morning when she looked like a flaming salamander on the wall, that he had never seen Mistislaus and thirsted after his power to help find the treasure. Being locked in a cellar gave him an unnatural amount of time for thinking, so his thoughts went around in all manner of convoluted circles. Always he arrived back exactly where he was—nothing could be undone by wishful thinking or regrets. Skyla was held captive in Herradshol, Mistislaus was dead, and he was about to be sold into slavery again. As for Illmuri, his plans for Skyla and the treasure of the Skyldings obviously had no room for Jafnar.

In spite of his distress, he eventually managed to doze. When he awakened, he was hungry, but he heard no sounds of Illmuri moving about above. He cursed and shouted, and still there was no response. If only he had Skyla's powers of moving things and changing substances, he would speak to the latch on the cellar door and get himself out of this dire situation.

He wasn't certain how much time had passed since he missed Illmuri, but he was famished. Finally he heard the door open above. Scuffling footsteps approached and the cellar door was thrown back. Expecting a package of food, Jafnar stood directly in the way as another body came flailing down upon him. He was knocked down and trampled by a pair of boots, elbowed, kneed, and when he tried to get up, he was knocked down again when the person charged him, head down like a goat, after first issuing a terrified bellow. Jafnar grappled with his assailant and was glad to discover that he was considerably larger than this intruder, so he twisted up the fellow's arms and sat on him with his face in the dirt, as he often did to the younger boys of his troupe.

"Now then, if we're to share this cellar, you've got to learn some manners, you little beast," Jafnar snarled, with an added twist of his opponent's arms. "The first lesson is that I'm the master down here and you've got to do as I say or I'll scour the floor with your face. Do you understand?"

"Jafnar? Is that you?" a familiar voice mumbled, somewhat muffled by dirt.

"Einka? Is that you?"

"Jafnar! I'd know that floor-scouring threat anywhere!"

Chapter Nineteen

Jafnar released Einka and helped him up. "I learned that the first time I was sold as a thrall," he said ruefully. "Now it looks like it's going to happen again. Illmuri's had a slaver here to look at me already. Is he rounding up the rest of you, too?"

"Yes, he's been chasing us all day," Einka said, sniffling and rubbing his nose on his sleeve. "He's going to sell us all as thralls?"

"I fear so. To get us out of his way when he uses Skyla to get our treasure. I knew from the start he couldn't be trusted."

"But you trusted him anyway," Einka said. "Now look where it's got us. You trusted several people you shouldn't have. If you'd minded your own business and stayed wild, this wouldn't have happened."

"I ought to bloody your nose for that," Jafnar said, but he found he was lacking in the conviction to do so. The truth of Einka's words smarted like salt in his wounds. With a weary sigh he sat down beside Einka, drawing a painful amount of comfort from the presence of his smaller friend.

Next to join Jafnar and Einka in the cellar were Lampa and Lofa, later that same day, or night. Their spirits were cheered somewhat to discover that Jafnar was there already, and the four of them spent the night curled up in one large heap, as they had in the old days. Sometime in the middle of the night Modga and Thogn were thrust down into the cellar. Jafnar immediately found himself with the job of soothing the fears of the younger boys, calming a terrified Thogn who was leaping about like a wild thing, trampling everyone, and preventing Modga from killing someone in his rage at being captured.

"This is all your fault, Jafnar!" he seethed, after Jafnar fattened his lip for him and slugged him in the stomach. "If I have to live to a hundred thousand, I'll get my revenge on you for this!"

"You won't live that long if they sell us to the mines," Jafnar said, "so you won't have to worry about it."

"And Skyla," Modga added. "This is all her fault. Hers and yours for tagging at her heels like a trained dog. You were an absolute idiot, Jafnar."

"I only thought it was a way for us to get our treasure and our birth scrolls. We got closer than we ever would have with just digging here and there."

"But we're going to be thralls!" Modga said. "Thralls are property! No more freedom than a horse or a dog! I'll forever rue the day you set eyes upon that witch Skyla. She put a curse on you with that plumabrot, I shouldn't wonder."

"Shut up, Modga," Jafnar said.

Thogn's hand reached out of the darkness and patted Jafnar reassuringly on the head. "Don't worry, Jafnar," Thogn's soft voice said in an encouraging tone. He was in one of his rare rational moments. "It will be all right when Ordvar gets here."

That stung Jafnar even worse. He had always been the leader of the wild boys, and now Ordvar had taken his place. Glumly he slumped against the wall, his eyes fixed on the faint outline of the door above. Presently a plan began taking form, clearing away the clouds of dejection and defeat. Beckoning to Modga, he whispered in his ear.

It took them some time to capture Ordvar. Illmuri threw food down to them twice, and they were expecting more when the door opened, framing a picture of Ordvar struggling in the grasp of Illmuri. It was the work of only moments. Modga and Thogn bent down and Jafnar leaped onto their backs. The younger boys then seized Jafnar's legs and boosted him vigorously right out of the cellar. He sprawled into Ordvar and Illmuri, bowling them over. Without waiting for a cue, Ordvar followed Jafnar's lead and pounced on Illmuri as he tried to leap up. They brought him down again by weight of sheer determination, although he was considerably taller and heavier. Fortune smiled upon their endeavor with unexpected kindness when Illmuri's head connected with a rock on the hearthstone, normally used for resting a pot on, but also effective for cracking skulls. With a startled exclamation he subsided on the hearthstone among the ashes in an untidy sprawl and lost consciousness.

Gasping, Ordvar and Jafnar looked down at their unconscious adversary.

"Is he dead?" Ordvar panted.

"I doubt it," Jafnar said. "There's not enough blood."

"I'll remedy that," Modga offered eagerly. "Somebody get me a knife!"

Jafnar dissuaded him in no uncertain terms. Quickly they hoisted the other boys out of the cellar. Then they rolled Illmuri in and commenced prancing around the trap door opening in self-congratulatory delight.

"We'll sell him to Otkell the Slaver!" Lampa and Lofa crowed. More practical, Einka looked around the house for something to eat. Soon a loaf of bread flew through the air, followed by a whole roasted fowl, boiled potatoes, and a cheese. Bites were taken without interrupting their cavorting, and the remainders thrown at someone across the circle in hilarious high spirits.

Abruptly, in the midst of the orphans' merrymaking, the door was thrown open with a crash, revealing a massive hooded figure on the threshold, blocking the only means of escape. The food and the dancers came to an immediate halt, the food forgotten, the dancers poised for flight.

"What's the meaning of this hullabaloo?" growled a deep, burbling voice that made Jafnar's hair bristle and his teeth start to chatter. Sunken little eyes blinked suspiciously, and the boys cowered back, horrified to find themselves in such close proximity to their old enemy. For several years they had disdainfully dodged his nets and traps and thumbed their noses at him with impunity.

"It's Otkell the Slaver!" Einka squeaked.

"One and the same, my lads! At last we meet on favorable terms!" Otkell lashed the air with a great snaky whip, sending the wild boys scuttling into a corner with the violence of one mighty crack. He kicked the door shut behind him with one heavy boot and advanced into the room. "Having a bit of fun in here, it looks like, with the meistari's food and drink. Thinking of escaping, were you? Well, we know how to deal with mettlesome boys."

Otkell opened the door and shouted out it, "Hakarl! Bring in those chains and collars, you worthless lump of cats' meat! Now where has the meistari taken himself off to? Shall we sit and wait for him to return?"

Hakarl stumped in, dragging the slaver's equipment and glancing at him askance, as if the circumstance of being consulted in any matter were entirely too foreign for his understanding to grasp.

"Yes, let's wait," Ordvar said quickly. "He'll be back any moment."

"Will he now?" Otkell mused with a sly grin. "It seems curious to me that he would leave, after taking such pains to tell me to be here just now. Perhaps he's changed his mind about shipping you out of Rangfara."

"Out of Rangfara?" Jafnar repeated in horror.

"And not to the Krypplingur?" Modga added with a puzzled frown. "I'm sure the reward was far more than what we're worth as thralls. That proves what a great dunce Illmuri is, doesn't it?"

"Not as great a dunce as you!" Jafnar snapped.

Otkell's eyes gleamed with the light of revelation. He chuckled, deep and sinister. "Well, well," he said. "You're the ones Ofarir put that reward on, aren't you? The ones the Krypplingur are turning Rangfara inside out for, aren't you? I can't see it myself, but whatever you've done, it's going to make me a wealthy man. Hakarl, you dog, let's get them into the wagon."

One by one the wild boys were caught and fettered, but not without a great deal of biting and kicking from the three youngest boys. Modga seized a rock to defend himself seriously, but Otkell and Hakarl put an end to his resistance and dragged him out, choking and thrashing, to the cart outside.

Thogn crept close to Jafnar, towering over him by a head, but as frightened as a small child by the tumult around him.

Otkell eyed Thogn and scratched one hairy cheek dubiously.

"Aye, that daft one's nearly as big as I am," he muttered to Hakarl. "That kind can tear your head off if they get worked up or affrighted. Stronger than five men when they get into a mad state."

"Don't hurt him," Jafnar said. "He doesn't want to cause trouble, but everyone is scared of him. All he needs is a little kindness and he's like a pet sheep. Put a sack over his head so he can't see and you won't have any trouble with him."

"Kindness!" Otkell grumbled, glaring around incredulously at Hakarl. "Is that what the slave trade has come to these days? Kindness? Well, you dolt, find a sack! I'm getting of an age that I don't care for any more broken bones."

A sack was fitted over Thogn's head without incident, then the collar was fastened around his neck and his hands bound behind his back. Moaning in protest, he was led away to the cart outside.

"That was easier than I expected," Otkell said with a gap-toothy grin, wiping the back of his red, hairy neck. "Now for the last one. He looks like a mean beggar."

Jafnar could see no sense in debasing himself with the frenzied and hopeless struggle the younger boys had indulged in, nor the undignified removal to the cart, carried by arms and legs. Ordvar and Modga had put up a noble fight, doing credit to themselves and the reputation of wild boys in general, as was expected.

"The least you could do is give me the chance to fight for my freedom," Jafnar said to Otkell. "Like men, one to one. If I win, the wild boys and I win our freedom."

"I've not got time for heroics," Otkell said in exasperation. "You forget yourself; you're a thrall now and thralls don't trouble themselves with honor and pride and that sort of thing. To be sure, it doesn't impress me in the slightest. Now don't be a beast about it; you've lost the game fair and square, and fighting against it now won't do you the least bit of good."

They bound his hands behind him and fastened the hateful thrall collar around his neck. Removing his first one had been no easy matter. He had gotten rid of it only after enlisting Ordvar into his small army of wild boys. Ordvar had managed to wedge apart the metal links with a stolen chisel, and with rapture Jafnar had torn the collar off his neck and flung it away over the parapets of Rangfara. That first day of freedom haunted his thoughts on this day that appeared to be his last as a freeman as he was led to Otkell's's wagon and his chain secured to a ring inside. A hide cover was tied in place and the horses started up with a fierce cracking of Otkell's whip.

The iron gate of the Kjallari was easily negotiated by Skyla in lynx form. She slipped through the bars, scarcely brushing them with her whiskers enough to get a taste of the paralyzing iron-sickness. As she padded through the vast and gloomy vaulted rooms she thought what a peaceful place it was, this temple of death. No one dared come here to torment her or betray her trust, and the shadow world of the mist people seemed almost close enough for her to walk through the flimsy barriers that separated her from her long-deceased ancestors. But this was forbidden, she knew, at least until she had the knowledge she needed.

Herrad had ordered the body of Mistislaus carried into the Kjallari and placed upon the stones in the central court, instead of just tossing him down the shaft without ceremony. Skyla inspected the body with approval at Herrad's unwonted display of respect. Nor had the Kjallari creatures dared approach the circle she had drawn around him.

Wearily she found her way to Skriftur's court. A very little light came from the openings far above, showing her lynx eyes enough light to find her way. Shifting shape, she nodded to the dessicated remains of Skriftur.

"Oh, Skriftur, if only you were here and could tell me what I need to know," she implored him. There was no answer.

She sought out the little rooms where Skriftur had lived during his mortal lifetime. His accommodations were still comfortably appointed, with very little dust. He had owned a straw bed, a table and chair, a lamp with extra wicks and oil, and a few small personal items, nothing that would stand in the way of his love for his records and his kinsmen.

"Thank you for your hospitality, Skriftur," she said, suddenly so tired she could scarcely drag herself to the small cot. She pulled up Skriftur's eider to her chin and fell into a dreamless sleep.

She had no idea how long she slept. When she awakened, she stretched every muscle and joint and sinew as if she could never stop stretching for the sheer relief and pleasure of it. Some inner clock mechanism told her she had slept far longer than usual, and in a moment her stomach told her the same thing with a noisy growl. Such a nuisance to feed and clothe and take care of, she thought, giving her empty belly a warning slap to silence it. Mistislaus was free of such burdens now, no longer enslaved by the rituals of eating and bathing, no longer tempted into unhealthy excesses by tasty food and captivating Dokkalfar ale.

She glided out of Skriftur's court, heading for the main stairs, but the sudden stink of Kjallari-folk halted her. They had come to the archway of Skriftur's court and looked within, searching for her. Also they had left offerings of food and drink. There was even plumabrot, swimming in a dark pool of plummy syrup, tantalizing her nostrils with its fragrance. Almost she accepted their offering; almost she put a piece of the plumabrot into her mouth, starved and unthinking. A quick whisper of the mist voices, and she dropped the plumabrot as if it had turned to a snake in her hand. Instead of fragrance, she now smelled the stink of rotting flesh and the corruption of the barrow. Throwing it down, she followed the unmistakable smell of Kjallari-creatures down the passageway until she came to the broad tunnel that led to the great charnel pit. It was a place that made Skyla shiver, just catching a whiff of the air from its deep maw. Here the unnatural creations of the Skyldings in their quest for the powers of life and death had been thrown down to destroy them, down the pit where all dead things were tossed. Unfortunately, the Kjallari-creatures had not died, and thanks to the warlike tendencies of the Skylding clan, they had a constant source of sustenance.

Something stirred within that dead darkness, scarcely more than a whisper, but Skyla heard and knew something was there, hovering and watching. She heard the stealthy pad of a foot, as in her nightmares of the Kellarman creeping closer and closer to her in the dark.

"Who are you?" she demanded of the dark. "What do you want?"

"You know who I am." The voice had such nightmare clarity that she wasn't certain if she heard it with her ears or if it went straight to her understanding without the benefit of physical speech.

"I am your guardian," the voice continued. "Your protector. Your mentor. Everyone who seeks me out will be given gifts of knowledge and skill."

"You are the Kellarman," Skyla said. "You gave me nothing but nightmares. You have no gifts. You seek only to destroy."

"To destroy is to build anew. To die is to live forever. You cannot understand, you are a mortal."

"Then why do you trouble me, if I can't understand?"

"Because you have inherited the wrongs of your ancestors. You will find no rest until justice is done."

"What must I do?"

"The Skyldings who created us gave us immortal spirits. They sought to create a race of perfect people. Gods over fields and flocks, earth and sky, who would protect and serve. They created the forms and brought them to life. But the spirits they gave us were wrong spirits. The Skyldings lacked the true power. Perhaps they became frightened at what they were creating. They gave us the spirits of criminals, beasts, and foul things. Perhaps it was the evil in their own beings they gave bodiment to."

Skyla thought of Ofarir and the secondhand spirit of Kraftugur that had pounced upon him at the first opportunity. With her retrieving spell, she had unwittingly provided that opening. Her Skylding ancestors had made the same mistake with their creations. She shuddered, remembering some of the forms the Kjallarifolk had been given.

"And what can I do about the mistakes of my ancestors?" Skyla asked, her voice sounding faint in her own ears.

"Join us. Be one of our leaders. You possess the Four Powers of creation and destruction. Think of the havoc we could wreak upon this world. Think of the revenge."

"I cannot! I wouldn't if I could! You are all unclean legions!"

"And the Krypplingur are any better? And Kraftugur? He has killed Mistislaus. I know, I have sensed the passage of a great one through the aethers. His welcome in the shadow world has touched even the depths of the Kjallari, but there is no joy for us, only the darkest of despair and rage. We can help you get your revenge upon those who have wronged you. Would you want Mistislaus to die unavenged? Is your love for him and your grief at his death so shallow? A falling leaf would leave a deeper mark."

Skyla clenched her fists as his taunting tone whispered through her skull. "Much you would know of how I feel. You have no heart, no soul, nothing but mindless rage against all living things and a lust for destruction. The word love on your foul lips is worse than the basest obscenity. I have no use for you or your revenge."

"You will one day, when you are not so haughty and self-righteous. When you are humbled sufficiently, you will come to the Kjallari and beg for my help. Those who have lost all come to me, as well as those who have obtained everything. We shall be waiting for you here, where you can easily find us. One day we will have you for our own, when you decide to exact justice upon your enemies."

Skyla drew a mark across the floor of the tunnel leading to Skriftur's court and scratched runes over it and around the arch of the entrance. She used the most inimical wards she knew from her clandestine dipping into Mistislaus' books.

"Beyond this line," Skyla said into the weighty darkness of the pit, "you shall not cross." A chill breath fanned her cheek, as if in affirmation, or warning perhaps, that she was still on the Kellarman's territory when she left the safety of Skriftur's hall.

Aboveground, in the gloomy halls of the Kjallari, she noted by the dimness of the light that the sun had gone down and the nightfarers' raucous voices were beginning. A sudden clashing and clattering at the front entrance gate sent her into hiding as a troop of Krypplingur opened the iron gate and drove in the Kjallari cart with its blind horse. A load of wretched carcasses, both human and animal, went down into the bottomless pit of the Kjallari.

"The Kellarman will feast well today," one of the Krypplingur said when the job was finished.

A larger Krypplingur promptly struck him a heavy blow on the back of the head, felling him to his knees.

"We don't make jokes about the Kellarman, you ignorant young pup! Not when the snow lynx might send any of us down that pit any time she wishes!"

As the cart lumbered ponderously away, through the gate and into the street again, a gray shadow trotted unnoticed beneath it. At the first opportunity Skyla took to the rooftops, leaping easily across the roofless intervals and traversing walls and roofs until she reached Athugashol. The street gate stood open, run aground in moss and cobblestones. No wild boys whistled from the Hall of Stars. There was scarcely a smell left of them, only a few rags and bones and a blackened firepit.

No grimly protective Guthrum squatted like a watchful old toad on the threshold of Athugashol. Skyla wandered in and out of the stable; Fegurd was also gone, along with the cart and harness. It all smelled abandoned, as if she and Mistislaus and Guthrum had never lived there. Skyla offered a few mournful yowls, sounding more like a desolate housecat than the terror of clan Krypplingur. A couple of old scavenging women scuttled suddenly from the tower, clutching a small bundle of rags, and disappeared into the Street of a Thousand Steps, looking back furtively.

Skyla wound her way up the stairs to the top of the small tower where her room had been. Nothing remained except the straw ticking of her pallet. Shifting shapes, she sat down on the straw and scratched it aside in the corner next to the wall. Down toward the bottom, where the straw was ground into fine shreds by use, she uncovered a cloth bag, rejoicing to discover that it was still there. All her rune-sticks, copied carefully from Mistislaus' old books, her amulets, bones, dead creatures, and other precious objects were still intact. It seemed a long, long time ago when her chief interests had been in making the mud people come to life, or healing the injuries of a mouse, or conjuring a new spirit for a dead lizard. In those days she had thought little of the fourth and darkest of her powers, which was the ability to drive out life from a living creature, to kill and destroy at a word. Suddenly her earlier experiments seemed nothing but child's play. She had not come so far as she had thought along the road to the knowledge of her powers. All her precious objects seemed amateurish, or downright useless. She threw the bag into a corner and pressed her face into her hands, wondering what she was going to do.

Now she pondered her choices, realizing that she might be forced to use the destructive side of her talents in order to protect herself. All her life there had been someone to take care of her. She had never been alone.

Alone. Absently she composed a tiny mud person from the dirt and bits of straw that settled to the bottom of her pallet. The tiny creature ran about on her hand like a friendly pet, a very small comfort in her grim situation.

Yearningly she thought of Ulfgarth and the simple days of her childhood. Thorborg was still there, and Hrysi and Hugi, and probably old dour Guthrum, by now. What a relief it would be to go back there and forget Rangfara, but nothing could ever make her forget the hollow ache in her heart that had replaced Mistislaus' love and security. A tear slid down her cheek and splashed on her hand, dowsing the little mud person with minuscule droplets. At once it doubled over and scuttled about in desperate death throes. Before Skyla's startled gaze, it quickly perished. With a breath she returned it to the dust state and brushed her hands.

It was time to go; she was still starving. Getting to her feet, she made the floor creak, a noise that suddenly silenced an almost imperceptible source of sound down below. Warily she cocked her head and listened with growing certainty that someone else was down there in the dimness also holding his breath and listening. She tied her bag of spells to her belt and shifted shapes, which resulted in a gust of wind that traveled around the little room and puffed dustily down the stairs.

On soft feet she glided down the cold steps, freezing suddenly when she definitely heard a footstep down below. Her whiskers twitched and her lynx instincts warned her that whoever this trespasser might be, he was not to be trusted. A few more steps down and Skyla could see the door at the bottom, standing slightly ajar. It moved slowly, closing, with Skyla trapped in the tower. With a mighty spring and a desperate scream, Skyla launched herself at the door, driving it open again into the face of whoever was closing it, rebounding off it and into the room. Out the door to freedom beyond, she paused once to look back. A cloaked figure leaped up from the ground and rushed to the door of the hall.

"Skyla! Wait! Come back!" It was the voice of Alvara. "I've got something to tell you."

Skyla paused, uttering an annoyed moan.

"Skyla, I know you're there. Listen to me. I'm your only friend in Rangfara now, although you might not yet believe that. Mistislaus is dead and the wild boys are all gone."

Skyla shifted shapes so she could talk to Alvara.

"Gone?" Skyla repeated.

Alvara nodded. "Illmuri has done away with Jafnar and all the wild boys. I watched him capture them all, but before I could do anything to save them, Otkell the Slaver got them. I imagine he turned them over to Ofarir for the reward."

"I'll go after them," Skyla said. "My clan brothers—my only kinfolk—"

"It's no use trying to get them away from Ofarir," Alvara said. "We have no way of telling what he has done with them. But there's no time for grieving now. You have so much that must be done."

Skyla pressed her hands against the rough stone of the doorway, not feeling, scarcely seeing.

"Let me help you, Skyla," Alvara continued. "I swear, you can trust me. You saved my life there at the tent, when someone tried to strangle me. We may as well name him—it was Illmuri, ever intent upon finding the treasure."

"I don't trust you," Skyla answered. "I don't trust anyone who claims to be my friend. The only friend I can claim is now dead, lying in the Kjallari. I wish I'd never seen these evil dark streets and never coveted that cursed treasure. I wish I was still a simple girl running free on the green moors. Now everything I've ever loved is gone. It's true what they say, I'm a curse to everyone who comes near me."

"Nonsense. There's no curse on you, just a heavy load of obligation. I'm not afraid. I'm here to help you, Skyla, to repay those obligations."

"What obligations?" Skyla asked guardedly after a moment of silence.

Alvara's eyes glowed as she spoke. "The obligation to avenge your ancestors. You are the only one left who can give them peace in their undeserved graves. Imagine how they are crying out to you for justice. Their killers are walking the streets where every cobblestone is yet stained with the blood of your clansmen. Is it any wonder you feel their presences and hear their voices?"

"The name my mother gave me was Skylda, which means 'duty.' Or 'obligation.' Perhaps this was what she had in mind when she gave me that name," Skyla said. "Revenge. What must I do, Alvara? I'm not skilled in using the powers of destruction. I never thought I would be anything but one who heals and mends, until I saw that creature Kraftugur kill Mistislaus. Now I know I can destroy him, and I will."

"Yes, and I will tell you how to do it," Alvara said. "Between us, we are no match for the Kryppling clan. With your skills of retrieval from the dead, however, we will have all the help we need from the shadow realm."

"The shadow realm is not a place I wish to go again," Skyla said. "Must I truly return there?"

"You must," Alvara said firmly. "There is one in particular that will be eager to help us. One who has endless reason for revenge upon the Krypplingur. But you alone can bring her here from the shadow realm. Are you determined enough to avenge Mistislaus and your clansmen, Skyla?"

"I am determined enough," Skyla said in a wooden tone. "The evil is already in me and has always been waiting. Now the time has come."

Chapter Twenty

Down below in the cellar, Illmuri regained consciousness. He sat a moment contemplating his plight, slowly shaking his throbbing head. After standing up, he pushed at the door and found it securely barred from the other side. It was ominously quiet above. He sighed and sat down, queasily cradling his head in his hands. Gently he felt for the bump, which was large and painful. Then he felt around in his various pockets and sleeve-ends and tied-up strips of cloth until he found one particular little packet. He opened it carefully and allowed a round orb the size of a small egg to roll into his palm. For a moment he rubbed his eyes, sighing deep breaths and rapidly muttering strings of iterations, then he commenced to gaze steadily into the brilliant sphere.

"Oh, Eyjarr, my friend and mentor," he murmured, resting his elbows on the table and rubbing his eyes a moment before beginning the summoning spell. "This time I have truly failed and destroyed everything. I should be put back in the lowest standard in Galdurshol, teaching small children their first runes."

"Are you sure you could handle it?" a dry voice inquired. An image materialized in the sphere, beginning with a wizened face with deep-set sparkling eyes and a long straggly tail of white beard.

"Now then, my scholar, why all this gloom and despair?"

"It's the Skylding boys," Illmuri said with a smothered groan. "They've escaped. I tried to win them over, but they wouldn't trust me for an instant. I've never seen such wild and unmanageable creatures before. Not even wild horses that have never seen man are as stubborn. Some element of essential rational human thought seems to be missing in their minds. I don't see how we can ever do anything with them, even if we do find them again."

"Don't worry so much. The problem with them is a lack of responsibility. Wild boys have no sense of belonging or dedication to a purpose. The only thing they are truly dedicated to is filling their stomachs with food they have stolen. You're not discouraged, are you?"

"Discouraged? Master, I've been outlawed and hunted like a beast. I've crawled through stinking ditches to save my own life. I've associated with murderers, thieves, half-trolls, cannibals, scavengers, and dabblers in all the evil arts, some of which I've never even heard of, but I can tell how depraved they are. I've eaten the most execrable things you can imagine. I've never suffered such humiliations, until I came to Rangfara."

"Good, good. Humiliations are very good for you. A young wizard needs a great deal of opposition to develop his spiritual qualities."

"After this, I shall be a very spiritual wizard indeed," Illmuri said gloomily. "There will be scarcely anything physical left of me to serve as the slightest interference. I wish I could at least rid myself of this revolting disguise."

"No, no, you still need it," Eyjarr said. "It will be most useful to you where you're going."

"I'm going somewhere?"

"Of course. You've got to get your wild boys back. It will be a marvelous exercise for you, my boy. You've always wanted to travel, you know."

"I'm going to leave Skyla in the control of Alvara?" Illmuri asked.

"Pish. Skyla's in no danger. She'll have tremendous fun tormenting the Krypplingur. Of course, she could become so enthralled with the dark side of her powers that she won't wish to return, in which case the Kellarman will gain possession of her, but I think she's far too clever for that. She'll experiment awhile, but she'll come around. Do sit down and eat something, won't you? You've got to keep your strength up. You're going to need every bit of it."

"I can't do what I was sent to do. It's impossible. It's too late."

The sphere glittered more brightly and the words of the speaker came into Illmuri's mind.

"You're too impatient, youngling. You expect them to want to be saved? You expect them to know the future, to have your vision?"

"Meistari, they've locked me in a cellar and now they're gone. I think it shows a definite lack of trust on their part. You might even say they hate me. They're not going to believe anything I say or do is going to come to any good. Only one of them seems to have a grain of reason, and that's the one Mistislaus was working on. But now Mistislaus is dead."

The hopelessness of his situation struck him an overwhelming blow. He had failed utterly. Then he calmed himself by looking into the clear, calm depths of the jewel in his hand until he was again speaking on the level of Eyjarr his mentor.

"Kraftugur has returned to Rangfara," Eyjarr said. "Not content with the desolation he spread the first time, he is back to finish off the Skylding clan completely. Wherever they are, they are in great danger, I needn't tell you. You must do what your masters sent you to Rangfara to do."

"I shall do it, Meistari," Illmuri said faintly. "As quick as I get out of this cellar."

"The time is getting short," Eyjarr said. "You haven't done as well as I expected, but this is a difficult problem. We are all waiting to see how you will resolve it. We have great hopes for you, my lad. You are the best in your standard at the Guild. It would grieve us exceedingly to see you fail now."

Illmuri brushed a faint sheen of sweat from his face. Still queasy from his head injury, he looked at the trapdoor above. "No more than it would grieve me," he said.

"Now you've got to buck yourself up a bit and put off this gloomy countenance," Eyjarr advised him. "It turns people right off you when you look as if you're standing on a bridge wearing a millstone around your neck."

"It's difficult for a man in my position to be extremely cheerful," Illmuri said. "My dear friend Mistislaus is dead, and his child ward is in the hands of a witch, and the only other survivors of the Skylding clan are lost somewhere. I myself am confined in a cellar. Tell me, are my mates at Galdurshol all having such a terrible time with their first callings?"

"No, you're by far in the hottest soup," Eyjarr said cheerfully. "You should count yourself as lucky. When you come out of this, you'll know something, one way or the other. Well, it's high time I was going. Don't give up, my lad. It's not entirely hopeless yet."

"Yes, I do feel so much better now," Illmuri said, stifling a moan of despair when he thought of the place Eyjarr was, while he had to stay in Rangfara. Home had never seemed so dear. Many times since his arrival here, he had pondered his insanity in wanting to become a worker of spell and magic. It was a hideously lonely business, fraught with terror and deceit. Other young men his age were living in agrarian contentment with wives and children, sparing scarcely a thought upon the mysteries of the earth's aethers and elements and the controlling thereof.

"Tut tut," Eyjarr said in mild reproach, reading his desolate thoughts. "I'm watching over you, laddie. If things should get too far out of hand, I know of an excellent retriever who can snatch you right back and set you on your feet again for another go-round."

It was not a particularly comforting thought. Illmuri shivered, remembering his last encounter with the shadow realm, brief as it had been.

"Then I'm to go after the boys?" he asked, but scarcely was the question across his lips when Eyjarr's apple-cheeked, smiling image faded from his sight with a genial wave of one hand, and he was alone once more. "To think—I once considered myself fortunate to be a son of the Galdur clan," he said to himself, shaking his head.

With no great enthusiasm he set about thwarting the stout door above his head. In his disguise, he was forbidden from employing certain principles of magic that would have greatly assisted him, so it took him far longer to find a means of sliding open the latch on the far side of the stout planks. Looking around, he saw the signs of the riotous feast and read the evidence of the struggle. In a very short while he knew exactly what had happened and who was responsible.

Since it was now daylight outside, he had no choice but to wait for nightfall before sallying forth. Acting upon a rumor he soon garnered outside an ale tent, he made a circuit of all the drinking booths, carefully scanning the occupants who dared defy the belligerent squads of Kryppling still searching every unsavory nook and cranny of Rangfara. At last he found his man, Otkell the Slaver, accompanied by the silent and gloomy Hakarl. Boldly Illmuri shoved aside the flap and entered the booth, dimly lit by a few rush lights, and seated himself at the table with Otkell.

Otkell wiped his hairy lips on his knuckles and brought his brows together in a scowl.

"I'm surprised you're still alive," he said. "Nearly every outlaw in Rangfara has been ferreted out. You're making mighty bold for an outlaw, coming in here this way and accosting a decent citizen."

"You're anything but a decent citizen," Illmuri said. "Much as I can see how you hate to discuss it, we must talk. What have you done with those boys? I know you were there in my absence. I promised to pay you well to deliver them to Eyjarr in Galdurshol.

Enough, I thought, to temporarily overcome your own greed and to inspire a brief spate of honesty, but it appears I deceived myself when I thought you had any decency that could be bought."

"Deceived! I was the one deceived," Otkell grumbled. "Those boys of yours are as deadly as vipers. You should have warned me they would try to escape."

"Escape! You let them escape? Where were you? Where did they go?"

"Escape they did, leaving me lucky to possess my life," Otkell retorted in an aggrieved whine. "You said it would be an easy way to earn three hundred marks in gold, plus a fat reward in Galdurshol. I never wanted to go to Galdurshol. Too many fire wizards down there for my taste, but I was tempted by your gold beyond any fellow's ability to resist. For Illmuri, I said, I would do it. You stole away my common sense and it very nearly cost me my life. Little fiends they were, always scheming to get away."

"What happened? How did they escape?" Illmuri demanded.

Otkell slowly swung his head to the right, then to the left, squeezing his eyes down to mere slits as if he scented something hazardous on the wind. Or perhaps he was having trouble thinking up another plausible lie. "I don't want to talk about it here." His boozy whisper was loud enough to be heard on the street outside. "Might not be healthy for either of us even to be seen together. Come to my camp in a little while and I'll tell you all about it."

Illmuri sighed impatiently and stood up. The fellow was right in suspecting listening ears, and certain things were best not generally known. "All right, in a short while I'll be there. And you'd better forget about your ale and join me or I'll start to think you're trying to avoid me. Neither of us would want to think that now, would we?"

Otkell grinned jovially and hoisted his ale horn to his lips. "Friends such as we are would never avoid each other," he declared with oily sincerity.

Illmuri quelled a nasty cold suspicion nagging at his gut as he made his way along the dismal Skurdur pathway alongside the ditch that gave the unsavory place its highly suited name. Illmuri wrapped his cloak around him more tightly and hurried toward the encampment on the east side of Rangfara, where the pony trains and wagon caravans stayed.

Midway, a half-dozen Krypplingur sent him scuttling onto a rooftop. With greater wariness and reluctance than he had witnessed in Krypplingur, they crept into the alley, weapons ready. Even from his perch above their heads, he could smell them sweating as they advanced. With uncanny predatorial instinct, they came directly toward his hiding place, as if homing in on his own thudding heart and sweating palms.

"On the roof, something hiding," one of them whispered, motioning to the others to spread out and surround the building.

Illmuri contemplated his only retreat, which was a harrowing leap to an adjoining roof. He stood up, gathering himself for the insane plunge. Suddenly the cry of a snow lynx wailed down the alley, coming from someplace very close. The Krypplingur froze a moment, then turned as one and galloped away in the opposite direction. Illmuri climbed down from his roof and prodded around in the shadows.

"Skyla!" he hissed. "Jafnar? Is that you? Come out, I want to talk to you. I never intended to sell you to Otkell or Herrad. I had a much better plan, something you would approve of. Jafnar? Skyla?"

No response, except some ominous scuttling sounds in the darkest corners of the alley. He gave it up, fearing that the Krypplingur might regain their courage and return to hunt the lynx.

Otkell's wain stood apart from the other caravans, shunned by folk with any sensibilities regarding the value of human life. A bed of coals cast a feeble light on the wagon and the horses tied to it. The animals snorted at the sight of him, sweating and trembling in fear. Illmuri could see they had pulled against their halters and torn up the ground, tying to escape. He was about to halloo out to Otkell, but the halloo died in his throat when he caught a faint whiff of blood smell. Warily he darted behind a pile of rock and watched awhile, seeing nothing except the wind currents fanning the coals and whipping away wisps of smoke. Finally he crept out to investigate, sensing no other presences except the ever-present mist people swirling around eternally reliving their terrors and triumphs. He shook his head to dismiss the visions that had marked him from early childhood as a gifted recipient of the Galdur blood of his father.

"Away!" he commanded silently, catching a faint gleam of eyes in the shadows. A hulking form backed away with a burbling growl. "Kjallari garbage, get yourself back to your pit," he snapped, adding a rebuffing invective that elicited a howl of pain from the creature in the shadows.

More of them would be coming from the Kjallari than he cared to deal with. Steeling himself, he moved toward the wagon, holding his staff in his hand without lighting it. Now he sensed a presence, ahead of him in the dark. With a brilliant burst of light, he lit his staff and beheld the scene before him. The carcasses of Otkell and Hakarl were strewn in the tall grass, shredded and mauled with a fury that made him recoil. A few paces more and he discovered yet another sad ruin of human flesh. It was one of the Skylding orphans. Cursing, he searched out the rest of them, all seven destroyed in the most thorough and hateful way possible.

Illmuri passed a trembling hand over his brow. Failed again. His mentors in Galdurshol had been mistaken in thinking he could ever save the Skylding clan from complete and utter destruction.

A low and beastly chuckle startled him with its nearness and he spun away, holding his staff before him.

"Not a pretty sight, I fear," rumbled the voice of Kraftugur. He leaned upon his axe, still red with gore. "Now it is finished, wizard. Run away to your safe towers and dusty books in Galdurshol and forget about Rangfara. You've failed yet again."

"No. The infamy of Rangfara is an endless knot in the strands of time," Illmuri retorted. "A wound without healing. I'll be back. The wizards of Galdur know the secrets of traveling the strands of the Norns. We'll meet again, Kraftugur, as many strands and lifetimes as it takes to eradicate you and your creatures below."

"There is no end to Rangfara's destruction," Kraftugur said with a mad chuckle. "My revenge will endure forever—unlike the Skyldings, who will perish at my hands a thousand times. Your wizards of Galdur are not the only ones who know how to manipulate the strands of history. Away with you now, while I'm still in a good enough mood to let you live. Until we meet again, wizard of Galdur."

He lurched away, still cackling, summoning his Krypplingur from the shadows with a hoarse bellow.

A sudden piercing cry sent the Krypplingur plunging away in terror. Illmuri stumbled back two paces, quenching his light in momentary disarray. Red eyes gleamed in the dark, lunging straight at him. He lit the staff again, barely in time as the creature came hurtling into the light, bloody jaws agape for his throat.

"Fordast! I birtu!" he gasped at the last instant, and the black shape veered aside with a strangled cry, but not before he got a good look at it. Beyond a doubt, it was a snow lynx, its silvery throat and breast blackened with fresh blood. Blazing eyes burned into his a moment, striking bleak despair and desolation into his heart, pulling at him as if he were standing on the edge of a pit. Then with a tormented cry, the lynx bounded away.

"Skyla?" he called into the dark. "Skyla! Come back! Let me

help you!" He extinguished the light and started after her, straining all his senses. He halted abruptly, seeing her standing before him in human form, her cloak blowing in the cold wind.

"There is no help for me," she replied. "Go away and let me destroy myself and the ones I hate."

"Skyla! No!" But she was gone, and the night was cold and empty.

About the Author

Elizabeth Boyer began planning her writing career during junior high school in her rural Idaho hometown. She read almost anything the Bookmobile brought, and learned a great love for Nature and wilderness. Science fiction in large quantities led her to Tolkien's writings, which developed a great curiosity about Scandinavian folklore. Ms. Boyer is Scandinavian by descent and hopes to visit the homeland of her ancestors. She has a B.A. from Brigham Young University, at Provo, Utah, in English literature.

After spending several years in the Rocky Mountain wilderness of central Utah, she and her husband now live in Utah's Oquirrh mountains. Sharing their home are two daughters and an assortment of animals. Ms. Boyer enjoys horseback riding, cross-country skiing, and classical music.